SO-AEL-800

LAUREL

THE CITY OF ANGER

"An open, bleeding slice of the U.S.A. *The City of Anger* reaches high peaks in its implication and forceful writing."
—*The New York Times Book Review*

"It has all the lurid impact of a byline account of crime."
—John Dos Passos

"Mr. Manchester knows . . . much about the desperation and degradation of slum life . . . and he knows a great deal more . . . about keeping a story in constant motion."
—*The New York Times*

"A tough, realistic novel."
—*The Nation*

Books by William Manchester:

Biography

DISTURBER OF THE PEACE: *The Life of H. L. Mencken*
A ROCKEFELLER FAMILY PORTRAIT: *From John D. to Nelson*
PORTRAIT OF A PRESIDENT: *John F. Kennedy in Profile*
AMERICAN CAESAR: *Douglas MacArthur, 1880–1964*
THE LAST LION: WINSTON SPENCER CHURCHILL; *Visions of Glory: 1874–1932*

History

THE DEATH OF A PRESIDENT: *November 20–November 25, 1963*
THE ARMS OF KRUPP, 1587–1968
THE GLORY AND THE DREAM: *A Narrative History of America, 1932–1972*

Essays

CONTROVERSY: *And Other Essays in Journalism, 1950–1975*

Fiction

THE CITY OF ANGER
SHADOW OF THE MONSOON
THE LONG GAINER

Diversion

BEARD THE LION

Memoirs

GOODBYE, DARKNESS
ONE BRIEF SHINING MOMENT: *Remembering Kennedy*

THE CITY OF ANGER

William Manchester

A LAUREL BOOK
Published by
Dell Publishing Co., Inc.
1 Dag Hammarskjold Plaza
New York, New York 10017

This is a work of fiction. Its characters and the events it describes exist only in these pages. Any specific resemblance to anyone, anywhere, is sheer coincidence.

Reprinted by arrangement with
Little, Brown and Company, Inc.
Printed in the United States of America

June 1986

10 9 8 7 6 5 4 3 2 1

WFH

To
MILTON BASS and GEORGE F. BENOIT

Think where man's glory most begins and ends,
And say my glory was I had such friends.
                    —Yeats,
                         The Municipal Gallery
                         Revisited

Publisher's Note

Over thirty years have passed since the first appearance of *The City of Anger*. First published in the United States in 1953, and thereafter in Britain, Germany, and Taiwan, it was reissued in 1962 and is still bought, read, and discussed. A number of its techniques — silent transitions, the use of plot as metaphor and counterpoint as irony — are widely imitated by successful novelists today. The book is indeed one of those rare first novels that survive as minor classics. Reread today, it is as powerful as when H. L. Mencken read the opening passages and enthusiastically urged the young writer on, as engrossing as when it was hailed on publication by John Dos Passos and Louis Untermeyer.

The vast majority of Manchester's contemporary readers know him as a writer of nonfiction. Before he wrote his best-selling histories and biographies, however, he published four novels, and the reviewers of each commented on his skillful command of detail — accurate detail, for his eye has always been a lens, not a prism. While working as a newspaperman and researching *The City of Anger*, he rented a furnished room in a black slum, eavesdropped on the weekly strategy meetings (held in a Turkish bath) of the exploitive politicians running through the city's numbers racket, and finally, at Maryland's Pimlico racetrack, found how a number could be fixed. His use of detail is both Manchester's strength and his weakness. Those who dislike it, particularly in his nonfiction, criticize him as a collector of trivia. But to Manchester the skills of narration grow out of the mastery of detail. It is a matter of taste. Faulkner is no less compelling than Hemingway; *An Appointment in Samarra* no more convincing than *Main Street*.

Whatever its flaws — and like all early work it creaks here and there — *The City of Anger* was immediately recognized as the work of an original mind exploring dark corners of urban ghettos then largely ignored by the press. In those days the births, weddings — even the murders — of blacks went unrecorded. They were, as Ralph Ellison had pointed out the year before, Invisible Men. Some of Manchester's techniques, notably his rendition of ghetto dialect, may seem quaint, though no quainter than the Mississippi dialects in *Huckleberry Finn*. And his use of the term "Mr. Charlie" in the novel's opening scene was picked up by Baltimore blacks and is heard almost as often as "honky."

The City of Anger proved prophetic. Its description of a race riot shocked Baltimore — *The City of Anger*'s city — and the last, ominous sentence in the novel foresaw more violence in the years ahead, more "fire next time," as James Baldwin later called it. In the early 1950s such pythonizing was unacceptable. Hamilton Owens, editor in chief of the *Baltimore Sun*, Manchester's newspaper, described his prediction as "ludicrous" and argued that "the colored . . . have been passive, are passive, and will always be passive." Truth is indeed the daughter of Time: in 1968 they ran amok and put vast tracts of the city to the torch.

But *The City of Anger* is more than a slum novel. Most of its characters are white; many are genteel. As a young reporter the author had access to all levels of society, to the governor's mansion and skid row, to the elegant Maryland Club and the penitentiary's death row. He was struck by the forces cutting across all classes, the elemental drives that knew neither breeding nor sex. It struck him that there were as many emotional have-nots in Green Spring Valley mansions as in ghetto hovels, and he recognized a striking similarity in patterns of conduct. More often than not it was hostility toward oneself. The palliatives for these walking wounded were alcohol or, emerging for the first time on a recognizable scale, narcotics. Others turned their rage outward. Yet violent destruction, in those years, was rare. Most frequently they became addicted to gambling, the mildest sedative for the emotionally starved, though the gambling was not always conscious: "Everybody bets but me," says the novel's numbers king, Ben Eric.

Perhaps *The City of Anger*'s most significant contribution to literary craftsmanship was its breakout from the postwar vogue of formless fiction. Critics had all but exiled Charles Dickens from his place in the history of letters. The "interpersonal relations" of fiction, they argued, should be as amorphous, as random, as life itself. Writers, Manchester replied, ought to be more than builders; they should also become architects. A careful reading of this work reveals that one of his postulates is Sir Isaac Newton's deceptively simple Third Law: every action has an equal and opposite reaction. The action of every character in the novel affects the others. The structure of the book is designed to express this. It begins as a circle of action and moves from segment to segment, taking up the people one by one. The circle contracts until in the last stunning passage we are at the hub, where all the forces and all the events collide.

And there Newton's Third, having reached its climax, yields to another familiar premise: that the whole is more than the sum of its parts — reexpressed, that we are more than ourselves, and that no being is complete without the understanding of another. *The City of Anger* has its strong figures. Police Commissioner Zipski — brilliantly played in the screen version by Ed Begley — is a rock of integrity against whom breakers of corruption and intrigue shatter and evanesce. Zipski's strength is his inner serenity. Most of the novel's characters (and, Manchester implies, most people) lack it. Their void cannot be filled. Searching for solace only exhausts and, finally, diminishes them. Their futile pursuit of what Jefferson called happiness — and he did not mean pleasure — becomes the actions that provoke the novel's reactions. Following their blind stumbling, seeing them blunder hopelessly into one another, inflicting pain that is repaid in kind, watching them finally merge in despair, we are swept up in the novel's catharsis and discover we have witnessed a unique study in the tragic plight of the loveless.

The Lottery, with its weekly payout of enormous prizes, was the one public event to which the proles paid serious attention. It was probable that there were some millions of proles for whom the Lottery was the principal if not the only reason for remaining alive. It was their delight, their folly, their anodyne, their intellectual stimulant. Where the Lottery was concerned, even people who could barely read and write seemed capable of intricate calculations and staggering feats of memory. There was a whole tribe of men who made a living simply by selling systems, forecasts, and lucky amulets. Winston had nothing to do with the running of the Lottery, which was managed by the Ministry of Plenty, but he was aware (indeed everyone in the Party was aware) that the prizes were largely imaginary. Only small sums were actually paid out, the winners of the big prizes being nonexistent persons.

— *George Orwell, 1984*

CONTENTS

The Rim of Darkness   *page 3*

The Track of the Rat   *page 96*

The Gestapo   *page 191*

— 555   *page 350*

THE CITY OF
ANGER

1

The Rim of
Darkness

THE city faced the bay. In the days of sailing vessels all the
people had lived in a horseshoe of homes circling the
downtown basin, and everyone could see the water, and
the land behind was wild. Now the skyline blocked out the bay,
and those who could had moved inland and built in the green
corridor of the Valley. But the horseshoe remained, a vast arc of
decaying houses running from sea to sea, walling the skyline in
and the suburbs out.

The politicians had split the arc in two. To the east thick wards
of Poles and Slavs curved down through the industrial complex
of East Bay, ending at the bay's end, where the river slipped into
the dark hills. And westward sprawled the foul Seventh District,
in whose cramped warrens a quarter million blacks lived, panting
hard against the white rim to the north.

The entire perimeter was tightly and corruptly organized, but
only in the Seventh did the voters buy themselves. They did just
that. They paid the district machine for the trouble of bossing

them, and the machine gave a little back and kept the rest. And this was but poorly understood that raw Thanksgiving eve when, on a cluttered street deep in the black Seventh, a policy writer who didn't even know who was keeping the rest gave a little back to a voter on his lucky day.

He was inside, paying off, and the crowd knew it.

Before the broken stoop twoscore blacks had gathered, spilling gaily into the street and completely surrounding a gaudy convertible parked at the curb. Behind the wheel a sleek young white man waited, lazily reading the Hearst comics and ignoring the noise around him — women chatting busily among themselves and policing their children, men calling happily to one another.

"Ole Pete, he done it this time!"

"Sholey did!"

"Tuhkey for Pete tomorrow!"

"Man, oh man!"

From time to time one of the younger blacks peered curiously inside the splendid car or, more often, pressed his face against the starred glass of Pete's first-floor window and stared eagerly at the shredded wallpaper and the stained, sagging ceilings.

"Tell me. What you see, Wiggie?"

"Can't see nothin'. They's all upstairs, doin' somethin'."

"Doin' *somethin'*! My oh *my!*"

The mob grew and grew restless. Two boys in corduroy hats sparred in a dirty patch of sunlight. An old man squatted on the stoop and lit his pipe. A baby cried plaintively over its mother's hushing. Suddenly a window upstairs flew open and the familiar odor of burning kerosene rolled out, followed by a dark, beaming face. The crowd let go a mighty shout.

"Gimme what you got, Pete!" they chanted. "Gimme what you got! Gimme what you got!" Pete turned away and then reappeared with an even broader grin and a wad of ten-dollar bills in each grubby fist.

"Wow! Wow!"

"Gimme what you got!"

"Fatroll!"

"Honeybucks!"

"*Hip*-gee!

"*Hipgee! Hipgee!*"

They surged forward, hands outstretched, eyes glittering with envy, and for a tiny instant their excitement lit up the cold and squalid street. Then Pete's wife, a large woman in a tattered navy pea jacket, stepped from behind a bunting of wash and pulled her husband away. The disappointed moaned below.

After a hurried, gesticulating conference, he returned. "Beer for *ever*-body!" he cried. "Be right down!"

The mob broke for the corner like a routed platoon, and the last children were scampering in pursuit when the front door opened and a white man came out slowly. He was thin and wan, with watery eyes and a furtive expression. He wore a soiled felt hat and a threadbare overcoat. The coat was too large for him, and he plucked nervously at the lapels as he came down the steps. In a mittened hand he carried an empty canvas bag.

From a shadow by the house a fat woman in an enormous stocking cap appeared and approached, crunching over the sidewalk's carpeting of rusting tin cans and trash. She offered a pudgy hand; the man shook it absently, deposited her quarter in his overcoat pocket, and drew out a small order book. She whispered briefly. He nodded, wrote, tore out a carbon and handed it to her.

"My, my," she chuckled. "Look lahk you et yore buhd already, Mr. Charlie!"

"Sure, sure," he muttered vaguely. The woman crunched away, her chuckle fading as she realized her name was unknown, and the man, who was called Charlie Bond, slipped the K-book in his pocket.

The convertible's motor turned over. The sleek young man opened the door. "Long time no see," he said sarcastically.

Charlie slid in with an apologetic little laugh. "It was that mob, I thought they'd rape me. Don't ever let me carry a load that big without I got protection."

They pulled away and shot down the narrow, cobblestoned

street, the young man silent, Charlie worrying his lapels and staring out the window. "Jees," he said wearily. "They sure love that do-re-mi."

"That's right," the young man said between his teeth. "And *you* give it to them."

"Well, I guess that's so." Charlie forced another laugh. "Five payoffs in a week, the man that broke the bank at Monte Carlo is me."

The wheel spun; the car cut a vicious corner. Charlie fell silent. He sank into his overcoat, throwing quick, nervous glances across the street. Six blocks later they drew up before a fire hydrant and he got out, brooding, and lifted the canvas sack from the floor board. "See you Friday, Moss. Hope we have a dead run."

"We better," Moss said grimly. "The boss don't like giveaways."

Charlie cringed. "You know I can't help it," he protested. "If a number hits, it hits. I don't have no way to fix that, Moss, you know that, Moss."

"Sure." Moss's eyes were winking oddly. "I just said the boss don't like to give away giveaways."

"But —"

Moss reached over and slammed the door and then was gone, sliding swiftly down the street, leaving Charlie spluttering and shivering on the empty corner.

Jees. They knew it wasn't his fault. He swung out savagely with his foot and sent an empty Campbell soup can spinning across the street. The wind caught it and rolled it against the door of an A & P, and a swarthy, aproned man looked out menacingly. Charlie hurried across the street, pulling at his hatbrim. The bastards, he thought. They never let a guy alone. They ought to be sued, the way they kick a guy around. He pictured himself in court, denouncing Moss and his unknown boss with cold scorn and, with the picture, relaxed.

At the second corner he entered a wholesale drygoods store, strode familiarly past the display counters, and pushed through a revolving door on the far side.

Parked outside was a battered prewar Mercury. The hood was

up, and a young man in a cheap fedora was peering at the motor. He looked up petulantly.

"I was waiting for you and I got to worrying, about the weather. Think it'll freeze?"

"Naw," Charlie grunted. "You got a month yet." Peter Wyne's automobile obsession was annoying, but he was a ride home.

"Well, I saw some ice in the gutter," Peter said as they jumped in. "If it freezes you get a cracked block, and that's expensive."

They drove back through the slum, following a zigzag pattern along the littered, ill-paved streets. Here and there a basement grocery loomed, its windows hung with skinny turkeys and before it two or three shabby blacks lingering on their way home that day before Thanksgiving.

"Bet some of them's your customers," Peter said, pointing.

"Why?" Charlie was immediately on guard.

"Well, a store like yours, down here I mean, they drop in sometimes, don't they?"

"We're wholesalers," Charlie said shortly.

"Oh, I keep forgetting."

Charlie gave him a narrow look, but Peter was guileless, so he settled back. He was thankful he did not have to write on holidays. It meant one less explanation at home.

At Crone Street a gleaming blue Cadillac swept by as they waited at the light, and Charlie craned his neck. A silver-haired little man in a loud sport coat was huddled over the wheel.

"Some trolley," he said admiringly.

"Coming home from Willoughby, I bet."

"Boy. Some people got it tough."

He saw himself in a gay Buick, speeding north to the track, giving a blond beside him the real lowdown on the horses. The blond was impressed, and as they stopped in traffic she snuggled up to him. Other sports, in lesser cars, looked on enviously. Charlie ignored them. He winked at the girl, produced a wad of bills, and asked her how she thought he ought to blow it.

"Well," said Peter, as they left the black section and crossed Kendall Square. "See you Friday."

"Sure," Charlie said woodenly, still in his dream. "Friday."

Peter turned down Linvale Place and pulled up in the middle of a row of old brick houses. Charlie got out silently, feeling the bite of the air. The girl's nose was wrinkled with laughter. He had just said something funny. He tried to think what it could have been.

"So long," Peter said.

"So long."

He trudged up the steps, fumbling for his keys.

His wife was in the front room, unlaxing with Mrs. Carter. "Let's unlax and wait for my husband," she had told her. "He'll be here in a little while." She hoped it would be a long while and thought it would be longer than it was. When the front door slammed she jumped. "Oh, my God," she said, sliding to the edge of the frayed Morris chair. "It's Charlie and he's home."

"I beg your pardon?"

"My husband, he's home."

"Oh, splendid."

Charlie thrust his head through the beaded portieres, grinning. When he saw Loretta's guest he gaped. She's gone and done it, he thought. There'll be no living with her now.

She waved a triumphant hand. "Mr. Bond, Mrs. Carter."

"Pleased, I'm sure," he said with profound respect.

"I *am* delighted," Lucy Carter murmured.

She was a handsome, heavy-breasted woman in her late thirties, with a surprising nose, an abundance of black hair, and the trim, hard lines of a bullfighter. Her grandfather had been a founder of the thoroughbred Guardian Club, and her husband had escorted her to the german every year until his untimely and uninsured death. The modesty of his estate had prevented her from joining the genteel retreat to the Valley suburbs, and she had remained aloof, till now, from the decaying neighborhood.

Charlie beamed. "It's really a treat, having you on the reservation."

8

Loretta looked pained. "Sit down, hon. Mrs. Carter, she's been telling me some very interesting things."

"Just a minute." He opened the canvas sack and drew out four coffee-stained Dixie cups, telescoped together. "For seedlings," he explained. "I collect them. From the people I work with."

Lucy's smooth brow arched. "Seedlings? This time of year?"

"Well, not yet. But you need an awful lot of cups, you know. I started late last year, collecting, and I ran out in May. This time I want plenty. So I won't run out."

Loretta sniffed impatiently. "He's got enough for all Rogers Park already. In the spring" — she rolled her eyes — "they're all over the cellar, so you can't get around, even."

Lucy nodded understandingly. She had been told Charlie was thrifty and believed it. As she believed everything she had been told about him. As she had to believe.

He tucked the cups behind a chair and sat down. He knew his wife disapproved but did not care. He lived for April and the long Sunday afternoons in the wasted little garden behind the house. He was leaning back, preparing to play the genial host, when a valve in his stomach opened and closed audibly. He stood up quickly. "Excuse me," he said, bowing away toward the drapes. "I'll be back in a sec — a second."

He disappeared up the stairs, and his wife sat in trembling silence by the scarred radio on the marble-topped corner table. She had known, just *known* Lucy Carter would call one day. In another time, under other circumstances, Loretta would have waited a lifetime for the inevitable peal of the chimes and died believing in their inevitability. But the time and the circumstances were as they were, and the caller had come, and that this had happened was to Loretta no more remarkable than would the arrival of a transparent, methylene-blue fairy godmother have been remarkable to her little Dulcy.

"I've noticed your daughter," said Lucy, studying an ornate goldfish bowl. "She is enchanting."

Loretta nodded brightly. "She's a trial, but we love her."

"I'd like to paint her some time. I have a little home studio, you know."

"Oh!" Breathlessly. "That would be *wonderful!*"

Loretta did not think Lucy's arrival a miracle. She had passed Dulcy by that much. But rationalization is no great improvement on faith, and, speculating as she waited for Charlie, she fetched props for her shaping dream. Did Lucy Carter think Charlie made a lot of money? Many thought so.

"It is amazing," Lucy was saying, cocking her head gently, "how children have changed."

"My brother Al says exactly the same thing."

"Your brother?" Lucy was tentative, poised.

Loretta had blundered. "He's a," she groped, "a clothing technician."

"Oh." Lucy tossed her head gracefully. "How nice." She was polite because she had been taught it was proper, and scornful because she had been taught that too.

She leaned forward suddenly. "Mrs. Mathias tells me you husband is in drygoods," she purred. "A buyer, I believe she said."

Her tone was edged, but Loretta missed it; business, Charlie' vague business, was pleasantly remote. Henrietta Mathias! O course! She should have known. Henrietta often mentioned Lucy

"Henrietta's a riot," she said with measured approval.

"I believe her husband's firm is in the neighborhood."

"The drugstore on Belton Avenue. He owns it."

"Really? I didn't know." But she did. Lucy had met Henriett that morning, on just such a foray as this. She sighed deeply she was not anxious to discuss it. In this square, high-ceilinge room, crowded with potted plants and chintz, Lucy looked an felt quite out of place.

There was a bustling in the back hall and Dulcy appeared taut and painful in a starched frock.

"My little girl," Loretta said simply, relaxing for the first time "She's in the first grade, same as your little boy."

Lucy smiled glassily. "How sweet."

"Mommie, Bobby won't play on the slide." Dulcy balanced pettishly on one foot, eying the stranger hostilely. Lucy looked away, to the goldfish bowl, the radio, and the bright, busy wallpaper.

"Play somewheres else, hon."

"But Mommie!"

"Well. If you're real good, you can go upstairs. But *real* good!"

"Oh yes, Mommie, yes!" She pattered awkwardly through the drapes and down the hall toward the rear of the house. Loretta clenched her moist hands. Where *was* Charlie?

Upstairs a toilet flushed audibly. He came down the stairs, buckling his belt.

"Sorry to keep you waiting, have to clean up when I get home." His wife glared at him, and he glared back. It wasn't his fault if he had trouble. He sat very gently on the shield-back sofa and turned to Lucy. "Loretta was saying as how you had . . ."

"Mrs. Carter's worried about the neighborhood," Loretta said and leaned back contentedly. She had not even begun to grasp why Lucy was worried. That was for Charlie.

Lucy folded her hands in her lap.

"As you know, Mr. Bond, my family has been on this land a long time."

"Hundreds of years, I guess."

Lucy nodded. "Over two hundred. The Kendall house covered this entire block at one time." She smiled. "Where our present home is, there was a ballroom. Here," she tapped her foot softly, "were the servants' quarters."

Loretta bit her lip.

"Well, times change," Charlie said uncertainly, wondering what this had to do with him.

"Yes," Lucy went on, with a trace of bitterness. "They do, and seldom for the better." She leaned forward. "Do you know a man named Patecka?"

Charlie considered. "It rings a bell," he said slowly. "A very faint bell."

"He's in the real estate business."

11

"Real estate. Oh! *Joe* Patecka! The blockbuster!"

— A frightening word on the slum edge, where white home-owners kept a solid, desperate front against speculators who would buy a house, rent to blacks, and destroy every equity in a neighborhood overnight. Charlie was eight blocks from the present border of the black belt. He knew it was slowly advancing toward him, but he had thought the buffer between protected him, that until there were blacks living at the corner, he was safe.

He still thought so. "What about him?" he asked.

"That's the person," Lucy said dramatically, "who is getting ready to wipe us out."

Charlie looked at her sharply. "Patecka? In *this* block?"

She nodded meaningfully.

He began to perspire. "How do you know?"

"I have connections in real estate."

"I didn't know he skipped blocks," Charlie said weakly, with a vague feeling he was being fouled. "There isn't a Nigra living in I'd say a quarter mile of here."

"I know. But he couldn't break in there, so he looked for a soft spot and found it back here. I've just learned he's having a house in this block appraised."

"*Whose* house?"

"I understand it's Mr. Redsedski's."

"That dirty kike!" Charlie was livid.

Loretta looked doubtful. "I don't think so, hon. I think they're Polish people."

"It don't make any difference," he said impatiently.

"No," Lucy said quickly, "it doesn't. If Patecka gets it, it will be full of colored by the first of the year. And then —— ?" She shrugged her shoulders in despair.

Charlie mopped his head, figuring rapidly. He remembered Patecka now, all right. Jees. In a month he could lose three years of mortgage payments. He felt like crying.

"What can we do?" he cried hopelessly.

Loretta was bewildered. She could not imagine why they were

so upset. "Excuse me," she said. "I think the kids are doing something upstairs."

She thought no such thing. But she could not stand the confusion here, and she was not altogether sure she approved of skill in business matters in any woman, even in Lucy Carter.

Lucy smoothed her ruffled blouse deftly. Loretta was right: Lucy had been told Charlie was prosperous. It was his penalty for deceiving his wife about his work. The casual mystery of his employment had lent it a romantic cast in the block.

"If Mr. Redsedski can be bought by one party," she said, "he can be bought by another."

Charlie shook his head. "What party?"

Lucy looked at him carefully. Yes, he would do that. He would not commit himself, not yet. She smoothed her skirt and fingered her hem, but Charlie, lost in his troubles, did not notice.

"My idea," she said, "is to hold a meeting of everyone in the neighborhood. We could have it at my house. Perhaps we can find a way." She brushed hair from a temple with an easy motion, lifting her breasts. "There has to be a way."

"God, I hope so. I sure hope so, Mrs. Carter."

Loretta tripped down the stairs, and Lucy arose.

"Oh, Mrs. Carter! You're leaving!"

"She's got a kid, too," Charlie said. "It's late." Loretta scowled at him.

"I really must go. Good afternoon." They saw her to the door. On the steps she turned. "I can count on you, then, Mr. Bond?"

"Sure. I mean, I'll be there." He closed the door and leaned against it.

"You look peaked." Loretta patted his chin softly. "A good thing tomorrow's a holiday." She walked back into the house, humming. "Imagine Lucy Carter paying me a call! You never thought she would, and don't say you did!"

Charlie stared after her numbly, rapidly adding together his special checking account and his war bonds, calculating interest, wondering if he could touch Moss for a couple of hundred and damning Redsedski, Patecka, and the whole insane pyramid of property values.

Dulcy came down the stairs a step at a time, a comic book clutched in her fist.

"Daddy, read to me! Read to me!"

"Sure, Princess."

They went into the front room together and he settled on the sofa. In the kitchen Loretta was singing to herself in a quavering voice. Dulcy leaned back and Charlie spread his thin legs to receive her. Jees, he thought bleakly, opening the magazine. They never ever let a guy alone.

Squat and elegant, the Guardian Club sat well back from a pleasant side street in the heart of the business district. The club was an anachronism and so was the side street. All the influence of the most prominent men in town had been necessary to keep it free of noise and commerce. Their success had been complete, however, and apart from the offices of a few specialists, there was only the club, surrounded by towering shrubs and silence, an asylum for the most prominent and influential men in town.

Today at cocktail hour the main drawing room was nearly deserted. The servants were thankful for that, for Jarvis Cameron was having a little party. Cameron was celebrated among his fellow members as a sportsman extraordinary, a hard rider and drinker with three heroic letters from Princeton and, more than incidentally, the entire stock of Willoughby Racetrack. But among the servants he was notorious for his quick temper and intolerance of delay. They hovered along the great paneled wall, rocking on their toes and watching him anxiously.

He sat in his usual corner, under the oil portrait of his grandfather, intent upon a dossier of penciled notes. Mike Holloway, coming in over the deep rug, observed with some surprise that he was whistling softly. Whistling was forbidden in the club, and usually Cameron was acutely aware of club rules. Since the war he had seen his world disintegrate: Bermuda invaded by the gasoline engine, Bar Harbor gutted by fire, and now, finally and most terribly, racing languishing and his own track in peril. Yet he kept up all the old traditions. Keeping them up was a Cameron's duty. Or so Jarvis thought.

He heard the heavy footsteps and looked up, his great florid face shining with hospitality. Holloway had not seen him look so young, or so happy, in years. The old eyes sparkled. He rose and held out his hand.

"Well, Mike," he said, speaking with the corrupt southern accent of the border gentry. "It's been a long time."

Holloway frowned slightly. He was a police inspector, and the key to him was that he liked people to remember his title. That was because he did not deserve it. He had a dull mind and had failed in every business when his father, using the best connections and the meanest pressure, forced old Commissioner Holzweig to appoint him. Holzweig had been dead a year, and all influence on the office had died with him, but Holloway was in for good.

He was an enormous, beefy man, and he eased his vast bulk into the leather chair gently, reproving the slight with silence. Then almost immediately, he forgot his displeasure in a sudden recollection. "The commissioner'll be a little late, Jay. Commendation ceremony."

Cameron set his papers aside. "Damned nice of you to fix this up. I understand he's difficult to meet. Martini dry?"

"Sure. What about Wally?" Wallace Gillette, Cameron's brother-in-law, represented a genteel county seat in the State Senate and knew everyone.

"Matter of fact, I'm going to see him with Wally, but I wanted a little talk with him first myself. Wally's out of town, and there's something of a time factor."

"Oh?" Holloway said hopefully. But Cameron merely ordered without volunteering more. He knew he could use the inspector without providing details. There was, however, one necessary, rather unpleasant, detail. "By the way," he said lightly, "I've asked Ed Sylvester to join us."

"*Big* Ed?" Holloway reddened and half rose. The detail was

15

unpleasant because Sylvester was a politician, and Holloway, childishly loyal, hated to be reminded of political influence in the Department. It had been necessary because Sylvester was entering the room.

He came in silkily, trailed by the club's black doorman. Big Ed didn't look like a Guardian clubman and wasn't. There was a plebeian lilt in his walk and a Slavic, almost servile, hunch to his shoulders. He was a large man with thick jowls, a small mouth, and tiny eyes. The doorman took his hat and he was bald.

Cameron rose in cheerful recognition. "Good to see you, Ed. Know Mike?"

They bristled like dogs meeting. "We been introduced," Sylvester said coolly. "Once," Holloway grunted, shaking his hand once and then sitting ponderously.

Big Ed ordered a Manhattan, produced a silver case, and offered cigars. He was his only taker. After a few fierce puffs he settled back and looked around. "Where's old Stoneface?" he said jovially.

"Stonefa ——" Cameron stopped. "You mean Zipski?"

"That's what they call him."

"Mike said he had a meeting. He'll be late."

Mike stared hard at the rug, but Sylvester ignored him and rattled on pleasantly about politics. Cameron listened attentively. Big Ed deserved attention. He was the leader of all the East Bay wards, one of the two most powerful bosses in town. His finger was in every municipal pie; among other things he held absolute control of the zoning board. Holloway had just begun to wonder what his connection with Cameron could be when they heard the front door swing wide and a harsh voice speak to the doorman. Big Ed killed his cigar and folded his soft hands and fell silent. Commissioner Zipski had arrived.

He stood in the hall, unbuttoning his greatcoat, a graying little man with a calm, impassive face and flat blue eyes. He was in uniform, and his arms were so short the black braid reached his elbows. He handed the doorman his coat.

"In there?" His delivery was singularly penetrating. "I'll find it."

He came into the drawing room, saw Holloway, and stepped over. The three men rose, Holloway automatically, Cameron expectantly, and Big Ed with sloppy ease. Zipski looked at each directly. "Gentlemen," he said slowly, as though it were a word he had just learned.

The inspector stumbled through the introductions.

Cameron's face cracked along old lines. "This is a rare privilege," he said heartily. "You're something of a legend, Commissioner."

Zipski bowed, looked sharply at Big Ed, and sat without a word.

Holloway excused himself. He sensed the Department would be discussed and couldn't bear that. To him everything was black or white, and the Department was beyond discussion. It had to be that way. Otherwise he would have been obliged to recognize the emptiness of his success in it. No one urged him to stay and he shuffled out.

"Drink, Commissioner?" Cameron suggested, settling back.

Zipski straightened and crossed his legs with a little jerk. "Thank you, no."

Cameron arched his brow in feigned disappointment and offered cigarettes, but Zipski merely shook his head. The package was replaced, this time with genuine regret. Cameron was proud of his imported tobaccos. At home they were a joke. His wife Madelaine swore she had once substituted a pack of stale Camels and he had not known the difference.

The commissioner dug into the side pocket of his tunic and drew out a scarred old pipe. He slipped it in his mouth unfilled, unlit, and upside down, and held it there, folding his arms and watching narrowly as the others ordered fresh drinks.

When the servant had gone he leaned slightly forward.

"Well, gentlemen?"

Cameron thought his manner odd, but Big Ed, who had studied him, knew it was calculated. Zipski had a way of making strangers ill at ease. In his work he found it very useful.

"I suppose," Cameron began, clearing his throat, "you know my brother-in-law, Wallace Gillette."

"Met him. Senator. From the country."

"Yes. Ah — the senator plans to run for governor."

Zipski nodded curtly without removing his pipe. "So I'm told."

Sylvester inspected his fingernails carefully. "I'm going to support him," he said.

"Oh?" The commissioner opened his mouth slightly and clicked the pipe against his teeth. They waited a long moment, waited for comment. But there was none.

Cameron took a breath. "The senator," he said, more loudly than was necessary, "is running on one issue — clean up the Seventh District and wipe out Ben Erik."

"And I," said Sylvester, turning his hand over, "am supporting him."

They waited a longer moment and heard only the clicking. Cameron lit a cigarette and still the pipe clicked. He took a long drag and then a much shorter one and then the pipe stopped.

Zipski was looking at Big Ed. "Why?" he said softly.

Sylvester slumped and grinned. "I thought you heard. Me and Ben don't get along."

"That's right, but nothing like this. This is war."

Sylvester shrugged and looked away. But Zipski was bearing in.

"It wouldn't be because Erik's fanning out, would it?" He took the pipestem out and ran it down the tight curve of his chin. "It wouldn't be because he's pushing the numbers into East Bay and picking up a few precincts? *Would it?*"

Big Ed forced another grin, but it was a fake. His eyes glittered tinily. "I had a hunch you knew," he murmured.

"It's my business," the commissioner said shortly, and the clicking started again.

"If you knew ——" Cameron began with heavy irony and sucked it back as the pipe came out, pointed directly at him.

Zipski held it so lightly, and it looked so big.

"I gather you're supporting him, too, Mr. Cameron."

"Well, I'm — I'm — well, naturally. Of course."

"Of course. Why?"

"Why?" Cameron flushed, stammered again, caught himself, and then reminded him he had the best of reasons.

Zipski nodded, playing with his pipe. "It wouldn't be because Erik's breaking out in other ways?"

"Well ——" Cameron began.

"Because policy's picking up track fans?"

"Well ——"

"Because Willoughby's running in the red?"

Cameron's cigarette singed his fingers. He crushed it out, abruptly lit another, and choked on the first puff.

"Just looking for a motive," Zipski said dryly.

Cameron indignantly stifled a cough. "If you know about all this, why don't you do something? After all," he added sarcastically, "lotteries are illegal."

Zipski palmed his pipe and looked him over carefully, as though for a mistake which must be there. "You're asking me to enforce the law," he said gently. "I'm only the commissioner of police."

"Only!" Cameron was confused.

But Big Ed wasn't. "We understand that," he said quietly. "But we also know you'd like Erik's scalp. That's why we're here. We can't do it without you. And you can't do it without us."

Zipski stared grimly at the wall, chewing his pipestem. It was true and it stung. His appointment, as an independent inspector unidentified with either Sylvester or Erik, had been entirely a fluke. The year before, a split between the bosses had permitted the election of a reform mayor, and Zipski had come in as reform commissioner. But the machines still held the City Council, and the mayor, essentially weak, had begun bargaining with them and now was helpless. The Department had returned to its norm — skillful fencing between Erik cops and Sylvester cops, all entrenched in the favor of men far more powerful than Zipski — and he, isolated and unallied, had been left to administrative routine and the loyalty of a few, a very few, old hands.

Big Ed rattled off the names of the minor suburban bosses. "They'll all be with us after the speech."

Out came the pipe. "What speech?"

"Wally's," Cameron said. "Senator Gillette's. He's going to kick off the campaign in about a week, with a terrific blast at Erik. Nothing libelous." He laughed nervously. "But damned near."

Zipski crossed his arms high on his chest and sucked the dead stem and pondered. So they were all lined up: Big Ed, threatened by Ben; Cameron, after the racing business that Ben's numbers had stolen; and Gillette, who needed a target. Some lineup. And Cameron was right: the law belonged with them. Zipski had wanted Erik so long and so hard he could almost taste the blood in his mouth. This was his chance. But he had to step into the lineup to do it. He didn't like the company. But maybe it was the only way.

Cameron had polished off his drink and was again genial. "Commissioner, we're having a few people out tomorrow afternoon, and we'd like you to come and stay over for dinner. Ed, here, will be there, and Wally, with his speech, and afterwards we can talk it over. Of course, if you have plans ——"

It was a decision and it had to be made now. Zipski juggled his pipe for a moment. "I can't come to dinner," he said crisply. "But I'll be glad to drop out later."

Big Ed nodded enthusiastic approval, and Cameron beamed. "Splendid!" he cheered. They set the hour and went over the route to his country house and then broke up, drifting toward the coatroom.

At the door Cameron added, as a calculated afterthought, "Perhaps Mrs. Zipski can come too? Mrs. Cameron is hoping to meet her."

He didn't mean it, and Zipski knew he didn't, and like the dinner it was out of the question anyway. "No," he said. "She can't."

Cameron murmured his regrets, and his wife's, and Big Ed winked. "That'll be two of us bachelors. My old lady's got the kids to worry about. Every holiday's the same. I guess the boss here," he indicated Cameron, "don't have that any more. His kids must be all grown. He's in what I call the granddaddy class."

He turned toward his host with a smile, but at that moment the doorman called him back to take a call, and he therefore missed the effect of his sally. Only the commissioner saw the darkness gather in Cameron's face and slowly fade. Only Zipski, hurrying toward his car, guessed at the bad luck in the Cameron home. He was, after all, a cop. He had been dealing with that kind of luck a long time.

The garbage men sprawled on the lip of the great bin, where the city's castoff food lay in huge piles, fetid and dank, and watched the crane come down. It floated slowly to their level, its jaws hanging open idiotically, and dug into the steaming heap of decayed meat, dried crusts, and soggy melon rinds. Then it swung wide, heaved up, and disappeared over a wall of laced cement pillars. Beyond, the fires of the incinerator flared brightly in the thickening dusk and the bare, sweatstreaked backs of the firemen wiggled and bobbed and bucked.

There were three men on the lip. The youngest, a pasty white youth in a rakish peaked workman's cap, fingered his blouse and stared vacantly into the smoke and flames. His dungaree trousers were caked with grease, his face was broken out, and his breath was asthmatic. As the crane swung out again he spoke to a small, light-skinned black curled on the ledge beside him.

"Bet Joe's the only boss when the checkers say, roll off that line, get goin', he's sorry."

"Yuh." Lou Dunton was bitter. Once he had been a driver, the foreman of a crew. A supervisor had found him junking — salvaging tin cans for sale outside — and now he was a crewman again.

"I bet Joe," said the youth, "he doan care if we never get home."

"Yuh," Lou said again.

Now the crane, worrying a thick mass of debris, caught the end of a jagged stick and tossed it, end over end, toward the three watchers. It fell short, but Lou cringed, and the youth, who was known as Snake, crawled off the ledge and retreated, snarling, toward a line of packer trucks waiting to unload.

"Do that on purpose," he cried, waving a filthy arm at the pillars. "Doan tell me!"

"Yuh," Lou muttered, spitting into the bin. "On purpose."

The falling stick had aroused the third man, who rose and stretched easily. He was tall, oddly built, with a long waist and crooked legs, and his skin was very black. High cheekbones sunk closely set eyes, and a wide, almost theatrical nose was conspicuously broken. He wore faded army fatigues, a rough woolen coat, open cloth overshoes, and an old felt hat with a tall crown and a narrow brim scalloped by the weather. His name was Sam Crawford, and that day he had fifty cents in the numbers game.

The crane teeth plunged into the pile again.

"My-oh-my," Sam said happily. "Looka there!"

Lou grunted and spat again.

Sam chuckled. "Ummmm-umngh! Man, that's a lotta stuff."

"A lotta rotten, no-good stuff."

"What you sayin'?" Sam's eyes twinkled. They were so close they gave his face a curious, top-heavy look. "That's betteren you get tomorrow, unlessen you been junkin' some mo'."

"You talk."

"Ummmm-umngh! Dig-er-up, dig-er-up, dig me up a fat, juicy tuhkey for a thankie-Thanksgiving. Hee-yuh!"

"Go on, talk," Lou said contemptuously and walked away.

One of the trucks detached itself from the line, rolled toward the ledge, and braked to a halt. A snag-toothed, ragged gray head appeared over the grimy window by the driver's seat.

Sam looked up cheerfully. "Them people is sholey in a hurry. They been sayin', 'Where that Joe?' since befo' you was up on the scales, even."

Joe leered. "Four ton, thirty-two pound. Four-thirty-two Friday number sure."

"Hell," Sam chuckled, "I got a system betteren that now. Dream system, best they is. Dreams I get."

Joe looked hurt. He rolled up the window, and Sam, running

around to the front of the truck, hopped in beside him. Slowly the truck backed toward the bin and stopped at the ledge. Sam reached over and pulled two bars by the shift, one after the other, and the truck body swung up and back and dumped their last load of the day on the heap below.

Joe never had to get out of the cab. His brother, a precinct executive in East Bay, had wheedled this job for him during the depression, and Joe had never found anything better. The work was light and he made a nickel an hour more than his men.

"Them dream systems is no good, Sam," he said. "You just know they can't be."

Sam shook his head cockily and climbed out of the cab. Outside, Snake and Lou were sweeping down the sides of the packer body. Joe rolled the window down again and called back.

"Snake, you hear about this new system Sam got?"

The boy leaned his broom against the rear wheel and came up to the hood. "Whatsat?"

"Jest dreams I get," Sam said defensively, looking down at the rough cement floor. He did not like Snake.

"Dreams!" Snake laughed. Joe shook his head, and Lou came to the front of the truck.

"What's a wet dream number, big boy?" he asked.

"They's all wet," Sam said solemnly. "Got to be wet to wuhk."

Snake laughed again, and Lou spat on the floor.

"Forget it," he said. "Ain't no way to beat numbers."

"That's right," said Joe, still wagging his head.

"Well, I got it beat." Sam was confident. "I got the big un today sure, you see. Look for it any time now. Seven-twenty-one."

He felt cozy inside. Today, he thought, today. Mr. Charlie Bond would be waiting for him at home, out front, and all the neighbors would be there. The stores would be open until nine, plenty of time for Lottie to get to them — and afterwards, maybe, a little load on for him.

Snake looked up tauntingly. "Boy, ain't you heard?"

"Heard what?" Sam mumbled, wondering if Fink Kerby, next door, would want a little load on too.

"Nine-oh-five hit. You lost, boy. Maybe your dream wasn't wet enough. Or maybe your system is the one is wet."

He danced toward the tailgate, doffing his cap and swatting the truck side with it.

Sam grinned weakly. His voice was uncertain. "That Snake, he say anything. He doan know no number. It ain't in yet."

Lou nodded positively. "That's a fact," he said. "Weighin'-in man got it. I thought you knowed, I'd of tole you."

"Nine-oh-five," Joe said softly. He had lost too. "Weighin'-in man."

Sam's smile faded slowly. He tried to keep it, but in a few moments nothing was left but a faint twitch at the corners of his mouth. He stood stunned, his bony wrists along his trousers, the thumbs against the seams of his fatigues, so that he appeared as a man standing at attention: a man in a misshapen old hat, open overshoes, and tight denim. A man who had just heard his orders, and hoped they were not true, and knew they were.

Then he staggered toward the tailgate, his eyes rolling. "You a liar! Dirty goddam liar! Where'd you get that lie, you liar, liar!"

"That's it, Sam," Lou called. "Weighin'-in man, lahk I tole you."

"Weighin'-in man, he doan know nothin'!" He was breathing hard and his lips were quivering.

"He got it all right," Joe said. "He heard it on the radio. Didn't have the heart, Sam."

Snake spat contemptuously and turned away.

Sam's mouth kept working, but his voice withered away. He stared blankly at Lou, and his long arms dangled helplessly by the ration pockets of his pants.

"Come on up in the cab," Joe called gently. "Ride up in the cab. It's warm up here, Sam, in the cab."

Lou went silently to the tailgate. He and Snake swung aboard, bracing their heels against the bottom, and Joe warmed the engine. After a while Sam walked clumsily to the side door and climbed in stiffly, and Joe pulled away from the bin. Outside the red, waning winter light deepened on the faces of the ugly stone houses, and men and women, bent half double in the gathering chill, hurried along the sidewalks. Long and fading streaks of day ribboned across the sky, and on each answering corner an arc lamp flickered on. In the cab Sam, his dead weight against the cab door, wept softly.

Across the black Seventh like a bent and wrinkled old arm lay West Concord, the main street of the poor. Along the upper arm, where the peeling frame rooming houses stood row on row, the street was wide and, in the winter, windswept. It narrowed until it reached the pit of the slum. Then it turned and headed straight for the river, ending in the wrist of the waterfront and the twisted fingers of the piers.

It was all cheerless, but the Elbow was the worst. And this was curious, for a hundred years ago, when the foul and sagging brick barns there were new and the hills around were green with farmland, when West Concord was a pike and the land beyond wild country, the gates had carried the names of gentlemen. The deeds still did. But the heirs of the gentry had long ago retired to the city's new edge, leaving the property to agents and asking no questions, never visiting the family homesteads to knock on the scarred doors of the past.

In the jungle behind the Elbow, where the alleys crowded upon one another like magpie tracks and the air lay mean and stagnant half the year and cold and dead the other half, Sam Crawford lived. He was buying half a split house on a corner where two dead ends met, and to meet payments he had rented the first floor to a junkman. The junkman was afraid the Crawfords would steal his junk and had padlocked the door at the top of the narrow stairs, so they had to come and go over a fire escape built by a former tenant, a chain of rusty automobile doors which bridged the sill of their kitchen window and the roof of a shed behind. The doors met on the branches of an old catalpa tree blossoming feebly in the eternal shadow between buildings.

In the winter they lived in the kitchen, by the wood stove where the only heat was. During the day it was all the world for the baby, dozing in his cardboard-box bassinet on the floor, and he wept bitterly when carried from it at bedtime. The little boy, Peter Paul, slept with him in the front room. Between them and the kitchen was the master bedroom, with the master bed, a creation of Sam's consisting of old upholstery springs stolen from a dump and bolted to a stripped packing case.

Lottie heard Sam coming over the automobile doors now, his overshoes thumping along the metal. He swung a ragged leg over the window sill and climbed in as slowly as he could.

"Honey," he said finally, his back sagging against the wall, "I done lost."

She said nothing but stood still, facing the stove, her thin back to him, her sneakers braced against a buckle in the floor. Despite the stove the room was cold.

"I done lost," he repeated in a low voice. "That number, the one I dream, it lost." In his voice there was a note of wonder, almost of disbelief.

"I know. Miz Kerby, she tole me."

That was the truth, but not all of it. Lottie hated the numbers, but their great need that Thanksgiving eve had almost brought her to share his faith. So when she stopped at Emma Kerby's to pick up her children on her way home with the wash, she asked Emma, who had a radio, to call over the winning number when it came in. Lottie was hanging diapers in the yard when she did. She thanked her kindly, finished hanging wash, and carried Peter Paul and the baby one by one up the shack ladder and over the automobile doors. She put them in the front room for their naps and stood, studying the stove wick and wiggling the bare toes in her tennis shoes, waiting for Sam. For half an hour.

She was exhausted. She always was on Wednesdays. With the junkman downstairs she could not use the washtubs there, and the others in the neighborhood always seemed to be in use, so once a week she hiked to the nearest municipal bath with her laundry. The bath was nine blocks away and the trip back, with the wet wash, a long stagger. Today the smashing of Sam's hope, and hers, had been too much. She was trembling.

He lowered himself clumsily into a rocker. The chair was frail and unsafe. He perched uneasily.

"I doan savvy," he said nervously, eying her still back. "It sure looked mighty awful good."

Lottie turned, her face tight. She was a small woman, with tiny hands and a little face, but her eyes were large, and when she was excited, as she was now, they could be alarming.

"*Mighty* good! *Awful* good! How many times I hear that?"

"Honey, you know . . . you know . . ." He fought for the right words and found nothing, and his voice died.

"No." She ran her eyes over him wildly, furiously, despairing. "I doan. I jest doan. I doan know why you can't do lahk other men, save and hep me and yore little boys. It's jest pitiful. We doan ever have nothin', doan eat nothin', doan do nothin', doan be nothin'. Jest go cold is all we do."

She danced frantically in the sneakers, arms swinging, face working. She had awakened the children. In the front room the baby was stirring with hunger, and Peter Paul had toddled to the doorway and stuck his woolly head around the jamb, his face wrinkled with curiosity. He wore an ill-fitting snow-suit Lottie had fashioned from odds and ends. The cloth was worn and poor, and despite new patches at the knees and elbows there were fresh holes there.

"Look at him, yore boy! Ever time I see him I'm ashamed! Doan have a heart left to fix his little coat, where it tore!"

She paused, and Peter Paul edged into the room, admiring the noise. Lottie turned to the stove and set up a clatter with the pans, and he giggled appreciatively.

Sam crumpled his hat in one big hand, studied it, shifted it to the other hand, crumpled it again, and again studied it.

He looked up imploringly. "It . . . it temptation me . . ." He stopped, groping wretchedly. It was hopeless. His shoulders drooped, and he looked down again.

Lottie was at the end of her wrath now. She wheeled and spoke slowly.

"It ain't gonna temptation you no mo', mister bossman. Hear?

27

No mo'! That dreamin' ain't gonna do no more temptationin'. Hear? You hear?"

He nodded miserably. She turned to the stove with purpose now, and Peter Paul, disappointed that the noise had stopped, disappeared into the darkened little room. Lottie opened the side window and took half a bottle of milk and a square of white margarine from the sill.

"Get yoursef ready."

A chipped basin stood on a Victorian commode under the single spigot. Sam applied himself to it with furious relief, scrubbing the grime away. When he had finished, the kitchen table was steaming with a vegetable hash and Peter Paul was agitating the flour-bag tablecloth. Lottie tiptoed from the front room.

"Baby asleep," she reported. They settled before the meal with a customary hush.

"Good Lord," she chanted, "Makeus thankful, Forthisanallourblessin's, Inchrisname, Amen."

After a few determined, businesslike spoonfuls she looked up with compassion.

"Honey," she said softly, "Mr. Kerby, he ask you to go shootin' in the mornin', remember?"

"Why that's so," he said, brightening. "Fink said that."

"More," Peter Paul demanded. Lottie dished out the little left, and they watched him chase it energetically with his spoon.

"My-oh-my," Sam chuckled. "That boy, if he doan ever do nothin' else, he sure eat good!"

Lottie tittered, and Peter Paul, attracted by this new noise, looked up and giggled with delight, and they did not mention policy again that evening.

They lay together on the makeshift bed and waited for the alarm. The hour before dawn was the best hour of the day for Lottie. The sounds of the slum were hushed, the last drunks had rolled home, or were under arrest, or sprawled quiescent in the alleys, and the rancid smell of morning had not yet risen. Under the last wave of night even the rats seemed asleep. If Lottie thought about it, she could almost see them quivering furrily in the pitch-black shadows lying in the damp gutters between backyard barrels and outside hoppers. She thought about it now, and she shivered.

Sam stirred. "Is you 'wake?" he asked drowsily.

No, she thought, still again under the army blanket. Not asleep, but dreaming. Her waking hours were his, but she must have this hour when the world slept with the slum and she could be, if only fleetingly, another person, shaping thoughts, creating images of life as it might be, of herself as she might be, and of him, yes even of him, as he might be.

Sam grunted, flopped over, and buried his head under a rag-stuffed flour bag, his pillow.

Poor Sam! She smiled softly in the darkness. He could imagine no other life than this. He hoped. He wanted to drive a packer truck. He wanted money. Most of all, he wanted to win the numbers game. Lottie longed for these things too, because he did and because they could bring comfort and security the family had never known. But they were the little hopes for her, good enough for the daytime, perhaps, or for the long hours of evening, when Sam was out with Fink Kerby. The hour before dawn was a special time. For it she saved her special dreams.

. . . The best time of the day, and now, in the smoky autumn, it had a sweetness and a savor setting it apart from even the hours before spring sunrises, when the air was new and the first birds sang on the branches of the dying tree in the yard. In autumn, late autumn, her dreams flourished best, for warm sadness, not warm promise, ran down the deltas of her heart.

All her favorite memories were of the fall. She remembered a faraway October morning in her first school, when the principal had presented her with a paperbound picture book for bringing to class each morning that month the cleanest hands and face. The afternoon before, her teacher had whispered the secret. She carried it happily home and in the ceremony next day wore a gay new frock, sewn through the night by her mother. She walked trembling to the blackboard, and after school she did not hear the catcalls of the boys. The book lay at home, unopened, for a week. Then one day she came home and found her mother poring over it, trying to decipher the print under the pictures.

The November she was ten her oldest brother had bought her the biggest doll carriage in all Montgomery Ward. The carriage body was of yellow wickerwork, and there were real springs, and steel hub caps, and an adjustable top. Turning her mind backward — it went backward so easily — she remembered prancing down the walk, crowing to her friends and singing to the doll under the hood.

Still another and later November had seen her elected president of the Carver High School Young Women's Art and Culture Society, an honor which lent glory to her whole fifteenth year. The society's adviser was a social worker. After the election she and Lottie sat and talked of the future. It had never seemed brighter. Lottie was to be a social worker too. She had wanted to be one very badly then, and looking back now from the rough embrace of an army blanket on a packing-case bed, it did not seem a bad want to have.

Here the autumns shattered against a bleak wall of winters. Of December heartbreak when her mother died and she left school to care for the family of men. Of December despair when war came and her brothers left and she came here with her father. Of February terror when he fell ill, a tubercular, unable, the Health Department doctor said, to work again.

The doctor had been kind. He offered to find room in the crowded chronic disease hospital, and when in her loneliness she refused, he found her a job as a waitress. Later the hospital took the old man against both their wishes, and she saw him only on Sundays and holidays on the great sunlit porch behind his ward. She saw him still. She would see him today. Even with a family she was afraid to miss a week, for twice, when the babies came, she had missed, and the following Sunday he was so wasted and pathetic she cried on the bus afterwards.

After the war her brothers drifted away, and Lottie settled into a life of work built around the dissolving image of her father.

The pattern was hardening when she met Sam. In his angular face there was a lost look appealing to her own lostness, and out of this had come love. It was not an abundant love. She had never known abundance. But it had the wry strength of a slum plant, and it prospered. Then, the following year, in the finest autumn of Lottie's life, Peter Paul was born. His birth gave her life a meaning; she had grown into that meaning and, with the second child, become another woman. Her father sensed this during their Sunday afternoons together: often his clawlike hand crept out to hers in the sudden fear that the woman she had become might abandon him.

Still it was not a full life, and she knew it. She did not complain. But each morning before the day began she gave herself to a dream of life as she would have it. It was a dream of clean air and soft light and freshness. Lottie had seen little that was new. She had always dealt with castoffs. But in her dream she was wearing a new dress and a bright tiara, standing in an enormous room with light streaming over her shoulders. Through a wide window behind her a pure wind blew from a warm sky, and as it blew it idled her shimmering skirt and billowed the great curtains hanging by the raised sashes. The curtains were the finest part of the dream. They were muslin, finespun and vast. And they were wonderfully, wonderfully white.

"Bug," Sam growled suddenly. "Go 'way."

"What bug?"

A fly whined lazily over the bed and slowly sunk toward them. Sam tracked it with his hand. It settled on the flaking enamel table by the bed.

Smack!

"Got him, goddam!"

The alarm rang.

A half hour later Sam heard the first wretched scraping against the bricks. He grabbed his gun, swung out the back window, and raced across the automobile doors.

Fink Kerby's appearance on the road was a signal for pedestrian

31

delight and driver wrath. He claimed defensively he was unlucky. There was really no way of telling. The wreck he drove was so far gone no one could have backed it out of a driveway without clipping a post or two. Besides, it was not a driveway Fink backed from, but the long and narrow passageway between his house and the next. He seldom tried it. It took too much out of the car.

Sam was halfway down the shack ladder when he heard a second, louder scrape. He slowed to a walk and sauntered around the far side of the house. It seemed impolite to watch from the back yard.

The car was edging out as he arrived in the alley. First came the exhaust, then the quivering fenders, and, finally, the shattered windshield with Fink sweating behind it. "C'mon," he cried desperately. "Get in!"

Sam did, hurriedly, and the car crawled out the alley to West Concord, Fink fighting it all the way. "Golly damn!" he yelled above the engine. "Some day!"

It was warmer than yesterday and brighter. The new sun dappled the Elbow sidewalks pleasantly, and over the brick housetops the sky was flushed. There was no one out to watch the car, and after the first block it stopped roaring and settled into a mild whiz. Still, it was a spectacle, and shortly after Fink limped into Howell Street, hugging the center line with a wobbling front wheel, other drivers began honking at him. He did not dare approach the curb. Once, pulling over for a snarling Cadillac, he had crashed into a parked sedan. He was uninsured. "I tole that poor man," he would explain philosophically, telling the story, "I said, if I had in-surance, I couldn't have no car, and what good's in-surance without a car?"

Now he said, "Beep, beep, beep. Alla time beep, beep, beep. If they in such a hurry, why they waste their time behind me?"

"Big folks," Sam muttered. "Big time folks, my, ain't they big."

"That's okay. Gotta do somethin'. Might as well beep, beep, beep. Doan bother me."

Fink was an oyster shucker. Once, long before, he had been an electrician's assistant, but he had lost his trade, with his friends,

32

in the deal that promoted him a house, a name, a car, and the fear that one day his old friends would square things. The deal was the Consolidated strike of 1943, in which Fink served as strikebreaker and scab captain. Since then he had lived with a name and a car in the fist of his fear.

Stuart Street was heavy with holiday traffic. Most of it seemed to be behind Fink. A whole parade of cars kept trying to cut around him and honking loudly when they found could not. Whenever one managed to slip by on the inside lane the driver glared at Sam, and if there was a family in the car, the family shouted indignantly. Sam shouted back, but Fink was indifferent.

At Pavilion Avenue a beefy cop was helping the light with his whistle. When it changed he tooted and gestured, motioning left turners through and ordering the others to speed across. Fink rattled up, the light turned yellow, and he stopped. The cop blew his whistle and motioned him through. Fink shifted gears, and the old car lurched forward and stopped again. The motor was dead.

He pressed the starter, and they heard a sickening click. The battery was dead, too.

"Oh, God," Sam groaned. Fink pressed the starter again, and again it clicked.

The cop came over, shouting, "When I say come I mean come. Who the hell do you think you are, boy?" The veins in his forehead stood out angrily.

Fink shook his head sadly. "My battery gone, mister. I'm jest stuck."

The officer stared, aghast. Then he wrenched the door open and pushed the starter himself. It clicked for him, too. At the same time the light changed and the lines of traffic began honking again.

He blew his whistle shrilly. "Shut up!" he bellowed. But the cars at the end of the line could not hear him, and they honked louder. He turned savagely to the car behind Fink.

"C'mon!" he yelled. "Give him a shove!" But the car was a

low Buick, and when the driver edged up and pushed, his bumper hooked under Fink's.

"All right, all right!" the policeman screamed. He looked as though he were going to cry. "You!" he pointed at Sam. "Get out and help!"

They untangled the bumpers and pushed the old car forward while the lights changed twice. Fink steered to the right, down a hill. When he began to pick up momentum, Sam opened the side door and jumped in. The cop turned furiously to the intersection again, shouting and waving the cars through.

Fink's motor wasn't catching. He was approaching the bottom of the hill, coasting slowly down the center lane, and it still hadn't caught. He turned to roll down a side street on the right, narrowly missing a new Ford coming up on the inside. The Ford skidded dangerously and then swerved outside, the driver shouting hoarsely as he passed. "Battery dead!" Sam shouted back, but the driver was gone and had not heard him.

Then, suddenly, the motor turned over. Fink turned in at the first filling station to have the battery recharged.

The attendant, a thin young man in faded khaki, was suspicious and demanded the dollar in advance. "On second thought," he said, prodding a shredded fender with his foot, "that'll be a dollar and a half."

"Dollar's reg'lar price," Fink protested. This happened often and he knew.

The man looked blank. "You want it fixed, yes or no?"

Fink looked from the man to the car. "Okay," he said sullenly. "You's the boss." He produced two bills. The attendant gave him a half dollar, and they waited in a corner.

Fink studied the coin. "Say," he began carefully, hunching forward and peering intently at the empty street. "I got me a new *Combo* yesterday."

Sam looked away quickly. *Black Combination* was a monthly magazine forecasting lucky numbers. One of its early predictions had come through, and it had been a steady seller since.

Fink rattled on. "Says, Christmas comin' up. Says, now's a time to zing it in, hit a big one."

Sam spat bitterly. "Well, well. Ain't that some dope for a quarter." The hurt was still there.

Fink was taken aback. He had bought the magazine because of Sam, because Sam's talk of numbers and dreams fascinated him. Fink had never heard of dreams like that before. "Course," he went on cautiously, "I doan claim nothin' for *Combo*. Never won nothin' for nobody I know yet. But this one say a Bible's the place for Christmas numbers. I doan know," he wagged his head skeptically, "but that's what it say."

"Bible? How that figger?"

The old magnet was drawing.

"Way *Combo* say it, ever year same numbers come up near Christmas."

"Funny. Doan remember nothin' lahk that."

"It's a way *Combo* figgers it. Takes a Bible talk for a day, lahk Luke, chapter two, verse sixteen. Two sixteen. That's a number, see?" He smiled happily.

"Ain't got no *Combo*." He had to make a show of resistance.

"Doan I tell you I got a *Combo*? Ain't you lissen?"

"Mebbe I'll have jest a little look."

Fink snorted. "Doan do me no favors."

Sam shut up. But he promised himself he would look at the magazine. Just look. He owed it to Fink.

The garage man was barking at them. "Hey, boy. Roll that junk outa here. C'mon, let's go."

They puttered past the suburbs and entered the Valley: the country opened up. An hour later they arrived at a long field freckled with tree clumps. Fink braked down noisily and the motor ended with a tortured wheeze.

Sam dangled an arm over the back of the seat and picked up his gun, a carbine he had smuggled home during the war. He kept it well oiled, with a patch in the muzzle and another in the breach. Fink carried a twenty-two. They had small hope of find-

35

ing more than a squirrel or two. They were there for a walk in the woods. Shooting was an excuse.

"See them trees?" Sam pointed. "Let's eat a sandwich there, then take off."

Fink nodded, and they started across the field. Dead leaves lay scattered across the thick grass. The day was warming up. There was a slight breeze.

"Right nice day," Sam sighed, watching the sun-flecked brush. "Sure lahk to get me a big fat un, mebbe two."

He pictured himself climbing over the kitchen window with a brace of squirrels swinging before him, calling to Lottie and Peter Paul, and as he finished his sandwich he reached for the carbine, pulled out the patches, and tucked them carefully in his blouse pocket.

Everyone was embarrassed but Jarvis Cameron, and he was indignant. Clearly, he thought, this was an unreasonable man. Equally clear was his duty to see that neither his morning nor his pocketbook was ruined. But the more he blustered, the more stolidly the farmer stood by his torn garden, and from the field of riders the sympathetic murmur grew stronger. What a ridiculous situation! thought Cameron.

"Come on, come on, come on," he barked, slapping his crop against his leg and taking up stirrups. "Fifty dollars is just absurd. It would buy you a new house."

The farmer looked at the leaning frame building beyond the field and then back to the robust figure in the scarlet coat above him. "No it wouldn't, mister," he said and spat vigorously.

"Well, almost. I'll give you twenty."

His first offer had been fifteen, and he had thought it would be snapped up. At most, he thought, the man would barter for five or ten more. Now a principle was involved. Usually Cameron was at his best in matters of principle. But in the wood the hounds had taken up the scent, and the longer he lingered here, the greater the fox's lead would be. It was intolerable. Surely twenty dollars would do.

"Fifty," the farmer insisted.

"Damn!" cried Cameron.

Behind him the forty riders adjusted stock pins, inspected flasks, and otherwise disguised their annoyance. There was nothing they could do. The Master led the hunt. But it was, they agreed, rather a bit of a nasty situation. Really, it was a shame, for the day had started beautifully, moist and crisp, ideal for the scent. The first hour's chase had been flawless. Then one of the whips had seen a disturbance of the fowl in this barnyard and here they had come, racing and shouting and plunging through the farmer's garden.

The farmer had come out of the barn, pitchfork rampant, and when he began shouting too they all pulled up in confusion and looked to the Master. It was his hunt. Further, he had done the most damage. His horse bridged five ruined furrows.

There was a baying in the far wood. The huntsman looked up uneasily. "They're tonguin', Mr. Cameron."

"I hear 'em," he said impatiently.

"Fifty dollars settle it," said the farmer, taking a fresh grip on the pitchfork.

There seemed no solution.

Then Madelaine Cameron detached herself from the nervous shuffling of the field and rode up.

"Jay," she said gently, poking at a wisp of gray hair under her topper brim, "everyone is waiting."

Cameron glared. "Goddam it, I know it, I know it, Maddy! But the man wants fifty bucks for his fool garden. Fifty bucks!" Still, he was glad she had come.

"It ain't a fool garden," the farmer shot back, knifing his fork into the soil. "You gimme it back and keep your damn money."

"Watch your language," Cameron said sternly.

"You watch yours."

"Jay," Madelaine pleaded. "It's only fifty dollars."

The Master slapped his crop against his thigh three times. Then he reached into his waistcoat, drew out a roll of bills, handed five to the huntsman, and turned to his wife. "I hope you're satisfied," he said coldly.

37

She smiled vaguely and started to reply. But before she could he turned abruptly and rode back through the field, and she was left with fading dimples and whatever it was she wanted to say.

One by one the riders wheeled and left; the huntsman paid the farmer and left too; the farmer swung the gate shut and locked it. Then he rolled a cigarette deliberately and lit it and watched the hunt disappear over a far ridge. The hunters were racing, hurrying to join the hounds, and from his gate he could see the buff britches of the last horsemen stretched taut across their backsides and, under them, the plunging buttocks of the horses. He walked back to the barn slowly, his pitchfork on his shoulder.

The last straggler was Madelaine. She was a wretched rider. Her husband galloped far ahead, a heroic figure in custom-built boots and a full-skirted coat, with a stock pin crowned by a perfect carat.

"Where is the little bastard?" she heard him shout merrily.

"Cast!" cried the whips.

"View halloo!" yelled the huntsman.

"Tally-ho!" bellowed Cameron.

With a great clatter they pounded after the fox, who vanished in a mass of weeds by a stream bed. The hunters halted, undecided.

Madelaine drew up beside a slight, windblown girl who had also been riding alone, astride a stallion. Whenever the horse moved the girl looked alarmed, and Madelaine thought she might like company. "Do we have him?" she asked her breathlessly, adjusting her hat.

"No. They're lifting the pack or something." The girl was the guest of another member. She had missed the end of the scene with the farmer and thought Madelaine must be a stranger also. It seemed unlikely so poor a rider could belong with the others. "Honestly," she said vehemently. "I think it's all so *silly*."

The mistake was a common one. Madelaine bore it gracefully. "Well," she said brightly, "I do hope we catch him."

"*You* hope?" The girl rolled her eyes. "God!"

Up front Cameron was in conference.

"Spaulding! What's the matter with the hounds?"

Spaulding, a puffy, weary man, had been leaning on his horse's withers, dreaming. "Got me," he said guiltily, looking around quickly in all directions. "Seem all right to me."

Harry Wilkinson, an old man in a frayed coat who had been Master before Cameron, joined them. "He probably crossed," he said. "It's thick on the other side."

Cameron eyed him sourly. "C'mon," he muttered, kicking out. "Damned hounds."

They rode down into a narrow draw and forded the stream, Cameron splashing ahead.

"Are we moving?" Madelaine asked.

"I suppose so," the girl said. "Yes, we are."

They crossed the stream and fell behind the others again. Madelaine was trying to place the girl. For several moments she frowned in thought and then burst out, "Alice!" The girl jumped. "You're Alice Saunders, Helen Saunders' niece, aren't you? You were Miss Skinner's."

Alice Saunders, Miss Skinner's, nodded.

"I'm Madelaine Cameron."

The girl looked at her warily. "Oh," she said. "Yes."

"My daughter was there for a while. A little ahead of you, I think."

"Yes," Alice said hurriedly. "I know. I mean," she added in confusion, "was she?"

"She was awfully good at hockey, you know. Really, terribly good."

The girl fidgeted in her saddle. "Yes," she said wretchedly. "Yes, she was. I mean, I heard she was." Then, rapidly, "Mr. Cameron is sort of the leader, isn't he?"

Madelaine smiled her vague smile. "He never misses a hunt. I'm afraid I embarrass him. I'm such a poor horsewoman."

"Oh." Cheerfully. "So am I!"

The field disappeared over a steep hill, and they tried to follow and could not. Farther down, the hill had a gentler face, and they went up this, sideways, calling out encouragement to each other. On top they found the others were well ahead. Before them a broad meadow stretched, speckled with the scarlet of the hunters and, far ahead, the weaving tan backs of the hounds.

"How pretty!" Madelaine lingered on the crest, resting and admiring the rolling grasses. "They teach riding at Miss Skinner's too, don't they?"

Alice had been thinking. "I've been thinking," she said, turning in her saddle. "I'm awfully sorry about what I said. About not liking the hunt. I mean, with Mr. Cameron in charge and everything."

Madelaine reached over and patted her hand. "My dear, don't be silly. I certainly don't mind. Between you and me, I find all this a little tiresome myself."

They rode down into the meadow and moved out on level ground. Twice Madelaine glanced at Alice. She was comforted that the girl appeared relieved. It wasn't surprising, for Alice had not been at all sorry. She merely wanted to change the subject.

The hounds were loping back and forth in a neat pattern, checking covers. Behind them the hunt staff was poised on a small rise, hunched forward, watching the brush.

Cameron was sweating valiantly. "Goddam farmer," he muttered.

Spaulding nodded mechanically. Wilkinson shrugged. There was a scuffling to the right front, and everyone turned to face it.

As they did, several things happened at once. A patch of brown fur shot out of a clump of bushes and scampered across the meadow. The dogs went boiling away in full cry, the horsemen headed after them, the huntsman bawled "Gone away!" and Cameron, beginning a yell of his own, ended with an outraged scream as his horse slipped and pitched him to the ground.

The field swept past, several of the ladies brandishing riding crops and shouting gaily. Madelaine and Alice were cantering up as Cameron regained his saddle and galloped wildly away. His cap lay on the ground.

At the top of the rise they slowed to a walk. "It's never happened before," Madelaine panted. "He must be just furious." She saw the girl smirking and lifted her chin.

Ahead lay a small orchard, another meadow, a copse, and, finally, a road and woods beyond. The fox was winning. He built up a long lead and jumped into the orchard. The pack, well-bunched, plunged after him. The brush was thick and the scent could easily be confused.

Just as the hunt staff vanished among the trees, closely followed by a charging Cameron, Madelaine saw a wisp of brown streak out the far side and disappear into a patch of tall grass.

"Oh!" she cried excitedly. "Look!"

Alice craned her neck but saw nothing. The hounds and the hunters were still in the orchard.

"What should I do? Didn't you *see*?"

The girl was confused. "See what?"

"The fox! The *fox*!"

Still no one came out of the trees. Madelaine dug her heels into the flanks of her horse, but he did not move.

"What are you doing?" Alice demanded.

Madelaine swung her legs out as far as they would go and whacked them against the horse. He sprang forward, moving steadily toward the orchard, and she clutched the reins frantically in one hand and clapped the other to her topper, slanting it tipsy over one ear.

She entered the orchard. At that moment a shot cracked out somewhere ahead.

The echo ricocheted against the trees and was followed by another shot, and then by another, and then by silence.

"Oh, Jesus," Alice breathed. "Jesus, Jesus."

The hunters and the hounds swept out of the orchard and bore down on the far copse. Now Cameron was once more in the lead.

Sam had been standing, tapping his magazine in place, when he heard the rustle in the bushes. Otherwise he would have

41

missed. Fink, sprawled under a tree, was still groping for his gun when the carbine spoke.

Whump, it said, and *Whump.* And as Fink sighted along his barrel it said *Whump* once again and shut up.

"Guess you done him in," Fink said, relaxing.

Sam flipped the safety over and held the gun in one hand, his fingers tight against the breech. Under the scalloped felt hat his eyes were bright.

"Sure did," he said slowly, moistening his lips. There was a thin sob in his voice, and Fink looked at him quickly. "I sure as hell did."

They crossed the clearing and stood over the mess. The fox had come out of the trees fast, head up and legs pumping, and Sam had led him wide and aimed low. The first shot had crushed his skull and started him rolling, and the second two had torn open his belly. He lay quivering on the ground, weeping blood on the rusty grass.

Fink stared at Sam and Sam stared at the fox.

"Man," Fink said nervously. "He real daid."

"Sure did," Sam repeated stupidly. "Sure as hell did."

His head hung forward, his eyes were glassy, and with his free hand he rubbed a growing dampness high on the left leg of his fatigues.

Fink backed away, fumbling with his shirt front. "Killed him daid," he said shrilly, trying to laugh.

"Sure did, sure did."

Fink looked down at the fox and up at Sam again. He was rocking slightly on the balls of his feet and rubbing, rubbing his trousers. The fox's blood dilated on the grass in low, rhythmic spurts.

Then the baying of the hounds penetrated to the clearing and Fink ran through the trees, to the bushes on the far side of the grove.

"Daid," Sam chanted softly to himself. "Daid, daid, daid."

Fink ran back. His face was wild.

"People comin'!" he shouted. "Boss people!"

Sam did not move. Fink grabbed his arm and shook it frantically.

"Sam! Real boss people comin'!"

The pack burst through the bushes and drew up in the clearing. They crept into a ring around the fox, whimpering. Still Sam did not move. Fink leaned against a tree, trembling.

Cameron crashed through the trees, fighting for breath, his great face crimson and sweat streaming from his horse. Spaulding and Wilkinson were behind him, and behind them was Madelaine, miraculously still in the saddle, her hat gone and her hair unbound and ragged on her shoulders. The others ranged up in the brush and for a long moment there was nothing but the sound of heavy breathing from the riders and the quiet crying of the hounds. Neither Sam nor Fink had moved, and the fox's spasms were dying away.

The huntsman came up. "Oh my God," he groaned.

With a tremendous effort Cameron controlled his lungs.

"You," he blurted hoarsely, waving his crop unsteadily at Sam. "You with the gun."

Sam looked up dully and continued to rub his crotch. The stain had spread. Cameron saw it. He slapped his chest fiercely, still gasping for air. "Stop that! Goddam it nigger cut it out!"

Sam turned. His face sagged foolishly. "Yessah," he said in an odd tone. "Yes indeed." He was the only one not listening to himself.

"Did you, did you kill that goddam fox?"

Sam nodded listlessly.

"Yessah, killed him daid."

"You dirty bastard!"

Cameron turned in his saddle, moved forward, and lifted his crop high. His face was twisted, he crouched forward, he began to swing.

"Jay."

He wheeled to face his wife. "What the hell do you want?"

"Jay, don't."

Madelaine's throat was very dry. Her voice sounded harsh. She was staring at the mane of her horse.

"*Will you shut your goddam mouth?* I'll handle this!"

Everyone looked away except Wilkinson, who had been watching the fox since he arrived and kept on watching it.

Madelaine was very white. Her fists, wrapped in the reins, were tiny knots. She glanced down vacantly. Her eyes bulged. She looked popeyed.

Sam, aroused at last by the towering figure above him, had backed against a tree. He was alert now, watching the crop slyly.

But Cameron did not strike.

Instead he turned on Fink, who had crept, like a scared animal, to the edge of the clearing.

"You," he barked. "Come here."

"Yessah, boss. Yes, indeed."

He came forward, fear rolling his eyes.

"What's your name?"

"I'm Fink."

"Fink what?"

"Fink Kerby. It's a name."

"What are you doing here?"

Silence.

"Wh —"

"Out hikin', boss. Jest out hikin'."

"With guns?" Cameron's scorn was brutal.

"Shoot a buhd maybe, boss."

Cameron waved his crop at the furry corpse. "Call that a bird, do you?"

No answer.

"Well, do you?"

No answer.

"What are you doing on this property?"

Fink looked up, pleading. "I didn't do it, boss."

Cameron's eyes glittered. "Then he did it, didn't he. Answer me, didn't he?"

"I said I did," Sam said.

He sloped against the tree, his seat flat on the bark and his head sunk back into his shoulders. The skin was tight across his cheeks, and he had to wrinkle his lips to keep them together. His hands were shaking. He rested them on his knees and still the fingers shook.

Cameron studied him coldly.

"Don't you know," he said slowly, "it's against the law to shoot a fox in front of the hounds?"

"No. Nobody tole me no law lahk that."

"Nobody told you."

"No."

"You filthy black swine."

A wave of shock passed over the huddled riders, something deeper crossed Sam's face, Fink cringed, and Madelaine turned her horse and left the clearing alone.

"Get out," Cameron said. To the huntsman he added, "See that they go."

He looked down contemptuously into the sullen, working face and then led the others away through the brush. The huntsman stood by the dead fox, waiting.

Fink staggered brokenly out of the grove, down the field to the car, and Sam followed, his long flat-footed stride sweeping across the grass and his head cocked to one side, as though listening for a faint sound which must not be missed.

In the car Fink collapsed, trembling. Sam drove, and he drove fast. After the second mile the flickering died out of his face, but the excitement lingered in his eyes, and he seemed strangely exalted.

Madelaine closed the glass door, squeezed her eyes shut, and twisted the cold water faucet to the far left. Then she screamed. The shower was powerful, there was no one else in the wing, and so only she heard the yell. Hearing it, hearing the full-throated roar, she drew herself up, filled her lungs, and shouted again, louder and more angrily. It was an unlikely scene: a thickset

45

woman in her early fifties, naked and quivering under the spank of a cold shower, bellowing like an enraged animal. Madelaine thought it unlikely. She came to the end of a breath, panting, and opened her eyes with wonder.

She could not understand why the hunt had upset her so. Her husband had insulted her in public before and she had forgotten it. In the pleasant, narrow little garden which was her mind the flowers were always neatly set out, the shrubbery just pruned, the grass freshly cut. No subversive thoughts dwelt there. Everything in her training had taught her to mend quietly whatever rents appeared in her life. She always had before. Why not now? She did not know. And so she shut her eyes again, threw her head back, turned her head up to the streaming shower head, and shrieked.

Cameron had been untroubled. He decided Sam's odd caressing of his trouser front had disturbed her, and for that he could make allowances. He made them on the way home, denouncing the Negro race while the black chauffeur blandly watched the curving road. The incident was best forgotten. Directly they reached home she should take a long nap. And trembling against the upholstery she managed not to flinch as he stroked her hand. She remained that much of a lady. Her training remained effective to that nice degree. When the car drew up at the portico she went straight to her room, undressed quickly, stepped into the shower, and let go.

She was at her dressing table a half hour later, humming softly, when her son Fred entered with a rush. He was a slight, serious young man with gentle features, delicate hands, and many convictions. "What's this about Dad?" he demanded indignantly.

"What's what about Dad?" she said, smiling. His earnestness amused her, as the earnestness of sons often does.

He sat on the edge of the bed, nervously patting the back of his head. He was clearly upset, but that did not bother Madelaine, for she seldom saw him serene. Since resigning abruptly from Princeton he had moved downtown, joined the staff of a pro-

46

gressive social agency, and thrown his frenetic young energy into the support of a half dozen liberal organizations. The very sensitivity which thus drew him conspired against his peace of mind. He and his father rarely spoke any more, and he had come today only to please his mother. On the way he had stopped and met a band of resting hunters. He had driven, furiously, here from there.

"This about swearing at you."

Her smile vanished. "Where on earth did you hear that?"

"At the club. From about fifteen different people."

"That club! After all your father's done for them!"

"Then it's true!"

"What's true, dear?"

"He did swear at you!"

"Freddie, you know your father."

"Yes. He did it, didn't he?"

"Oh, Freddie, he didn't mean anything."

"I know what he meant."

"Where are you going? Freddie!"

But he was gone. She turned to her dressing table and studied her image in the mirror, then reached uncertainly for the rouge.

When his son came into the library Cameron was still in his riding clothes, telephoning the track. He looked up casually and continued to talk, jotting notes on a scratch pad, and when he had finished he hung up and rose to leave as though the room were empty. Madelaine's brother had once said Cameron had two sets of manners, for guests and for the family, but there was really just the one for guests. At home he had no manners at all.

"What's your hurry?"

"What's my hurry?" His tone pegged the idiocy of the question. "I've got company coming, boy. Got to dress."

"To be polite, I suppose."

"That's right. What about it?"

Fred flushed. He carried himself very close to the surface. "How about being polite to my mother once in a while?"

Cameron thrust his short neck forward. "What?"

"How about swearing at the hounds — if you have to swear. I suppose you have to."

His father didn't understand. He perched on the desk and looked grave. "Your mother's upset, Freddie. Very upsetting incident on the hunt."

"Does that mean you have to treat her like a hound bitch?"

Cameron started and then began to redden himself, for the third time that day. "Who do you think you're talking to?" he demanded harshly.

"I think you made an ass out of yourself today. I don't mind that so much, but you made an ass out of my mother, too, and I want to know who in hell you think *you* are, doing a thing like that, to her, in front of people." He spoke very rapidly, agitating the back of his neck with nervous fingers.

Cameron lit a cigarette deliberately, blew a cloud of smoke into Fred's face, and attacked under it.

"Listen you." His voice was low. "You, with your asses and bitches. You that can't work with decent people, have to work with niggers and kikes."

Fred twitched. Cameron leered. His son's inversion of his own bigotry was a tragedy of his middle age. "Hurts, don't it? It ought to hurt. You, you're ashamed of *me*. What a laugh that is. Ashamed of *me*."

"I didn't say that."

"Don't tell me. All right. You listen for a change. I'm fed up with your Red ideas. Stay away from here if you don't like it."

Fred tried to check the cringe. "I don't come here to see you," he whispered.

"And your mother feels the same."

"I don't believe it." The whisper lower.

"We'll see what you believe." He slid off the desk and glared. It was a brittle glare, breaking fast. "A hell of a swell family this is. A son that's a Red." He paused, breathing hard. "And a girl that's a whore."

Fred lurched to his feet, but Cameron was moving swiftly out

48

the door, into the hall. The glare shattered, but Fred did not see it. Sarah, the maid, crossing into the library with a tray of potato chips, saw, but she was an older woman, well disciplined, and she did not slow her step or otherwise show surprise.

The first guest was Nora Tracy, a faded little woman with a throaty, finishing-school voice. She was a native of Memphis and had been married three times and was now single.

"That Floyd of mine!" she giggled as Sarah took her wrap. "Honestly! All the way over here he said, 'Miz Nora,' he said, 'yo sho cain't be too cayful whay-ah yo pahk, cayahsin' if'n yo pahk wrong, them *police* they poun' yoah cah, they *poun'* it hahd!' He really thinks when they impound it they pound it, you know, pound it with a hammer!"

She burst into shrill laughter. It was nothing malicious with her, but merely something endemic with unmarried southern women.

Cameron chuckled and led her into the main room, strutting. He was gallant in a plaid jacket and flannel trousers, and his gray hair was slicked back.

"Old fashioned, Nora?"

"Oh, darling!"

The bell rang again and Madelaine, running down the stairs, answered it. Helen Saunders and her niece, Alice, were outside. Alice was nervous.

"Are we early?" Helen asked weakly, peering about. She had promised Alice they would be late, and now she anticipated a row afterwards.

"You're just on time."

"Willie always called it garbage," Nora was explaining to Cameron, exhibiting the fruit in her glass incidentally and specifically the fact that the glass was empty. "You knew Willie, didn't you? My second husband."

"Willie? Oh, sure. Hey, let me get you another."

"Darling!"

"We brought up the rear," Madelaine told Helen. "We were

the very last. It was so nice to have company back there." It would not do to ignore the hunt altogether.

"Sorry I missed it," Helen lied.

Alice looked desperate. "May I have a drink?" she asked.

"Oh, I'm so sorry. Sarah!"

In three swift gulps it was gone and Alice sought the maid herself.

"She knew Jan at Miss Skinner's," Madelaine said.

"Yes," said Helen. "What a nice song!"

The musicians were singing:

> All I want for Christmas is my two front teeth
> My two front teeth, my two front teeth
> All I want for Christmas is my two front teeth
> Tho I can with you Mewwy Chrithmath.

"They played hockey together, or nearly did. I mean at the same time."

"Yes," Helen said. "Oh, they're going to sing it again! Sing it again!" she called. They hadn't been going to, but they did.

The doorbell rang and Helen joined Nora, whom she detested.

In the hall Cameron enthusiastically greeted a jaded man in tailored tweeds. "Well, Symonds! Fine day! Have a drink. No? Glad you came. Damned glad."

Helen jerked her head toward them. "I gather Smith Symonds is interested in Willoughby," she said dryly.

"What?" said Nora. "Oh, that c-razy song!"

The music swelled noisily, and only Sarah's practiced ear heard the bell peal. She opened it on Mike Holloway, burly in a shapeless overcoat. "Jay!" he bellowed, coming into the foyer. "Goddam it, Jay, I'm thirsty!"

The drinkers turned, surprised, and Holloway grinned impishly, the grin explaining that his boorishness was only a joke, that this was just the old inspector having his little fun. Cameron pranced across the foyer, twisted his hand, and grandly presented him with a martini. They disappeared among the guests.

Fred sat in the darkened library and watched the party. It looked unreal from there, a burlesque of itself. The front room was crowded now, and the guests, like marionettes, pirouetted and bowed and danced up to one another, saying things they did not mean, smiling at people they did not like, while the music, now maudlin, now giddy, mocked them though they did not know it.

He wondered if life were better this way. Certainly it was politer and, if you were used to it, more pleasant. On the whole morale was high in the other room. Whether the marionettes were happy was unimportant. They thought they were. Then he was wrong to wish the straw were blood and the canvas flesh. The puppets did not want life. The mere suggestion would annoy them. Perhaps, he reflected, he was himself only a marionette with twisted strings. Possibly no one was alive, quite possibly there was no real life and could be none. He stared bleakly into the artificial light, as a bathtub suicide stares at his slashed wrists, watching them leak blood under water.

"Highball, anybody?" Alice was staggering. No one heard her.

"Nora, you're spilling your drink."

"What, darling?"

"Look at your drink, Nora."

"Darling, I *can't!* I'm looking at *you!*"

Cameron had Smith Symonds against the sideboard.

"Erik won't last, Symonds. Take my word for it. I can't tell you how I know, but I know. He's only a crook, a crook with pull, maybe, but what does that mean? Look at Binaggio."

"Sorry. I've examined this thing very carefully, Cameron. It simply will not wash. Who'll come to the track when he don't have to leave the drugstore? We'll always have the book, and when the book's too big, the track's a flop. It's too big here. Much too big."

"Erik isn't a bookie, Symonds. Never wrote book in his life."

"Same thing. Worse. If they bet the book at least they're following the track. At least they're interested. Policy is just another step away. Anyway, that's where the money's going."

"You can't sell horses short, Symonds. They'll always be horses."

"Horses." He laughed shortly. "Who wants to look at a horse?" He walked away.

There was a fluttering at the door, and Sarah ushered in Big Ed Sylvester, looking conspiratorial under a snap rim turned down all the way around. He nodded familiarly as Cameron hurried into the foyer.

"Nice party. Where's Wally?"

"Hasn't come yet. Look." He took his hat and led him to a corner by the hall telephone. "Remember — this is our only deal." Quite apart from the coming drive, Sylvester had performed certain services for him in the City Hall, and he was anxious that no one, not even his family, know of them.

Big Ed grinned. "I'll remember if you want, but I'd rather forget."

"All right, all right. Just forget everything, even with Wally."

"Right. Customer always is."

The party quieted as they moved into the room. The louder guests were hushed by their friends.

"Alice, stop laughing!"

"I'm laughing!"

"Well, stop it!"

"I can't!"

Big Ed came in behind Cameron, carrying his bulk daintily, with a prancing little step. He was only a name in the Valley, and the other guests watched curiously. Cameron had told them he was coming, and that Zipski would be out later. But Zipski was just a name, too, and they wondered, with the idle interest of the indifferent, which was which.

Wrong he might be, Fred decided, but he doubted it. Not even puppets could perform so badly if they were well in hand. No, his strings were not fouled. They had been, and unsnarling them had not been easy, but now they were untangled, if puppet he really was, and he doubted that, too. The real snag lay there before him. He could almost see it between the unctuous Sylves-

ter and his father, now urging arguments on the impassive Symonds in a last, desperate surge.

He watched Big Ed: fat, sleek, pompous, shrewd — the man,
one would think, least likely to succeed at a Valley party. Yet
there he was, moving with oily grace among the women, avoiding
the openly hostile and chucking the hospitable under their sagging
chins. He had a gift, Fred grudgingly admitted, a gift of false
charm which somehow warmed and persuaded even those who
knew how dishonest it really was. His uncle Wallace had it too,
and so, he supposed, did the poisonous Erik. Fred wondered with
grim amusement whether, when they put their heads together,
they hypnotized one another.

Yet it was a mistake to laugh at a genius which could draw so
chaste a hermit as Zipski to its councils. Fred loved bureaucratic
gossip, although his sources were sharply limited. His job at the
agency was largely clerical, and the agency head, a militant liberal
who parted his straight gray hair in frank imitation of Henry
Wallace, had lost his few influential friends since the war, and
then had lost himself in martyrdom, and now knew nothing of
the city. But Zipski was decent: Fred knew that. The month
before he had gone wearily from department to city department,
gathering data for the agency's annual report on discrimination,
and only at police headquarters had his questions been answered.
The policemen had been no politer than the others, but they
had to answer. Zipski had ordered it. One of his first moves as
commissioner had been to announce that matters of public record
were public to everyone, and when a police clerk had telephoned
and indignantly asked if this included such as Fred, Zipski had
replied that it did.

Someone turned on the light.

"Hello, Freddie. Didn't know you were in here." It was Inspector Holloway, holding an empty glass and a small platter and
swaying. "Wanna drink?"

"No, thanks." He wondered what Holloway would have done
if he had said yes. Obviously he had come here to escape the
crowd.

"Chip?"

"Thanks." Fred took a fistful.

"Careful. Spoil your dinner."

"Oh well. I'll probably lose it anyway."

Holloway was tiresome. Fred knew that. Still he did not leave. He could not without being rude, and to that extent he was a marionette.

In the other room the party was approaching a climax, with Cameron leading it. Usually he let his guests carry the final heights but Symonds had been firm and Wallace had not arrived. His hair was rumpled. He lurched.

"Everybody drunk?" He beamed at Nora. "You drunk?"

"Oh, *darling!*"

"You?"

"Not very," Alice mumbled, eyes woozy. "Not very *very.*"

The musicians began singing and everyone joined in.

> *Oh they cut down the old pine tree*
> *And they hauled it away to the mill*
> *To make a coffin of pine for that sweetheart of mine*
> *Oh they cut down the old pine tree.*

"Here it comes," said Helen. "Oh, baby."

> *Oh* CUT IT DOWN!
> *Oh* CUT IT DOWN!
> *And they hauled it away to the mill*
> *To make a coffin of pine for that sweetheart of mine*
> *Yes they cut down the old pine tree.*

"Here *what* comes?" asked a thin, smartly dressed woman.

"Stick around."

"OH CUT IT DOWN!" Cameron bawled. "OH CU–T IT DOWN . . ."

"I see." The woman nodded. "I suppose that's his outlet."

Madelaine was in a corner, talking to Sylvester. She looked up quietly. "The man with the fiddle has a nice voice, I think."

"Looks drunk to me," he grunted.

"Yes, they cut down the old pine tre-ee-ee," everyone sang, hoping that would end it.

"OH CUTITDOWN, CUTITDOWN," Cameron bellowed.

Smith Symonds backed toward the door, but Nora and Alice joined their host, screeching the chorus off key. Helen and the smartly dressed woman disappeared into the hall. Madelaine smiled at her husband. Big Ed appeared to be falling asleep.

The musicians crooned wearily:

> For that sweetheart of mine
> Yes . . . they . . . cut dow-n
> The o-ld pi-ne tre-ee-ee.

"OH CUTIT, CUTIT, CUTIT, CUTIT DOW–NN! YEAH, CUTITDOWN!" Cameron roared, his right hand deep in Nora's bosom and his left groping for Alice's. They leaned against him, brackish drinks in hand, chanting wildly.

> For that sweet-heart of pi-en
> Oh they cut down the o-ld mi-en tre-ee-ee . . .

"WOW! WOW! WOW! CUTITDOWN!"

The saxophone player huffed and the accordionist tried to keep pace with the shifting rhythms. The fiddler, who did look rather giddy, sawed away, smirking foolishly.

Holloway had become enmeshed in a series of remarkably silly statements and was frantically trying to defend them. He really hadn't thought Fred was listening.

"Why shouldn't Zipski come, Mike?"

"It's never been done!" Holloway blurted, furious at being caught. "The Department's above politics! The old man never would've done it."

"That's absurd. Far as I can see, he's just going to talk to them. Holzweig sure did a lot more than that when he was commissioner."

"Oh yeah?" Holloway said hotly. He regarded any reflection on Holzweig as a personal affront. "And what makes you think they'll just talk? I know Zipski. I bet the whole Department gets a shakeup."

"Well — why not?"

"Why *not*? It was good enough for the old man!"

The front door opened without a ring and a tall, slender man in a black homburg and formal topcoat stepped into the foyer. He stood stiffly by the clothes closet, quietly putting his things away, and then walked down the hall and stood, amused, watching the party. He wore his silver hair long, and his eyes were Madelaine's, drawn with a sardonic cast. None of the celebrators noticed him. The musicians wanly hoped he was a neighbor protesting the noise. The fiddler smiled sternly.

Then Holloway saw and sat upright. "Wally's back."

Fred nodded indifferently. Then Sarah, who had been frantically trying to attract Cameron's attention on another matter, saw too and said so. He started, gave a little shout, and pounded out and pawed him affectionately. Sylvester minced behind, fat hand extended.

"He's staying to supper?" Holloway asked, hoping to change the subject.

"I guess so," Fred replied, adding, without a breath, "maybe corruption isn't good enough for Zipski."

"Oh, hell, that's a lot of talk," the inspector said indignantly.

"Then why does he want a shakeup?"

Holloway was sly. "Suction, that's why. He wants suction."

"With who?"

He jerked his head toward the other room and nodded meaningfully.

"With Big Ed? Oh Mike, come on."

"I'm telling you, Freddie. No other reason."

56

"You sound like one of Ben Erik's men. At least they've got good reasons for being against changes in the Department."

"Don't tell me you take these stories about Ben being the numbers boss seriously!"

"I don't take anything seriously."

"Then why get excited about Zipski?"

Fred yawned. "I don't even take you seriously, Mike."

Holloway stood, annoyed at last. "You're young," he said feebly and left.

Everyone was leaving. The party was breaking up. Nora and Alice were moving it to the club. What they were moving, it developed, was themselves, a reluctant Helen, and two amiable young Princetonians down for the holiday. Wallace had gone upstairs. Big Ed was nodding on the couch. The rest of the guests were gone, and Madelaine had vanished into the kitchen. Cameron sadly saw the dregs to the door. He really wanted to go with them, he said, and meant it, but the family always spent Thanksgiving together.

On the portico Alice giggled something about one Cameron who was missing. Fortunately he was too groggy to notice, and Helen hurried her down the drive.

He closed the door weakly and leaned against it. In the front room the musicians were packing silently. Fred walked out of the library, his first drink in his hand.

"Well," he said cheerfully, "they cut down the old pine tree."

His father looked at him stupidly.

"Cut it down," he said.

They filed into the candlelit dining room sluggishly. Only Wallace wanted the meal. Sylvester had dined with his family at noon, and the others weren't hungry. They sat and dawdled.

Usually Cameron dominated supper, but he was exhausted from the singing and sat with glazed eyes, mechanically sipping his warm cocktail and stifling belches. In the beginning conversation flagged, for Madelaine was busy with Sarah, Fred was thoughtful, and Sylvester still seemed drowsy, but once Wallace had taken the edge off his appetite it picked up, for he was in good spirits. He had just returned from a tour of the state.

"The counties want me," he announced confidently. "It's practically unanimous."

Big Ed perked up. "They want you in the city, too, Wally." He winked familiarly at Fred. "On the east side they won't settle for anybody else."

"I'm a cinch in the primary if I can get city support."

"And a fat cat to pay the bill," Cameron grunted, turning to his shrimp with obvious distaste.

Wallace chuckled and reached for a roll. "The cat I have is fat enough."

"Don't be too sure. Symonds turned me down cold tonight."

"Oh!" Madelaine was distressed. "I'm so sorry, Jay."

But Wallace was undaunted. He could not take Willoughby's losses seriously. As a young man he had learned the sport's quicksilver quality from a mutual friend, Cameron's Princeton roommate, who had inherited a big track on the Gulf shortly after graduation. That track had suffered alarming reverses in the beginning but had, with the help of Cameron and a few others, pulled through, convincing Wallace that racing worked that way — something always happened, someone always stepped in to carry you over the rough spots.

He bolted his roll. "Don't worry about Symonds. When we get through he'll be begging you for shares."

"I hope so." Cameron sat back listlessly, waiting for confidence to return. "What a joke if your speech should fall flat."

"Fall flat!" Big Ed almost shouted, jarring everyone to attention. "It'll fall about as flat as the atomic bomb."

"Maybe," Cameron said reluctantly. "You can't tell."

"I can tell. It'll split this town wide open, that's what it'll do. I'm not guessing. I *know*."

"Ben's been looking for trouble for a long time, and the boys know it," Wallace said. "All we have to do is run up the flag, my flag. They'll cheer." He looked to Big Ed for approval. "Right?"

"Dead right."

Fred sat up. "You're going after Ben Erik?" he asked his uncle.

"You bet. We all are."

"But why you? I mean, why doesn't Mr. Sylvester, here, do it himself?"

His father leered. "Thought you knew all about politics."

Wallace reached for a cigar with an easy gesture, practiced against the day congratulatory reporters trooped in. "Because I'm a hick, Freddie. A city slicker wouldn't have a chance."

"I don't get it."

Big Ed waved a fat forefinger. "If I tried it, young man, I'd be sunk."

"Why?"

"Same reason Bill Meck, say, or Maury Warrick, or anybody else in politics would be. I wouldn't back them, and they wouldn't back me. Too risky. Build up a city man and he's liable to get ideas and try to break out of his district — the way Ben has. Only way you can line everybody up is from the outside, with a country man you can trust," he nodded at Wallace, "from a place like Cornwall County."

Wallace poked the cigar end into a candle flame and puffed. "That's where the big hick gets his chance," he said softly.

Madelaine peered anxiously across the table. "But you aren't *really* a hick, Wally."

"Why not?" he chuckled. "Hicks vote like everybody else, and they're loyal. It's a loyalty I can use." He spoke as though it were a device.

Wallace rolled on, ringing the changes on Big Ed's discovery of unsuspected Erik strength building up in his powerful East Bay organization wards, of the dealings of Erik men in the legislature and City Council and, finally, of the undercover spread of Erik's racket. "We wouldn't have a chance if he weren't up to his neck in numbers," he ended.

Fred felt contentious. Once he had admired the dedication which kept his uncle living on, alone, in the old Gillette home, too poor to marry and too proud to sell his vote. But that was before he discovered that for Wallace, honesty and poverty, like loyalty, were only devices.

"What makes you think Erik is behind policy?" he demanded.

Everyone looked at him. "Why, even I know that," Madelaine said.

"Sure. But can anybody prove it?"

His uncle's eyes twinkled. "I rather think the police can."

"Mike Holloway thinks the commissioner wants to shake up the Department."

Wallace drew tentatively on his cigar. "I daresay."

Big Ed rocked back. "I guess one of the first men he'll try to move is an old friend of mine," he said slowly. "He's wanted to boost Rudy Morelock to inspector for a long time. Well — let him! That's fine! It's fine for Rudy!"

Wallace looked at him sharply. It wasn't that simple. Captain Morelock was chief of the vice squad, one of Big Ed's key men. Ed had always fought his advancement, not because he could not use an inspector, but because control of the vice squad was vital to him. If Morelock were promoted the squad could fall into unfriendly hands. Sylvester's intrigues were subtler than Erik's, but there were dark streets in East Bay, too, and the last thing he wanted was an efficient police detail prowling down them.

Yet the risk was better calculated than Wallace thought. Morelock was approaching retirement age anyway, and so was Zipski. For the next month any new vice captain would be busy in the Seventh District, and when Erik had been beaten, Sylvester expected to name the new commissioner and, through him, Morelock's permanent successor.

Cameron brushed his supper aside and ordered another drink, and then another. Madelaine watched with compassion; she knew of the staggering deficits at Willoughby and how crushed he had been by Symonds' snub.

Fred's differences with his father flared up but once, and it came to nothing, for Cameron was by then convivial again. Toward the end of a long story about a black jockey, he told how the man had won a large purse one afternoon and dropped it at dice that evening. "He was so broke," he chortled, "I had to give him a room in the family block. He couldn't pay a cent for months. Matter of fact, he's still there."

"Probably still broke, too," Fred said casually.

His father looked blank. "What?"

"With the rents down there a man's lucky if he ever gets even."

Cameron glared. Since Fred's early college days the legacy of old houses had been a battleground between them, and they were about to refight its entire history when Madelaine coughed reprovingly, there was a shuffling of feet under the table, and Big Ed rubbed his chin.

"That jockey reminds me," he said suavely. "The meeting starts down south week after next, don't it?"

There was a nervous pause; then Cameron turned from Fred and swung into a technical discussion of Gulf tracks, bent upon entertaining his guest even if he must leave his son unrated this once. The interruption was welcome. Willoughby's autumn meeting days were running out, and for once he was glad a state commission regulated him. Racing interest would shift to the tropics, to the big winter season there, and he could crawl into his quiet office and lick his wounds and hope Erik would be beaten by spring gate time.

He rattled on, drinking through dessert, and was finishing his fifth highball as the others finished their coffee. Madelaine was about to offer everyone a second cup when the bell pealed.

Sarah admitted Zipski. He gave her his coat and stood in the front hall, erect and somehow even smaller in civilian clothes, casting a clinical eye over the ruins of the party. His hands were locked behind his back in a crisp pose of authority, and his entire bearing suggested that this was an official call, and that whatever business was to be done with him should be done quickly and efficiently and now.

61

Cameron pushed his chair back and lit a cigarette, his hands wavering and catching at one another like a reformed drunk's. "Excuse us," he muttered. "Time for business."

"Let's go into the library, gentlemen," Wallace said, and he and Big Ed rose together.

The men left the room in a bunch, looking more like directors leaving a board room than diners from a family table.

Fred followed his mother up the stairs. She stopped at the second landing and turned. "Why do you bait your father like that?" she asked.

"Do you have a minute?"

"Of course, silly."

"Can we talk?"

"Oh, Freddie!"

They went into her room and sat by the casement windows. The windows looked out on a little park behind the house. In the center was a birdbath and on either side cement benches and winter grass. Sere leaves from the trees above littered the grass, and soon a handyman would come to rake them away, for the park was now well kept.

It had not always been so. Years ago the grass had been tall and tangled among wild shrubbery, and Fred and his sister had played there together. There were no benches then, no birdbath. A tottering old garden swing had listed by one of the trees, and against another, the largest, stood a bird shelter, with trays for water and seed. The shelter had been Madelaine's idea. The children adored it. The park became a sanctuary, there were always birds there, and one May day when Fred was eight and his sister ten they held a party, with lumps of suet tied to the trees, to welcome back from the south their pets, a nest of orioles. When they tired of birds they played in the swing or hid from one another in the bushes.

Then Cameron, who thought the park an eyesore, decided it would be ideal for garden parties. He shooed them out, had the grass shorn, the shrubbery cleared away, the shelter torn down,

62

and the swing destroyed. But it rained at the first two parties and he never planned any others. The park had been deserted since.

Now a pigeon descended quietly upon it and Fred spoke softly to his mother.

"I didn't think you wanted to talk to me any more."

"Oh, Freddie."

"Well, that's what he said."

Madelaine was exasperated. "You know your father. You know he doesn't mean what he says half the time."

"Well, I wasn't sure."

"You ought to have been," she answered gently.

They saw the bird hop about in the darkness and then fly up, hovering over the benches.

"Maybe he's an old-timer, looking for the shelter," Fred said. "How long do pigeons live?"

Madelaine was not listening. She watched the bird flicker across the bar of light from the windows and then disappear. "Have you seen her?" she asked.

Her voice was cloudy, and she thought perhaps he had not heard her. "Have you? Seen her?"

"No." He stared down at the park.

"Oh. I thought you might have, in your work."

"But I know where she is."

"Oh where!" He did not answer, and she reached out and touched his hand. "Please. Please. I've got to know."

He hesitated. "It's not a very nice place. I don't think Dad would like you to go there." Then, before she could answer, he added bitterly, "I'm sure he wouldn't want you to see her, not even here, if she came looking for you."

She caught her lower lip between her teeth and held it there lightly, running her eyes over his face. "Your father is not a simple man ——"

"I don't find him hard to understand." His voice was cutting.

"That's because you *don't* understand him. You couldn't, not and talk to him the way you do. She does. That's why he mourns for her so."

"Him! Mourn!"

"Yes, Freddie. More than you can ever know. He's sorry about you. He wanted you to turn out differently. Most fathers do, though you don't realize it and neither does he. But he really grieves for her. That's where his heart is, down there, where she is, wherever she is."

"He hates her," he said, with the conviction of a hater.

"Yes. Because he loves her so."

He shook his head without understanding. She waited, hands in lap.

"I'm not sure myself whether you ought to go." He was weakening.

"Freddie, I have to. If you know anything, you ought to know that. And you do know it, you do, or you wouldn't have told me you know where she is." Her eyes were reproachful. "It's been a year, Freddie. A year!"

He stood abruptly. "Do you think she wants to see you?" And added, tenderly, "I understand she's not very pretty."

"I think she does," she said quietly. "I have to think she does."

He drew a notebook from his pocket and wrote three addresses inside, then tore out the page and handed it to her. "The first is where she lives. The second's the lunchcart where she works. The third's where you'll probably find her."

"Ollie's Famous Bar," she read and folded the paper carefully and slipped it in her bosom, as women do who were young when the bosom was sacred. She smiled with silent gratitude, and he went downstairs alone.

As Sarah handed him his topcoat the library door opened. Fred caught a glimpse of Zipski sitting behind the desk with his arms folded tight across his chest. Then the door swung toward him and Wallace came out, sipping armagnac. He waved cordially. "Going so soon? Stick around, have a drink."

"Sorry, I have to. Thanks just the same."

"When you coming out to the real country to see me?"

"Sounds like a fine idea." He buttoned his coat hurriedly.

"Make it real soon," Wallace chuckled. "I may be moving one of these days." He winked slyly and turned toward the lavatory.

On the portico Fred hesitated, turned, and walked around the house to the park. He stood for several moments under the trees, by the benches banked with leaves, watching the empty bath. Then the light went out in his mother's room, and loud laughter floated out from the library, and he walked slowly down the drive to his car.

Dying with the autumn, the sycamore leaves twisted free and floated to the brick sidewalks and lay there under the late November rains. They fell in layers, forming soggy mosaics, and the trees were bare, and there was mud in the gutters. The leaves lay against the shiny brick, the mud was matted thick in the drains, and the winds of early winter were everywhere. Indian summer had been short, and some thought warm weather would return, but a cold air mass swept in from the bay, and there were snow flurries in the mountains, and that night a kerosene stove exploded on Crone Street, killing three black children.

The father was arrested, and six blocks of Striker Street were torn up, and all the tradesmen were furious. The Valley Public Library announced it would move into new quarters after the first of the year. A Tenpoints candy salesman and an East Bay waitress married, and the *Evening Star* deplored a hasty decision in the Department of Commerce. The American Totalisator Company prepared to move its equipment from Willoughby at the end of the fall meeting. A flue seam split in a Three Forks rooming house, driving fifty-eight people into the street, and a Whiteoak painter surprised his helper tippling shellac and fired him. Rotary dedicated a boys' club. A former Congressman, the first vice-president of an investment banking firm, and a time-keeper at the Consolidated plant, died. Railroad police chased ten deadbeats from Holden Station. The Citizens' Committee for Better Government reported no reply from its letter to the mayor expressing disappointment in his reform administration.

Two blacks assaulted a taxi driver on West Concord Street and fled with $7.32. Inclement weather forced cancellation of an oyster roast at the Seventh District's Central Democratic Club, a workman was injured when a pile of trash exploded mysteriously at the municipal dump, and $35 was stolen from the purses of three choir singers during a rehearsal at the Church of the Nazarene. In the 800 block of Lockton Street, two girls who had grown up together joined the Sisters of St. Francis. The State Tuberculosis Association opened Christmas seal sales with a goal of $424,700. The Daughters of the American Revolution protested the burnishing of a tarnished war memorial, and five blacks were injured when their 1927 Dodge crashed into a safety pylon. The Catholic War Veterans sent certain recommendations to their Congressional representatives. Vandals defaced the Schlitz beer sign under the Striker Street viaduct. In Sticktown, the body of an unidentified man was found floating under Jake's Wharf. My Ideal was the favorite in the first at Willoughby, a Drexel Boulevard poultryman was arrested for dyeing turkeys yellow, and a fifty-year-old boilermaker cut his throat in the washroom of a Howell Street bowling alley.

And the sycamore leaves, the last leaves, twisted slowly free and floated to the sidewalks, forming withered lemon mosaics under the naked trees, against the shiny bricks, as the wind swept wildly around corners and up alleys, beat against doors and murmured by the windows of the sleeping and moved on swiftly and wetly in the night as the late November rains drummed along the blacktop, as the thick mud matted in the drains.

The Saturday morning after Thanksgiving, Hoot Vogel walked red-eyed and breakfastless through the Elbow to Swinton's Paint Store, marched rapidly with mincing steps to the back of the floor, and laid a puny fist against the wooden quarter-barrel on the rear counter.

Everything about Hoot was puny. He was a slight man with ragged blond hair and a pinched, instinctively troubled face. Even so, his clothing was inadequate. A denim shirt stretched tightly across narrow shoulders, filthy black pants sawed conspicuously at his crotch, and from each split shoe a gray toe protruded. He did not own socks.

Hoot stood at attention, the fist before him and the fingers of his left hand stiff and straight against his trouser seam. His wet eyes blinked rapidly and the withered muscles along his jaw quivered. Otherwise he did not move. Presently George Swinton left his inventory lists and came over, but if he had gone into the back room for a half hour, Hoot would not have changed position when he returned.

"Money?" The storekeeper might have been asking a dog if it wanted to go outdoors.

Hoot thrust his fist forward a few inches. Swinton opened it, removed two damp dimes from the palm, and pocketed them.

"Got your bottle?"

The rigid fingers of the left hand darted inside the shirt front, produced an empty pint flask, and held it out. Swollen knuckles gripped the flask stubbornly, and Swinton had to wrench a little to free it. He did not seem to mind.

He slipped the bottle under the barrel spigot and flipped it on easily. He was a big man, and he cultivated this trade because he knew he could handle it. Other hardware dealers, less splendidly endowed, refused to carry methanol.

"Hear they had a rodeo up the park yesterday, caught near twenty smokes. You in that?"

The red eyes, still to the front, snapped damply.

"Where'd you sleep last night? The station?"

Hoot said nothing. The bottle filled. Swinton replaced its cork, produced a gay red poison label, sealed it against the glass neck, and swung toward his customer. The fist on the counter opened clumsily and clawed at him.

"Wait a minute," Swinton snarled suddenly, pulling the flask out of reach. "I asked a question." He leaned forward menacingly. "Was it the station?"

The eyes became very small and beady and the jaw wobbled. Hoot nodded stingily.

Swinton relaxed. "All right." He handed back the bottle. "I just wanted an answer to the question I asked, that's all."

Hoot put it back in his shirt, wheeled, and walked out through the odor of varnish and fresh shavings, carrying with him his infinite dignity. Swinton, watching him narrowly from the rear, observed the tautness of the trouser seat across his frail buttocks and the way his run-down heels drew his legs in a faint bow.

Outside on West Concord, Hoot stepped lightly for two blocks, entered an alley, walked to the rear, and turned sharply into a dark and grimy passageway between buildings. He groped briefly in a heap of unsavory debris and came up with an empty gallon jug, took this to a water tap in the alley and filled it to a scratch two-thirds from the bottom. The jug in one hand and its cap in the other, he returned to the dark corridor. He was sweating now, and when he set the jug on a broken orange crate he looked quite exhausted, as though he were at the end of a long chore.

Gingerly he lifted the flask from his shirt. In the dim light he examined the poison label with approval, removed the cork, and sniffed the contents. Then he carefully mixed the wood alcohol with the water in the jug, pouring slowly, for his hand was unsteady. The water took on a cloudy, smoky appearance, and Hoot, perched on the crate and cradling the capped jug gently, shook it until the quality was uniform.

Satisfied, he unscrewed the cap and with an effort hoisted the jug to his frail arm, his forefinger in the handle ring. He opened his raw mouth and puckered his lips, as an infant puckers at the promise of a breast, and gulped noisily for several moments, the thin liquid seeping down his throat in cloudy waves. Then he put it down heavily and rested his shoulder gently against the foul brick, gasping.

He lingered so for ten minutes. Gradually the quaking in his hands subsided and a faint blush crept into his cheeks. He sipped languidly at the jug mouth for another quarter hour. Then he filled the pint bottle, slipped it under his shirt, replaced the jug under the debris, and stepped jauntily back to West Concord.

His eyes were bright and his face had lost its anxious look. He skipped across the pavement to the shabby, sagging façade of Ollie's Famous Bar.

Ollie Wetlek had inherited this place from his father. When Ollie was a boy and his father was in his prime, it was a respectable workman's tavern, but then the Elbow changed character and the character of the bar's customers changed with it. Ollie had loved his father, and he tried to buck the tide for a long time. Then he gave up and let the building go to ruin. Now he was middle-aged and sad. Still, he was a good man, and he eyed Hoot hostilely.

"What do you want?"

"Where's Rube?" Hoot's voice had a thick rasp.

"She's workin'. Be here in a few minutes. No, you can't stay here."

Hoot had started for one of the booths in the rear. He paused uncertainly, and as he turned toward the door with regret the chain in the ladies' room rattled and the door opened.

"Hoot!"

An enormous black slattern, grotesque in straight gray bangs and gaudy gingham, tottered toward him. He grinned toothlessly. She hugged him grimly.

"He won't let me stay here," Hoot said petulantly.

"Not without a drink," said the bartender. "Positively."

"Hell, I'll buy you a drink," offered the woman, who was known as Annie. Ollie looked troubled, but he served them.

They took two beers to the rear of the tavern, where the old woman enthusiastically exhibited a miniature shuffleboard game played with iron wafers on a long wooden table. Ollie polished the bar resignedly. Annie was his best patron, the only one who never ran out of money. The source of her wealth was a mystery to the Elbow and had been for twenty years. But it was genuine.

Shortly before noon, as Hoot and Annie were at the height of their second game, the door opened and a third customer entered.

She was a lanky, flat-chested girl with unkempt straight brown hair, and she dragged her feet as she walked. She was wearing a plaid blouse and loafers and slacks which had been dirty for a long time. Her hands were thin and red. There was a wary look in her eyes, a looseness in the dark skin underneath, and a hardness in the lines around her mouth. Her face seemed unnaturally old, but she might have been unnaturally young. She could have been twenty-five. She could have been forty.

Ollie watched her approach the bar slowly, her eyes averted, and when she reached it he placed a brimming shot glass before her. She picked it up deftly and threw it down an open throat. Still watching her, he refilled the glass. Still avoiding him, she picked it up and drank, in rapid sips this time. When she had finished she leaned forward on a forearm and looked at him steadily, with only a faint flickering of yellow in her eyes.

"Brother Ollie, I will now have a beer."

Her voice was husky. It carried to the back of the room. Hoot peeked around the last tier of booths. When he saw her, he gamboled down the aisle. He stood there grinning foolishly and presently Annie followed, pouting.

"We got to finish, Hoot," she said fretfully.

"Hoot here left a call," said Ollie sarcastically.

"Go ahead, Hoot, finish your game," the girl said wearily.

He ran his tongue over swollen gums. "Let's talk in the back."

The girl drained her schooner and thrust it toward Ollie, shrugging resignedly. He filled it at the tap.

"I wouldn't of let him stay, Ruby, only Annie, she wanted somebody to play with, you know how it is."

Annie spat on the floor.

"I got to do somethin'," she said loudly. "This stick gives me the creeps."

"Forget it, Ollie," Ruby said. "Come on, dreamer."

She slouched back to a corner booth, holding the beer high, like a chalice. Hoot pattered after her, chortling silently.

"Play with me, Ollie," Annie sulked.

"Okay, I might as well. I should of closed till Monday for all the business I get."

He slipped a nickel in the juke box by the door. They went

to the shuffleboard table, and the machine hammered out a harsh hillbilly tune.

"Well," said the girl, "you got a ship."

Hoot giggled and nodded enthusiastically. "That ain't all I got, Rube."

"No, I guess not. You got a little change, too."

He giggled again and patted his trousers pocket meaningfully. It jingled. "Thought that Swinton'd hear it sure. I forgot till I got inside what a crook he is, how he'll take what he can get. I most died."

"You got a jug hid?"

"I got one hid and I'm gonna get five more, only not all at wunst."

"Where'd you get the cash?"

He shook his head merrily.

"I'll bet you got it at the station."

A gleeful nod.

"Hoot, you want to miss that ship?"

"Nobody saw me, Rube. We got it made."

She looked at him with compassion. "We, huh?"

He nodded solemnly. "Just us, Rube. Us and the jugs."

"Happy days."

"That's right, Rube."

She hunched her thin shoulders forward and drained the schooner. "Ollie," she called, "get me a hard one. I got gloves on my teeth something awful."

He left the game and brought her a double shot, looking at Hoot sharply. He left and she put it down empty on the narrow table.

"Hoot, you know better than that. I'm not going on any joy ride with you." He looked crestfallen. "It isn't you, Hoot. I'm staying here."

"It's a good ship for winos, Rube, real good." His voice was pleading.

"A good ship! Where?"

" 'Rico." His voice was very small.

She looked startled. "Hoot! You aren't going there this time of year!"

He nodded miserably. "Oh, Hoot!" She was genuinely distressed.

"It's a good boat, Rube. We could lock the shaft right here and smoke in 'fore we get out the bay. Smoke in all the way over, don't have to leave the number two deck even. Just over'n back, just you'n me."

"Oh, good bloody Jesus!" she said incredulously. Ollie left Annie and came over suspiciously.

"What's the matter?" he demanded.

"This crazy bastard is riding a flatboat to 'Rico," she said wonderingly. He looked at Hoot with pity and Hoot looked reproachfully at her.

"You don't have to tell everybody," he whispered hoarsely.

"He wants me to smoke in with him."

Ollie was outraged. He grabbed Hoot's flabby shoulder and yanked him from the booth spluttering.

"Rube!" the little man shrieked. She watched him with faint amusement. Ollie heaved him down the aisle.

"Come on, you dirty little runt with big ideas. Get out! You think I don't know what you was up to, with your slimy, your filthy face and your dirty, no-good mind. Get out!"

"Rube! Rube!"

Hoot pitched forward, his runny eyes rolling wildly and his spindly legs buckling, clutching the bulge in his shirtfront. Ollie shoved him profanely out the door, slammed it shut, and came back sweating.

Annie wobbled down the aisle worriedly. "What's the matter?"

Ollie wiped his hands on his apron. "That little sonofabitch." he panted.

Ruby winked. "It wasn't that bad, Ollie. It's just out of season."

He looked at her stupidly.

"Where's Hoot?" Annie asked.

"He wanted me to take a little trip with him, and Ollie got sore."

"Where?"

" 'Rico."

"On a flat?"

Ruby nodded, half smiling at the gaping bartender.

"Too cold," Annie said positively. Then she walked into the ladies' room, slamming the door noisily.

"Honestly, Ruby, I don't get you," said Ollie. "I just don't."

"Well, get me a drink," she grinned. "With some life in it." She yawned. "Six jugs!" She shivered. "Jesus!"

Annie pulled the chain.

Here she was known as Ruby. Elsewhere she had been Po-Po, Jan, Janice, and once, for a week in New York, Mrs. John Smith. Her aliases changed casually with her habitat. Po-Po, an early, inscrutable corruption of her own, survived to school age, when it was replaced by Jan and then Janice. Mrs. John Smith was a common name for a common transgression. Ruby was the most casually given of all. Ollie had christened her after a ring she wore her first evening in the bar, and although the stone had since been pawned, the name stuck, for she had never offered another. She now thought of herself as Ruby, for although the alias was new, all her life until now had been a becoming. Becoming Ruby.

She was born in the Valley and made a tiresome debut at eighteen. She was a dull and rather plain girl, and this fact, together with the great expectations of her parents, cast awkward shadows almost before she was out of short dresses. Her mother blamed her slowness on a premature birth. That was unsound. She came early, but she was a healthy infant. Even as a child she liked to be handled, although even then the wrong people did it: nursemaids, governesses; strange women who came and cared for her and left with little investments of a child's love, and never returned. She was slow. It took her two years to walk,

73

and her father thought she would never talk. He said so often: indeed, he may have been partly to blame, for she was a nervous child, appalled by disapproval.

Yet he loved her. He spent far more time with her than most fathers would, and his concern over her stemmed from his awareness of her. Whether she returned his love is doubtful. She was anxious to please him, but that was probably because he was pleasant when pleased and very unpleasant when not. She would try to talk. But she could not, not until he gave up in disgust. She loved her mother, but it was a veiled, cautious love, for her mother always acted as her father's emissary. Loving Madelaine, her daughter discovered early, was rather like loving the Virgin Mary. First one must be reconciled to a terrible God.

Fred grew up ignored by his father: whenever he was at fault, his sister's lack of example was held responsible. One day when she was eight and he six, Cameron found them playing with matches in the field behind the garage. She would light a clump of dried grass, it would blaze, and they would both blow it out. Cameron watched this repeated several times. Then he walked over, picked up a badly frightened Fred, and whipped him, his dreadful eyes on her all the time. She tried to flee, but he caught her with his free hand and made her watch. Afterwards he let the boy go and lectured her on the danger of fire. But she did not hear him; her mind was still on the whipping. Years later she mentioned the incident to her brother, curious to see how much he remembered. He remembered nothing.

At school she was in trouble almost from the beginning. It seemed she could do nothing right, and this was because she rarely understood instructions, and never principles. If a teacher listed a series of multiplication problems on the board and called on a number of girls each day for the solutions, she would eventually memorize the answers she heard. But she could not grasp the theory of the multiplication table, and when the examples were changed she was lost. Eventually she mastered the table by rote, but the why of multiplication remained a mystery to her

She was dropped back one class and then another. Each failure precipitated a crisis at home and finally, in self-defense, she began to cheat. Ultimately she was discovered.

Her teachers suggested remedial help. Her father was outraged. There was nothing wrong, he told them, that a thrashing and a little classroom discipline would not cure. He spoiled a rod and Miss Skinner's spared a child, declining to continue with her, not because she had cheated, but because she could not keep up with her classmates without cheating. Cameron could not understand. To him her delinquency was responsible for the disgrace, and to him it was a disgrace.

She was transferred to Ivy Hall, one of the plush and utterly incompetent boarding schools on the outskirts of Philadelphia dedicated to the daughters of indulgent families. Life at Ivy Hall was lazy and seldom exacting. Days were passed riding horseback, playing tennis, and studying posture and fashion, with a little innocuous courting of grammar sandwiched in at odd times. Evenings, ostensibly for supervised study, were spent exchanging obscene jokes, smoking, and, in the upper mains, in secret drinking parties. The attitude of the authorities was sophisticated. Ivy Hall provided social prestige without inconveniencing parents or children. It offered gentility and custodial care.

Here, beginning in her fourteenth year, Ruby vegetated. She still was not up to even the meager academic requirements of Ivy Hall, but Ivy Hall did not object. Further, she had profited by her experience at Miss Skinner's. She became an artful cheater, developing her young cunning to an extraordinary degree. As she moved into her late teens she carefully chose the primmest teachers. Before an examination she would carefully ink crib notes on the inside of her thigh, and during the test period her skirt always rode high, with the examiner chastely looking the other way. Oddly enough, she was never caught, though she naturally acquired a reputation for being brazen.

Even here it was possible that with understanding, under careful guidance, she might have become an average student. She would never have been more, for her mind had been stunted too early, but she could have acquired the fundamentals of an education.

The difficulty lay in the rubrics of her society, which did not demand such achievement and even scorned those who were too painstaking in their search for it. The gauds of education were indispensable. It was essential that she bring home passing marks. But it did not much matter how she got them. Her mother knew she used cribs, and all her classmates knew of the inked notes on her thigh. No one ever reproached her, and several girls even paid her the tribute of imitation.

If Ruby had been a pretty girl, and the influences brought to bear on her had been different, none of this would have mattered. She would have survived her education somehow and married an acceptable young man who would have been amused, and in turn would have amused his friends, with tales of her classroom deceit. That was what others wanted for her and therefore what she wanted for herself.

But she was not pretty. Her legs were too thin, her breasts too small. At a dance her eyes were always flat and lifeless. Her mouth never parted; it gaped.

This does not mean she completely lacked sex appeal. Few women do. With the vast machinery civilization has created for the Rubys of the world she could be made attractive and even desirable, and was. But machines can do only so much. When the last false curl was deftly laid against her neck, when the padded brassiere was strapped in place, when the sheer silk hose and the tailored dress were slipped on and the custom-built shoes buckled and the gay chemicals smeared on, she could stir men's lust, but not their devotion, as she might have if left alone. Even in the middle teens, when masculine naïveté is at its height, she was not the kind of girl for whom boys keep themselves chaste. She knew this, and because she had a low opinion of her own worth, she accepted it.

She lost her virginity at fifteen, while summering with the family at a Virginia resort. The seduction was cruel, as adolescent seductions are. Afterwards she and her lover parted in mutual horror. But far more cruel to her was its sequel. By fall he was boasting of his achievement. Janice Cameron, he told his friends, was a good lay.

Immediately her reputation swept her into a wild popularity with Valley boys attending prep schools near Philadelphia. At seventeen, she had a lurid past. Like most promiscuous girls, her enjoyment of sex was small, and she never knew love. With a pathetic yearning for real affection, she followed one adventure after another, waiting, always waiting, for the change which would bring her life warmth and meaning.

Men scarcely thought of her as a person; she was an experience to be enjoyed and later discussed. Other girls regarded her scornfully or tolerantly, depending on the state of their own affairs. Her mother, quite unaware of the reason for her popularity, was enchanted to hear of it. Her father hoped her studies would not suffer, and was gratified to learn they did not. Fred, who could not be kept ignorant, suffered quietly.

As the boys moved into college they became more demanding. Dance week ends were no longer satisfactory; indeed, they could be damaging, for by now to be seen with Janice Cameron was no character reference. Week ends in Philadelphia hotels were suggested. Partly because she was becoming older and less satisfied with the company of the younger girls at Ivy Hall, and partly because she found the pitiful attention which went with her wild reputation exciting, she agreed. She forged notes from Madelaine, asking the headmistress to release her for family occasions. They were not challenged, and she became bolder.

Her secret was a casualty of the war. As long as her bed companions remained in school her chance of exposure was slight, for they also had standings to consider. The service removed that risk for them; the military was not interested in such activity. In the spring of 1944 a young naval officer on leave persuaded her to spend the Easter holiday with him in a Manhattan hotel. She wrote Madelaine that she hoped to graduate this year and would remain at Ivy Hall, bent over her books, as testimony of this. On

Easter Sunday Cameron herded the family into the car and drove to Ivy Hall for a surprise visit. At the very moment they were confronting an astonished dormitory proctor, she was ringing room service, inquiring in a thick voice what had become of the fresh fifth her husband had ordered.

Ivy Hall expelled her. Turpitude within its walls could be tolerated, but absence without leave could not. Otherwise parents would withdraw their children in droves. The headmistress regretfully bade her goodbye. She could not imagine who would take her suite.

Her father would not speak to her. Her mother could not. She herself was defiant. She was also thirsty. She had been drinking a great deal during the past year; after late excursions she had felt a need for morning bracers and had kept a bottle in her rooms. Here she missed it. During the long, awful days when Madelaine was attempting a reconciliation between her and Cameron, she nursed herself in her room with contraband from the library sideboard. It was her first solitary drinking and would eventually have been discovered, if Ira Pike had not come home.

Before the war Ira had been known to the Valley as a tall, quiet, rather handsome young man who would one day inherit a massive amount of money and social prestige. He had been one of the first to enter the army when conscription began, and now he was one of the first home. In 1944, that was enough to give him an almost mystical glory. There was more. He had been a company commander through the North African and Italian campaigns, in the assault wave at Omaha Beach, decorated with the Silver Star, and wounded at St. Lô. The Valley, unaccustomed to the ways of returning heroes, opened its heart to him. The first week he was home he called on Ruby.

The Camerons were enchanted. Why their daughter had been chosen they could not imagine — he had scarcely known her before the war, and was closer to a half dozen of her friends. Her father, whose notions of propriety antedated the mandolin, had thought his daughter's reputation irreparably damaged. Surely, he had told himself, no decent young man would be seen with her. Now he believed himself wrong and was pleased. Madelaine was relieved to see the household relax. Ruby was undeceived.

Five years later, when Ira was committed to a veterans' hospital, hopelessly schizophrenic, the Valley had all but forgotten the tribute it once paid him. His record was by then a tarnished and disreputable thing. The poor boy, they said, bobbing their heads smartly in sunny drawing rooms. The war, they said knowingly, was to blame. Some, for whom war was still a splendid thing, denied this and blamed Ruby, but that was unjust. For if she was to blame for Ira, as Fred later pointed out to his mother, who was to blame for her?

But these were questions unraised until long afterwards, when the great Welcome Home Party the young Valley set threw for itself was in the small hours of the 1940's and ready to close down. In the winter of 1944–45 it was just beginning. Ruby and Ira were the first Guests, but they were not long alone. Through the months which bracketed the last summer of the war the heroes continued to stream home in swelling numbers. They were still checking in at the Stuart Klub and the Valley Tavern early the following year. By then a moratorium had been declared on heroism by bewildered parents, but had come too late. Enough hasty marriages had been contracted, enough problem drinkers had been spawned, and enough of a Party spirit had been generated to assure a hard and brilliant core of Guests who would not be daunted and would not go home.

In the beginning most of the men came from the Valley and the wealthier suburbs, for that was where the money was, and money was the one requisite for participation in the Party. There were a few from other quarters of the city, but their number was never large. Afterwards this changed. When their money ran out the Valley men ran out too and were replaced by petty gamblers, flush deadbeats, and itinerant musicians.

The girls were more cosmopolitan. Ruby was from the Valley, and there were several of her friends who had married or become engaged to unstable men during the war. But there was a large representation from the middle economic classes of the city, and there were three girls who had married Valley men elsewhere and come home with them after discharge.

No one had any illusions about himself, no one considered himself more than a vehicle for dissipation. In the women, where this seemed most extraordinary, it amounted to a perversion of all normal instincts, of all hope for security. Of maternal love there was none. When a child arrived, everything possible was done to turn it over to its grandparents; if there was a divorce, and children usually meant divorce, the mother kept the baby only because the increase in alimony would more than meet the expenses of a black housekeeper. Children did not change a Guest's status, nor did divorce. After the decree the girl moved back with her family, if she lived nearby, or into a furnished room if she did not. Inevitably she fell in with another man: usually he was the cause of the divorce in the first place. Frequently she married him though the proportion of such marriages dwindled as the waning years wasted the beauty of the divorcees.

The pace varied, for most of the men had indifferent employment. Their jobs were inconsequential, and they never held them long, but they were enough of a consideration to give the Party a manic-depressive pattern, with intense binges followed by agonizing, desperate hangovers. The constitutions of the Guests may have had something to do with this, though no one seemed to think of them much.

The normal length of a manic phase was about five days. It usually began casually with the meeting of several couples at the Tavern or the Klub, reached a climax in a waterfront rooming house or an Atlantic City hotel, and ended with lovers' quarrels, tapering off, and blank, meaningless stares. The number of Guests varied. Sometimes there were as many as twenty; sometimes as few as three. Their conversation was incredible, their language basic and monosyllabic. It was amazing how long they could talk about nothing: about how drunk they had been, or were, or were going to be; about clothes; about scandal. There was always a lot of scandal. Toward the end the debauchery would reach fantastic levels: mock abortions, excursions with narcotics, public performances.

Fred called them a lunatic fringe and he was right. They were a tiny, unbalanced minority. The more literate liked to think of themselves as a lost generation, but that was inaccurate: they constituted, not a generation, but the red and ragged edge of a generation. There was never more than a score of Guests at one time, and the number of hangers-on was less than half that. And in each case the seeds of the sybaritism had been sown long before the war. But because they were all abnormal they were blind to their unbalance. The tightness of their circle protected them from the world. Within their defenses they erected shrines of conduct the gayest outsider would have thought preposterous. To be drunk was good. To be very drunk was very good. Promiscuity was daring, sexual experimentation amusing. Heresy was forbidden. If a Guest announced he had enough to drink, or a husband protested his wife's interest in another man, he was ridiculed. "Oh, don't be stuffy," he was told. It was the opprobrium of their culture. No one could be stuffy and remain.

In time the Party ended; one by one the Guests drifted away, or went broke. Ruby's departure followed the inevitable discovery, and inevitable crisis, at home.

Cameron had left her alone because he refused to face the obvious. Everyone else knew. At the club it was open gossip, and even Madelaine had heard the less unsavory details from Fred. Privately she had reasoned with her daughter a dozen times, and because she was an artless woman she had left each session convinced she would reform. But for nearly three years Cameron was serene.

This was because Ruby had set up a pact with Candy Harrison, a young divorcee whose mother lived in a suburb on the western edge of the city. Candy was in many ways like Ruby, but she was prettier and more resourceful. She also had a baby, and this complicated her life no end. Fortunately for her, her mother, like Madelaine, was pliable as long as she was convinced Candy was not, as she put it, "up to real mischief." The pact, which was an elaborate variation of Ruby's schoolgirl intrigue, worked this way: at the beginning of a spree, each girl telephoned home she would be staying with the other for a few days. If the spree ran over, the calls would be repeated. Because Candy's mother and the Camerons were indulgent, and because they did not dare challenge their faith in their children, it worked. Candy's little son was no handicap to her and both girls could frolic without sacrificing security.

The arrangement broke down the first week of 1947. Ruby's drinking had become steadily worse; once, after the celebration of a professional football victory, she had blacked out for nearly two days. This alarmed Candy, but when she became reproachful the merry Guests suggested she stop being stuffy. On Christmas Eve Ruby was insensible before dusk; only after a two-hour shower could she be persuaded to call home and inform her mother she would spend the holiday with the Harrisons. Christmas was always a family event with the Camerons, and when the word reached Cameron his suspicions were actively aroused for the first time.

Two hours after hanging up, Ruby was out again. The Party moved three times in the next two days, and twice she had to be carried. The combined efforts of four Guests, led by Candy, brought her home sober three days before the New Year. Immediately she was seized with a mild attack of delirium tremens, her first, and stayed in her room, pleading illness. Fred and Madelaine were frantic. He wanted to call a doctor, but his mother, after a long session at the bedside, demurred. She could not have been more wrong. For one thing, Ruby's tortured psyche was begging for liquor. For another — and this Madelaine could not have been expected to know — nothing could have locked the door behind her daughter more securely than the pleading, "Don't upset your father."

The morning of New Year's Eve Ruby called Candy and ordered her to be in the drive at four o'clock. When Candy objected, she threatened to expose her. Candy agreed.

At four exactly a furious honking broke out before the portico. Simultaneously Ruby, haggard and drawn, appeared before her family in the front room. She tried to smile. She looked ill.

"I'm going to Candy's for New Year's," she said brightly. "Isn't that nice?"

"What!" Cameron was incredulous.

"Why Daddy! It'll be such fun!" Standing under the arch, folding and unfolding her hands to control their shaking, she looked like a little girl asking for her allowance. Madelaine's eyes filled. Fred stared into the fire.

"Look here ——" Cameron began, rising. But she pretended not to hear him. She tried to smile more gaily — and grimaced horribly — and turned and ran out the door.

" 'Bye!" she cried.

When he reached the door, Candy's convertible was rolling down the drive. He caught a glimpse of her corn-colored, closely bobbed hair as the car dipped down the cement apron and, as it swerved to the right, of his daughter, erect on the leather seat, her face still twisted in what she thought was a smile. He thought he saw her wave, but he could not be sure.

Madelaine, with an enormous effort, persuaded him not to call the Harrison home. It would only drive her away, she argued. Cameron agreed reluctantly. He promised a showdown when she returned. Three days later she telephoned from Richmond.

He was not supposed to know the call was from Richmond, but the Richmond operator, suspecting from their thick voices that her clients were unreliable, checked Cameron's number with him and then told Ruby to go ahead, please.

"What the hell ——" Cameron began.

" 'Lo, Daddy. 'Lo? 'Lo?"

"What in God's name are you doing down there?"

"I'm at Candy's," she said feebly, knowing the game was lost and not much caring. "Candy's, Daddy! I'm gonna be ——"

But he had hung up. He was thumbing the pages of his telephone directory furiously, looking for Pinkerton's National Detective Agency.

The following day the girls were found in a cheap Norfolk hotel with two sailors. The sailors were questioned and released. Ruby and Candy were returned home.

Cameron had his showdown, but even as he strutted and bellowed and implored he knew it was no good. He ended by ordering her from the house: his shame and his outraged pride admitted no other course. But he really hoped she would defy him and stay, and while she was packing he sent Madelaine in to persuade her to. Then he holed up miserably and awaited the news. A half hour later the front door slammed, and his wife came in.

"She's gone."

"She didn't even say goodbye!"

For the first time in their marriage he cried.

She came back twice at Thanksgiving. On the first visit she was drunk and relaxed, with the strange ease of an alcoholic in the early stages of a siege. The second time she was sober and nervous. It made no difference to her father. He was excessively polite on each occasion, exhibited great interest in the reports that she was now modeling for a department store, now waiting on table, and, with a display of self-control startling to the family, saw her courteously to the door after dinner. This year she had telephoned her mother she could not come. Cameron immediately left for the club and rode alone in deserted pastures until darkness came down upon the woods.

Ruby's modeling, such as it was, sprang from her continuing liaison with Candy. In the Harrison house the exposure produced no real crisis. Candy's mother had long suspected her deceit; when it was unmasked she was not especially shocked. She was, however, unbearably reproachful. How could her daughter *do* such a thing to her, she asked a hundred times. Within a week she had become unbearable. Candy left her baby with her and moved into the downtown room Ruby had rented with money from Fred. She was gay. Never in the history of the world, she declared, had two girls gone without in a flourishing city. If worst came to worst, they could always go on the street. As a matter of fact, she said, that would not be necessary. As a matter of fact it was, though Candy did not admit it, for her definition of sin was loose.

She had an admirer who hired models for a downtown store. He was delighted to find places for them. Their only expense was a cheap partition he insisted be constructed across the middle of the room. Willie Merrick, Candy explained, had always been fastidious.

The work was absurdly simple. They were required to appear at women's luncheons and teas and parade before guests for an hour or two, changing frocks every fifteen minutes. Willie made the arrangements in advance. They had only to prance between tables, pivoting every few steps and murmuring the price to whoever appeared interested. If they found it inconvenient to come on a given occasion, Willie was understanding. There were other girls and he managed.

Candy rarely missed. She loved to wear nice clothes, and her commitments to Willie, an exacting employer in other ways, restricted her with other men. With Ruby it was different. She knew she was not an attractive model and would not have been hired if Candy had not made it a condition of her own employment. She was also afraid she might be seen, if not by her mother, then by her mother's friends, for the teas and luncheons were popular with the older Valley set. But the most important reason for her absenteeism was her drinking. Willie told her bluntly he would rather she not come if she could not come sober, and since she was rarely that, it seemed best to stay in her room.

Candy's affair with Willie lasted long. She modeled for nearly two years, building up a wardrobe of fashionable clothes with her salary and spending her nights with him. Both she and Ruby saw less of the Party — Candy, because Willie was not fond of her old cronies; Ruby, because she had passed that subtle line which separates the amateur drinker from the professional and preferred to be left alone with her trade.

Inevitably the end came. This time the fault was Candy's. On her way home one December evening she ran into Ed Sykes, an old Party Guest. Ed was disconsolate. He and his wife had quarreled. Candy offered to buy him a drink. In the bar they met a mutual friend; the friend had an apartment for which he had no immediate use and the key to which he slipped Ed under the table. One drink led to a dozen others. By midnight Candy and Ed were in bed.

All this might have been explained away if there had been time the following morning to prepare a yarn, for they were both wily liars. But they were not even permitted a night's sleep before Helen Sykes, who had traced her husband to the bar and there wrenched the truth from the woozy friend, burst in on them. A hysterical scene ended in bloodshed. Helen tackled Candy, they wrestled, and before Ed could pull them apart, Candy's face was rent and spurting blood. Ed took her to a hospital. He was badly frightened. He called her mother, who came to the accident room and took her away. Two days later he called Ruby. By then Candy was en route to Florida with her mother and Willie had learned the sordid details from a vindictive Helen.

Ruby went directly to the hospital. She inquired at the information desk and was handed an envelope addressed to her. Inside, a single sheet read:

> *Darling* ——
> It's simply awful to leave like this I know tho I
> *am* sick and just can't cope with things — take the
> clothes — don't write 'n' I won't — Helen was
> *AWFUL* — it was perfectly horribly *DREAD–*
> *FUL* — Bye ——
>
> C.

She went home, dressed carefully, and walked to the department store. She hoped she looked chic. She did not. Her hair, despite a frantic combing, was hopelessly snarled. Her clothes fitted loosely and her face had suddenly become quite old.

She had trouble finding the employees' entrance — it had been so long. The lunch-hour break was erupting in the business departments as she started up the long, weary stairs. Above a door opened wide and straight from the pages of *Seventeen* came the girls in Accounts Receivable, sandal-shod, balloon-skirted and gay, running just behind the noon bell. Ruby stood meekly aside, a creature apart. They glanced at her curiously as they passed and on the landing put their heads together, whispering and looking back.

She plodded heavily to the second floor, to the models' locker room, and waited there. When Willie came in he did not see her. She greeted him feebly.

"Crissake!" he said, aghast. "What are you doing here?"

She fussed with the buttons on her blouse and then, suddenly aware that her hands were shaking, pressed them against the bench by her skirt.

"What's on today, Willie? Where do we go?" She tried to look at him, but her eyes fell.

"What's on what? Where do who go?" He was immaculate in a pin stripe suit and a knitted tie, and his fat red face was petulant.

"I — I'm ready for work, Willie," she stammered, her eyes on the locker room floor. "All set."

He started perceptibly. Then he walked over to a full-length mirror in the wall. When he spoke, it was to the glass.

"I'm sorry. Really, I am, I'm sorry. We're going to have to let you go. We're cutting back, orders, economy move, and we just have to let you go. Glad, 'course, glad to consider you when there's an opening."

He wheeled curtly and walked from the room. At the door he glanced back quickly into the mirror and saw her image. She was in the same position, her hands pressed against the bench, her eyes on the floor. He had really forgotten she was still on the payroll.

Outside on the street she leaned hopelessly against a show window. Her hands were folded against her breast now, and her lower lip quivered out of control. After a while a policeman began to look at her suspiciously, and so she went home.

She arrived in the room exhausted, threw herself across the

87

bed and wept. For two years she had been utterly dependent upon Candy and had become a virtual invalid. She had known Willie did not want her at the store, and so she had holed up with one bottle after another until she was nearly always drunk and often helpless. Her physical resistance had dropped steadily. She had a cold most of the time, even in the summertime, and her d.t.'s had returned twice. Her care of her personal appearance had dwindled to nothing. She had lost what little appeal she had, and now that her generation was older, a return to her collegiate popularity was unlikely.

All this she understood as she sobbed miserably in the disheveled room which had seen so much sick pleasure.

She lay there for nearly four hours, crying intermittently, and when she rose she had a plan. She knew Candy would never return, and so she sold her clothes and bought a bath, a shampoo, and a permanent wave. She found a suit to fit her wasted figure and hunted a job. By the evening of the following day she was a waitress in a downtown hotel. She moved her belongings to a new room and began to save.

She did not know whether the sane approach to living would work for her, or even whether she wanted it to. At the time a change was clearly indicated, and so she made it. It worked for over a month. For a month she drank nothing. Then she disappeared on a four-day bout and returned to no job. She bought more beauty treatments, applied at another hotel, and this time behaved herself less than a week. The third time she found she had been blacklisted in the hotels. She celebrated this news with ten martinis in the hotel bar, left the bar with a salesman, and lived with him for two days. Then, without permanent or shampoo, she was hired to work behind the counter of an Elbow diner. Thereafter, the Seventh District was her home. She drifted from job to job. Sometimes she was sober for days at a time. Other times she was too drunk to leave whatever furnished room she was renting. Most of the time she was in an alcoholic haze, able to handle the simple work required in the diners. Since she would work for almost any salary, her employers were satisfied until she became wholly unreliable. Then she would move on.

Through her customers she became acquainted with the floating derelicts who hung about the waterfront's Sticktown. There were a few women of uncertain age and background among them, but most of the drifters were men. Each morning they appeared on the streets of the lower metropolitan district, begging nickels and dimes. With a day's take they would visit a cheap hardware store, buy a pint of wood alcohol, mix a batch of smoke, and retire to the empty houses and the beached barge hulls. They reappeared around nightfall, sponging flophouse money. If they did not get it, and they often did not, they returned to hole up along the piers. The women lived with them, sometimes with all of them, sometimes with just one. Ruby moved along the fringes of this crowd, sleeping with the men, drinking her own cheap whisky, and avoiding the smoke, whose fearful reputation she knew. Her first waterfront excursion was with a former naval commander, her second with an old ship caulker, and her third with Hoot Vogel. She was sinking rapidly. Through Hoot she had come to know the barge captains, men so far gone that the cadging of change on street corners was beyond them. Barge running was a way out, a dangerous way to be sure, but still a way. Shipping companies, hauling large cargoes from port to port, were obliged to hire men to tend lines and maintain signals and watch for leaks. The responsibilities were light. In a heavy sea, however, the weight of the barge menaced the men on the tug. It could capsize them. And so, when the swells ran high, it was common practice to hack the hawser in half, collect insurance for the cargo, and list the missing man as "lost at sea." He was a nameless, unmourned drunk who knew the risk and was paid for taking it.

The barge captains drank smoke, not by the day, but by the week. They were men without memories. They rarely knew the year and never the month. The life of a bargeman was short, for if the sea did not get him, the smoke did.

Hoot introduced Ruby to smoke. She sipped it languidly with him late one night, mixing it with a little whisky she had left. There were no aftereffects, for she had swallowed much less than she thought. Toward dawn one morning two weeks later a friend of Hoot's staggered into her near Sloane Square, on the waterfront, and invited her to join him in a derelict barge. She went along, but she had been ready to pass out when he met her, and after one tin cupful she did. At twilight she awoke to find him dead and stiffening in his rags beside her.

Since then her work had been steadier and her bouts less frequent. For over two months she had been working at the Unique Lunch, living in a room over a rummage store and hanging around the bar in off hours. She still drank heavily and had to be put to bed almost nightly by the black woman who ran the store and lived behind it. But the twisted hunchback who ran the diner tolerated her, and she had not missed more than one day's work at a time. The opportunity was always there. Hoot's call had not been his first. But she always refused. She had seen the face of death and turned her own away. How long she could keep it there she did not know. But she was making a supreme effort.

This was not only the most impossible neighborhood Madelaine had ever seen: it was also the most improbable. She had always been dimly aware that there were people who led sordid, inadequate lives in dark and insanitary places. But these people! And these places!

She had parked several blocks away, locked her car, and gone first to the rummage store. The black woman there was overwhelmed. She had never heard of Janice Cameron, and she did not associate the tramp she knew as Ruby with such splendor. The best Madelaine could get out of her was that her tenant was out.

In the stool line of the Unique Lunch she sat painfully apart while the shabby clientele eyed her curiously. She was shrewder here. When the crippled manager approached her timidly, she simply asked him if he employed a slight, straight-haired brunette. He replied, lisping and wiping his hands apologetically on his greasy apron, that she might be found at the bar around the corner. She headed now for the third address Fred had given her.

West Concord was very narrow at this point, paved with nine-teenth-century cobblestones and lined with early Victorian houses of dingy brick. The sidewalks were scarcely wide enough for two to pass. Trash littered the gutters, there were broken windows in nearly every house, and in the air was the dead smell of stagnant sewage. The very people on the streets seemed forsaken. Most of them were blacks, ill-clad and undernourished, with numb, hopeless faces. As Madelaine came to a deserted and particularly desolate stretch of sidewalk a door was flung open ahead and a scraggy, ragged little white man in tight clothes hurried out and down the street toward her. She shrank against the wall to let him pass and observed with astonishment that he was weeping.

Ollie was washing glasses when she came in. He stopped to stare. She pretended not to notice. Here, as in the diner, she would be a freak. She had anticipated this and decided that since the only impression that mattered was the one she made on her daughter, she would dress for her alone. Even so, she was un-comfortable.

"I am looking for a girl," she said lamely.

"Yes, ma'am." He held his mop like a truncheon.

She cleared her throat. "A young girl, rather slender, with straight brown hair and brown eyes. She has a tiny scar on her right eyelid. You probably wouldn't notice that," she added. Immediately she felt silly. Ollie continued to gape.

"Yes, ma'am."

"She is employed by the — ah — restaurant on Horrigan Street. As a — ah — waitress."

"Oh. That would be Ruby."

"No, no. I'm afraid ——"

"That's what we call her here. Yes, ma'am, you mean Ruby." He nodded emphatically.

"Ruby," she repeated vaguely.

"She's right back there, last booth on the right."

She walked down the aisle slowly. When the back of the tangled, bowed head appeared over the booth something quivered in her breast and for the first time she thought perhaps she ought not to have come. Madelaine was not ashamed of her daughter, any more than she was ashamed of her husband. She knew she could not judge those she loved. Yet with this sudden pang she realized, if only for a moment, that she herself might be judged and even condemned.

Ruby looked up and saw her mother standing beside her, smiling uncertainly. She had been sitting hunched over the table, making wet, sloppy circles on its surface with an empty shot glass. For a moment she did not recognize Madelaine. She had not eaten since the evening before, and the liquor had reached her quickly. She focused slowly.

"Hullo," she said dully, setting down the glass with a trembling hand and studying the circles on the table.

Madelaine smiled brilliantly as she slid heavily along the facing bench and reached for her daughter's hand. It was withdrawn brutally. Inadvertently she upset the little glass.

"I'm — I'm sorry. Oh, love!"

She leaned forward, still trying to beam and looking quite unhappy. Ruby set her fingers on the bare edge of the table and stared vacantly at the last circle she had made. She was trembling. She appeared about to cry.

"Mummie," she whispered hoarsely.

"Dear!"

She reached again, but her daughter pulled her hands back quickly and laid them in a neat little pile in her lap. Madelaine had hoped for a welcome and counted on truculence. She was not prepared for this. She shook her head and blinked. Then she opened her purse and fumbled for a cigarette.

"Light me one," Ruby said suddenly. Madelaine noticed how coarse her voice had become.

"Ollie!" He came over. "A drink." He turned to leave. "Wait

a minute." She looked at her mother hesitantly. "Want a drink?" Madelaine nodded, lying. "Two drinks." He went away.

She drew deeply on her cigarette, still shaking. Madelaine noticed that her nails were chipped flat and caked underneath, and this surprised her, for the hands of all the waitresses she had ever seen had been immaculate.

"Are you a daytime drinker now, Mummie?" Her voice was taunting. Oh dear, Madelaine thought, perhaps I should have said no.

"Sometimes," she said casually.

"Me too. Sometimes."

"Yes, dear, I know."

Ruby snickered shrilly. Now I *have* offended her, Madelaine thought. The huskiness in her daughter's voice sounded odd. With sudden solicitude she wondered if she were ill.

The whiskies were before them now. Madelaine had not had time to decide whether or not to drink when the other glass was empty and on the table. She sipped her own tentatively.

"There are a great many colored around here," she said in what she hoped was a sprightly voice.

"Yes," said her daughter, suddenly quite gray. "And now I must puke."

She rose quickly and went into the ladies' room. There was a racket inside, for the walls were thin. Annie passed the booth on her way to the juke box and eyed Madelaine rudely as she did. Ruby came back, the cigarette slanting from her mouth. She sat down, removed it, and deliberately wiped her mouth on the sleeve of her blouse.

"Ollie!" He came over. "Two more." Annie strutted by, leering. "We call her Annie," she said to her mother.

"Really?" Madelaine sipped her drink desperately.

Ruby dropped her cigarette into one of the puddles before her. It turned brown and lay there obscenely, like a corpse.

"Well," she said flatly, staring at it.

"Well?" Madelaine answered in a little voice.

93

"What's on your mind?"

"Oh." I must not get hysterical, she thought. I must not. I must *not*.

The fresh whiskies arrived and Ruby threw hers down. Then, on a sudden impulse, she reached over and tossed down both her mother's, her second and what was left of her first.

"Sorry," she said with a wild grin. "Sometimes I'm a big daytime drinker." Her eyes were bright and her breath quick.

"It's all right. Everything is all right. You ought to know that, dear."

"Yes. Ollie!"

"It's awfully hard, never seeing you."

"I suppose. *Goddam it, Ollie!*"

"Dear, don't you think . . ."

"Think what?"

"You could talk to me, for just a little bit."

"Sure. Two more, Ollie."

"I don't want another, dear."

"Sure. Ollie, two."

"Isn't there some way . . ."

"Some way what?"

"You could come out, maybe visit us, once in a while."

"Why?"

"We do miss you."

"Oh my, oh my *Christ!*"

Ollie brought the drinks. Before he put them down he wiped the table top carefully. Ruby watched him like a nervous cat, and when he left picked up a glass in each hand and drank both rapidly.

Madelaine watched with profound pity. "Oh, love!"

Her daughter looked up with terrified eyes.

"If only, only, just once, you could see your father!"

Ruby was gone. She swung her legs out of the booth together, in one motion, like a vaulter clearing a high wire, and ran into the ladies' room. Madelaine heard her retch several times. Then she came back and stood by the booth, tears streaking her unwashed face, her thin chest shaking. She looked like a child, in from play, begging comfort, and finding none, or none she wanted, or could take.

"Mummie," she said with a swollen voice. "Go 'way."

Madelaine rose quietly and walked to the bar. She handed Ollie a five-dollar bill and walked out, and she did not look back. On the street outside she stood very still for a moment, and a raw wind crept up her skirt, and she was cold. Acrid smoke from the Consolidated plant was drifting across the Elbow. She coughed several times on her way to the car.

An hour later the tavern door opened and Ruby came out slowly, looking like a whipped terrier. She stumbled over the cobblestones, down into the next block, and in a littered, familiar alley pitched headlong over the prone figure of Hoot Vogel. He giggled when he saw her.

"Here," he murmured happily, handing her the flask.

She pulled painfully to a sitting position and leaned against an empty tar barrel, rubbing her side. When she saw the bottle she took it and tilted the neck down.

"Oh balls," she said wretchedly.

Then she drank deeply, with great open swallows.

2

The Track of
the Rat

THE snow began on Wednesday. At first it was a sticky, wet snow, melting on pavements and spattering pedestrians, but at dusk the temperature dropped, and by ten o'clock the narrow streets were covered. Softly through the night it sifted down in great powdery layers, and by morning the city lay under a thick coverlet at which a million risers plucked feebly, struggling to open doors and wading to trolley stops where no trolleys came. Still it fell, speckling the faces of early Christmas shoppers, deepening on parking lots and frosting the medieval spires of the Catholic Cathedral, stitching the eaves of the Elbow and the Valley with the same shimmering thread. And after the snow came the wind, howling in from the bay, tearing trash can lids loose and flinging them against fences, sending the hard white silt scudding before its raw gusts. Drifts hung in the dark alleys that night, and there was an epidemic of broken oil burners in the suburbs.

In the slums it was a time of great suffering. The snow seeped into the huge, drafty Civil War period buildings and stayed, for there was no warmth to melt it. Privy doors froze shut, and on sills milk turned to ice. Old women warmed themselves over kerosene stoves, and little children, watching their breath form in the cruel air, wondered why Christmas should be white. Men doubled the cardboard stuffing in broken windowpanes and sealed it with Scotch tape, but the tape would not stick and the wind blew the cardboard away and filled the shabby rooms with whistling agony. It was hard for everyone. There had never been a winter like it. It had never been so cold.

They were on the twentieth floor: that was the excuse. Zipski liked to sit shirtless by the window, reading the morning paper before breakfast with his thick suspenders loose in his lap and his starched shirt in another room. He could do it here. It was the one advantage of the apartment. There were no other twentieth floors in the block, and so Edna had given in and permitted it.

He heard her in the kitchen, darting from pantry to stove, from refrigerator to sink, clattering among her pans and bowls in a crescendo of activity. Her preparations were highly complicated, partly because she made large breakfasts but also because she insisted that everything come out even. All the dishes were timed, and she was quite skillful, but there was a busy stage at the end and this was it.

He grunted approvingly and turned the page.

It was just dawn. Away to the southeast the sun was rising over the dark band of the river, its bright wands glittering across the frozen wastes of the city. On the snowbanked streets below a few huddled figures scampered, and an occasional icebound car crawled, and a thousand icicled traffic signals winked red and green, red and green, mechanically awaiting the rush.

Zipski read on.

"Hell," he growled suddenly.

In the other room Edna paused and stepped spryly to the door. Her jolly mouth was drawn in a scolding line. "Bernard Zipski!"

"Sorry," he said automatically. "They got it wrong."

"That's no excuse." She returned to the stove, her duty done, and in a moment called, "What did they get wrong?"

"Just the time of a political meeting. Nothing important. They say eight and it's eight-thirty."

"Is *that* all?" She attacked an egg with a spatula and delivered it, intact, to the waiting plate. "As if you care!"

"Well, they ought to get it right." He flipped to another page, his sense of precision still outraged. "They never do."

The sun was growing stronger, shortening the dull shadows on the worn rug, and here and there points of light twinkled in the room: on the swinging brass pendulum of the grandfather's clock, on the square toes of Zipski's high black shoes, and, behind him, on a silver frame. The frame stood alone by a black leather box on a broad table, and its isolation, and the expression of the boy in the picture it bore, lent it a peculiar dignity. The boy was a patrolman, and he wore the high-crowned policeman's cap that went out with Repeal, and he wore, even in youth, his father's steady, impassive look. It was an old picture, and cheap, and the detail was poor. But it had been the last one.

Zipski held the paper closer, rereading a short item. He was on the last page and approaching the end of that. Edna knew just how long it took him to read the paper. It was one of the things that had to come out even. He was folding the sections together and laying them on the window sill when the clock chimed and she called, "All right! All right, old man!"

The dining room was large and crowded with knobby, involved furniture. The entire apartment was like that; Edna had been determined to find a place for everything from the house. Yet somehow, despite the overcrowding and the involution, she had managed to give the chaste rooms the richness of her own personality. Zipski did not like apartments; coming in through the lobby at night he felt like a unit; yet once beyond their door he could settle among the warm smells of mahogany and old leather and damask and feel at home. It was a small miracle, Edna's specialty.

"Well!" She spread her napkin with a quick, nervous jerk of her fingers. "What's what today?"

"Same thing. Trouble everywhere."

"Isn't it awful?" She shook her head smartly, and the bun of silver hair behind twinkled in the fresh sunlight.

Zipski ate methodically, with his gray face gently bowed and his thin ankles neatly crossed under the table. Occasionally he would nod slightly or murmur agreement, but otherwise he let his wife ramble on, gossiping of his sister's grandchildren, of her niece's new home, of all the myriad details of life in the two families. They were enormous families, and Edna was devoted to them: to the new marriages, to the babies, to the housekeeping of the women and the slow struggling of the silent men. In the lower East Bay neighborhood where they grew up all the men were strugglers. It was one of the rules of living there. Zipski was the hardest struggler in the family, and until he became commissioner he had been a winner.

Now he finished the last sausage. He laid his fork across the plate and reached for his pipe and filled it. It was well lit, and Edna had slid the thick mug of black coffee before him, when he told her what was really in the paper.

"There's a little piece from the State House," he said casually. "That job is still open."

"Say! That's good news. Have you heard anything?"

"Just a formal letter yesterday. I only wrote last week."

"Well, there's plenty of time." His retirement was six months away. "If only they don't get into a lot of red tape. The way it is in the city — goodness!"

All Edna knew of the past year was that what had promised to be the crowning glory of his career had been an agony of frustration. Politics was a mystery to her, and so she blamed the change on municipal routine. She worried about him. She knew how badly he had been hurt. For the failure everything is simple: he has been cheated and that is that. But the defeat of a big man is large and complicated and hard on those around him.

"I'm sure it'll come through," she said.

"Let's hope so." He rose and went after his shirt.

It was a large apartment, and they could have afforded a maid, for there were just the two of them now, but neither would have thought of that. Edna put the breakfast dishes to soak and began her dusting, thrusting a determined rag into the stubborn corners of the ornate furniture and moving systematically across the dining room. She would rather have done the front room first, for it faced the industrial east and was the dirtiest. But she always left it until he had gone, for the picture and the box were there, and she did not want him to come upon her and find her going over them, going carefully over them. He would not like that and she knew he would not.

The killing had a very special place in Department history, for it had been Prohibitions's last, but Zipski never spoke of it. He had refused the medal, and Commissioner Holzweig had brought it out in its leather box and given it to Edna, and she had kept it all these years, with the picture, and Zipski had never spoken of them. When she asked him to sell the old house and move he had agreed, but he wanted no reasons. He knew all the reasons, and he did not want, and did not want her, to speak of them. And on that bitter day when the killer, caught in another crime and brought to confession — on that long day of driving rains when the killer was hanged, he had not spoken at all.

He appeared in the serge tunic she had carefully pressed the night before. "About that job," he said, fingering a brass button thoughtfully. "I'm going to tell them to write me here. I wouldn't want it to get around the Department."

She nodded pertly, and he went to the closet and struggled into his greatcoat. His hat was on, and he was at the door, when she called, "Old man! It's cold. You better wear ear muffs."

"Ear muffs!" He sniffed. "Ear muffs!" And went out without them.

She shook her head and went to the dining room and took out the metal polish.

Zipski hated the self-service elevator. He considered it a conspiracy against his dignity. The twentieth was the top floor, and as the first passenger going down he had to stand at the control panel and, when someone wanted to get off at the lobby, push the right button. In uniform he felt ridiculous. The Christmas before, an elderly woman had actually tried to tip him, and when he indignantly protested to Edna that night she had burst out laughing.

But this morning there were no other passengers. He rode smoothly to the ground floor and stepped swiftly to the street.

His driver was waiting by the black Lincoln, stamping on the glazed concrete and slapping his arms and watching his breath form in shapeless puffs and disappear. The sun was well into the sky now, but there was no warmth in it, and when he saw the commissioner he saluted gratefully.

"Morning, sir." He opened the door.

"Good morning, Tucker. Raw day."

"Yessir."

Zipski saw the vivid pink in the man's face and paused. "If it's cold as this tomorrow, better wait for me in the car. No point freezing."

"Yessir. Thanks."

He was in the back seat, arranging the steamer blanket on his lap, when he noticed it.

"Tucker! This isn't my car."

The driver turned around. "No, sir. Yours is being fixed again. This is Inspector Holloway's."

"New."

"Brand new," the driver said and pulled away from the curb.

"What happened to his?"

"Well, that's — uh — being held, sort of." It was considered bad luck to speak of promotions, and Zipski had not yet appointed an inspector to fill the vacancy his own advancement had left.

"I see. Thank you."

The apartment house was on the outskirts of the city, and the Lincoln moved rapidly down the deserted streets, its chains clicking rhythmically. Twice they passed well-bundled patrolmen who saw the license plate and stood awkwardly at attention as they raced by. Zipski sat erect in the middle of the back seat, listening with one ear to the staccato bark of the police radio in the front seat and remembering, and going over, the harsher passages in Wallace Gillette's speech.

The mark of the season was everywhere, in windows, on light poles, and in the wide canvas signs hanging over the downtown streets. In the shopping district a crew of scaffolded workmen moved stiffly before the face of a tardy store, hanging evergreen, and a block away three mission women in black overcoats and bonnets had tuned their brass instruments and were bravely ringing out the first carol of the day.

Zipski opened the right window a little to let the cold air seep in. He breathed deeply, drawing closer and closer to decision with each breath, and when the Department building loomed a scant two blocks away he was ready, he had a plan. After the speech tonight every outpost in the world beneath the Seventh District underworld would be alerted, and so he would start today, before the declaration of war, before the barricades were up.

The driver slid to the curb, jumped out, and held the door wide. Zipski strode in and halted for a moment in the inner hall, peering about. He saw a heavy man with grizzled hair and a seamed face talking to a sergeant.

"Morelock!" He beckoned.

The man came over quickly.

"How long since you thrown a tap?"

The question shouldn't have been embarrassing. Officially, Morelock hadn't tapped a line in months. But Big Ed Sylvester paid him more than the Department did, and for Big Ed, he had.

"Why?" he said warily.

"You know where Ben Erik lives?"

Morelock brightened. "I sure do."

"Been out that way lately?"

"Not in years." He really hadn't, because the last time he had bungled, bleeding the wire in the middle of a call and tipping Ben off. "But I can find it all right."

"Good. See me in about ——" He drew a massive watch from his trousers and looked down. "See me at nine sharp."

Morelock nodded, smiling, and Zipski headed silently into the building, moving quickly down corridors of habit.

Ben Erik straddled the custom-built stool in his overheated bathroom and tried to urinate. As usual, he despaired. He leaned back on his haunches, furiously lit a cigar, and flipped the match into the pool below.

"Ah, frig it," he muttered. He looked at his watch and spat disgustedly. Fifteen frigging minutes.

Ten minutes was par for Ben. After ten he usually tightened up and ended by quitting. Later, when the pressure became unbearable, he would run to the nearest toilet and let go. But this morning he had too much to do. He could not humor himself. Come on, he urged himself desperately, come *on*!

He crouched on the horseshoe seat in reverse. Lately his legs had begun to protest against the long sessions of standing, yet he could not bring himself to sit as a woman sits. Built into the tile wall above the plumbing was a reading rack with the latest copy of *Quick* clipped to it. It was a family joke. Ben turned the pages sluggishly.

He had spent over five thousand dollars on psychiatric advice and given up when the best efforts of the best men only told him what he well knew. On a February night twenty years before he had been shot while relieving himself on a country road. He was waiting with his trucks on the shoulder when a competitor tried to wipe him out. His wound was slight. One slug passed through the flesh of his thigh as he rolled under a tandem axle. But the damage to his nervous system was irreparable. Bad news, or any excitement, tied him up for hours. The lilt in Paul Gormley's voice that morning had been enough.

Squatting thus, with one hairy forearm on the porcelain sheathing, he might have been a monastic at devotions. There was a piety about Ben's face in repose, an almost ecclesiastical peace his men never saw. He was always bossing them, or fighting to reassure himself he should be boss, and so they knew only his apelike frame, his shrewd eyes, his reptilian mouth. But here, as he wrestled with his private trouble, there was a curious softness in his face.

"Ah! God*dam* it! Ah!"

Ben strained.

The vegetation outside the window was very thick. In the summer, when the treetops and the lacing vines were in bloom, it was impossible to see the street. There was a reason for this. Ben had built the house in 1934, after trumpeting his withdrawal from the rackets, and had carefully camouflaged it to hide his new business from his new neighbors. The screen had been successful, and for Ben this was a double triumph, since he had chosen the neighbors with purpose. He had made his home in this discreet and unfashionable corner of the city because he wanted nothing about him so much as mediocrity. He wanted to be among common people so that the uncommon people, those he feared, could be quickly identified when they appeared among them. Here, he calculated, he could pose as a political amateur while he quietly built his power in the Seventh. It worked. His home precinct, indeed, became his best, for the neighbors were unsuspicious. They accepted, as the world accepted, the myth of the Erik retirement, and to insure the acceptance, his wife cultivated them socially. He himself remained aloof. That, too, was part of the plan, for the fable of Ben Erik flourished best in the absence of Ben.

Among these branches, bare now and heavy with snow, something remarkable was happening. A squirrel, dropping from a vine branch, had alighted on the back of another and larger squirrel passing on the branch below, and they were hopping awkwardly together along a twig just outside the window. Ben saw them as he was about to give up.

"Well I'm a son of a bitch," he chuckled. "What do you know about that."

So diverted, he urinated.

He was buttoning his trousers in triumph when his wife called up the stairwell: "Ben! You Ben! Come down here!"

He walked down heavily, trying not to hurry. "How many times I got to tell you not to yell at me like that?"

She eyed him placidly. Gloria was a big woman with a great mop of white hair. She had never attempted to keep her figure, and so she rather dominated him.

"Paul's downstairs in the office. The boys," she jerked her massive head toward a closed door off the foyer, "are in there."

"They can cool their cans. I'll be with Paul a while anyways. He's got some kind of news, and the way he talked this morning, not what I'd call good news."

She frowned. "Big Ed?"

"Ed you don't have bad news about. Ed *is* bad news."

"Well, I don't know what else there is."

"It could be a lot of things. Say." He brightened. "You know them squirrels outside? I saw one carrying a buddy on his back, you know, piggy back. Never saw that before."

"I'll tell Otto to clean them out. Jody could see them. It could give him, you know, a start."

"Well, I wouldn't do that." He paused doubtfully. "It might be just what he needs, a little excitement."

"No excitement, the doctor said, and he knows."

Ben snorted. "Doctors don't know nothing, is one thing I know." He went downstairs briskly.

Paul W. Gormley, police magistrate and representative to the State Legislature from the Seventh City District, was grooming his mustache in the cellar. Actually, the mustache wasn't a mustache and the cellar wasn't a cellar. Paul affected a little hair on his upper lip after an actor he admired, and the ground floor affected cellar windows to deceive tradesmen. Within the concrete walls of the foundation, beaverboard partitions had been erected, and inside these, air-conditioned and brilliantly lit, was the core of Ben's business. It looked like a broker's office. But at this time of morning brokers' offices were at the peak of their rush, and here there was no one but Paul, sitting under an enormous blackboard, massaging his fuzzy lip with a tiny bristle brush.

He heard the door above close, rose quickly and straightened his coat, and was slumped again in his chair, casually polishing his glasses, when Ben danced in.

"Brrr! B-rutal out, eh? Think of the poor horses!" He watched Paul carefully, but there was no answer. He cleared his throat. "God, you scared me this morning. So mysterious!"

"Scared is what you ought to be."

"But you should of told me why, then."

"On the phone? Does Abbott tell Costello everything on the phone?" Paul drew an onionskin manuscript from under his shawl collar. "Gillette gives this at Big Ed's club tonight. The newspapers got copies."

Ben studied the speech and Paul studied Ben. Outsiders wondered at Ben's prestige. In public he seemed weak. But outsiders never saw him on his home grounds. Even at his Central Democratic Club he hovered in the background. This was different. This was business. Ben knew all about that.

He finished and tapped the speech on the table. "I can keep this?"

"Well — Better burn it."

Ben tapped. "Any of our people know about this? Thorpe?"

"Nobody I told."

Tap, tap. "Any word from Meck? Warrick?"

"No time yet."

"Big Ed. How does he take it?"

Paul shook his head.

"As if I didn't know. As if I couldn't see that greasy Spik hand in every line."

Tap, tap, tap.

Suddenly Ben was livid. He slapped the speech across the desk, and it fell with a sharp crinkle.

"Bastards!" he said hoarsely. "Dirty bastards! 'Gangsters'! 'Parasites'! From them in the Valley, with their high-class talk. With

106

more fakers than India. I feel like singing, know what I mean? Just to get them out where I can look at them," he pounded the desk, "the whole dirty bunch," he pounded, "just to get square!"

Paul shook his head dismally. "A fine square we'd be."

"But who'd get hurt in the long run?"

"Us. We would. Look, Ben." Paul leaned forward. "I went over this whole thing with Sol soon as I got it. Sure, he says. We can sue. And if we sue everything comes out." He said it again, trenchantly: "Everything."

Lawyers, Ben thought contemptuously. Always thinking about law.

He calculated rapidly, juggling the dollars, the men, and the election districts in one vast motion, until his mind was a kaleidoscopic, distorted map of the city, with moneybags clustered on the weak squares and massed, huddled little figures where he was strong. Nearly all the figures were in the Seventh. The rest were with the money in the disputed wards, and these were unreliable. He had a few people in minor city jobs, and they would be useful, but the rest of the outside people would be sucked up by the tide. The tide, alias Big Ed You-Take-the-West-Side-I'll-Take-the-East-Side Sylvester. With the heat on, Ed could kill Ben's coming strength in East Bay overnight. Certainly Ben couldn't count on the other district leaders. He had what they wanted. This was what they had been waiting for. All he had to work with, really, when you came right down to it, was the Seventh.

"If we fight," Paul said with a faint whine, "we're hung." He fingered the thick knot in his tie and pursed his lips. They were loose and full and a little indecent. Gloria called him Liverlips.

Wolves, Ben thought bitterly. Waiting in the night. Waiting with Gillette.

He cleared his mind of the city and concentrated on the district. It leapt up, a kidney-shaped pattern of precincts and wards dovetailing together in a framework of strength, Ben's strength. Here the vote was solidly his: when the thousands of blacks swarmed out of their cold-water tenements on election day, herded together by his men, Ben Erik meant free oyster roasts, and parties at the

Central Democratic Club, and the buck outside the door at the poll. Here the leaders were blindly his; the legislators and councilmen were hopelessly tied up in the racket, and two of the three magistrates were bought and paid for, with papers in a safe-deposit box to prove it. He saw the district with a great forked stick across it, marking off their bailiwicks. In the crotch of the fork was Judge Russell, an independent. Ben had tried everything short of murder to unseat him and had ended by doubling the pay-off for all the cops under Russell, converting him into a sort of magisterial eunuch.

"Trouble," he said absently. "Trouble, if I don't watch out."

Paul gestured impatiently. "Honest to God, Ben, I don't see anything bad, really bad, here. A mess, sure. But it'll blow over. Look. It'll cost a little money. There'll be a few you can't reach. So what if we lose a few and the papers raise a stink? So what happens? Nothing. Nothing happens. Stop worrying, you'll be back on the couch again."

Ben shook his head. "We'll fight, our way. No libel suits."

"How, for Crissake? The only one you blow up with a bomb these days is yourself."

"Leave me find a way," he said doggedly. "I got some other things to think about first."

Quite a few things, he thought. Operation cutbacks and spies and courts and money. A lot of money. A tremendous lot. The bill for police protection alone ran to $200,000 a year now, and most of that was for ranking officers: patrolmen got only five dollars a month and a bottle of whisky at Christmas. This Christmas that would not do. The $200,000 would run closer to $350,000 — over a third of a million, he thought bitterly, and all the suction he had with the top gestapo now was one headquarters lieutenant. Police protection was just one item — there would be others — how many he could not foresee. And his income would be less. He would have to draw back everywhere, pulling out of all white neighborhoods, abandoning all new drops, losing all the trade he had taken from the bookies, from the tracks. In the strongbox behind his bed Ben had $232,000. In a fight like this, how long would that last? Not long. But maybe long enough.

The outer door slammed and a scrawny, balding man came in, blinking uncertainly and shaking the snow from his overcoat like a wet dog. He dropped a brown paper lunch bag on one of the desks and nodded at them cheerfully. "Hello, Mr. Erik. Hello, Mr. Gormley."

They ignored him. He accepted the snub stoically, hung up his coat, brushed it carefully, and began thumbing through a sheaf of machine tape playsheets at the far end of the room. This was Henry Loomis, the manager of the policy bank. Fifteen years before he had left high school with a brilliant record in mathematics and the dream of a Rutgers scholarship. The dream had flared out pitifully the day of the examination, and the shattered boy compromised on a night-school course in bookkeeping.

"I guess I better go," Paul said. "What do I do — nothing, or what?"

Paul knew more about the business than anyone except Ben, but he hated a fight. Ben knew that and despised him for it, but he needed him. He stood slowly, preoccupied with Loomis's quick birdlike movements. God, to have a job like that, so simple.

"Get the delegation talking Jim Crow. Gillette's always voted for it, and Cameron's track don't let niggers in. We can tie him in on this, anyway. Make 'em a couple of race bigots. Put it over big."

Paul nodded, adjusting his glasses. "How do we keep in touch with you?" Ben did not sponsor his men publicly.

"Nobody comes here but you, understand? If it's an emergency, and I mean real emergency, the others use my direct line. Tomorrow we find out which way everybody jumps." Paul turned to leave. "Wait a minute." Paul turned back reluctantly. "I got a job for you."

"A job, Ben?" He laughed nervously.

"Write me a speech for Thorpe." Robert Thorpe was Ben's

State Senator. "Make it dirty, like this." He gestured with a finger, showing how. "Give it right back. I'll be around this afternoon, four or five o'clock, to see how it looks."

"My God, Ben, I got court!"

"Get Wein to take it. No, don't tell him why. That's what he's for, a jam like this."

"Okay." Paul drew on his sharkskin coat listlessly. "What about Russell?"

Ben smiled thinly. "By morning no grift for the judge himself on that run."

Paul went out, bouncing on his toes a little from habit.

Ben stood by the desk, worrying the manuscript on the floor with his foot and thinking.

"Hey Henry," he said finally. "Burn that."

"Okay, Mr. Erik."

He went up the stairs slowly.

Immediately above the bank was the library. Ben liked to think of the two rooms as dissimilar, for if it was important to have the syndicate here, protected by the immunity which normally covered the homes of district leaders, it was also distasteful. So he had sealed off the ground floor with soundproofing and decorated the library with pine paneling, false book backs, cerise drapes and a fireplace. Somewhere Ben's decorator had failed. The library was the bank in greasepaint.

Here, as Ben conferred with Paul, Moss Bailey baited Otto Lutsche. Otto was a dull Swede with a saving touch of pathos. During Prohibition he had been Ben's bodyguard, and now he ran errands for him. Otto adored Ben: his mind was a slate from which he read whatever Ben had last written there. Last week Ben had said Wipe Kijowski was a cinch to win the title. The opinion was now obsolete, for Pete Manzer had knocked Kijowski out in the fourth round, but no other had been offered to replace it, so Otto hopelessly defended it.

"I saw the whole thing on television," he said doggedly. "The referee was fixed."

Moss mimicked him. "I saw duh hull ting on duh tell-a-vi-shun. Duh re-fe-ree hit Wipe on duh head wid a mal-let." He puckered his lips and ran a forefinger over them, "wubble-wub-ble-wubble," like an idiot child.

Otto was furious. He never knew how to deal with Moss. "Don't gimme no wind," he growled. "I'll hit *you* on the head." He tried to think of something insulting to add but could not.

"Look at him." Moss grinned. "What a pan. It's so horrible it can't be real. It's a mask, like they used at Brink's."

The others watched sourly, not because they pitied Otto but because Moss did the thing badly. Ben had six pickup men handling his policy writers. They were all here, for after Paul's call Ben had ordered Otto to bring them in. Normally their mornings were their own, and they had sworn at Otto bitterly, but they had come, for a pickup man's job was soft and paid well, and they knew if they crossed Ben he would quickly find replacements.

Two were blacks, two were Jews, and one was a devout Cath-olic. Moss Bailey, the sixth and least reliable, was the youngest. Ben had hired Moss on the recommendation of Eddie Finch, one of the blacks. Eddie had met Moss at a hot tea and jam party on the west side and thought the boy had spirit.

Eddie had spirit. It was about all he did have. He was a small, jumpy man who had once been a musician and now lived with a growing family in a black apartment house. He had played drums for an odd-job band until the end of the war, when the sudden slump in the entertainment business marooned the band in a Striker Street dive. The leader quit and the others decided to split up and singleshoot. That was fine for them, but very bad for the drummer, and Eddie was flatpocket when his present wife picked him up and gave him a couch in her apartment and found him a job. He was so grateful he married her. They still lived in the same apartment, but there were two children now, and when he wanted to practice his two-beat finish he had to go outside, to a cave club around the corner. He still had his own drums, but his wife would not let him play them in the apartment.

The others had all been with Ben in the old days. Izzy Friedman and Milt Feinblatt were cousins and looked alike. Both were fat, both wore bifocals, and their faces were scarred with acne. Milt was fatter and his voice was softer. It was so soft you could hardly hear him in a crowded room. During Prohibition they had worked in one of Ben's cutting plants, stirring burnt sugar, oil of rye, and glycerin into the vats of raw alcohol. They were hard workers, and late in the era, when routine kept Ben in the city, they ran everything in the county for him. Now they were old men, and Izzy had become peevish, but they still worked hard and were still dependable. They lived with their wives in a large house near Rogers Park. Every night the four of them went to the movies together.

Joe Murdock, a chain-smoker with a sharp face, was the other black collector. He was the best of the six, and Ben knew it. That was about all he or anyone else knew about Joe, except that he lived quietly and was the smartest black man they had ever known. Not even Joe's wife knew he was a college graduate. He had come up from Louisville in 1927 and worked his way through C.C.N.Y., stoking furnaces in office buildings at night. When he went home with his degree he thought he was a made man. But he couldn't find a job. No one would take him seriously. Everyone thought either Joe or his diploma was a fake. Or said they did. "Where'd you get that, nigger?" they asked, and "Who done that for you?" and admired it, clucking, "Say, that's a right narce job." Then they told him to get out. Finally he burned it and became a truck driver. He began driving for Ben in 1932. For ten years now he had been managing the writers in Judge Russell's wards, the toughest run in the district, and for the past nine months he had been working with Paul Gormley in the shadow of Sylvester's East Bay Club, setting up policy drops as fast as Paul found precinct executives.

The Catholic, Hugh Slade, hated all the others. He was a bald, walleyed man in a shabby suit carefully pressed at home. Every evening he sat up while his wife did the ironing, eating animal crackers and regaling her with stories about Ben. He hated

Ben most because his hatred sprang from fear, and he feared him most. He thought Ben hated him, too, but he was wrong. Ben felt sorry for him. Slade had been one of Ben's salesmen in the Volstead days. He was neither bright nor efficient, and if he had not had such a large family, Ben would have fired him long before or broken him to writer. Slade lived with his wife, nine children, and thirty-eight installment payments a month in a frame house in the district.

The pickup men made a hundred twenty dollars a week. Each had some thirty writers who drew a straight ten percent commission on all bets. Writers got about seventy dollars a week. Their commissions ran much higher, but they had to split part of the take with their subwriters — newsboys, bartenders, and shoeshine men who worked for them.

Otto had tried to be first a pickup man and then a writer, but he had never understood arithmetic, and so he failed. He blamed arithmetic, which he distrusted. He was convinced Moss was a fraud and that if he only knew arithmetic he could expose him. Now he turned the pages of *Titter*, trying to ignore Moss's taunting.

"May-be," Moss intoned, dangling his arms and affecting a simian pose, "may-be duh doity ref give Wipe a Mickey before duh fight. Ya-ah!" He stuck his thumbs in his ears and wiggled his fingers crazily. Otto sweated and pretended to read.

Joe lit a fresh cigarette from a dying butt. "Better quit," he suggested lazily. "The boss's grandson's upstairs sick. He might hear."

Jody was not Ben's grandson, although Ben cultivated the impression he was. Ben and Gloria were childless; they had taken the boy in when her niece's marriage foundered.

"Gimme it straight, Pop," Moss said, dropping the imposture and rocking on his pointed toes, digging the taps into the thick carpeting. "You bet on Manzer and collected heavy. You couldn't of bet on Kijowski. You couldn't be that stupid. Kijowski's a punk and you know it."

He leered insultingly. Slade watched him with bright eyes. His wife would love this.

Moss's nose was beginning to run, and there were flickers of pain in his stomach. He kept grinning at Otto, the grin becoming glassy as the light in his eyes faded. He cracked his knuckles rhythmically. *Gotta have sugar*, ran through his mind. *Gotta have sugar, sugar, sugar.*

Izzy glared. "Do you have to do that?" he said testily. "I mean, is it absolutely necessary?" Moss ignored him and stepped up the rhythm.

"Where's the boss?" Eddie asked suddenly. "This was such an emergency."

Moss tapped his foot loudly, keeping time with the tune as he drove it through his mind. *Sugar, sugar, sugar. Sugar, sugar, sugar.*

Izzy stormed over to the window, fished indignantly in his vest pocket for a cigar, and did not find it.

Sugar, sugar, sugar.

Otto exploded. He threw down the magazine and stood, spluttering.

"You wisenheimer, you no-good! Kijowski's five times as good as Manzer. In a fair fight he'd win — he won Tuesday, only that referee, he give Manzer all the breaks. I saw it! On the television! Manzer's no good, like you, you no-good! Kijowski's a champ, a real champ!"

Then Otto's luck turned bad. As he talked, Ben came in and stood in the shadow of the doorway. "Kijowski's a punk," he said casually, walking into the room. "He stinks."

Moss grinned, and Otto, his rage ruptured, stood silent and shaken.

"About time," Izzy said fretfully, taking a seat by the fireplace. The others arranged their chairs in a semicircle with him and looked at their watches.

Otto was hurt. "No he don't, Ben," he said weakly. "He don't stink so much as Manzer."

Ben brushed by him and sat in a tall chair under the false book backs. "Much worse, Otto. Do me a favor and get me a pad upstairs."

114

Otto left quickly, relieved at the chance, and the others waited expectantly.

Ben took a deep breath. "Boys," he said, shifting his eyes across theirs, "we got a fight on our hands. Some people want to give us a hard time."

He began at the beginning. The significance of Jarvis Cameron surprised them: they were only vaguely aware of competition for gambling and had scarcely heard of either Cornwall County or Wallace Gillette. Ben skimmed over Wallace's speech quickly, flushing a little and making notes on the lined pad Otto brought him as he talked. When he touched upon the police situation he was very gentle. For the older men it all had a familiar ring and they took it easily. Only Slade looked scared. Eddie Finch was merely curious, and Moss, tense on a couch, his tongue hanging dry between his teeth, was not listening. He was overdue where he ought to be and was beginning to feel it.

"So," Ben finished, "as you can see, it won't be exactly a cinch. You," he pointed a pencil at Joe, "will have the toughest time. Tougher than your writers, even."

Joe frowned. "Russell's gestapo can't stand much heat. He rides them pretty hard."

"Exactly why it's so tough for you. When you pick up today, tell your writers no more action. Tell 'em to send their people over the line, either line. By tonight I want an average on every writer you got, what his take is. I'll pay it —" he patted his wallet pocket "— here. But you got to move around, get the money out, keep the organization in shape for when the heat's off."

Slade had been working his lips, shaping a question, and when he finally got it out he was so excited his voice broke. "How about us, with families that we got? Suppose we get arrested, if it's hard like you say. Then what?"

Ben looked at him sharply. "I got a family too, but I don't worry about no gestapo. Nobody else does either if he watches what I tell him."

"Well, I don't want no trouble."

Inside, Slade's heart was pounding. He had never confessed

115

his job in the syndicate to his priest. A job was a job, he had always told himself, and this was as legitimate as any other. But he knew it really wasn't, and the thought of facing the priest from a cell terrified him.

Ben was persuasive. Slade was the only one here who wanted to quit, but there would be others out among the writers, and the pickup men would have to deal with them.

"Me too," he said cheerfully. "I hate trouble, too. Frig trouble, I always say. Better frig it before it frigs you." Into the laughter he added, "We got nothing to worry about provided we're careful."

He turned away, watching Slade obliquely as he talked to the others. I got other ways of coaxing, mister, he thought. This racket isn't going to smash up over a yellowbelly.

He outlined the shifts in writer locations necessary for each pickup run, the increases for cops, and how to get in touch with Thayer Cross, the syndicate lawyer, in a jam. They were supposed to know that, but there had been so few raids lately most of them had forgotten. And he told them, with an eye on Slade, how to squelch queasy writers. "Say it's no skin off your ass, as far as you're concerned, but I get nervous habits when people working for me don't do what I want."

"We going to lose a lot of money, boss?" Milt asked. "Like in the beginning?"

Ben wet his lips and managed a smile. "Multiplied by ten and you got an idea," he said. Multiplied by a hundred would be more like it, he thought.

"How about the suction we got?" Joe asked.

"I thought about that, but there's no time like the present."

Ben went to a kneehole desk in the corner and picked up the phone. He dialed a number and waited impatiently while the other end rang. He never called police headquarters direct. Usually he reached his lieutenant there through Paul, but Paul would be out now, lining up the councilmen and the legislators, and so he was calling his emergency link, an old organization man he had placed as criminal court bailiff. But the municipal switchboard was unattended. "Who you got to know to get Main seven thousand?" he complained.

He slammed down the receiver and turned to face Moss.

Moss was twitching uncontrollably. "I got to go, boss. I really got to go."

Ben was annoyed. "Come on, come on, get in the game. We still got the new odds to go over."

"I got a doctor's appointment. I think I got a virus grippe. A doc's gonna look me over. Sorry, boss, I'll get it from Joe later." He fled out the door, leaving a confused silence behind.

"What's the matter with that guy?" Ben demanded, picking up the phone again. Otto snickered and the others looked embarrassed.

The switchboard was still dead. "What a city," he muttered, hanging up again. "I pay taxes and I can't even get anybody downtown to answer me when I call."

It was nearly noon, and the second race at Willoughby would be run at two o'clock. In the little time left, Ben drew up revised odds, starting with an increase of from 750-to-1 to 800-to-1 for payoffs on the big book — bets of fifty cents or more. The loss in income would be enormous. He would drop an average of between $2,000 and $3,000 a day. But Ben was not interested in money now. He was bidding for survival. He had to crush the doubts which would rise among his constituents. Otherwise they might lose the habit he had so carefully twisted into their lives.

He saw them to the garage under the house, where Otto was waiting in the big Cadillac. They came and went this way to avoid suspicion in the neighborhood.

Ben drew Joe aside. "Tell that Moss kid he's got to be careful or we drop him. He's too nervous."

Joe blew the stump of his cigarette to the cement floor and stepped on it. "Bad business either way. Only one way to drop him right. This is no time for that."

Ben shook his head. "Anybody gets in my way now I make a time. Tell him that, too."

"I don't like it," Joe said thoughtfully. "This whole thing don't feel good."

"Forget it." Ben laughed and shoved him into the car with the others. "There's always a way to fix it." He slammed the door and went inside.

When Moss Bailey left Ben's house he crept four tortured blocks and hailed a cab. The driver wanted to talk, but once Moss had given the Crone Street address he didn't try to answer. He couldn't. His skin was alive with a crawling itch, and a thin electric thread of pain was vibrating along his trunk, and he knew if he once opened his mouth he would lose all control and scream the flat animal scream of the panicked hype.

There was a patch of shadow in the corner of the cab, and he lay white and wide-eyed in it, sniffling and listening to the dashboard meter ticking off the separate seconds of his agony. He hooked his heels under the rod on the floor and locked his knees, straining to keep them rigid and wishing he could die for a while, until the ride was over and he could soak up the peace of the needle. He told himself he was a board the cabbie was taking home, an old plank to be sawed up and hammered into a table. He tried to stiffen and a twitch rippled through him and suddenly there was another image, a saw, a razor-sharp buzzsaw of pain slicing and tearing into his gut.

Ben you bastard, he thought. Ben you no good frigger. Holding a sick man's sickness against him, keeping him until he wants to, maybe will, die. The tears of his suffering welled up and trickled down his face. Ben you Ben you Ben you bastard. He unhooked his heels and drew his knees to his stomach.

The driver merely thought Moss had a bad cold. He rattled on about the weather, taxes, and the prices of the Christmas season.

"It's a crime, know what I mean, the way they mark everything up when everybody's got to buy. I went down last Saturday to get my kids some things, some little things . . ."

The tale was a long one, and it reminded him of another.

Moss heard him through the curtain of his anguish and prayed for green lights and thin traffic. The meter clicked: thirty cents. They were nearly there.

Some hypes carried their own needles, but if you were picked up it meant six months in the House of Correction, and a pickup man could not risk a search. Further, it was a steady hype who could find his vein in a panic, and Moss was needle shy. The opening of his arm always terrified him. He could never have given himself a shot.

The cabbie braked before a red light. Three blocks to go. Moss squeezed his eyes shut. The light turned green: the cab gunned forward. The meter clicked: thirty-five cents.

He jerked his hand into his side pocket — froze as a spasm twisted across his groin — and then jerked it out. The cab drew up before a familiar lamppost. He spilled two quarters into the driver's hand, got out carefully like an old man, and walked rapidly on stiff legs across the cracked pavement and up the grimy stoop. If an angel had opened the door he would not have been surprised. Black Hebe, his angel, did.

The Hebe bulged in his filthy sweatshirt. "Hullo, boss," he greeted him lazily. "Thought mebbe you was kickin' it, didn't need no chef no mo'." He was a coal-black man whose name was inexplicably Abe Goldman.

Moss hurried past him and a scarecrow in rags rose from a darkened corner of the foyer, his mouth working frantically.

"This here's Frank," Hebe said genially. "Frank's a cotton shooter. Got cotton for Frank?"

But Moss was gone. He ran up the shaky staircase, past the single unshaded bulb in the second-floor corridor, and disappeared into the stale smell of a rear room. Hebe looked at Frank with contempt. "Missed again," he spat. "Hog." The scarecrow settled back into the forlorn shadow, his mouth still working.

Upstairs Moss tore off his overcoat and jacket and collapsed on a worn mohair couch. He was plucking ineffectually at his cuff button when Hebe shuffled in.

"Help me!" His eyes rolled out of control.

Between them they unfastened the sleeve and Moss pushed it back, gripping the upper arm with his left fist and watching the veins swell.

"Same way?" Hebe asked.

"Right up the pipe."

Hebe fixed the jolt. He opened a number nine capsule deftly, shook the white powder into a teaspoon, and heated it over an oil lamp near the shaded window. When the powder had melted he poured it through a cotton filter, into a small syringe. He approached the couch, grinning.

Moss's eyes were shut, and he could not see him, but above his panting he heard the footsteps shuffling across the linoleum, and his heart hammered.

"Quick. *Quick!*"

Hebe's grin was suddenly gentle. "Here it comes, boss," he whispered and slipped the needle into the scarred knot beating with a pulse of its own under the white thumb.

"One," Moss whimpered as the syrup seeped into his starved blood. "Two." Hebe drew out the blood-flecked needle. "Three. Four. Five. Six. Seven. Eight. Nine. Ten."

Somewhere a streetcar rumbled in its track bed, and somewhere the cry of a child echoed in a narrow alley, but here there was only the whiz of slowing breath. Hebe crouched over the limp arm, holding the empty syringe like a spent penis. His smile lingered and his eyes were bright.

Moss opened his eyes and smiled back idly. "Over the hump. Black Hebe daddy."

Hebe came back, teeth flashing, eyes crinkling. "I'm happy when you're happy, highpockets."

Moss rolled on his side and plucked three crumpled bills from his pocket. "Cheap at half the price," he murmured.

He turned on his stomach and closed his eyes and did not open them for half an hour.

Rattus norvegicus, slum-bred, never runs in the open. He

follows a wall, or a fence bottom, or a baseboard, scooting along with his head slung low, feeling his way with his whiskers. He makes his holes in corners, or in dark patches behind outside hoppers, sliding in and out on his belly, leaving the ground around his nest packed and smooth. Anything that moves in his narrow track he bites.

Like a slum rat Moss Bailey crept along the thin and warped wall of the old hall and down the stair treads, his heel taps ringing in the dusty air. At the last landing he paused and looked around quickly. He was alone. A cracked mirror with a tarnished gilt edge, a relic of the house's past, sat in a recess. He strolled over indolently and combed his hair, stroking the puffy sideburns with loving fingers.

He remembered the cab ride vaguely, and not at all as it had been. There was a meal between him and his hunger now. Maybe, he thought, I ought to stow a finger of codeine in case I get caught again. But the thought begged decision, and in the sweet aftermath of the drug he could decide nothing. He set the idea aside and stepped out into the winter sunlight, gulping cold air.

A little black girl was playing on the icy walk. He flipped her a quarter. She chased it down the pavement crowing, caught it, and turned and waved. He waved back, grinning slack-jawed.

He looked at his watch. Twenty-five minutes to pickup time. Might as well walk.

Ollie Wetlek's bar was six blocks away. Moss made it in less than ten minutes, drumming his taps along the broken sidewalks. Approaching the bar he felt a rhythm pounding in the air. He pushed the door open and suddenly the noise was all around him, a swelling wave of jukebox jazz and profanity, sprinkled with soap bubbles.

Ollie stood by the nickelodeon, gesturing with a suds-soaked arm and twisting the tuning knob to the left. "It's my joint," he shouted, "and I'll turn it down or off, all the way off if I want."

Beside him Annie was spluttering. "Goddam you, you want

to lock everybody comes in here in a cage." But she was really on the defensive. She had been playing with the knob while Ollie washed his mugs, and her finger had slipped.

"No more talk, now," he warned. "No more gab or I turn it off all the way. Crissake. A man's got to have some peace in his own place."

From behind an oil stove in the corner a young mother, with the peaked face of a mountain girl, looked up and stopped rocking the burlap bundle in her arms. The bundle wailed fraily and she gave herself to it again, cooing softly.

"No more talk, no more jabber, no more fun," Annie fumed, turning in defeat to the ladies' room. "You Communist."

Moss leered. "Thought you had a band in here. Heard it half a block away out in the street."

Ollie wiped the final suds from his arms. "Beer?" Moss nodded and he drew one. "She's lonesome. All her friends went away, left her nobody to play shuffleboard with."

Moss sipped. "Seems to me I haven't seen that Rube around last week or so. They was great friends, wasn't they?"

Ollie shook his head sorrowfully. "Two weeks they been gone. I don't know if they ever get back, bad weather like this."

"*They* get back?"

"Her and that runt, that Hoot. They took a flat to 'Rico, or I think they did." Ollie looked puzzled. "Funny thing, you maybe don't believe it, in a lot of ways she's a nice kid."

Moss jeered: "Frontways or backways?"

"No, no, really nice." He shrugged his shoulders and added, with a burst of memory, "Day before she left a woman come in here all done up, a real lady, and they had a talk."

Moss slammed down his empty glass. "If she's anything but a friggin' whore drunk, I'm Stoneface Zipski. Last time I saw her she didn't even smell *human*." He wrinkled his nose to show how she did smell.

"No, I mean it." Ollie was dogged. "They sat right back there." He pointed to the last booth, and as he did the door of the ladies' room opened and Annie came out, arranging herself. She eyed him hotly. "Who you pointin' at, Jellybelly?" she shouted.

The men collapsed in laughter, the mountain girl tittered, and Annie rushed over to the shuffleboard, swearing loudly, and began flinging the iron wafers against the stained plaster.

In a moment she was calm again, sipping beer from the quart tankard which bore her chalk inscription, "Aney," and reading, from her inexhaustible store of comic books, a tattered copy of *Kid Eternity*.

Moss buttoned his coat. "Got to pick up. Your slips in?"

"Charlie was here fifteen, twenty minutes ago. I never have much. Too close. If they're here, they just as soon go see him. They think it's luckier that way."

"If there's any luck around, the bank don't get it," Moss said darkly.

"Losing? Don't cry on my shoulder. You rob me plenty enough." Ollie held up the spread fingers of one hand. "Five hundred bucks I must've lost before I got smart."

"We're making all there is to make," Moss said at the door. "It's just some people are jealous and some of 'em wear blue suits, and they're maybe gonna take a few of us downtown."

Ollie rolled down his sleeves, studying the soiled flannel cuffs. "If that's the case you can count me out from here in. No dough subbing anyways."

Moss paused. Then he returned to the bar, staring at the bartender and holding his right thumb between his teeth. At the rail he took it out abruptly and held it high, gripping it with his fingers. Ollie swallowed hard and nodded hurriedly, with sharp little jerks. "Okay," he whispered.

"So long, Fatboy," Moss said scornfully and slammed the door behind him. The slam jarred the door's curling yellow shade and it flew up, rattling dryly in the empty barroom.

"Whatsat?" Annie cried slyly, looking up from *Kid Eternity*. "Givin' up numbers, are you?" Her laughter was oddly like the crackle of the shade. Ollie ignored her. He disappeared into the back room. The young mother tiptoed out, closing the door softly with one hand and cradling the child with the other.

He reappeared carrying a small Christmas tree. "Jingle Bells! Jingle Bells!" he sang merrily, "Jingle all the way!"

Annie watched him, catlike, over the comic-book edge. "No more numbers here, Ollie?"

He hummed to himself, anchoring the tree to the end of the bar and dressing it with lights shaped like Santa Clauses.

Still she watched. "Do I have to see Charlie to put in my bet after this?" Her voice rasped like a file.

On each green finger he slipped an ornament.

"Do I?" As though she ever played the numbers. "Hey Ollie, do I?" The comic book was tightly rolled in her fists, and her eyes were bright beads against rotting leather.

He reached to fix the shade. "Guess I'll have to get new stuff for the juke. 'Silent Night,' and all that. Carols. People will be asking for 'em."

But when he drew the cord to the bottom it slipped from his fingers. The shade clattered and Annie cackled harshly and he looked at the little Christmas tree with despair.

Moss found Charlie Bond bent over his squat pinball machine, trying for 150,000. He had one ball left, and he had to hit the thin chrome bridge marked "Double Score" with it. It was worth a try, for it meant ten free games, and afternoons dragged wretchedly until payoff time.

The machine, here as in all the drops on Moss's run, was Moss's idea. He had persuaded Ben to install them as a gimmick to attract customers, and if they worked out Ben planned to put them in drops all over the district. But they weren't working out. Moss's psychology was all wrong. The real jonahs, who supported the syndicate, did not want other channels for their spare change. If they had an extra nickel, it went on the number-of-the-week the Reverend Wilson Small passed out in his Gospel Tabernacle each Sunday night — and rang from the steeple bell if it hit — or on one of the obscure systems advertised in *Black Combination*, or, with the persevering individualists, the one number which would be cherished, year after year, until it hit. Only chippies were attracted by a bagatelle, and if they tried it and liked it, they would go elsewhere, to the neon emporia on Striker Street, where the quarter machines were. Here the only steady patron was Charlie.

The door stuck, as always. Moss put his shoulder against it and burst into the long, shallow room lined with empty vegetable bins and bare shelves.

"Hello, crazy. You still playing that crazy thing?" Moss knew the machines had failed, and Charlie's fondness for his annoyed him.

Charlie looked up absently, fingering the shooting knob. "Wait a minute," he said.

Ping!

Out of the alley on the right the ball spun and bounced against a tiny rubber tire marked 2,000. The motor chattered excitedly, lights flashed on the scoreboard, and the ball popped in and out of a 5,000 hole. More chatter, more lights. The double-score slot lay directly ahead.

"C'mon, Crissake, I'm in a hurry," Moss grumbled, perching on the store counter.

The ball worried the side of the bridge, balanced precariously for a moment, and then slipped down the side, lost in a clatter of minor tallies and a final feeble display from the scoreboard. Charlie deliberately tilted the machine. "That tears it," he said bitterly, biting his lip. He had wanted those free games badly.

"You done that too late," Moss snickered. "Tilt it on the first shot, you save yourself a lot of time."

Charlie swung behind the counter, rapping his knuckles on the linoleum top with chagrin. He dreaded these sessions with Moss. "You were in a hurry, you said," he muttered sullenly, stooping down and lifting the canvas bag from under the counter. "My stuff's all here. I was loaded with action all day." He looked up into a loose face and tiny pupils.

"What's the matter, you want to get rid of me?" Moss asked vacantly, reaching for the case without looking at it.

125

Charlie's disappointment dissolved in the quicksilver fear which always poisoned his defiance of Moss. "No, no," he said hurriedly. "I just thought, from what you said, you wanted to go."

Moss opened the bag, ignoring him, and thumbed through the bundles of green slips, each carrying, in Charlie's painful handwriting, the transparent code: "Five cans spaghetti, three cans beans, four dozen radishes," or "Two boxes baking powder, one potato, nine jars peanut butter."

"Okay," he said at last. "How many winners you got today?"

Charlie's laugh was forced. "None, I hope. None at all."

"For you that'd be a record." He lifted the bag and dropped it on the counter with a significant thump. The knots of change in the bottom clanked dully.

The door opened and a short, burly black in a checkered cap came in panting and clutching a coin. "Hi, boss," he said. "Gimme ——"

"Too late," Charlie snapped. "You know that." Latecomers were a problem. There would be no harm in this one, but a line had to be drawn.

"Couldn't get here no faster, boss. I got a real zingeroo here, just lahk last time. I got two bits say so."

Last time was eighteen months before. He had won thirty-five dollars with a dime then, and no day passed he did not savor the memory.

Charlie shook his head. "Sorry, chief."

The checkered cap scowled. "Over Mister Ingram's they take after one o'clock. Done it myself."

Moss looked up stonily. "Beat it, punk. Take your grift somewhere else."

The man went out, twisting his cap at an angry angle, and Charlie knew he had lost a customer.

"You shouldn't talk that way," he said plaintively. "I get a quarter from him regular."

Moss squeezed the bag shut. Ingram was another of his writers, and it was no concern to him which drop a player chose. "Never mind. I got more important things to think about. The bank's in trouble."

"Trouble?" Charlie's voice trembled. Moss's predecessor had recruited him with the assurance that the racket was safe. "Law trouble?"

Moss lit a cigarette and blew the smoke in Charlie's face. "Something like that. Some politicians want to make a little noise. Probably nothing will happen. We just got to be careful, take care of the gestapo better, is all."

Charlie fingered the linoleum. It would have to happen today. Still, he had never touched Moss before. It was worth a try.

"This comes at a very bad time for me," he said. "I got a little trouble myself, at home." Moss looked up expectantly, and he hurried on. "Nothing serious, only we got a blockbuster after our block and somebody wants to sell."

Moss did not understand. "So what?"

Charlie threw out his hands, as though the explanation lay there. "Real estate goes way down, you got no idea how far."

"Makes no sense," Moss said, wafting another cloud of smoke across the counter. "Anyway, how does it figure with the bank?"

"Well, I was just thinking, I worked here pretty steady two years now, I was just wondering if the bank could maybe let me have a couple of hundred for, well, until I could pay it back out of my take."

Moss shook his head, took a drag on his cigarette, and kept his chin wobbling, less in reply to Charlie than in time to a secret song only he heard.

"Oh." Charlie gulped. "Could *you*, maybe, let me have just a little?"

Moss did not seem to be listening, but he was still wagging his head, and finally he said, "Nope," softly. The Hebe's belt was at its height now, warming the corners of his body. He felt far away.

Charlie slumped. "Well," he said dejectedly, "it was just a thought happened to occur to me."

Moss came back slowly. "The trouble the bank's in is nothing for you to worry about. A few writers will have to move around a little. Not you yet. Maybe later. Just watch things, be careful, and call me if you get in a jam. We buy the lawyer."

Charlie felt a cold finger on his heart. He saw himself in jail, an outlaw. He saw Dulcy mocked by other children and Loretta, stunned, filing for divorce.

"Sure." He swallowed again, hard. "The bank's pretty good the way it takes care of people, fixes them up like that." He figured rapidly, moving his lips. His losses had been large lately, but he knew that was abnormal. Inevitably the law of averages would swing the pendulum back. "I wonder," he said slowly, "I wonder how a guy, a writer, would make out on his own. Away from the bank. Not so good, I guess."

Moss stared with disbelief. Then he began to laugh. In the beginning it was a light laugh, but once it had begun he lost all control over it. It swept into the vacuum left by the fading belt and left him sobbing against the counter.

Charlie giggled sympathetically, wondering what it was all about.

Moss wiped his eyes. "No," he choked, "a guy on his own wouldn't make out so good."

"Like I said," Charlie tittered foolishly, "no good at all."

At the door Moss turned. "Any bets you get this afternoon, tell them the odds go up tomorrow. How much I don't know yet, I'll tell you later. But both books get more."

He went out, swinging the canvas sack against his coat, and disappeared down West Concord toward the garage where he kept his convertible, his shoulders shaking gleefully in the wan sunlight.

Then, alone among the empty shelves of his empty store, Charlie recovered. "I don't see anything funny about that," he said aloud, with great wonder.

He returned to his calculations. If he could survive the first week without disaster he would be in business for himself, and it would be far more profitable than working for the bank was.

He couldn't see why the bank should object. He represented only a fraction of its earnings. If there was a protest he could kick in a small fee, the way concessioners did.

It was an idea. He wondered if it would work. Possibly it would not be necessary. Possibly there was enough money on Linvale Place to beat the blockbust without him. But he doubted that.

He checked the day's hoard of used coffee cups under the counter, eyed the pinball machine longingly, and reached for his coat. After lunch at the Unique he would retire to Ollie's for a beer and a little heavy thinking.

At home Charlie preserved the lie that he was a drygoods buyer by a simple ruse. He told Loretta his boss was a widower who resented his employees' families and had been known to discharge men whose wives called them at work. She had never visited him, either here or at the store where she thought he was, nor did she doubt him. But the June before, the son of a cleaning woman who attended homes on Linvale Place had opened a fruit stand just above the Elbow. The boy did not play the numbers, but the fact that he was there meant Charlie must detour each day on his way to the diner.

He followed this detour now, sliding along the icy pavement, for he had forgotten his rubbers, and reflecting on the day's number. There was a run on seven-nine-three. The night before a Consolidated truck with permit plate 793 nailed to its tailgate had crashed into a store front on Thawe Street, and nearly thirty of Charlie's bets had followed the hunch. He hoped the number didn't hit. With the luck he was having, he never knew. But, he reminded himself again, it could not last.

Joe Ferrara, the neighborhood patrolman, was inspecting automobiles in a No Parking zone on Horrigan Street. Ferrara supplemented his income by permitting all-day parking for a small fee. He carefully tagged those who did not pay. As Charlie passed he looked up fretfully.

"When you gonna start driving to work?" he demanded. "I give you a special rate."

"No car. You know I got no car."

Ferrara spat lustily into a snowbank. "Business is awful. I lost five customers this week. Same as always. Every Christmas bad."

Charlie swept the snow from the sidewalk with his instep. "Things aren't so bad for you as you might think. It's just possible, I don't say for sure now, but just possible you might get a little extra bonus from us this year."

Ferrara was interested. "Yeah?"

"That's what I hear."

"What's up?"

"A little trouble, political is the way I get it."

"Maybe some heat, huh?"

"Maybe. But I aren't worrying."

"Naw, you got nothing to worry about, Mr. Bond."

"Not down here, I don't think."

"Naw, we take care of you, Mr. Bond."

"Come over Ollie's later, Joe, I buy you a drink."

"I be there."

Charlie crossed to the Unique, whistling in the cold air, and Ferrara went about his inspection with new vigor, wondering what form the new graft might take. In that neighborhood he could have doubled his income if he knew the law and his beat. But he didn't know either, and so he had to be satisfied with his cheap parking racket and the monthly fin from the bank. All in all, he was a poor excuse for a cop.

Gloria Erik was in the back bedroom with Jody. He lay grave and curly-haired, listening to her read. Under the tall ceilings and the drapes cascading from the high valances he looked absurdly tiny. Now and then a phrase would strike him, and he would giggle, and a faint flush would creep along his cheeks, but most of the time he watched her with the awful solemnity of the very young, his dark eyes shining in his white face. Jody was five years old and convalescent. His mother was in Mexico, honeymooning with her second husband.

Ben opened the door softly and tiptoed in. Gloria did not hear him, nor did she see him creep up behind her, but Jody did, and when Ben cried "Boo!" and grabbed her shoulders, the bed shook with small laughter.

Gloria twisted around indignantly. "I told you what the doctor said," she snapped. "He said no excitement."

Ben winked at Jody, who smothered his laughter in the quilt. "And I told you what I say, that docs don't know nothing."

"*Ben!*" She slammed the book shut. Jody stopped giggling and looked at them with alarm.

"Come on," Ben said firmly. "One thing me and docs see eye to eye on is naps. Pull the shade down, Granny. Jody goes to sleep."

Clearly the boy did not approve, but neither did he protest. He never did, and that bothered Ben more than anything else. A kid that age, he told himself worriedly, ought to put up a scrap now and then.

Gloria was still cross in the hall. "You know better than that," she scolded. "If he don't have a high regard for the doctor, how will he ever get well? Honestly, Ben!"

He steered her to the top of the stairs and whispered, "Come on downstairs. Something I got to tell you."

She clucked formally on her way down, but her snappishness faded quickly. Ben never confided in her unless he was in trouble or about to take a big step with the business, and she knew of no big steps left there to take.

He closed the library door and leaned against it. "Doll," he began and hesitated. Then he went on, more gently. "Doll, I'm in a jam." He did not look like a man in a jam. His color was his own, and his hand, reaching for a cigar, was steady. "Not much of a jam. At least I don't think so. Nothing to worry about." He meditated, biting the cigar. She waited with folded hands while he lit it, puffed, and examined the end. "I thought you might like to know," he said finally and sat down.

She shifted uneasily. "I hope we don't have any bad trouble."

He sucked on the cigar and shook his head confidently. "Nothing like that. Leastways nothing you or anybody else'll hear about." He puckered and blew a smoke ring toward her. It sailed out, quivering, and flattened and ducked over a bridge lamp. "Only thing is," he said casually, "a little publicity, maybe some of it not so good."

"Oh!" She sat up straight. "Ben!"

"Nothing about the family that I look for. Just me," he said, shaping the wet end of his cigar into a spike and pointing it at himself accusingly. "Just the old man."

Gloria sat back, confounded, making question marks with her hands. Then, with an exasperated "What *is* it!" she leaned forward again, pleading with every line of her vast body.

And then he told her, as she had known he would, with that terrible clarity which always came to him in moments of crisis.

He always teased her when she could least endure it, and that was the index to their marriage. Ben was vain: it was his weakness. Others unconsciously addressed themselves to the Erik legend they had absorbed before meeting him. They thus indulged him, for Ben cherished the myth: that was his vanity. Gloria did not, for there had been no legend when they met. There had been only Ben, and despite the great turnover in their lives since, she still saw him as she had then. He took his revenge by taunting her when he was closest to the fiction, in a fight, in a corner, with the law closing in and his chances knifing into the danger zone.

It was strange she should not have seen this, for he had never been closer to his ideal of himself than when they first met on a cold and bloody Chicago street corner in 1914. The First Ward vice kings were warring that winter, and Ben, small and dark and fresh from the North Side, was a minor pug on the pay roll of one of them. That afternoon he had been caught alone in forbidden territory and badly beaten about the head. He was leaning against a doorjamb, trying to stop the blood with a soggy handkerchief, when Gloria passed. She was large even then, self-reliant and unafraid, and she took him to the home of a friend and washed and bandaged his torn face.

They married the following year. Ben was working in a shabby faro racket then, and because Gloria had graduated from a Madison Street scullery to a cashier's desk, she was making better money than he and so controlled him. Then Ben's boss tied up with O'Banion, and Ben went with him, and Gloria was through. For as he found his manhood he drew into himself more and more, until her role had subtly changed from protector to confidante. She had married a failure to rule him, and when he became successful his success undercut her and left her alone. She responded by ignoring it, and this was the sin his vanity could not forgive.

When O'Banion was murdered in 1924, Ben was running three stills for him in the Twentieth Ward. He had seen the war with the Gennas coming, and when he read the papers that day he rushed home and picked up Gloria and drove to Detroit, where he had money banked. But Detroit wasn't safe. The city was swarming with Torrio men, and in a week he was in unorganized territory, negotiating with the small bootleggers. He told them a retail pool would cut their merchandising costs and persuaded them he was the man to run it. It was a beginning, and it was enough. In three months he had his own cutting plant, in six months he had two, and by the end of his second year all his former partners were working for him. For the first four years he was one jump ahead of the sheriff. After that, the sheriff was one jump ahead of him. No one could touch him.

The opposition in the trade was negligible. In the early thirties a small coalition formed to fight him, but it never had a chance. Its leaders were wiped out the spring after his wound. The massacre came one dreadful night on the lower bay beach where the boats came in from the sea. Six men were cut down as they counted cases on the sand. Ben was called before the Grand Jury, but the two survivors refused to testify and no indictment was handed up. Thereafter his fable was secure. Smalltimers worshipped him. Policemen were terrified of him. When beer came back he became a popular figure, like an enemy hero in a defeated country after a war.

With this popularity his political organization was begun. It was an auspicious time for Ben: the machine of a city-wide boss —

who had led, among others, Big Ed Sylvester and old Commissioner Holzweig — was collapsing through sheer inertia, and the neglected Seventh was wide open for someone who could capitalize on the racial consciousness borning there. Ben gathered around him a group of bright young lawyers and impoverished aristocrats, pouring into their campaigns profits from his growing numbers syndicate. By the late thirties he was known to the city generally as a powerful political force. The informed knew him as a successful monopolist. Among them it was believed his control of policy was absolute.

It wasn't quite. Locally it was, but Ben's business was not altogether local. In the winter, when the big races moved south, his daily number came through the indispensable teleflash service of the Marsh Sports Daily. Old Chicago wounds made his relations here poor. For information from the Gulf he was obliged to pay fantastic rates — they grew more fantastic every year — and he had to work entirely without layoff betting, the splitting up of a suddenly popular number with other wholesalers in other cities against the chance it might come in. Until now this weakness had been a detail, like so many others unimportant. Ben maintained a surplus adequate to deal with the most preposterous freaks of luck and never let contributions to his councilmen and legislators dip into it. Now that surplus would be pledged to the fight against Gillette. Now details became important.

But they were still details. He could still survive anything short of catastrophe. The odds were still with him — still a thousand to one in his favor. It is hard to lose that kind of lottery.

So Ben decided to let the constellation of events wheel on. It was his choice to make and he made it that way.

He finished his cigar and his précis together and dropped the cigar into the smokador as he had dropped his plight into Gloria's narrow life: deftly, with finality. He had been over it twice, once artfully for the pickup men and once honestly for himself and, because he needed her here, for his wife. But now he was ready. Now there would be no more talk.

"I guess it'll be hard," she said doubtfully, wondering what he expected of her. "But I guess it's been hard before, too, hasn't it? Hasn't it been harder?" It seemed to her it had, but she could not be sure.

He stared at her myopically. "What? Oh sure. Plenty harder." He rose, through with her. "Don't worry, Doll. Like I say, nothing to it. Do the old man good." He opened the door and waited on the threshold. "Lunch?"

They went down the hall together silently, Ben thinking, Gloria fumbling in the world into which he had taken her. Before they reached the dining room she was resentful. His business was his, he had no right to worry her with it. She decided to put it all out of her mind and return to her insulated life, where there was no struggle or insecurity and Ben was a man to be bossed. Ben had known all along she would do that. Otherwise he would have told her nothing.

By 2:15 P.M. the Cadillac was back in the garage, the pickup men were huddled with Ben in the library again, and downstairs, in the bank, Henry Loomis and his sorters were approaching their daily orgasm of sweat. The results from the second race, Ben's first, had just come in. The number was nine.

Henry carried his portable-stepladder to the blackboard, ran up it, and wrote the single digit above a maze of figures representing the day's take, by pickup runs. Then he picked his way between the sorters' desks to the corner where he kept his books. From a choked shelf he took down a fat ledger, opened it to a marked page, and under the proper date entered in his tiny handwriting, "Willoughby, 2d, $33.90." He circled the nine to the right of the decimal point, left the book open, and took up his vigil again, mincing along the aisles, humming softly to himself.

Twenty sorters were working at a furious pace. On each desk was a wooden case divided into ten cubbyholes labeled with numbers from zero to nine. Into these they were dealing heaps of brightly colored paper, the hole depending upon the first number of a slip. The colors represented the different runs. After the fourth race the winners were divided by color and each pickup man took his, Joe the blue, Moss the green, etc. Each had small marks identifying his different writers, but that was not the bank's affair.

The bank's job was to catch up with the track. Each sorting was ten times as easy as the last, and since every race took the same length of time to run, sooner or later the track was sure to fall behind. The time of the overtaking was important, however. Usually it came between ten and fifteen minutes to three o'clock. That meant the sorters had a few minutes to rest and smoke before the last spurt. If they didn't finish the second number by three, when the fourth race started, they would be late, and that was bad for business.

Six of the men and three of the women were Puerto Ricans. Otto had recruited them when an unscheduled airliner, New York bound, broke down at the Municipal Airport and left its passengers destitute. Seven others were black women who lived in the district and used their afternoons to supplement family incomes. A retired fireman, a former haberdashery clerk, and an overweight jockey were the best workers. The worst worker was an elderly white woman named Gladys. She was a widow with a feeble-minded son, and she had taken this job because she had to be home with him mornings. Gladys's responses were slow. She could never finish her pile of slips. The retired fireman always helped her. He was cheerful about it, but her incompetence worried her, and she was afraid Henry would fire her.

Now in the race against time he stood behind her, humming under his breath, looking over her shoulder. His humming and the crackling of the slips were the only sounds in the room. She clutched her wad like a pack of cards and dealt, with trembling hands, into the little bins.

The clock over the blackboard read 2:20 P.M. Henry cleared his throat abruptly, and Gladys, startled, jumped and dropped her slips. They scattered along the floor like wild leaves on a windy street.

"Oh!" she gasped. The others looked up to see what was the matter. Henry, horrified, dropped to his thin knees and scooped

136

them up. She scrambled to help him, her seamed face drawn in a tremendous frown of fright.

"Never mind," he said frantically, forcing them into her hands. "Go ahead! Go ahead!"

"I'm awfully sorry ——" she began tremulously.

"No! Finish!" He pointed indignantly at her desk, and she turned to it wretchedly, and the room settled back into its tense silence.

At 2:27 P.M. the telephone rang again.

"Yes," Henry whispered hoarsely, his pencil poised over a printed yellow form. "Okay, go ahead." He listened a moment and then jotted, filling in the blanks:

WIN	PLACE	SHOW
$5.40	$4.40	$2.80
	4.30	2.80
		2.70

$5.40 + $8.70 + $8.30 = $22.40 — Total Mutuel Prices

Ben's syndicate used the digit to the right of the decimal point in the total price pools of three successive races, and when that figure was in Henry circled the four there and read it back with deliberate emphasis: "I get four. One, two, three, *four*. Right? Right." He hung up and fled to his ledger.

With the fireman's help Gladys had finished, and all the sorters were standing for a moment, stretching. They were running a little late, but it had been a very busy day, with over 65,000 slips. Every day would be busy now until Christmas. Every plasterer, every caulker, every janitor in the district would be leaving two bits, or four bits, or a dollar, with his writer each morning from now on. He would painfully calculate his potential winnings and spend the day budgeting them, with so much for the tree, so much for the dinner, so much for the electric train, so much for the tricycle. In the evening, after the results were in, he would fight with his wife and go to bed in despair, waiting for morning and its fresh hope.

"Okay!" Henry cried. "It's nine-forty something." He leapt on the stepladder again and marked the four with a deep chalk line beside the nine.

The sorters slipped rubber bands around the eliminated slips and pushed them to the corners of their desks for Henry to count later. They dealt nine smaller piles from the remainder, produced more rubber bands, and stacked all but those in the number four bin with the others. They were abreast of the track now. It was two minutes to three o'clock.

Ben came down the stairs. This was part of the daily ritual: the revelation of the winning number.

He stood by the blackboard, arms akimbo, inspecting them. A beat-up bunch, he decided. Well, no wonder. It was terrible work. He was lucky to have enough people, any kind of people, to do it. Then, with a sudden sense of guilt, he defended himself from himself. He didn't make the world. Somebody had to sort slips.

Secretly they worshipped him. He was the Chief, whose visit always capped their day. They never thought of the racket as a racket, any more than a soldier on parade thinks of war as evil. They never thought of Ben as a racketeer. He was the boss, the Old Man.

Gladys was openly admiring the squat of his shoulders when he looked up and saw her. She glanced away timidly.

That woman has got to go, he thought angrily. She can't keep up with the others and she's a nuisance. Always staring. Let her take her troubles to somebody hasn't got troubles of his own.

The others smoked furtively or slumped forward in postures of fatigue. Some were players, personally interested in the fourth race. Their own numbers had been eliminated and were among the bales of paper Henry was collecting from their desks and depositing in the big wire baskets under the ledgers. None had ever won. They knew the odds against them and had small hope of winning. But they followed policy as many players did, for the feeling of belonging.

The telephone rang, and Ben, who always took the last call,

sat and picked up a pencil and a yellow form and answered. "Menotti?" There was no one on the other end. "Abe?"

The line clicked. It was a tap. Somewhere, someone was listening.

Ben jumped up, holding the receiver like a weapon. The sorters froze. Henry looked up anxiously from the ledger.

"What's the matter, Mr. Erik? Bad news or something?" He could not imagine what was wrong. The betting in the nine hundred and forties had been light, and whatever the results the bank had won heavily.

Ben's face was wet. He crouched half out of the chair, trying to decide whether he ought to hang up, and as he swayed there in indecision he heard Abe's voice, curiously muffled, on the other end.

"Sorry, boss. That was a tough one. Had to check the board."

"No!" Ben was horrified. *"No!"*

"Boss?"

Ben swung the receiver to the hook and nearly put it down. Then he lifted it and spoke carefully. "Good to hear from you, my friend. How many votes you think I can count on in the Senate? *Enough to . . . squeeze by . . . I hope.*"

He prayed Abe would remember.

The line was silent for several moments. Then Abe answered easily. "Sorry. *Three's* the best you can get. You can't get no more, not the way it looks here, than *three.*"

"Well, thank you a lot anyway," Ben said formally. He hung up and settled back, wiping his face. Christ, I'm soft, he thought. I know they're coming. I got all the time I need, and I think of first things last. Three years without the code and only an old hand like Abe, remembering the way he had, had saved him. Well, he told himself bitterly, you'll learn. In the Pen, maybe, but you'll learn.

Henry was impressed. "Gosh, Mr. Erik, it's tough if the Senate's weak, with all the big bills you got coming up." Politics fascinated Henry. In his early days with the bank he had hoped

Ben might pluck him from his ledgers and send him to the legislature.

Ben was snapping back. "Sure. Sure, we'll make a few deals, fix it up." He winked, and Henry nodded enthusiastically. "You don't need no breakdown," Ben said abruptly, tearing up the blank yellow form. "The last number was three."

"Makes it nine-four-three," Henry announced, writing it down efficiently. He peered up at the blackboard and quickly leafed through his records. "Last time it hit was March 5. One hit before that, back in '45. A smalltimer, Mr. Erik."

Henry liked the rare ones to come in. It gave his ledgers a balanced look and was vaguely associated with sympathy for the underdog.

The sorters rapidly went through the rest of the slips and sifted out the winners. There were twenty-nine in the big book and twenty-five in the little, at 350-to-1. Henry took them to his desk as the others cleared away the debris. When they were ready to leave he had finished figuring.

"Not bad, Mr. Erik. We done all right today. Took in over thirty grand, pay out less than nineteen. A good gross, I'd say."

The figures flickered through Ben's mind as he reached for the winning slips. Par for the bank was $9,000 net. When it ran under $5,000 he went into the red. With his emergency economy every day would be a loss. Today's profit would give him that much longer to ride out the storm.

He cleared his throat. "I wish you'd all listen to me for just a moment. We're going to change our place of work starting now. It won't be here. Otto'll take you where it is tomorrow. Kid upstairs is sick, I want to try somewhere else for a while." He had decided not to tell them the real reason: they would find out soon enough, and there was nothing they could do about it.

They looked at him with astonishment. Henry protested. "Otto don't take me, Mr. Erik. I come myself."

"He will tomorrow."

"But — the blackboard! The equipment!" Henry had never heard of anything so absurd. What a way to run a business!

Ben scowled. "Never mind the equipment. What we can't take tomorrow we'll get there later. Meanwhile you'll have to use your head, work without it."

"But ——" Henry was confused.

"What?" Ben was curt.

"Where will it be, the new bank?"

"It will be where it will be, is all you have to know."

"Oh. Oh. Yes, Mr. Erik."

Ben swung up the stairs angrily, leaving Henry white and hurt among the sorters. That creep, he thought, with all his questions that I haven't got time for.

At the same time he knew the phone tap had jarred him. He would have to learn again, from the beginning. If he let the frayed edge of his nerves get caught in the machinery of the fight he would lose, and he could not lose, he told himself, he could *not*.

He took the winning chits to the safe behind the dining room, counted out the stacks of prize money, and tossed them in a wooden box. None of the pickup men knew where the safe was. Otto knew, because he brought the cash here every afternoon after lunch. Ben's emergency reserves were in his bedroom strong-box. Not even Otto knew about that.

In the library the pickup men were gaudy in suede shoes and pastel silk shirts. Ben insisted they dress in the height of sporting fashion and accompany the writers to the winners' homes. It was his way of advertising the syndicate.

Warning the writers of Gillette's attack had compounded the inevitable rush of gathering cash and slips, and private worries had been snapping at their heels since morning. They were on edge. Moss was an exception. He was as pleasant as he had been unpleasant four hours before.

Ben sat at the little desk, pushing out the money. Moss had ten winners and led the others. He tried to take it lightly. "I keep my customers happy," he grinned at Ben, stuffing the packets of bills into his canvas sack. "Let 'em win a lot, they come back. Good for business."

Izzy cackled. "Sure, maybe you can work for them when you get canned here."

"That's right. It's a kind of insurance, you might say."

Ben watched Moss draw the loaded bag shut. In the old days, when the racket was new, he had armed his men. Later holdups had become rare and he had taken their guns away. He wondered if he should give them back now and decided not to: the risk would be too great.

Moss saw him pondering and worried. He nagged his writers because he was convinced Ben resented high winnings. That Bond, he thought, or, today, that Ingram, is getting me in trouble. When the other pickup men lost heavily his scorn was vicious. With his twisted values he believed every misfortune must have its scapegoat.

"Starting tomorrow we get a new bank," Ben told them as they left. "Where I don't know yet. Otto'll take you tomorrow."

"Trouble?" Joe asked.

"Just a phone tap. Watch everything you do. Keep your nose clean and in a jam act dumb. A month, maybe two months, we're out of the woods."

He saw them to the car. Crowded against the upholstery in their vivid shirts, a canvas bag in each lap, they looked like a troupe of unhappy clowns leaving for a circus parade.

Shortly after 4 P.M. Ben drove to Paul's office and spent the rest of the afternoon with him, finishing Thorpe's speech. Darkness was coming down upon the city as they turned out of the alley behind the office building and headed north. Thorpe lived on the outer fringe of the district, in an old stone house he had inherited from his father. His other legacy, his name, accounted for his usefulness to Ben. If dipsomania was a political handicap, tradition was not, and the tradition of a Thorpe was as great as that of a Gillette or a Cameron. His childhood friends had long ago broken their ties with Thorpe. Still his name looked good on a ballot. For Ben it was good enough to justify an investment of fifty thousand dollars in unpaid, and unpayable, debts.

The Pontiac swept through an ill-paved, dimly lit suburb — Ben had lost five precincts here to the reform slate in the last primary and had struck back through the Bureau of Streets and Highways — and approached a drive-in restaurant. "I'm hungry," he said abruptly. "Let's grab a bite."

He pulled into a vacant space by the order window, and a boy in white duck trousers with a face reddened by the cold appeared from a side door. He had been warming himself inside and did not welcome business.

"Two hamburgers and a Coke," Paul said.

"Double it," said Ben, and the boy went away, surly.

Paul glanced down at his briefcase. "Pretty strong stuff. Think he'll take it?"

"Not only that. He'll give it when and how I tell him to."

"The sooner the better, I guess."

"Tuesday would be fine, I think. He speaks Tuesday downtown. Monday night we tip the papers, give out advance copies."

Paul smiled wryly. "Maybe we shouldn't give Thorpe an advance copy. He might tip somebody."

Ben chuckled and rolled down his window, and the boy gave him the cups and sandwiches with a bitter look.

Amy Thorpe received them in the front hall. She was a slender, long-suffering woman in her middle fifties, with blue-gray hair and a strained look about the eyes. Ben thought this remarkable. "She looks like a rummy and never touches a drop," he often told Gloria wonderingly.

"My husband is not well," she said, staring at him with open hostility. "I believe he has retired."

"My, my. Nothing he ate, I hope." Ben winked at Paul.

"Not at all," she said starchily. "Something about you I believe."

Ben stepped back. "You see?" he told Paul. "It's got around already. I knew it would."

"I should think so," Amy said. "It's been on at least three radio programs. There may have been more, but we've only heard three."

"On the *radio!*"

All right, he thought, I'm an old man and I fall into traps, get a tap when I'm not ready, have to move my bank overnight if I can find a place. But this is dirty. If a speech is given at nine o'clock, then it isn't given before nine, and nobody talks about it, at least not over radios, until then.

Paul wet his lips. "I forgot about the release," he said in a low voice. "It said for morning papers, and after the evening papers were out I guess the radio stations just went ahead."

Ben turned on him. "You forgot? Jesus!" Couldn't anybody think any more?

Amy stood quietly on the foyer carpeting, enjoying his discomfort. "He really isn't well," she told him after a pause which clearly said, if you're *quite* through cursing, we may talk. "However, if it's absolutely necessary, he's in his study resting."

Thorpe was sprawled on a Victorian sofa by a dying fire, sipping from a dark glass. The coffee table beside him was littered with choked ashtrays and empty bottles. A radio sat on an end table, and as his wife opened the door a powerful tide of Wagnerian music swept through the double doors and into the eddies of Ben's consciousness.

"C'mon in, Chief," Thorpe cried gaily, flipping off the radio with the careless grace of the very drunk. "Les have tall one for the wake. Crusaders takin' over." His stringy white hair was matted on his forehead, and his flabby face was blotched. He waved a fat forearm and burrowed in the soft cushions. "You, too, Amy, this . . . your . . . party . . . crusaders . . . over." His gaiety vanished and his voice died and he looked at Ben stupidly.

His wife went out and closed the door so gently it did not click. Ben looked down at him grimly. "Get the speech, Paul."

There were ways to handle Thorpe so he would stay handled. Ben did not like to use them, but he was quickly settling into an old and familiar attitude. In a crisis, anything went.

Thorpe stared at him suspiciously. "Wha' speech? Don' wanna read speech, heard all 'bout it. We're done, Erik. Done, done, done." His eyes were soiled celluloid shining dully in the firelight.

Ben's face split in an ugly grin. "What a caricature! Like he didn't know, Paul." He picked up a straight-back chair and dragged it across the room, spinning it around and perching on the edge. He jammed his knee against the coffee table. His face was a few inches from Thorpe's, and the smell of stale whisky was all around him. "Your speech, Senator. Your speech you're giving Tuesday."

"Haven't . . . haven't written it yet." Thorpe's lower lip quivered. He hiccupped suddenly.

Paul handed the manuscript to Ben and backed toward the door, ruffling and smoothing his mustache with alternate strokes of his forefinger.

Ben leaned closer. "It's already writ, Senator. We writ it for you. You don't have to do anything but read it. Wasn't that nice of us, Senator? And you don't have to even thank us."

He waited pitilessly in the growing quiet.

Thorpe hiccupped again, explosively. "Wha' do I say?"

"You say, Senator, you say that bastard Gillette, that no good frigger, you just say what you and me know, that he's a rotten sonofabitch. Not that way of course, but that's what you mean and that's the way you say it."

Thorpe looked as though he was going to be sick. Ben jerked back, but the old man controlled himself with a habitual spasm. He lay still, the firelight playing across his face.

"Wally ole frienda mine, good fella Wally."

"Sure." Ben bore in. "That's what makes his double-cross so dirty."

"Never turn back ole frien'." Thorpe was edging, looking for a way out.

"That's right, Senator. That's the way to be. I like that, I really do. And here's a guy, get this, a guy you known all your life, he slips the knife into the best friend you got, the best friend you'll ever have."

Thorpe's eyes popped. "Whosat?"

"*Me.*"

The old man swallowed deeply and tasted the sour after-drink in his throat. He had leaned over backward to avoid a trap and in his drunkenness had fallen into it.

"So I guess you'll be giving this speech everything you got," Ben said, slapping the script on the table. The glasses and the empty bottles rattled tunelessly. "Won't you, Senator?"

Thorpe nodded listlessly. He knew what it would be — the hammering headache, the rage in the audience, the insults afterwards, and, after that, the long drink. Still he nodded. There was nothing else he could do.

Ben rose suddenly, jolting the table with his knees. The glassware rattled again, and one of the bottles fell over and rolled wobbling to the edge.

"I'd leave this here with you, Senator, but it's the only copy we got, and you might lose it." He looked down at the rumpled shirtfront and grinned. "You get awful careless sometimes, Senator. We'll get some mimeographed. In the meantime I'll ask the representative from the Seventh District here to read it to you."

Thorpe started to say something, changed his mind, and poured himself a full drink. Ben clapped his hands together, as though he were summoning a servant. "Come here, Paul. Read it slow. It won't take long."

Paul walked across the room nervously, avoiding Thorpe. Then he stood by the fireplace and read, the script close to his face. Ben lit a cigar and sat in an antique chair by the door, puffing and nodding approval at the climaxes. When Paul had finished he applauded vigorously. In the small room it was deafening.

"Well, I guess that'll be all." He stood and pulled deeply on his cigar. "Unless you got some questions, Senator."

Thorpe hiccupped and shook his head. He stared after them as they went out the door, and when it shut behind them he hiccupped again violently and reached for the radio switch.

Amy saw them to the foyer in silence. When they were gone she stood back from the curtains, so they would not see her, and watched them climb into Ben's car, her mouth drawn in a bitter line. They had not even taken off their hats in the house.

On the way back they stopped at a pay station, and Ben arranged to lease a barn outside the city for the bank. After the tap he was afraid to talk business from the house. The barn had housed one of his cutting plants in the old days, and he knew the owner. The location was bad, which meant the payoffs would be late, but that was unavoidable. The bank would be safe there, and Ben would be even safer. He climbed back into the car with a relieved grunt. "Let the sonsabitches come," he chuckled. "Tomorrow this time, nothing in my joint smells of policy but money."

Paul laughed politely. Later, as they approached his home, he watched Ben in the darkness, wondering if he were up to the fight. He had handled Thorpe beautifully. You had to give him that. But Thorpe was a clay pigeon. Wallace Gillette wasn't clay. Sylvester wasn't. And if they got that square commissioner started, anything could happen. He made a note to see Ben's stationhouse captains in the morning, then remembered what they had told him about Zipski and struck the note out.

Maybe the whole thing would flop, fade away. But Paul knew there was little chance of that, and staring hopelessly at the ice-scarred sidewalks he wondered if there was a way out for him.

Ben dropped him at a corner and drove on alone. He stopped at a newsstand and bought a first edition of the morning paper. Under the snow-capped street light he read the lead story.

GILLETTE ATTACKS ERIK
POLITICAL WAR LOOMS

State Senator Accuses Boss Of
'Fantastic Apathy' in 'Crime Beehive'

State Senator Wallace Gillette (Democrat, Cornwall) rocked the city's political status quo to its foundations tonight in a sizzling speech aimed at Benjamin I. ("Ben") Erik, powerful boss of the city's Seventh District.

Charging that Erik presides with "fantastic apathy" in a section which has become "a swarming beehive of crime," Senator Gillette asked:

"Why does he do nothing? Why does he roost non-chalantly over this nest of evil? Why? Why? Why?"

Then he answered:

"Because he has outlived his political life. Because he has grown fat in his tyranny, as all bosses do."

Speaking before the East Bay Democratic Club, Senator Gillette, who is known to have gubernatorial aspirations and has strong support in the counties, demanded that the city "clean its own house."

In a bid for support from Erik's fellow bosses, the Senator declared he was "certain" no other political leaders were "aware" of the "turpitude" in the Roaring Seventh.

"He is afraid to let them see," he charged. "He sulks in his foul cave and shamelessly barters the votes of his craven stooges for political gain, ignoring the dreadful plight of the people he has betrayed."

Seven numbered points, condensing Gillette's charges and his demands for action, followed, and then the story jumped to an inside page. Ben read it all, dispassionately. When he had finished his eye wandered to a smaller head farther down the page.

SYLVESTER BACKS GILLETTE OTHERS TO 'WAIT AND SEE'

City political leaders were playing a "wait and see" game tonight following charges of corruption in the Seventh City District.

There was one notable exception.

He was Edwin ("Big Ed") Sylvester, in whose East

Bay Democratic Club Senator Wallace Gillette (Democrat, Cornwall) leveled the accusations.

Benjamin I. ("Ben") Erik, target of the attack and a Sylvester foe, was not immediately available for comment.

Others said they would study the situation and perhaps caucus later.

The poll, by districts:

Maurice Warrick, titular chief of the lightly held First City District, reserved comment until . . .

Ben folded the paper carefully, tossed it in the back of the car, and drove home slowly, lingering at each stop sign and rocking on his chains until the road ahead was deserted. As he entered the drive he saw the light in Jody's room. Gloria was reading him to sleep. He parked outside the garage and entered by a side door.

The telephone was ringing. It stopped as he turned at the first landing, and when he entered the hall he saw Otto had answered it. "Lemme take it," he said, quickening his step.

Otto cupped a hand over the mouthpiece. "It's the papers, boss. You want to talk or no?"

Ben took the receiver from him. "Hello? Hello?"

"Hackett, Ben." The voice rustled carelessly. "Heard about the big speech?"

"Hello, Joe. Yeah, I heard about it, all right." He tried to sound angry, but Thorpe had exhausted him. Come on, old man, he told himself, let's go.

"Want to say anything for us? If you don't, I couldn't get you."

"Sure, Joe. Lemme think." He thought. "You can say," he said at last, "I think Gillette's a dirty, smeary rat, without he's got the guts of a rat. This thing. You know what it is, Joe. He wants to be governor. I'd like to be governor, too. Who wouldn't? But not Big Ed's governor. Not that bad. I happened to know, or have some idea, this was coming, on account of Ed asked my help seven, maybe eight months ago, said he was dealing for Gillette, told me he'd give me anything, the zoning board even, if I wanted it, if I'd blow my district his way. That's what he said,

Joe. It's the truth and I can prove it. I don't have to tell you what I said back. I don't ask my people to vote for no man without it's for their best interests."

"I can use that?"

"Sure. And one other thing. You can tell any of my so-called friends, have to think this thing over, study these so-called charges, they can come into my district any time and look around, see what they can see, and I invite it, and that's more than I can say for theirselves."

"Got it. Anything else?"

"Anything else you can think of is all right with me. Fix it up nice, Joe." He hung up. Otto was admiring him.

"You sure told him, boss."

"Yeah." He wondered absently if Joe believed him. Sometimes reporters weren't as smart as you thought they were.

He climbed the stairs slowly, worrying about himself. He was going through the right motions, but something was missing. He was slower. He wondered how much that mattered. With a ball-player every step mattered. When his legs started to go, he went too. Ben's legs were shaky, no doubt about that. But, he figured, I'm no ballplayer. This is a different racket. Still, he would have to get in shape.

He was in the shower, flexing his flabby biceps, when Gloria looked in.

"Who do you think you are, Charles Atlas?" she laughed.

"You get out." He glared savagely. "Get out of here right now, quick."

She darted out, still laughing, but in her room she stopped abruptly. For the first time in thirty years she felt sorry for him. He looked so pitiful, like a small boy parading before a mirror. Her pity warmed her, and as she turned her head into the pillow she felt suddenly strong.

When Charlie Bond arrived home that afternoon he found his wife in their bedroom, swathed in a chintz kimono, stuffing her brassiere. Stuffed, it gave her figure an adequate bulge of what she called class and he called cleavage, and preparing it was a ritual with her before every public appearance. Tonight was the night of the block meeting. The brassiere lay on the bed, padded and nearly ready for wear.

"Jees!" he whistled, staring at the taut cups. "Some knockers!"

She eyed him coldly. "Charles Bond, you're the most commonest person I know."

He winked slyly and, as she spun haughtily toward her dressing table, picked it up. "Sometimes I wonder," he wondered aloud, "How many wom ——"

"Put that *down!*"

He dropped it on the bed hastily. "What's the matter?"

"You're nothing but vulgar," she said irritably, picking it up and turning her back again. "Just vulgar."

"Not as vulgar as some people I know," he replied ineffectually.

He went back down the stairs, stamping angrily on the treads. They had been married seven years, and she had never permitted him to touch her little breasts. Sometimes in bed his curiosity was overwhelming, but whenever they struggled she twisted away and ran into the bathroom and locked herself there until he came and apologized. Afterwards he would be filled with a sense of frustration and shame.

In the living room the Hearst paper lay open to the gossip columns. He refolded it with a grunt, read the comics, studied the sports page carefully, and turned briefly to the news. Senator Wallace Gillette was speaking that evening before the East Bay Democratic Club. Deep political moves were in the making. Some thought the power of Ben Erik, Seventh District czar, would be challenged.

Charlie laid the paper aside, pondering this. He wondered what it would be like to be a boss, rich and dangerous. He saw himself in a swank office, surrounded by hoods, ordering Congressmen about, killing legislation, dealing heavily with labor leaders and tycoons. If a rival boss crossed him he would rub him out or have him deported. In high school, civics had been a dull chore for Charlie, but politics was mysterious and exciting. It was Edward Arnold, lighting a fat cigar in a paneled study, or Edward G. Robinson, roaring through the night in a big Cadillac, the trunk packed with stolen ballots. He read the story to the end, wondering who Ben Erik was and which district was the Seventh.

The front door slammed and Dulcy pattered into the room, leading little Kenny Carter.

"Dad-dy," she began with a deep breath, "can-I-go-to-the-Carterses-tonight?"

"Gosh, Princess, I don't know," he said absently, worrying her curls with an open hand. "I'll have to talk it over with Mommie."

"Mom-mie," she wound up, "says-it's-okay-with-her-if-it's-okay-with-you."

"Well. We'll talk about it later."

They ran out with little shouts, leaving him unsettled. He did not want her to go, for the evening promised to be unpleasant, but whenever Loretta left a parental decision to him he was lost. She was always doing that, he told himself indignantly, always passing the buck.

Supper was a tug of war, with Dulcy demanding to know if she could please, please go and Charlie arguing weakly. Loretta was neutral. She wanted to leave Dulcy behind as much as he did, but she could never resist the temptation to thrust an unwelcome choice upon him.

"I'll call Ed Gardner," he said finally. "If he's taking his kids, you can go."

"Oh, Daddy!" she clapped her hands in triumph. "They're going! They told me! They're going!"

"Well," he said doubtfully, "we can always leave early." He looked to Loretta for approval. "I guess there isn't any harm."

She tossed her head indifferently and said nothing.

Dulcy pushed her chair away and danced gleefully out of the room. Charlie watched her go with a familiar pang. It hurt him to see her go and always had, since the first day, when a masked and antiseptic nurse introduced them and then whisked her away, a tiny and bewildered infant winking in the strange light. Dulcy was Loretta's doll, loved with the professional love of a mother. But she was her father's idol.

They took their coffee into the living room. Loretta drank hers black and thought cream a ridiculous extravagance. Charlie, who really wanted cream, poured in milk and stirred it thoughtfully. "Did you talk to Mrs. Carter today?"

"Henrietta did, and she said she's certain it's the Redsedskis. Isn't it terrible? How could they!"

Pete Redsedski was a plumber who lived on the other side of the street. Twice in the past week he had been seen in George Mathias's drugstore with Joe Patecka. It was enough to indict him, and for the block, in its present terror, indictment was conviction.

"I thought maybe Mrs. Carter's friend, the realtor man, had heard something."

"Henrietta said she hasn't heard a thing. But everybody's sure it's the Redsedskis."

"I guess it is, all right," he said desolately. "I wonder what Patecka's offering?"

Loretta pursed her lips. A week before she had known nothing, and cared nothing, about property values. The excitement of the neighborhood had turned her into a blazing enthusiast. "Henrietta has a friend, lives over near Jackson Place, where he broke that first block. She says he paid nine thousand dollars for a vacant house nobody'd lived in for years."

"Nine thousand!" Charlie wondered whether Redsedski was getting that much and whether he could have had it if he had reached Patecka first.

"Easy money," Loretta said spitefully, "if you don't mind selling out your neighbors. Like Henrietta was saying just today, it's positively unchristian."

Charlie frowned. Henrietta, always Henrietta. She and that fat husband of hers, with his drugstore to make them rich and no worries, no real worries like he had to drive them crazy.

"Wonder what Patecka'd give us if Redsedski sold," he said.

"Peanuts, that's what. They got a flat three thousand on Jackson, that's what Henrietta's friend told her."

"Only three thousand! Jees. I didn't know it was that bad."

"That or nothing, is what Patecka tells people."

They paused, calculating. After three years of payments, Charlie's mortgage was just below four thousand dollars. "Nothing," he said. "That's what it'd be for us."

"No, the loan company'll take the loss just to sell. Patecka's the only one'll buy even for that."

"A lot of difference it makes. Either way we're busted." Yet it did not seem real yet.

"Oh, it's a fine business," Loretta said vehemently. "Fine for him. Cramming them in under stairs, in cubbyholes, wherever they'll go. There's always some will. Thirty or forty to a house, ruining nice neighborhoods."

"I saw that over on Fine Street the other day," Charlie said. A few blocks away three old houses had been split into cheap apartments and were swarming with indigent mountain people. "Course, that's white."

"It'll be black," Loretta said tightly. And it would: white slums were merely transitional. They never paid. A white man could live anywhere, and only floaters would rent there, but a black, any black, had to find what he could within the belt.

"But why did he jump us?" Charlie cried, throwing up his hands. "There's nothing bad, black or white, around here."

"What I hear is, he heard about Mrs. Carter and come here."

"Mrs. Carter? What's she got to do with it?"

"Well, you know, some people think she's snooty, and in a way she is. Like Redsedski being a plumber, she's never spoken to them."

She had never spoken to Loretta until the threat of Joe Patecka loomed, and Loretta had once been bitter about the snub. But her bitterness had dissolved in that visit of the week before.

"Myself, I think she's a real lady."

"Her little boy's just Dulcy's age," Loretta said relevantly.

They heard her small step on the stair and into the living room she came, smiling, turgid in a starched red frock. "My dress," she said simply, perching on the couch. "My party dress."

Loretta looked up sharply. "Who told you to put that on?"

"Nobody." The child's face lengthened. "I just wanted to, Mommie."

"For Pete's sakes," Charlie said resentfully. "She's going out, you want her to look nice, don't you?"

Dulcy looked down at the rug. Her father was stronger than she was.

"It's the only real good dress she's got," Loretta said crossly. "She's got to go to a kids' party Thursday. It'll be dirty."

"Well, you want her to look good, at her best, at Mrs. Carter's, don't you?"

The unanswerable argument. Loretta pressed her lips in defeat.

"Blame Joe Patecka," he said wryly, and Dulcy smiled again. She took a comic book from the magazine rack by the couch, unaware of his eyes running over her.

Loretta switched on the radio. It warmed up in the middle of a local news broadcast, and a familiar name jerked Charlie upright.

". . . will denounce Benjamin I. 'Ben' Erik, the mysterious and powerful boss of the Seventh District, as an evil force in the city tonight. Gillette, who has been mentioned as a gubernatorial possibility, said ——"

Loretta switched stations.

"Turn it back!" Charlie shouted.

She did, in surprise, and then mumbled she did not like to be yelled at, but her voice ran under the announcer's and was lost in it.

". . . and therefore must go. The chief abuse named in the address, prepared for delivery this evening, was the practice of numbers writing, illegal gambling based on pari-mutuel returns."

"Jees!" Charlie sat very straight in the Morris chair. Loretta looked at him blankly. The announcer droned on.

"Seasoned political observers see a city-wide split as one possible result of tonight's speech. Gillette, as a popular and respected outsider, may draw a number of party stalwarts dissatisfied with the spread of Erik influence, these observers reason. It is almost certain that Edwin 'Big Ed' Sylvester, east side politician, will join forces with Gillette. Sylvester is said to be harboring certain grievances against Erik. An investigation of gambling practices in the Seventh District seems almost certain. Elsewhere, ice capsized a tug . . ."

"Jees!" Charlie said again. Where *was* the Seventh District? And from that corner of his mind where he shelved his West Concord routine each evening, he remembered Moss Bailey's warning.

Loretta shuddered. "Politics is a dirty business," she said, drawing on her store of accepted judgments. "It's a wonder nice people bother to vote at all."

"Turn it off," he ordered. "All they got is bad news. I don't believe half of it."

Not half of it, but all of it. All of it, magnified and remagnified until he was blinded by a vision of ruin and disgrace.

Then, moving up the stairs with lockstep tread toward his best suit, he collided suddenly with the specter of Joe Patecka, now fully shaped in his mind.

Jees, he thought, leaning heavily on the banister. They never ever let a guy alone.

The rain fell tenderly, spraying their faces as they eased down the icy steps and freezing on the sidewalk before them. The street was crowded with other couples, and some children, avoiding the sheer walks and slipping down the cleared street toward the huge old Carter house.

"Oh Daddy!" Dulcy cried. "See all the people!"

"Why, there's Henrietta," Loretta said. "Yoo-hoo, Henrietta!"

"Yoo-hoo!" Henrietta called and waved. But she did not wait for them, and her husband did not even turn around. Nor did the others. They speckled the shimmering tar under the high, old-fashioned street lamps in twos and threes, families drawing together in the shadow of the blockbust.

A black woman in sheepskin came toward them, headed for Jackson Place. They stared at her with open hatred. Look at her, the stares said. Just like the Nigras, to move in where they aren't wanted. Shiftless. Dirty. Wanton. Drunken. The colored. The Nigras.

The woman darted between them with a frightened step.

And they plodded on.

A mob, hurrying forward into panic.

Pete Redsedski watched them between the slats of his cheap Venetian blinds, chewing the end of an unlit cigarette. On the breast of a flowered sofa behind him his wife wept inconsolably.

"Looks like they're going to Miss Lucy's," he drawled bitterly. "Yep. First ones turning in there."

Flora Redsedski broke into a fresh spasm of sobs. She tried to talk but was incoherent. Her husband turned and eyed her hostilely. "Let's see now," he said, scratching his thin chin, "what was it you was telling me about Miss Lucy?"

She buried her head in a sea-green pillow, an Atlantic City souvenir.

He dug his thumbs into his trouser pockets. "You were saying, the way I recall, you said, hang around with old Joe, she'll come on her knees. Yep. That's what you said. That's what we need. No harm in that."

Her wailing drowned him out.

He peered through the blinds. "I think everybody's there," he said. "Mathiases, Wynes, Bonds, old Doc Hegel, Miss Freda — yep. Everybody."

She put her fingers in her ears to block him out, but he ignored her. "There's a stranger, out front of Miss Lucy's. Seems like he's looking them over. Maybe he's there to make sure we don't get in. Think that's it? Think that's why he's there?"

She thrust her gray head deeper into the pillow, and her weeping came muffled through it.

"Think that's it?" he barked, edging his voice with malice. "Think so? *Think so?*"

She looked up from the sofa with swollen eyes, pleading. He watched without compassion, chewing the cigarette tip, and turned back to the window.

*   *   *

The man in front of Lucy Carter's house was not there with her permission. He was a drunk. He stood shin-deep in the loosening slush, begging change from the neighbors as they turned up the walk. The others ignored him, but as the Bonds came up he stumbled forward and formally asked for a cigarette, and Charlie gave him a quarter, for that evening he felt sorry for the whole human race.

"The poor guy," he muttered, listening to the chatter of his own teeth. "He'll catch his death."

Lucy watched from a little window by the door, scowling. She tried to imagine what her father would have done if a drunk had stationed himself outside their door. And as she did she knew it was pointless, for when her father was alive there were no tramps on Linvale Place, nor anywhere else in the neighborhood. None would have dared come. And a Patecka, or a Redsedski, or a Nigra who tried to move east of Kendall Square, would have been horsewhipped.

The thought warmed her, and her welcome sparkled as William, her man-of-the-evening, opened the door.

"My dear Mrs. Bond," she murmured. "How nice you look. And how sweet your daughter is! Good evening, Mr. Bond."

Loretta nodded her practiced nod and Dulcy stared curiously. Charlie, embarrassed by the manservant and the paneled foyer, fawned.

"Gosh, Mrs. Carter, this is a swell place you have. Thanks for the invite. Thanks a lot." He bowed repeatedly, like a mechanical bird.

Lucy smiled palely. "William. Please show Mr. and Mrs. Bond and their daughter upstairs."

When they had gone she looked out again at the drunk, now leaning against a lamppost, hands apocket, hat askew. He shivered abruptly as she watched, and she was struck by the alarming thought that he might freeze there. *That* would be nice.

The upstairs drawing room was large and, at the moment, crowded. There were seventeen families in the block, and all but the Redsedskis were represented. Loretta found a seat by Henrietta, and Dulcy found Kenny. Charlie found no one. He perched awkwardly on an ottoman beside a mannish young woman he took to be Freda Treacle, the voice teacher, and wished there were an ashtray near, so he could smoke.

Freda had inherited her house, as Lucy had, and supported herself by giving lessons of doubtful value to the children of old friends. One of her pupils, a girl with an animated face and closely cropped hair, was on the other side of her, and so she simply turned her back on Charlie. He sat silent.

But elsewhere the room was filled with talk, the gay and desperate chatter of people pretending, while the moment lasted, that the meeting was social. They had been meaning, they told one another, been meaning to see more of the neighborhood for so long, and wasn't it nice of Lucy Carter to have them all in. And wasn't her house nice. And wasn't she such a nice person.

And all the time they were listening for her voice on the landing, dreading the moment they must face her. For they were all broke, every last chuckling one of them.

Next to Freda sat Dr. Francis Hegel, a wistful homeopathist who constantly denounced Socialized Medicine in the hope that it might bring him an aura of prosperity and perhaps, with the aura, prosperity itself. He was talking earnestly with Amanda Lunt, an aging virgin in a hip-belted suit who thought the younger generation behaved disgracefully. Amanda had brought her father, to whom she had dedicated her life. He crouched beside her, shrunken in a shrunken alpaca jacket, blinking meekly at the tide of conversation which rolled up to him and always stopped just short. After the Lunts came Newt Hucker, listening with glassy-eyed enthusiasm to the daily routine of a housewife from another part of the block while his mind, a relentless auditor, ran down the pages of the ledgers in his antique shop, pages it knew well, reaching totals it knew and hated. Then, perched on a Victorian love seat, Mrs. Lucinda Wyne and her son Peter folded their waxlike hands in their sharp laps and smiled identical smiles whenever anyone looked at them. Finally, in the corner, the

Henry Stephensons read the evening paper under a common bridge lamp. She read the front section and he read the back. They finished together, switched silently, and read on. Every night they did this at home — any evening Charlie could peer across the street and see them so — and the moment they had come into the drawing room they had spotted the paper and headed for it and split it up. Without a word.

Downstairs a final door closed and the small talk reached a crescendo of terror, falling away hopelessly as they heard the relentless step on the stair, the rustle of the brocade, the pealing hospitality.

The Stephensons dropped both sections. Thirty faces looked up and sagged.

Lucy swept in, the dark sheen of her hair crowned by a fresh gardenia. Behind her was a small gray man in winter flannels, carrying a briefcase. The older neighbors recognized him as a member of her late husband's law firm.

"This is Mr. Wilson, everybody," she cried. Thirty tongues wagged acknowledgment. "We did mean to start earlier, but you know how it *is*. I do hope no one has been bored *too* much."

The thirty deplored the suggestion. How you carry on, they said.

Charlie twisted around on the ottoman to look up at his hostess and found, with some confusion, that she was looking down at him and smiling her pale smile. As she looked, everyone else looked too. He wondered uneasily if he were in the way.

"You *poor* man, with *no* chair. William!"

"It's — it's all right," Charlie stammered. "I really don't mind, honestly."

"William, bring Mr. Bond a chair. Something he can *sit* on."

Wilson snaked across the room and bent over Hucker, the unofficial neighborhood historian, to discuss a question of obscure title. The others, sensing a moment of reprieve, broke into a torrent of fresh chatter.

William entered with two wicker chairs and put them by the door. Charlie, on one, found Lucy easing herself into the other.

"My," she said, moistening a finger and lifting it to the gardenia absently, "it must be hard on you, coming out like this after a busy day at your office."

"Oh, it's nothing, really nothing." Charlie watched the gesture, wondering if Lucy's cups were padded and deciding they were not.

"You know," she whispered impishly, smoothing the skirt along her upper leg, "sometimes I wonder what men do all day, when they're supposed to be busy with business."

"Oh, you'd be surprised. You'd just be surprised." He measured her with an obvious eye and winked, and she laughed gaily.

Charlie lit a cigarette carelessly, suddenly unconcerned over whether an ashtray was near. You never know, he decided. He gave himself to new thoughts, letting the hot finger of desire caress him gently.

Lucy sighed contentedly and rested her hands in her lap.

Loretta saw and approved, buttressing her hope that Lucy would accept them. She heard Dulcy and Kenny playing behind her chair and remembered all she had heard about the german.

The rest of the room watched and speculated. Lucy was known as a practical woman. They decided she must be convinced of Charlie's usefulness and, so deciding, became themselves convinced.

Wilson drew away from Hucker and cleared his throat. The room leaned forward, with hope now.

"I suppose everybody here got stopped outside by that bum, as I was," he said with a twinkle. "I don't know about you, but I've been wondering. Think maybe he's a spy for Patecka?"

Lucy led the laughter and the others joined in nervously.

"Well," he went on, "I guess he isn't. But the point I want to make is, don't underestimate this man. He's a shrewd one. He hasn't been beaten but once, by businessmen down on Winecoff Street, three or four years ago."

Charlie perked up. "Pardon me," he said and stopped, frightened by the sound of his own voice.

"Go ahead, Mr. Bond," Lucy encouraged him. "What were you going to say?"

"Well, the only thing is, I was just wondering, I never heard about that deal, that down on Winecoff Street. I mean, how was he beat down there?"

Wilson nodded approval. "A very good point," he said thoughtfully. The room nodded with him, and Charlie lost his fright. He waited, rather pompously, for the answer.

"Down there," Wilson explained, "everyone banded together. They just didn't let him get a foothold."

"Same as we're doing here, I guess."

"Well, yes. Much the same sort of thing."

The others swung their attention from Charlie to Wilson and back to Charlie again, like spectators at a tennis match. If the whole thing could be settled without their help, that was agreeable. Then, to their great surprise, one of them spoke.

"Well, not *quite* the same thing," Loretta quavered, leaning forward anxiously. "I mean, that street, whatever it is ——"

"Winecoff." Wilson was annoyed.

"Well, didn't you say it was a business district? Not residential?" She was miserable under the stare of resentful eyes, but she knew her husband's instability.

"Same principle," Wilson began and went into a detailed explanation of Patecka's only defeat.

Charlie, sharing Wilson's annoyance with Loretta, was suddenly aware of Lucy against him. She had slid over until the chair legs, and then their legs, touched.

"Why so sober, sobersides," she whispered, pretending to watch the lawyer.

"Oh, nothing," he whispered back. "I was just thinking about that old drunk outside." The caress of desire was suddenly rough, and his breath came quickly.

She laughed softly. "I guess everybody lets go once in a while, wouldn't be human if they didn't." He let his cigarette ashes spill on her skirt and dusted them off hurriedly, feeling giddy.

Wilson finished. Loretta, unconvinced, caught him up.

"Yes," she said, "but there's a big difference, isn't there? They had one hundred per cent cooperation, didn't they, and nobody needed Patecka's money, like I guess the Redsedskis do."

Dr. Hegel cleared his throat, an extraordinary process. The spectators shifted to him.

"Wilson's right," he announced, as if that ended it, adding, finally, "It's identically the same principle."

The claque joined in with the strenuous arrogance of the terrified. "Why yes," they echoed, nodding smartly. "He's absolutely right," "It's the same," "It's identically the same."

Not a word in the chorus for Loretta. For she had profaned their faith, the confidence in a quick solution. To deny it was treason. Yet she denied it still.

"But it *isn't* the same!" she cried, wringing her hands. "If it is, where are the Redsedskis, why aren't they here, with us, working against this person, this Patecka person?"

Lucy's voice was dark music. "My dear Mrs. Bond, they weren't *invited*. We didn't *want* them in our home."

She smiled wistfully into the sudden silence, and Loretta cringed, white and pitiful, with the snub a pennant fluttering over the room.

At that moment there was a loud thump behind Loretta's chair and Dulcy burst into tears. She ran into her mother's arms and everyone relaxed in the disorder.

Henrietta sat up indignantly. "Well," she said, "without reference to this particular meeting, I think maybe if everybody was nice to Flora Redsedski, and him too, it might help."

"Dear, dear, dear," Lucy sang. "If that were all there was to it! But I think we're being just a teeny bit naïve. Being nice . . ." she cocked her head comically, as though weighing the suggestion ". . . no, I think not. Being *nice* won't do." And she smiled again into the small laughter that followed. Henrietta pouted, beaten.

Wilson, sighting down the blade, stepped forward briskly.

"I think we have to face facts," he said, rubbing his hands together and addressing himself to Charlie as one who would understand. "We have heard that Patecka has a prospective buy in this block. That's one fact." Charlie expanded and nodded with the others. "Patecka has been seen with Redsedski. That's another fact." Profoundly aware of Lucy beside him Charlie nodded again, more vigorously. "A reasonable conclusion is that Redsedski is considering a sale. Now then," he concluded, brandishing his hands, "what are we going to do about it?"

He was still looking at Charlie, and presently everyone else was looking at him too. Loretta, muffling Dulcy's sobs on her breast, watched dully.

Charlie leaned back as far as he could and found himself in a box. A box whose sides were the chair back, Freda Treacle, the wall of eyes before him, and Lucy's urgent thigh. A box whose top was his panic and whose bottom was his pride.

"The only answer I know," he hoarsed, sucking saliva into his dry throat, "is money. Money to fight money is the only answer."

Wilson savored the wisdom of this and bowed, but he said nothing. Nor did the others.

Charlie leaned back again and felt the box about him. "I guess we all ought to chip in, as the feller says, chip in a little, maybe on a loan basis, to help this Redsedski, in this jam he's in, out."

His throat was a dry pipe, and it seemed to him that if he kept talking he would bark.

"That seems reasonable," Wilson agreed, patting his hands together like a man offering token applause. "How does the rest of the room feel about it?" A brief hum rippled from wall to wall. The room thought it reasonable, too.

But then, just as the image of the box was dissolving, the sides tightened in again. "What would you say, Mr. Bond," Wilson asked, "what would you say a proper contribution would be?"

Charlie was caught, finally and completely caught.

"Oh," he croaked, begging for time. "Well," begging, "I suppose twenty ——" The wall of eyes fell away and Lucy's leg was sharply withdrawn. He took a deep breath, and when his voice came again it was a high squeak. "That is, what I meant to say was, I guess I, personally, could manage a couple, that is, two hundred bucks."

Two hundred bucks! *Jees!*

Lucy was there again, and everyone was smiling except Loretta, whose face was pressed against Dulcy.

"Well," Wilson said jovially, offering more than token applause now, "that's fine, that's really fine, Mr. Bond. I daresay everyone here is grateful to you." Yes, everyone agreed; yes, they were quite grateful.

Several women reached for their coats, and Charlie started. "That isn't, well, it isn't all there is, is it? I mean, somebody else. . ." He trailed off in horror.

"No, no," Wilson assured him lightly. "Not at all all. I think everyone can manage a contribution of perhaps fifteen dollars?" The room murmured assent. "Good. I'll undertake to see Redsedski tonight. I'll let you know what he says, just as soon as I know."

Lucy announced brightly that William was ready with coffee downstairs and the migration there began. But the Bonds were not staying.

At the door Lucy was effusive. "Really," she bubbled, "we *must* see more of each other. It's been *so* nice having you." She squeezed Loretta's slack hand and looked long at Charlie and closed the door softly, noting with satisfaction that the drunk was gone.

On the street the inevitable reaction set in. Only fifteen for the others. The figure burned in his mind. He had supposed it would be at least a hundred apiece.

He tried to justify himself with Loretta. "It was a thing, you know, a thing I had to do. They expected it of me."

"Sure," she said bitterly, picking up Dulcy and hurrying on ahead. "Sure, sure. The big man with the big roll to throw around. Mr. Generosity."

At home he tried again, but she would not listen. "I take no interest in your business," she said and walked out of the room.

Later that evening Wilson called. He had seen Redsedski and

sounded puzzled. Redsedski had listened to the terms of the loan, burst into harsh laughter, shouted his acceptance, and then shoved Wilson out the door.

"I don't know what the matter was, but anyway he took it. We'll sign tomorrow morning. No interest, of course. He wouldn't have taken it any other way."

"Okay." Charlie hung up gloomily. Something twisted in his stomach and he knew he would have trouble that night. His trouble. His peculiar trouble.

The Bonds had walked out on a party. It was not a party when they left it and would not likely have become one if they had stayed, but once they were gone and the tension had gone with them, everyone relaxed. Freda Treacle and her protégée discussed elocution by the sideboard. Dr. Hegel denounced Oscar Ewing to a sympathetic Amanda. The Wynes admired Lucy's most cherished heirloom, a framed Continental Army commission. Lucy herself fluttered from group to group, beaming and clucking, and the others postured, or ordered William about, or simply basked in the pleasant memory of Wilson's mastery. Wilson himself was at the Redsedskis, and since his were the only sharp eyes among them, no one noticed the Henry Stephensons slip from the room, slide into their coats, and disappear out the front door, into the rain.

Perhaps not even Wilson would have seen them. People rarely did. There wasn't much to see, really. Stephenson himself was nondescript as a steward in a Pullman diner. He was a sober little man in steel-rimmed glasses and a mouse-gray suit he had worn, year in and year out, until the cuffs were frayed and the cloth along the elbows and knees was so thin you could see through it. His wife was a faded, shapeless woman with heavy eyebrows and a faint mustache. Her uniform was a woolen suit and Red Cross shoes. In the summer the suit jacket gave way to print blouses, but she had never been seen without the skirt. She made it last by wearing a tattered slip around the house.

Stephenson was a proofreader. His salary was small, and much of it was spent placating his wife's mother, a senile woman confined to, and obsessed with, her bedroom. It was cluttered with hundreds of gimcracks and gewgaws she saw advertised in her favorite pulps. She had insisted successively upon air conditioning, a built-in radio-phonograph, a television set, and a bed with a hydraulic push-me-up. Now she was demanding a public address system to call for help if she should be attacked in the night. She was seventy years old. The Stephensons never argued with her. They merely listened and then looked for the money, never admitting, even to themselves, that her mind, like a mudpie baked in the sun, had cracked and disintegrated.

They tramped down the wet street one behind the other, like strangers, and when they drew abreast of the Bond house they turned, as if on signal, and faced each other.

"I won't be long," he said. The street-lamp light glazed his glasses, and she could not see his eyes.

"You're sure you got it?"

He fumbled in his inside coat pocket and nodded, then left her and plodded into the darkness. When he had disappeared she crossed to their house alone. Under the mustache her lip was twitching. It looked like a smirk but was only nervousness.

When Stephenson reached Jackson Place he hailed a cab and gave a downtown address. He perched on the leather seat in the rear, memorizing the driver's number, wondering what the insurance would bring if there was an accident. At his destination he counted out the fare laboriously and left no tip.

He pressed one of a row of doorbells under the mailbox row of a plain brick building and poised with his hand on the knob, like an old tomcat waiting to spring. The buzzer buzzed and he rushed into the foyer and up the stairs. Behind him the door banged.

Joe Patecka met him at the landing.

Joe was humming his song-of-the-day and tucking his tie-of-the-day into his suit coat. They were fetishes with him. Every morning he carefully chose one of a number of hand-painted ties which hung in his wardrobe and, with it, a song. Today's tie was a sultry blue. Today's song was *The Hucklebuck*.

"The cab was forty cents," Stephenson gasped urgently.

Still humming, Joe handed him a dollar.

"I got change," he said halfheartedly.

Joe shook his head absently.

"It's just I got to watch every cent," Stephenson said apologetically. "You know, Mother . . ." His voice trailed off in surprise that Joe not only did not know Mother but was not interested in her.

Joe turned into the office and Stephenson followed. It was a small, square room with a dust-streaked window facing a dark alley. An ancient roll-top desk stood against one wall. Opposite it were several walnut filing cases. There were two chairs, and in these they sat.

Joe turned his bland oval face to the cobwebbed ceiling. "Well, what happened?" He resumed his hum in a softer key.

The room was warm and Stephenson's glasses had clouded. He took them off and wiped them on his lapel, talking as he wiped, holding the lenses up to the light as he told of Wilson's sophistry, and setting them back on the bridge of his nose carefully, with satisfaction, when he reached Charlie's surrender and flight.

Joe looked down and scratched his thick hair. "Wilson's a friend of Mrs. Carter?" Stephenson nodded. "Mrs. Carter, who's she a friend of? Never mind, I know. She's a friend of herself, that's who she's friendly with." His joke delighted him, and he chuckled silently. Stephenson smiled one of his rare, weak, humorless smiles.

Under a paperweight on the desktop lay a pile of sales contracts. Joe yanked the top one free and held it out. "See if that looks okay to you."

Stephenson took it, wiped his glasses on his coat again, and studied. The wording meant little to him, and he knew his wife would examine it carefully before they signed, but he read it through to the end, from habit, looking for typographical errors. There were none and he handed it back.

"Seems all right," he said tonelessly.

"Seven grand, that's what you said."

"Yes. We think it's a — ah — fair price."

"Well, that's it, anyway."

"Plus the — ah — the . . ." He fumbled deliberately, and Joe looked at him vacantly.

"Oh!" He remembered. "The bonus."

They had agreed Joe would match whatever the neighborhood loaned the Redsedskis. Joe was very proud of this feint. Stephenson had told him of Mrs. Redsedski's wounded ego, and he had convinced her that if her husband appeared publicly with him and permitted him to appraise their house, Mrs. Carter would come around. Now he had siphoned off the block's ready cash and was ready for the big kill.

Joe calculated. "I figure four hundred and ten extra. Right?"

Stephenson did not think this was quite right. He thought Joe ought to pay his fifteen dollar ante in the Redsedski kitty. His chances of ever getting it back, he argued, were less than slight. They haggled briefly and Joe gave in. He knew Stephenson had no intention of giving Redsedski a dime, but he felt expansive. He was buying Stephenson far more cheaply than he had expected. He had been instructed to go as high as ten thousand for a house, any house, on the street.

He wondered idly who Charlie Bond was and how much he was worth. Stephenson appeared impressed with him. If Stephenson were smart he would go to Bond tonight, before the papers were signed, and milk him for anything he could get. But Joe knew Stephenson was not smart. If he were, he would not be selling for seven thousand. He debated finding a witness and signing tonight and dismissed the idea. The morning would be time enough.

"All right," he said, pushing back his chair and standing. "You and the missus be here at nine tomorrow. You can get off work?"

"My business is near."

"Good. Next week we pass the papers. I'll get the zoning cleared right away. You got a copy of the deed?"

Stephenson passed it out from his inside coat pocket and then clung to his chair in indecision. "When do we get an advance?" he asked hesitantly. "You know. An advance."

"Well, ordinarily ——"

"It's, you know, Christmas coming soon. We would like a little advance."

Joe grinned. "Okay." He clapped him on the back impulsively and wished he hadn't as Stephenson stiffened in his old suit. "I'll have a grand here tomorrow. Just for Christmas."

Stephenson spilled down the staircase, his thin soles pattering excitedly as he hurried home to pack, and plan, and study with Mother her catalogues of P.A. systems. The door downstairs slammed jubilantly.

Joe heard it, listened intently for a moment, and then reached for the telephone bolted to the desk side and flipped the receiver off, quickly, like a gunman in a Western.

He dialed operator and gave a county number. The line rang twice and then answered.

Joe cleared his throat. "Is Mae there?" he said loudly. "Say, maybe I got the wrong number," he went on, as he had been taught. "Oh." The party was there, crackling instructions. Joe listened with astonishment. "Out *there?* Okay, okay. No, I got nothing else. Right away."

He locked the office swiftly and rattled down the front stoop. As he swung into his Buick for the long drive his thoughts returned pleasantly to Christmas, and he changed his song, humming *Oh Come, All Ye Faithful*. He stopped for the light at the corner and peered at his watch. It was 10:50 P.M.

The light changed and he slid forward, pointing the Buick's flat snout north, toward the snow-bearded hills above the city and the fields beyond.

Toward the home of Jarvis Cameron.

※　　　※　　　※

At 11:30 P.M. he pulled into the drive, switched off his lights, and stepped out on the glittering crust of the lawn. The freezing rain had formed a skin tough enough to hold him, and he groped across it to the lone light over the portico.

Cameron answered the door himself. He was casual in a velvet smoking jacket and mules. His beefy face was florid. He held a drink in one hand and waved Joe in with the other.

"Come in, my boy, come in! Been waiting for you. Fine night for waiting. Couldn't, just couldn't be better, eh?"

He winked gaily and turned toward the open door of the library. Joe followed, looking around curiously. He had been here once two years before and remembered little. Since then all business had been transacted by telephone or in his little office.

Cameron closed the door and freshened his drink. Joe hoped he would be offered something but was not.

"Heard the radio?"

"Tell you the truth, Mr. Cameron, I been so busy with papers I had no time. Was it something I should've heard?"

"No, no, no. You'll hear all about it in the morning. Just a little politics, Joe." He winked again. "A little game we're playing."

Joe wondered if the old man were drunk or simply elated over a piece of good luck. Certainly it could not be the break on Linvale Place. Nothing had been said about that yet. Indeed, Cameron appeared to have forgotten it. He babbled on with obscure wit, commenting on the tricks of political strategy. "It's a game," he repeated. "Played for big stakes, sure. Biggest there are. But still a game."

"I guess that's right, Mr. Cameron. I never had nothing to do with it."

"In a way it's like our little real estate business. That's a game, too."

Some game, Joe thought. If it were sport to parlay one old family block into a slum operation that now threatened to push the city's color line forward eight blocks, Johnny Mize was Rockefeller.

Cameron had stopped, abruptly as he had begun, unwound. He stared dully into his drink, and Joe, watching him, saw he was less drunk and elated than tired. The silence grew. In his uneasiness Joe began to hum the old carol softly.

"Cut it out!" Cameron snapped, and Joe stopped. Then, without looking up, he asked wearily, "How was the deal?"

"Real good, I think. We got the Stephenson house for seven grand and a four hundred plus bonus, for what the neighbors drained theirselves for."

Cameron glanced up and smiled. "Good boy." Then he offered the drink and Joe took it gratefully, deciding the old man was all right after all, trying to recapture the flush of his triumph.

But he could not do it. That moment had passed and this one was flat. Joe sat in this flatness, trying to think of something to say, knowing he had said it all, or all Cameron wanted to hear, and wishing he could hum.

He was sipping his drink awkwardly and toying with his tie when the bell rang again.

It was Wallace, brisk and confident.

"I don't think there's any question about it," he barked in the hall, peeling off his long topcoat and his homburg. "We've got him on the run. You heard the radio? Good. Seen the paper? Here. Read it and gloat."

They came into the library, and Joe stood clumsily. He thought Wallace must be Cameron's partner, or a real estate investor, or, perhaps, one of the officials at Willoughby. For all their ties, he knew very little of his employer. The racetrack was a mystery to him; Cameron rarely mentioned it. Joe assumed he had been hired for the usual purpose of making a rich man richer. It had never occurred to him that if Willoughby were flourishing he would not be busting blocks, or sweating rents from their new tenants, or working for Cameron at all.

He stood there a full minute. Cameron, deep in Wallace's newspaper, had forgotten him, and Wallace himself was busy at the bar. Finally he coughed and looked up from the rug, into Wallace's insolent eyes.

"Who's *that?*" Wallace demanded.

Cameron glanced up. "One of my people. He's all right, Wally. Joe, meet Senator Gillette. The Senator's going to be governor one of these days."

"Pleased to meet you," said Joe, greatly impressed.

Wallace nodded curtly and returned to the bar. Joe sat down, holding his drink with both hands, searching his memory for the name. The only senators he knew were in Washington. Joe did not know about state senators. He was barely aware of the legislature.

Cameron finished the story and gave a little cry.

"That's it! My God, it couldn't be better. It couldn't, Wally!"

Wallace smirked across the room. "They were with me all the way. It's a popular fight."

They ran on, discussing details. Joe finished his drink dejectedly, feeling the loneliness of the outsider and wondering what it was they were celebrating. When Joe celebrated, he wanted noise and lights and music around him. He could imagine nothing more depressing than this drear room, surrounded by the dead air of the country.

He stood again. This was none of his business. He did not understand it and he resented it. "If you don't want anything else, Mr. Cameron, I better go. I got to get up early, and I want to take my kids downtown, show 'em toyland."

"That's right, you have three, haven't you? Wally, here's a man with real Christmas trouble."

Wallace considered his drink sourly. Parental problems annoyed him, even among constituents.

Joe was stung. He wondered how this senator he had never heard of before had been elected, wondered if he had ever voted for him.

Cameron folded the paper carefully, left it on the desk, and escorted him to the hall.

"You'll sign that house in the morning? Fine. Better start hitting the others in the block right after Christmas, while they're still broke. This couldn't come at a better time."

It was true. Joe's best bargains were closed in the last days of December, when his clients were numb from the bullying of the season.

"We're having a little trouble on Fine Street, from deadbeats. You know, usual thing, slow paying, want credit." That was a sign of the season, too.

Cameron winked. "Well, you know what to do, Joe. We can't play Santa Claus." At the door he added, "By the way, now Linvale's started you can count on a couple hundred bucks extra for those kids."

Joe braced himself on the steps. "Gosh, Mr. Cameron! I mean, thanks!"

"That's all right, you earned it." And he had. Without the rentals he had faithfully brought in, Willoughby would never have survived the autumn meeting.

As Cameron closed the door he heard Joe crunching over the yard's thin skin of ice, humming loudly in the night.

After supper Sarah had laid a fire in the library. Cameron kindled it now, turned out the lights, and listened to Wallace, watching the flames run swiftly from andiron to andiron.

"This is confidential. Zipski's decided to transfer every policeman with rank out of the Seventh, and put in new captains, new lieutenants, and new sergeants from East Bay. All Big Ed's men. Not," Wallace chuckled, "that he likes *that*. He just doesn't have much choice. They're all either Erik's or Ed's."

Cameron grunted noncommittally.

"But that's only the beginning. The big thing Zipski's doing, the thing that'll make all the difference, is in the vice squad. He's completely replacing it."

The fire sprang up suddenly, washing the room with firelight. Shadows danced in the corners, the moon shone wanly on the snow beyond the windows, and in the darkness by the hearth Cameron sat, listening.

"First he's going to kick Sylvester's man, Morelock, upstairs —

make him an inspector. The new vice captain'll be a hustler, a real cop."

"Cops," Cameron said suddenly.

"I know. But we can count on this one. I've heard about him. He's good, Jay."

"He better be."

Wallace bowed gently, thinking of his campaign war chest. They had been close all their lives, but with money between them they might as well be strangers. Wallace was a salesman, the drive against Ben was his product, and Cameron, the customer, was wary.

"What about Erik's magistrates?" he demanded. "Can't they ruin everything?" With every bench appointment in the Seventh but one, Ben had always been able to stop the trickle of cases Morelock brought in with dismissals or light fines.

"Impossible. We're going to by-pass them." Zipski, he explained, had met with the State's Attorney, and they had reached an agreement. If a bad magistrate threw out a good case it was to be taken directly to the grand jury and then, after indictment, to criminal court. "They'll be convicted just like that." Wallace snapped his fingers to show how.

"Well!" Cameron's face opened up. "That's more like it."

"Erik won't be a pushover. He's sharp as ever. Zipski had Morelock tap his phone this afternoon. Ben was talking to his stringer at the track and switched right into code."

"Like a fox." Cameron shifted the fire with his poker. "God. I suppose you get that way, outside the law."

"In politics, too, Jay."

"Well, yes, but it's not the same."

"No," Wallace said dryly. "Of course not." Cameron looked at him quickly, baffled by the irony, but Wallace merely lit a cigar. "I'd give a lot to know what he's thinking tonight," he said. "In fact, I'd give quite a bit just to know what he's doing."

"Oh!" Cameron had almost forgotten. "I can tell you what he was doing just before your speech. He was out at Thorpe's."

Wallace sat up in a cloud of smoke. "How do you know?"

Amy Thorpe had called after Ben left with Paul. She had been listening at the door. "She was upset, poor woman. Can't blame her, with all she's been through. I told her not to worry, it was nothing."

"But you didn't mean it."

"Of course I did! What's that old sot to us?"

Wallace puffed until he was nearly obscured. "It's hardly unexpected, of course, but that doesn't make it any easier. He can hurt us."

"Damned if I can see how. My God, he's been whoring for Erik for how long? Ten years? Everybody knows that."

"No, Jay. Everybody doesn't. Everybody in politics does, and so does everybody who knows Thorpe. But that isn't everybody."

"But it's been in the papers."

"I've been in the papers, too, yet I daresay that man of yours never heard of me until half an hour ago. Politics is a business. People are interested in the business they're in and rarely in any other."

"But what does poor old Thorpe have to sell?"

"The same thing I have. Old Granddad. Old tradition."

Cameron frowned. Expediency was one thing; Wallace speaking of his family as though it were a pedigree to be hawked in the market was something else, something he knew as bad taste.

And Wallace, watching the disapproval flicker across his face, marveled at the tightness of his mind and for an instant envied him.

They went on, assaying Ben's position and the trap around it, like generals before a siege. It was past two o'clock, and the last embers were crouched under the firedogs, when they heard Madelaine's step upon the stair. She came in, neat in a housecoat, and turned on the lights.

"My, it's stale in here!" She looked at her brother reprovingly. "Those cigars, Wally."

Cameron cringed in the sudden light. "Was that necessary?" he scowled. "We are enjoying the fire."

She puckered. "Now, Jay. Don't be stuffy."

"Stuffy," he repeated flatly. That was a word. He had heard that word before.

She turned to Wally appealingly. "I ask you. What can you *do* with a man like that?"

Wallace fingered his glass uneasily. The artful warfare of women always left him at a loss. The weaker the woman, the more subtle her attack. His sister was the weakest woman he knew and the subtlest. He gathered that she wanted him to leave. Or perhaps she wanted to know what they had been talking about.

Cameron heaved his bulk out of his chair and strode over to the window, his back to them. "Go ahead," he said with heavy sarcasm. "Empty the ashtrays in the fireplace."

She glanced at him swiftly and then did just that, smiling furtively at her brother. "I have to be sure they're out," she murmured. As though he did not know.

It was her phobia. Early in their marriage she had toured the house after every party with a pitcher, filling the trays with water. The morning after a particularly brutal night her husband came upon a soggy dish of shredded tobacco and, baffled and outraged, had ordered her to stop. But she still had to be sure they were out.

Usually she waited until the first floor was deserted. By coming in now she had told her husband, in their silent language, that something was on her mind. He waited impatiently, one foot on the window sill.

Now the last ash was dumped and she sat, addressing herself to Wallace. "You know, I'm a stranger in this house. Just a stranger! Do you know today my husband told me a man with a name I never heard before, Polish I think it is, would be coming here *regularly*? And I don't even know *why*?"

That was it, then. Or was it? Cameron could not be sure. Sometimes it was many things. When there was a third person present it was often many, for she knew his patience would be longer.

He turned back to them. "I thought I explained. I must see

him here now. There is a very good chance our telephone may be tapped."

She threw up her hands. "You see? Telephone tapping! Have you ever *heard* of such a thing?"

His tone sharpened. "If you followed your brother's career more closely, you might understand."

Wallace cleared his throat. "I spoke tonight, Maddy. You see . . ."

She clapped her hands and cried, "Oh, I heard it! On the radio! It was simply wonderful!" They fell silent, abashed. "But what does that have to do with Mr., Mr. . . ."

"Patecka," Cameron said. "Very little, my dear. But the man we are fighting is highly unscrupulous, and there is no limit to the lengths he'll go to. In his business, tapping telephones is elementary."

"Oh," she said meekly. "Is there something wrong with the Polish man?"

He flushed. "Not unless you think there's something wrong with having a roof over your head," he said, his voice rasping. "It's just that . . ." he faltered and added vaguely, "different people look at different things differently."

She giggled and glanced demurely at her brother, their pawn. "There's not much I can say about that, is there? I mean, about having a roof."

The last of the fire crackled savagely. Wallace rose. "I really must go," he said wearily. "I have a crowded morning."

If Madelaine had anything else to say with him there, it would have to be said quickly. There had been a time when he would have stayed to please her, but there had been so many such situations his reservoir of patience was exhausted.

"Why, you ought to sleep here, Wally. We have plenty of room."

"Thank you. I have a room at the Highland, and I'm sure I have messages there." He started for the door, and Cameron followed.

"Well." Doubtfully. "If you have *messages* ——" She made it

sound mysterious, as to her it did, and Wallace was annoyed.

"It's very important that this man Erik be beaten, Maddy. Important for the whole state. Every taxpayer has a stake in this fight."

She nodded enthusiastically, trailing them into the hall. "I know. Oh, I know! I know more about him than you think I do. We've been talking about him and that vicious machine of his, down at Alma's."

"Alma's?"

Cameron chuckled. "Alma Whiting's Civic Club, for the beautification of the community."

"Oh, yes," Wallace remembered, "I know her. Had a call from her the other day. Very interesting woman. We need more like that."

"I understand from Mrs. Whiting," Madelaine said, "this Erik person just thrives on the ignorance of the Nigras."

"He does," her brother declared, striking a brief pose, "and one of my first acts as governor will be to do something about just that."

Cameron looked askance, then let it go. They would settle it later. But Madelaine rushed into the pause.

"That's what Alma says, and that's why we're going to have our bazaar, our annual bazaar, you know, with policemen to watch out, down there. And all the profits will go to Wally! Erik's victims will be supporting *us!*"

Her husband stared at her. "You're going into the slums?"

"With policemen. For Wally."

"Oh, for God's sake!"

Yet she had him. Wallace was sympathetic. The more the people knew of the conditions which bred Erik's power, the stronger they would be, he argued, and Cameron, who knew better but could not say so without bringing his real estate operations into the open, was reduced to inquiring which neighborhood it would be.

"West Concord Street," she told him, with an odd catch in her voice. "The Elbow."

Wallace nodded approvingly. "That's one of the worst."

"Well," Cameron grumbled, yielding. He owned no property there. "Just as long as you stay away from the old block."

Madelaine laughed. "Between you and me, the Whitings have a block of their own, and it's closer to the Elbow than ours."

Wallace left, chuckling. Outside a wind was rising, cuffing the shutters of the old house.

She had to be sure they were out. No matter how long she tossed, until she was certain, until she knew, exhaustion could not drive the image from her mind. And so she stood in the kitchen, hunched over the sink, washing ashtrays in the silence before dawn.

Madelaine had never seen a real fire, but sometimes, sitting by her window at dusk, she had watched the last burnished edge of day and imagined she was there, fleeing ahead of it, racing for the safe shadow of night. She would sit twisting her handkerchief until darkness folded her in. Then she would rise and quickly go to the door, scolding herself softly. "Don't be a silly," she would whisper, "you silly."

Afterwards at the supper table she would timidly suggest Venetian blinds for the house, but her husband never let her buy them. He rarely did anything she asked. Sometimes, when she was feeling sorry for herself, she thought it must be sheer perversity with him. Later she would be ashamed. Surely, she told herself, if ever a woman had been lucky, she had been lucky to marry Jay Cameron.

They had been young together. The Gillette house stood five hundred yards from the Camerons' on a rolling tract of land in northern Cornwall County. There were no other children for miles, and when the Gillettes were young they had played with the Cameron twins. They thought them a godsend, for Wally and Maddy were gregarious, outgoing children who really wanted to live in the city, with clouds of boys and girls swarming about. Not the twins. They avoided others and would have kept to themselves entirely if their father, a retired brigadier, had not disapproved. Occasionally, when her husband was at the height of one of his terrible rages, Madelaine would remember him as he had been then, a meek little boy cowering behind the lattice-work under his front porch and weeping when his father stormed down the steps and ordered him out. Or rather, correcting the memory, she would see two little boys, for there were two then, identical and inseparable.

It was so easy to forget Peter. He was such a shadow, flickering behind the latticework with Jay or romping with him in the shrubbery behind the house or lying with him on the spring lawn, playing the obscure games only they understood.

Once the Gillettes had thrown their home open to the country-side. The brigadier had come, herding his wife and children before him and insisting she mingle with the others while he watched the boys. But the moment she was gone they burst into tears and wept until she returned. She scolded them and they promised to be good, but when she was gone again they set up another howl, and then another, until the despairing brigadier left them with her and went with the men and got very drunk.

Another time they decided they would live in the great oak tree behind their house. They built a shelf on the lower branches and announced to their astonished parents they intended to stay there. Their mother's persistent coaxing brought them down, but even so, they spent their afternoons there all summer, giggling and crowing and fussing behind the screen of leaves while Wally and Maddy scampered about below and indignantly demanded they come out.

That tree. Madelaine could still see it, sprawling against the October sky, ugly and cruel and hideously green.

The air was thick with autumn that Sunday, and the brigadier decided upon a walk in the country with his family. The week before he had presented each of his sons with a rifle, and he wanted to demonstrate target firing. Peter couldn't go: he had a bad cold, and the doctor advised against exercise. Jay wanted to stay with him. So did their mother. But the brigadier would not hear of it. And so Peter sat in the sun parlor, his nose against the glass, and watched them disappear into the woods with Jay's new gun. And was left alone with his.

The Gillettes heard neither shot. They did see the doctor's buggy whirl up the road and the doctor rush into the house, but even so they knew very little until weeks later, when the brigadier advertised the property for sale and Madelaine's mother drew the story from Mrs. Cameron. They had found Peter lying beside his rifle under the tree, a bullet in his heart. A few feet away, its feathers muddy with blood, lay a dead sparrow. The house had been deserted. The family was away. There was no older person to stretch out a hand to Peter, to show him how to hold the gun while he picked up the bird, and so he went down. Reaching for a sparrow.

Mrs. Gillette kept everything from her children. Jay was stunned and quiet. He played alone, first under the tree and then, when his father ordered him from there, in the lair he and Peter had fashioned under the porch. At first his mother reproved him. Later she left him alone, for she found whenever she tried to draw him out he would ask her to take him to the cemetery. Once she did. She was overcome when she found he only wanted to caper in the grass around the headstone.

The day the Camerons moved, Wally and his sister were told they could not say goodbye to Jay. They watched the movers from their attic window. It was raining, and beyond the van the brigadier was shuttling doggedly between his carriage and the porch. Toward the middle of the afternoon he escorted his weeded wife to the carriage seat. Behind them Jay trudged, little and white and lost in his slick raincoat. He disappeared behind a wall of boxes. Later they went over and watched the movers finish, but the house was nearly empty, and it was so quiet and lonely they went away quickly, disappointed and vaguely uneasy.

Madelaine did not see Jay for eleven years. She scarcely recognized him when she did. Wally reported from Princeton how he had changed, but she could not believe it. It was incredible that that shy boy could grow up to be anything but retiring, and ridiculous to suggest, as Wally had, that he had become an athlete, a campus hero.

Yet he had. Wally brought them together at a dance during Madelaine's last main, the autumn before America entered the war. She was amazed. "How have you been?" she faltered, drawing back from this ruddy giant with the elastic undergraduate smile. "Well, I hope."

"Dance?" He said it casually and, before she could answer, swept her into the waltzing crowd.

"My, you're sure of yourself," she whispered uncertainly, falling into the clichés of the young.

"Sure." He elbowed another couple aside. "Say, you've turned out to be quite a flower."

She blushed as they blushed then and followed him timidly to the veranda railing. He pointed to a dashing young man in French blue. "That's where I'm going, as soon as I graduate. Maybe before."

"Oh! I should *hope* not."

"What? Why, we've had a whole bunch of Princeton men wounded already."

She felt his hand gentle upon her arm and they were back in the swaying ballroom, dipping between the planes of intersecting light under the dazzling chandelier, tossed in a whirl of soft gauze skirts and spinning, tightly trousered legs, while from the lantern-decked bandstand a singer crooned earnestly, *There's Someone More Lonesome Than You.*

Through the lilting darkness he waltzed her, into the morning, the morning after that, through Indian summer, into early winter, and when he sailed he left his picture with her.

From France he wrote daily. His letters were characteristically short and stenographic and dwelt chiefly on the depravity of the French. Her answers were longer, if fewer. A lady, her mother reminded her, never replies to a gentleman within three days and under no circumstances writes more often than twice a week, war or no war.

They announced their engagement the third day he was home and were married in April, 1919. He joined an investment banking firm and they built their home in the country and settled into the serenity she had planned while he was away. But it was not a time for serenity, and her plans were soon swept away by the time it was — by marathons, bunion derbies, bunny hug coats, harem skirts, Fatty Arbuckle, Red Grange, and all the other strange and wonderful enthusiasms which flourished in the big bull market of the twenties. Cameron loved it. Madelaine hated it, for she was at bottom a sedate young woman, prim and uncompromising with sin. Yet looking back later over the quarreling years of their early marriage, years since dissolved into submission and self-reproach, she sometimes felt she had let life pass her by then, when her generation was young and undespairing. It was a time for abandonment; for the abandoned, each day had been a careless triumph. Her husband had triumphed so, and so had all their friends, while she spent her days fretting over the children and her nights worrying about him and the sad state of the world. She had worried when there was no need for worry, and when it all ended she had no heart for smugness. The same forces which ended their gaiety struck her down also.

The crash wiped Cameron out. He came home one day wide-eyed and shaken, muttering pitifully to himself. She wrung her hands over what he might do and watched anxiously while he did — nothing. For three years he stumbled through a series of tragic failures with grants from the brigadier. Then the old man died the week before his eighty-fifth birthday, and with his money and the income from the family block Cameron plunged into a successful career in racing, beginning with a string of horses and ending with Willoughby. Throughout the thirties the track was a sound investment. It prospered — and with it Cameron himself prospered again. It was a perverse prosperity, based upon bitterness and a hidden sense of guilt, but it was nevertheless real. Nothing had been wrong with the country, he told Madelaine. The depression was temporary and would have soon ended if the Democrats had not wanted it to continue. He rebuilt his shaken life into a hatred of Franklin Roosevelt and found the reconstruction sound. He had followed the party line when it was party time and the hangover line when that time came. The secret of his strength was that he never doubted. It was no small strength to have.

And slowly, so slowly neither saw it, Madelaine faded. His great energy sapped her until she withered and died as a person and became less his wife than his echo. Whatever he said, she said; whatever he thought, she thought too. He was a man following a familiar path across unbroken snow. She was trailing in his footsteps and leaving none of her own. In the trailing she lost herself, lost everything so completely she came to believe, as he did, that the loss was a trivial one. Then the children grew up and she found she was, he was, wrong.

Even in her most searching moments she doubted her daughter could have been saved. The seeds of the tragedy were too deeply sown for Madelaine to have seen them. Fred was simpler. She knew Fred. He was judgmental as she was, intelligent as she was, uncourageous as she was, with her capacity for indignation and her bent for compromise. But he had not compromised yet. She was glad of that. What he had not compromised she did not know. In her mind it was vaguely identified with socialism and the New Deal, and so she could not approve. When he shrank from combat duty, when he quit Princeton protesting the club system, when he fell in with social reformers, she believed, with her husband, that the shame was great. But even in disapproval she was proud his color was still his own, that it had not been drained as hers had.

Cameron knew his son was an enemy, his wife a treacherous ally. He had told Madelaine of Willoughby's plight in the interests of household economy, but not even she knew of his slum dealings; she thought, as Fred thought, that he owned the one block, and knowing how valuable it had been in the pit of the early thirties she had disregarded her son's attacks on the slums, had told herself it surely could not be that bad. The trip to West Concord had shaken that faith. It was as though she had found a forgotten closet in her own home reeking with the stench of a clogged urinal.

And so, when Alma Whiting called and reported the club would hold this year's bazaar in the slums, Madelaine had said she would be delighted.

Alma was astonished. Madelaine was one of her duty calls — normally far too busy for anything but bridge and perhaps a few inactive committees. The receiver rattled her confusion.

"Yes," Madelaine repeated, "I think it would be lovely. I'd love to do it."

"It'll be rather grim," Alma said doubtfully.

"Yes, I know," Madelaine began and then, deciding explanations could be dangerous, swiftly added, "— so I've been told."

Alma's Civic Club — everyone called it that over her protests — was an offshoot of the Country Club and met there once a month. The paper membership was very large, for it was far easier to say yes than no to Alma, but attendance was small. Generally, in matters of this sort, it was limited to Alma and a half dozen other women, all her cronies.

She was a large, bony woman with gray bobbed hair and an expression of persistent cheerfulness. She had survived her husband by twenty years now and was very proud of that. Opinion among her friends, which included nearly everyone of her age in the Valley, was split over whether she was a genuine Samaritan or an incorrigible meddler.

When she announced at the organization meeting that the neighborhood they would visit was the Elbow, the cronies applauded.

"Oh Alma, that's just the place, I've heard about it," they chortled, and "How you do find things out!" and "My husband will have a fit, just a *fit!*" and "Well, let him." "Yes, just let him."

Madelaine feebly suggested some other place might be better and they turned around in their chairs and eyed her coldly.

"Now, girls," Alma boomed pleasantly. "Maybe Maddy knows

a more typical spot. I certainly don't" — she choked with laughter — "qualify as an expert in these things."

The cronies twittered disagreeably. Madelaine tried to think of another street in the slums. The only other neighborhood she knew of was the family block, and it certainly couldn't be *there*.

"I don't qualify either," she said feebly. "I just thought there might be some other place. I suppose this is as good as any."

The women turned back smugly, exchanging glances. The tiniest flicker of revolt was rare under Alma.

"Splendid!" she cried merrily. "Now we have nearly two weeks, and of course there's all our Christmas merchandise from last year, but there's still a lot to do — awnings, car pools, and so on. We'll have to work out a lot of details right away, because I promised to let the police know the arrangements in advance."

"Police!" someone squealed. *"My!"*

"You don't think we'd go down there with*out* police," someone else called, and a murmur rippled across the room.

Alma smiled. "They're going to give us a special guard." The ladies nodded approval. "I had to call your brother this morning to get it done," she said to Madelaine.

Madelaine was surprised. She would never have dreamed of calling Wallace during business hours, any more than she would have called her husband.

Alma reminded them as they left to bring any recruits they could find, for the only way to defeat Bossism, as she called it, was through education. Her targets, her examples of Bossism, began and ended with Ben Erik.

Madelaine spent that week, and the one which followed, working on plans for the bazaar. At first things went very badly. No one would help. But after Wallace's speech acceptances flooded them. Overnight Erik had become a symbol to the Valley, a community scapegoat.

Thorpe's speech compounded the uproar. In delivery it was a failure. The papers reported half the audience walked out before he had finished, and none of those left applauded when he sat down. But in the city at large it found surprising support. Cameron's name was brought into the fight for the first time, and there were reports that one militant black organization planned to throw a picket line around Willoughby at the spring meeting.

Madelaine, violently partisan, threw herself into the bazaar work with fresh vigor. Now and then, looking up from her inventories of ornaments, shiny, and wreaths, spangled, she wished there were someone at home to talk with. Fred came out so seldom. Cameron should have been interested, but he was full of himself, and when she approached him he was so amused and condescending she left him, discouraged, and did not try again.

Here, as always with him, she was defeated. Her married life had been a pattern of defeat and frustration. Yet she thought herself lucky to have him. It had been a mosaic of sorrow. Yet she cherished it. Perhaps because she loved him.

She loved him, but she wondered if she understood him. In their thirty years together he had never mentioned Peter's death, but she knew he drove to Cornwall County each year and spent the anniversary of his brother's death by the grave. She had heard it from friends who lived near the cemetery, not from him. He never shared his private thoughts with her. It was as though she was a casual member of the household and his real marriage was to someone else, or something else. To the memory of Peter, perhaps.

But these were old wounds, and their scars were thick. Now and then, when his touch was rough, he could run a telling finger over them, but not for long. She had learned to survive. His secrets were his and hers were hers, she told herself, as though she had any to share. She believed this so firmly, and so steadfastly refused to speak unless she had special cause, that often she missed matters as important to her as to him. This nearly happened the week after Thorpe's speech.

One afternoon Cameron came home whistling. He whistled his way across the portico and into the front hall, chucked her merrily under the chin, asked what Christmas presents she was wrapping and whom they were for, and then went into his study and closed the door, taking the evening paper with him. She stood over the gifts with her vague smile, wondering why he was so gay.

That night Alma called and told her. "Why, haven't you heard?" She was breathless. "My dear, you must have. It isn't possible. They're going to expose him, send him to jail!" She made it sound thrilling. Madelaine was thrilled.

"Why, I hadn't heard a word, not a single word. Is he arrested yet?"

He had been neither arrested nor even threatened with arrest. "But it's coming. You'll see. It's coming. Why, he's through! Listen."

She read the story from the evening paper, the same paper Cameron had taken to his study. It was very long, and she was wheezing when she finished. Madelaine watched the study door as she listened, wishing she had a paper of her own. She did not understand it all, but it sounded exciting. Sixty ranking policemen were being transferred from station houses in the Seventh District. There were rumors of a vice squad shake-up.

"So you see," Alma wheezed, "it's practically over."

"Well, I don't know," Madelaine said doubtfully. "I think we ought to go ahead. With the bazaar."

"Well, I should hope so!" Alma was indignant. "I should just hope so! But we've got him now, we've really got him." She liked the taste of blood.

Madelaine was relieved. She had worked so hard. She would have been terribly disappointed if it had been called off. She thanked Alma and hung up.

In the next moment Cameron picked up the extension in his study and dialed. She lingered in the hall for an instant, wondering if she could risk eavesdropping. Suddenly it occurred to her he might catch her. The thought frightened her, and she ran up the stairs breathlessly, running a trembling hand along the banister.

Safely in her room she turned out the lights and crept into the chair by the window, chiding herself. "Don't be a silly," she whispered, "you silly."

The grounds below were frozen fast, and, as she watched, a fresh snow began to fall, scuttling before the wind in wild gusts, like thoughts in the mind of a lunatic.

3

The Gestapo

ZIPSKI was clean. There was no doubt of that. Sometimes he thought he was the only man in the Department who was — thought that in all this vast machine oiled by graft and powered by something called suction, only he was incorrupt. Then he remembered there were others, a few others, as clean as he. Cleaner, perhaps, since they had not threaded their way through the maze of cogs and cams to the machine's top. Cleaner. Perhaps. But, he reflected bitterly, only a little less powerful, a little less responsible. For with the machine adjusted and readjusted by hands reaching in, tinkering with its shafts, the man at the top was not in control. Zipski could pull a lever or push a button or twist a dial, but the machine had a way of breaking down. The Department had a way of developing stoppages.

So he handled this one himself, going through the files personally, picking the replacements. Then he called in Griesel, the effeminate male secretary he had inherited, and dictated the orders.

"Send a carbon up to Records," he said at the end, leaning back in his worn serge and reaching for his pipe. "Bring me the original."

"I'll be glad to take it up to the Comm room," Griesel said, swishing around the desk eagerly. He could hardly wait to spread the news.

Zipski watched him narrowly, as a man with a fly swatter watches a fly, waiting for it to land. Griesel paused at the threshold.

"Did I ask you to take it?" the commissioner inquired mildly.

"Well, no, but ——"

"Just bring it here, like you're told."

The secretary went out, prancing hippily, and Zipski wished for the thousandth time he could fire him. He couldn't because he was the protégé of a Second District ward executive named Como. Griesel had suction with Como.

In the next room the switchtop desk flew open with a petulant slam. Zipski lit his pipe and went to the window. Below, the new shift was tramping away from the building, blue figures bobbing beside the ribs of new snow at the sidewalk edge. He watched them with his gray old poker face, the face which had not changed in forty years, the face of a hundred Department jokes. Zipski went to a masquerade when he was young, rookies were told. No one told him to take his false face off at midnight, and he forgot about it, and it became part of him.

He had never lost his prejudice against headquarters, picked up on an East Bay beat when the mask was new and he was a patrolman; and he watched the departing shift with faint scorn. Leave me in the sticks, he had always said. Don't send me downtown. His bias for the sticks was part of Zipski's popularity. His popularity was why he had been brought downtown.

He was still at the window, puffing at the dregs of his pipe, when Griesel came in and put the sheets on the steel desktop. "There it is," he said pettishly. "Sir." He waited a moment and then went out.

Zipski climbed the stairs slowly, holding the paper away from him, as though afraid he might soil it. Through their plate-glass windows the Communications Room force saw him coming, and everyone was quiet and busy as he walked in. The sergeant came over timidly.

"Yes sir. Something you want, sir?" Several of the younger policemen glanced up curiously from their switchboards. Zipski was almost unknown here. He hated this tangle of equipment. It made him feel obsolete.

"Orders," he said, thrusting them at the sergeant. "I want to see them go out."

He stood over the trembling patrolman at the teletype, crowding him so the man could scarcely work. When the message was sent he spun away without a word and strode from the room, down the stairs to his lonely office, to wait for Holloway.

In ten minutes he heard him bellowing in the anteroom and heard, almost simultaneously, Griesel stammer over the intercom: "Inspector Holl ——"

"Yes," Zipski cut in. "I'll see him."

Holloway wore all his commendations on duty. In uniform he looked like a French admiral. He was regarded throughout the Department as a comic figure, but because he had all the rank he could conceivably get and had nothing to gain by intrigue, he was Zipski's confidant.

"Well," he shouted, coming across the floor, "you done it."

Zipski nodded gravely.

"Who goes next? Lieutenants? Sergeants?"

"Both. Monday."

Holloway swore and dropped recklessly into a chair. His very size muffled the sound. He stared vacantly across the desk, the crimson slowly ebbing from his neck. "I still don't believe it," he said at last. "So far as I'm concerned it's still a phony baloney."

It wasn't. He knew it wasn't. Not even Holloway, insulated in stupidity and ignorance, could work in the Department and not know Erik's strength within it. But his loyalty was absolute, and he was prepared to spend a lifetime denying the obvious.

"Phony or not," Zipski said quietly, "they all move."

Silence. Then: "What about Morelock's squad? Going to shake that up?"

Again the grave nod. "In fact, I'm doubling it."

"What happens to Morelock?"

"Inspector."

"Well." Holloway flushed again. Then he had been right. Zipski was courting Big Ed. With his reverence for authority, Holloway could never have understood that Morelock shrank from promotion, or that Big Ed preferred him as captain. "He'll take your old slot on the east side?"

"That's right. You'll keep the west."

"Who's getting vice?"

"Seaver. I haven't told him yet."

"Seaver." Holloway worried an ear with a huge paw. Then, grudgingly: "He's a good man. Of course, with that many men it'll be a good job."

"It'll have its moments." Zipski rose and went to the window. The relieved shift was coming back, drifting along the walk in twos and threes. "All they let it have."

Holloway studied him. "Meaning what? You're the one that goes for this stuff. Myself, I never saw money change hands, or any of that. I wouldn't know Erik if I saw him."

"Why do you think you haven't seen him in court?"

"Maybe what they say isn't true."

"Maybe it's summer out, we only think it's cold." He paused, watching the last stragglers climb the stone steps below. "Here I am. Waiting. I could have Seaver sworn in and on the street today, but I wait. Why? For word. From the top. And the thing scares me, I'm getting so it don't bother me any more, I even sit down and talk their language, giving this, taking that."

He finished and came back to the chair and sat down.

Holloway squirmed in his tight seat. This talk confused him. He felt the old man was definitely slipping. Lack of Department confidence in the commissioner was to him like disbelief in God.

Zipski drew his tobacco pouch from a desk drawer and filled another pipe. "Don't get me wrong," he said over the flaring match. "I expect to have almost as much fun as Seaver."

Holloway picked vigorously at a clogged nostril. "You better watch out. You go after Ben Erik you're in real politics."

Zipski nodded slowly. "Funny. I was thinking the same thing." He blew out the flame.

They had never met, but Zipski knew Ben and Ben knew Zipski. Their memories were scarred the same way; they were professionals. In Ben's position anyone but a professional would have skipped Zipski and looked for other targets. Of all the men in the city's public life, he was the least controversial. Until Ben went after him.

Tuesday night the syndicate mounted its counterattack. Thorpe was to address a meeting of Seventh District women. At the podium Gormley handed him his speech. Simultaneously, a fleet of Western Union messengers delivered copies to all newspapers and radio stations.

It began by charging the mass police transfer was a whitewash of deep scandal, and though there had been no suggestion of scandal before, the very intensity of the assault lent it weight.

Then came the master stroke: a documented history of negotiations between Zipski and the State Police, for a training job when the city retired him.

Ben had learned of this the evening before. For years he had paid a clerk at State Police headquarters a retainer for such information. The arrangement was rarely of any use, and he had often considered discontinuing it. "Never let your premiums lapse," he now told Paul, winking happily as he handed him photostats of the letters. "Never know when you'll need the insurance."

Ordinarily the letters could have been easily explained. Zipski was ready for retirement, and there was nothing extraordinary in his wish to stay a policeman. But the disclosure came at an awkward time. The negotiations were incomplete, and so Zipski was obliged to refuse comment to reporters' questions. This in itself was suspicious to a public conditioned by Wallace's charges. And in political circles the letters were dynamite.

The position Zipski was after had been created by the last legislature. The salary was fat and the requirements inconsiderable. The State Police wanted Zipski. Clearly he was the most qualified man available. But every politician had a candidate for the job. Specifically, Big Ed Sylvester had Rudolph Morelock.

Big Ed was furious. He felt that in some obscure way Zipski had tricked him, and he sulked as the lesser bosses, so carefully groomed by Wallace for the coalition against Erik, saw the plum they too relished slipping away. They joined Thorpe in howling for a Police Department investigation. Zipski bogged down in denials and explanations, and Seaver remained unappointed.

Cameron was in an uproar. The subtleties of the situation were hopelessly beyond him. He could not understand what had happened, and so he spent his days badgering Wallace and his nights stalking his study, drinking and fuming.

Wallace was worried, not because he thought the libel of Zipski serious but because he saw it obviously was not. By the end of the week its worst effects were dissipated. With almost incessant haggling and bartering he had placated first Big Ed and then the others. The storm was rapidly clearing. But why Erik wanted the delay Wallace did not know, nor could he find out.

He called on Zipski to see if Zipski knew.

Griesel received him obsequiously. "The commissioner's just going over some reports, Senator. You won't need an appointment."

Wallace waited casually with his homburg tilted to the back of his head.

"The Senator from Cornwall County," Griesel called over the intercom, sounding important. "He'd like to talk to you, sir."

"Did he tell us he was coming?"

"No, sir, he didn't ——"

"Ask the Senator to wait."

Wallace heard the static drawl and smiled at Griesel's confusion. "I should have called first," he said amiably. "I'll just sit down and wait."

The secretary's admiring eyes followed him across the room. Wallace felt them and they warmed him. One of his immutable rules was never to show impatience with a clerk.

Another was always to enter the office of anyone of importance with a joke, however feeble. "Where's the swag, Commissioner?" he grinned, coming through the doorway with the intercom's permission. "You can tell me."

Zipski pointed at a chair. "Sit down and tell me what you know about this guff."

He looked tired. His integrity had never been attacked before, and Thorpe's speech had hurt him more than he had thought possible.

Wallace hung his homburg on his knee and sat on his overcoat. "It's practically over," he said, throwing up his hands in a gesture of dismissal. "His straw man's in pieces."

Zipski didn't mean that. "Why did he do it, is what I want to know. He isn't going to get anywhere this way. Why the stall?"

Wallace's hands sank slowly. No help here.

"I was hoping you'd tell me. You know more about these things than I do."

Zipski shook his head. "I don't know anything about politics. I'm just a cop. This is over my head. You might say it's above the law."

Wallace ignored this. "How about your new people? They find anything?"

"A little," Zipski said cautiously. "I think we can move whenever" — an eyebrow bent slightly — "your friends decide we can start."

Wallace was annoyed, but he let it go. "Anything new on the bank?" he asked lightly.

"Nothing since the tap. That was a mistake. It scared him. We've had people watching his house, but they haven't seen anything."

"Can you trust them, the people you got watching?"

"Yes," Zipski said acidly, "I can."

"Is he still operating there, do you think?"

"No. In fact, as of this moment he isn't even living there."

"Not *living* there!"

"No. He's been leaving the house every noon and not coming back until night. Yesterday we put a tail on him. He spotted it and shook it, and last night he didn't come home."

Wallace groaned. "He could be anywhere, then?"

"Could be." Zipski turned rudely to the papers before him and ruffled through them. "Most anywhere."

Wallace rose and donned his homburg. "I've got a meeting with Big Ed at three," he said shortly. "I think we'll give you a testimonial." The implication was that he did not, at that moment, deserve it.

When Wallace reached the threshold Zipski looked up owlishly. "How did Willoughby end the season?" he asked. "Lose a lot of money?"

Wallace went out, pretending he had not heard, forgetting another and feebler joke he had planned for the door.

At five o'clock that afternoon Big Ed reluctantly joined him in a statement pledging confidence in Zipski, and this was released in time for the first edition of the morning paper. The later editions carried Morelock's promotion to inspector and Seaver's appointment as vice squad chief.

It came too late. Ben had bought his time shrewdly and used it well. He had used nearly all of it for work and wasted very little on sleep, and when Otto brought the paper to him in the partitioned barn loft, he read it with red and tortured eyes.

But he read it all, savoring every paragraph, and when he had finished the rough floor was strewn with newsprint. He leaned back on his cot, feeling gay and a little giddy. "Raiders coming, Otto," he called in falsetto. "Gonna getcha, getcha, getcha."

Otto giggled loudly across the beaverboard wall. "Yeah. Look at me. I'm *terri*fied!"

He appeared in the doorway, naked and shaking as though in

fear. The shakes wiggled his slack paunch loosely, and Ben burst into laughter.

The telephone by his cot rang.

"Hello? You bet. I seen it, all right."

Otto raised a musclebound arm for attention. "I'm going down, take a shower."

Ben cupped a hand over the receiver. "How is that shower?"

"It was rusty, but I fixed it good."

"I'll be down later."

He returned to the telephone as Otto's fleshy feet pattered down the barn stairs. The caller was Paul. Ben questioned him anxiously.

"You been to Murdock's? Good, good. Only don't bother him no more. He's got to be on the ball, understand? All the time. Okay. Just so's you understand." He listened for a moment and then broke in. "Look. I got to get some sleep. Call me about" — he looked at his watch — "about seven. Let me know what happens. Yeah, yeah. So long."

He hung up and turned his head into the pillow. Otto came back ten minutes later, dripping from the shower and wheezing from the climb, and found him in a deep sleep. His dreams were all of Bull Hoover.

Bull Hoover was a cop. Or so he said. When neighbors asked him what he did, or when a stranger meeting him at the beach in the summertime asked what his line was, Bull always answered, "Copping." With a swagger.

But the real cops did not call him that. They called him a clerk, and that is what he really was, a file clerk who worked with cops. He had a uniform he wore at all times. He was entitled to wear it, though not required to, for his work did not bring him into contact with the public, and he was not allowed to carry a gun or make arrests.

Yet no one in the Department was more belligerent in uniform than Bull. Riding home on the streetcar he would sit rigidly on the front seat, watching the traffic, muttering black threats against the double parkers and watching his impressed fellow passengers with satisfaction. And if, striding heavily from the trolley to his house, he saw children playing in the street, he would stop and lecture them sternly. Among them he replaced the bogey man. "The Bull'll get you!" they would shout to one another after he had passed on. "Look out for the Bull!"

At work he was meek and inconspicuous, fastidious with his files and servile before authority.

He was nearly sixty and entirely bald, a sleek old man with small eyes, a little belly, and a nervous habit of running his tongue over his teeth without opening his mouth.

He had christened himself. When he came to the Department he was asked if he had a nickname. "I was an athlete in school," he said modestly, unaware two of his classmates were on the force and could identify the lie. "They called me Bull." It was so funny it stuck.

Secretly Bull believed he was a victim of discrimination. In his early years with the Department he was eager and loyal, but with the onset of age and the repeated rejection of his applications for transfer to a beat — always for the same discouraging reason, varicose veins — the belief grew, poisoning his devotion. Outwardly he was the same, bustling among his record folders, fawning when anyone approached. But in the locker room, where he did his heavy thinking, he seethed with a sense of injustice.

Bull's immediate superior was a Lieutenant Walter Gregg, a bluff, outgoing type toward whom Bull felt no bitterness. Gregg was everything Bull wanted to be: husky, handsome, and often commended. Moreover he had tried, he had honestly tried, to see that Bull's transfer was approved. Bull knew that. It was all in the files.

It happened that Bull, through those files, could be very useful to Ben Erik now. He was in fact indispensable. Ben knew that, because Gregg, through Gormley, had told him. Gregg was Ben's pipeline to police headquarters.

Gregg had learned that the enlarged vice squad would be situated in the west end of the Record room. There Seaver would be, and there his men would report when they spotted a numbers drop. Bull could not be expected to overhear their reports, at least not all the time, for his file cabinets lined all four walls of the room. But it was not necessary that he should. After Seaver ordered a raid the policemen would dictate warrants to the squad clerk, and after that the warrant carbons would be dropped in a wire basket for Bull. Between then and the departure of the officers with the approved warrant at least twenty minutes would pass — time for him to telephone a warning ahead. Numbers paraphernalia was small and easily removed. Bull Hoover, with a few calls, could cripple the Department's drive.

The problem was to convince him he ought to do it, and at this Gregg worked steadily, as Ben was furiously shifting drops, in the week of debate over Zipski's negotiations with the State Police. Gregg himself had no regular business in the Record room, nor would he make business there. The risk was too great. It had to be Bull.

Bull was no stranger to corruption. His powers of self-justification were enormous, and on half a dozen occasions he had sold folders to Gregg for small sums, assuring himself that in a Department so shot through with depravity and callousness someone else would take them if he did not, and that they were probably unimportant anyhow. Ben's record had been returned to Ben that way. Sometimes the thefts were discovered. When they were, Gregg simply reported to his captain that the files had no locks and anyone in the building had access to them. Locks were never supplied. Zipski's predecessors had lacked interest, and Zipski himself, with his profound distrust of administration machinery, felt records were unimportant.

Selling out to Erik in the middle of a vice drive was something else, however. The leak was not unimportant, nor would it be sprung unless Bull sprang it. His conscience was finally drugged with a heroic dose of Gregg's sophistry and $5,000 cash. Gregg got another $5,000. The bribe cost Ben nothing, for Zipski's transfer of his ranking policemen to East Bay had cut his Christmas bonus costs in half.

On the morning of the day Wallace made his unannounced visit to Zipski, the day the bosses fell back in line against Ben, the details of the fix were settled in an all-night lunchroom just off a highway east of the city. The settlers were Gormley, Gregg, and Bull. For once Bull was in mufti.

They met in the first streaked moments of daylight on the diner's steps. It was important that the policemen be at work, in uniform, on time, and they had to hurry.

Paul was waiting impatiently in a bulky plaid overcoat and a fuzzy hat with the brim slanted over his face. "Let's get inside," he said quickly, frosting the air with his breath. "I'm frozen."

"Officer Hoover," Gregg began formally, "I'd like for you to meet ——"

"Can that," Paul snapped. "No names."

Bull had begun to nod in acknowledgment, and his face fell. Paul grudgingly thrust out a heavily gloved hand. He could not offend this one. "Pleased to meet you," he mumbled. "Now let's get in*side*."

Behind the counter a one-armed man in white duck and a Legion button was making coffee. "Good morning, gentlemen," he said cheerfully.

They hurried past without a word and he followed to the last booth in the line. "Everybody want Java?" he asked when they were seated.

They did. Bull added hesitantly he would like scrambled eggs. He looked to Gregg for approval, and Gregg looked at Paul. "All right," Paul said with a trace of irritation. "Eggs."

Bull was staring at the empty sleeve. The man saw him. "Iwo," he explained, pinching the limp cuff with his one hand.

He was lonely and wanted to talk, but no one answered. Paul was annoyed, Gregg was embarrassed, and Bull was frightened by Paul's annoyance. The man went away, disappointed, and they huddled.

"You got the money all right?" Paul asked Bull. "Good. All we'll need, all we want from you, is the address. Nothing else, unless the knockoff boys already left when you call. If they have, say that."

"Just say they left — just that?" Bull was flicking his tongue over his teeth rapidly.

"No. Not just the address, either. Here's how it works ——"

The coffee was coming. Paul stopped abruptly and they waited in silence as it slid before them.

"Here's how it works," he began again, watching the white duck back disappear behind the grill. "You're the only one got this phone number."

"What number?"

"The one I'm going to give you."

"Oh, oh, pardon me."

"It's a private phone, unlisted, and you don't have to know where it is. Better you shouldn't. It was just put in yesterday, and nobody will ever be calling that number but you. Got it?"

"Yessir."

"All right. When the man answers he'll say, *Black's Delicatessen*. That's the man you want. If anybody else ever answers, they won't, but if they should, and say anything else, you hang up, see? And clear out, see? And don't do anything, not a thing, till you hear from Gregg, here. See?"

"Okay." In a little voice.

The eggs came and they waited again.

"Now," Paul went on when the one-armed man had gone. "When this guy says *Black's Delicatessen*, you say, *Would you please send a loaf of bread and a quart of milk to* —— and give the address. Remember that. If you forget, ask your boss, here."

"I'll remember."

"Good. If the knockoff squad is gone, say *That milk you sent to* —— and the address — *it was sour*. And hang up. Okay?"

"Yup."

"You know where you'll be calling from?"

"Pay phone, if I got time. Downstairs. But maybe sometimes I'll have to use an inside line, I don't know which."

"It's unimportant."

Gregg had been hunched over the table with his finger tips pressed together, dreamily studying a Varga calendar and looking as though he were not listening. But he was. "That number," he said suddenly, without looking away from the calendar. "You better give him that number."

"Fort." Paul's mustache twitched slightly. "Two seven six oh."

Bull repeated it after him solemnly in his scratchy tenor.

Then Gregg asked, "What about the guy on the other end? You should've brought him."

"He's a Nigra." Paul jerked his head toward the counterman. "The hero would remember us."

They left Bull's eggs untouched.

The man behind the counter wistfully watched them go.

The street lamps had been turned off. Outside the day was gathering in puddles of dirty light.

So it was arranged, and so it worked. The first day there was some trouble, not unanticipated. Captain Seaver was restless and had sworn out six warrants in advance against drops he knew from his own street time. He held the filing duplicates until after the raid, not because he was suspicious, but because he was too busy picking his men and planning his operations to give them to Bull.

Therefore these six had no warning. But four of them needed none. Ben remembered Seaver from the thirties, when he was the only patrolman in the lower district who would not join his payroll, and he knew Seaver knew about these four. When the raiders arrived, the drops were gone. In the others two writers were flushed. The newspapers made a great thing of their arrests, the cases were taken directly to the Grand Jury, and the State's Attorney, following his announced policy of swift judgment, prosecuted the following day. Otto was in the sheriff's office, paying the fines, immediately after the trials.

And there, it seemed, the fanfare ended. Seaver's men went out every day and returned empty-handed. Bull worked flawlessly.

All his life he had awaited a touch of excitement to color his drab days, and now it had come he met it magnificently. He was everything that Ben, anxiously watching from his county retreat, hoped he would be — cunning, bland, and fast on his feet, fast enough to keep the information coming and avoid the faintest suspicion in the Department. No raids could go out without his knowledge. Policy slips were in the drops for only a brief period, a period well bracketed by Bull's hours of duty in the Record room. His job kept him wandering from one floor to another, picking up folders, and it was a simple matter to slip into a pay phone booth on the first floor or, if all the booths were occupied, to wander into an empty office and place the innocent call to "Black's Delicatessen."

At Fort 2760 Joe Murdock waited. The phone sat on the dresser in his bedroom, and he never left it during the day. Beside it was another phone, also unlisted, for the relaying of Bull's reports to the pickup men, whose numbers were on a typewritten sheet tacked to the bedroom wall. Only Murdock knew the number of his second phone. It was not for incoming calls at any time, from anyone, for any reason.

Joe here meant no Joe with the writers in Judge Russell's territory, but they were idle anyway, and Ben told Paul to see they were paid and their players directed to drops elsewhere. That was secondary. This was primary. Ben knew he could trust Joe, and a man he could trust was more valuable here, with those two phones, than all the writers Joe had carefully nursed over the years. Indeed, his value, and Bull's, were incalculable. In the week that followed Seaver's first day the vice squad brought in but one man, charged, in a moment of exasperation, with disorderly conduct. The case was tried, before Paul Gormley in the Thawe Street station house. Paul dismissed it, observing, for the reporters, that Captain Seaver reminded him of a shadow boxer.

Ben was less whimsical. Through Thorpe he charged the smear had failed, renewed his demands for an investigation of Zipski, and suggested Wallace might well look to Cornwall County if he wanted a house to clean. The tide of public opinion ran heavily in his favor, and even the newspapers were doubtful.

Zipski did not understand it, nor did Wallace, nor Sylvester, nor least of all Cameron, but each had an answer. Zipski was sure Ben was using lookouts, and he and Seaver planned false leads to confuse them. They failed. Wallace believed Ben had shut down his drops, and Big Ed thought he might be operating with street writers. But when they called on the commissioner they were presented with copies of Seaver's reports, showing heavy activity in known drops — until the raiders appeared. Cameron was convinced the police were simply inefficient. He sent Joe Patecka out one morning to place a policy bet, and when Joe brought him the slip he forwarded it by Western Union messenger to Zipski, who directed Seaver to raid the drop, a poultry store, at noon. That morning it had been headquarters for two busy writers. By twelve o'clock they were gone. Under a row of skinny turkeys an aproned clerk was asleep. They had to shake him to wake him.

The patrolmen were as harmless as ever. Their new commanders made fierce speeches at each roll call, but in reports to Holloway they pointedly asked if Seaver failed in plainclothes, what could be expected of men in uniform?

The other district leaders, committed to the fight against Ben, did what little they could to hurt him. Big Ed maneuvered a resolution through the City Council condemning the numbers racket, and directives went out to all municipal departments, providing summary dismissal for anyone caught with policy slips. But there was nothing else. By the beginning of the second week the great drive was floundering. Stranded with it were Wallace's ambitions, Cameron's hopes, and the flagging interest of a city.

On the first day of Bull Hoover's treason, Ben Erik lost a writer. Charlie Bond quit the syndicate and went into business for himself. He did it with a telephone call from Ollie Wetlek's bar late that afternoon. The call cost him thirty cents, for he dialed a wrong number with the first dime and hung up the second time when Moss Bailey's mother answered. He had never called Moss before, and when the old woman spoke he thought he must have made another mistake. He was very nervous.

Six weeks before, his desertion would have been unimportant. People were always dropping in and out of the racket's lower levels, and although a wildcat writer had never been taken lightly, in the past he had been permitted to ride for a time to see if he would break himself on a bad number. Now, with the syndicate jittery over Seaver's first two arrests and unaware of Bull Hoover, a break in the dike could become a flood.

But Charlie did not consider it desertion. To him it was normal business. People in business did this all the time, and there was no reason why he should not cut free if he chose. It was his risk. Still he was uneasy in the booth. He knew Moss would not like losing him.

"Hello, hello, hello." Moss's mother's voice was faintly Polish and edged with pique. Charlie had hung up before without an explanation.

"Is Mr. Bailey there?" Charlie asked unevenly, certain he had wasted his last dime on another wrong number.

"Which one you want?" In the background children were shouting and an old man was hoarsely demanding attention.

"Mr. Moss Bailey," he said, disappointed that this was it, after all.

"He just come in. Moss!" she shrieked. "For you!"

There was a dull thud on the other end as she put the receiver down, then silence.

Charlie hoped Moss was in a good mood. He had picked today because he thought he would be. An hour before, they had paid off two winners, Charlie's worst record in a week. Yet Moss had been unreproachful.

He was hoping this hope in the quiet booth when a loud whistle shattered his eardrum. He jerked his head away and rubbed his ear. Harsh laughter crackled over the line.

"How's that!" Moss cried. "How's that, you sonofabitch!" His mother's telephone was an old-fashioned upright model, and he had held the receiver against the mouthpiece.

"Moss?" Charlie said uncertainly. "This is Charlie. Charlie Bond."

There was no sound for a moment, and then Moss said, "Bond!" incredulously, and then "Bond!" again, this time with disgust. He had thought it was someone else. Charlie felt a weakness in his bowels. But he went ahead bravely.

"I wanted to tell you, I got something to tell you."

"Can't it wait?" The implication was it had better.

"Well, not really, not exactly, no."

"You had a knockoff or something? We can fix it."

"No, nothing like that. Thing is, I've decided, you know . . ." He struggled for words.

"I don't know and I'm busy." The phone rustled as Moss flexed his arm, pumping home the new stuff, the half-hour-old stuff.

"Well," Charlie burst out, "I'm going into business for myself. Singleshooting. Like I told you once I was thinking of."

"You're *what*?"

"Sure," he rushed on, "I've decided. My mind's made up. Starting tomorrow."

"I don't get it." The receiver rustled, pumping. "You drunk?"

"No, I don't ever drink." He hurried to explain, anxious to finish. "I'm going to write for myself, be my own bank, keep the slips, do everything in my place."

"You can't do that," Moss said flatly.

"It's a free country."

"It isn't allowed."

"Who don't allow it?"

"We don't. Us. The organization. We don't allow anybody to leave, at least not now, and nobody but us writes. That's the way it is and that's the way it's going to be. For always. So forget it."

"That's a monopoly," Charlie spluttered. "They got laws against things like that."

"Yak, yak, yak."

"Yak, yak, yak yourself." Charlie was angry. "I know what's going on. I don't want to get caught in your politics. I live my life and you live yours. Pick up your bag any time, it's yours.

Only don't come around for no slips, understand? Because what I write I keep."

They argued. Charlie rooted himself in stubborn repetition, and Moss, with the drug socking away at his heart, was too weak to fight. He drizzled away into a thin whine, pleading with Charlie to wait another day. Toward the end he came back strongly with threats, but they were useless. The receiver lay wet in Charlie's hand and the veins in his neck bulged, but he would not give in.

He worked to end the conversation, shortening his answers, and when Moss's last threats had been turned back, said pleasantly, "It's been fine working with you, really fine. See you sometime."

He dried his hand on his overcoat and took another grip on the clammy rubber, waiting. For a moment there was nothing. Then the line clicked and the drone of the dial tone broke evenly. He hung up with relief.

Ollie made change for him and he returned to call Loretta, explaining he would be working late that night on an underwear shipment from Buffalo. She listened listlessly and did not ask when he would be home. Since the night of the neighborhood meeting she had treated him so, and they had drifted into a chilly truce. Afterward he went back to his store and spent the evening building sorting bins.

While Charlie talked to Loretta, Moss was calling Ben Erik. Moss thought Ben would share his alarm, for he thought he must know how shaky the other writers were.

But Ben did not. He was overconfident. Bull Hoover had made him so. He was so insulated in his overconfidence and so isolated in his hideout he could not feel the pulse of the syndicate, and Joe Murdock, who would have felt it for him, was as isolated as he.

He was also tired. Moss had awakened him. "Where's this guy?" he yawned. "Where's he write?"

"In the Elbow, boss."

"Yeah, I know that neighborhood. He's probably got one eye." He thought for a moment. "In the middle of his forehead."

"He's pulling out completely, boss. A singleshooter."

Ben yawned again, thought of Seaver, and snickered. "Let him pull. A peanut peddler like that don't bother me."

"Let him go!" Moss was amazed. "Just like that? What about the others?"

"What about them? They're happy, aren't they?"

"They're nervous."

"Well?"

"If one guy gets away with it, and it gets around, a lot of others might try."

Ben was silent. If you knew what I know, he thought, you'd know how glad they'll be to stick around.

But Moss did not know. He only knew Seaver had pulled two men in and the writers were skittish. He felt a little that way himself. "Look," he said. "I can call Seaver tomorrow, from a pay station, give him this guy's address."

Ben wanted no raids. Whether a writer was operating in or out of the syndicate was academic: he would be blamed if there were any convictions. The one thing which would starve Seaver and ruin Wallace Gillette was a blank docket.

But he could not tell Moss that. Bull was only as safe as his secret. So he hedged. "This nut might squeal."

"He don't know much."

"He knows more than the gestapo, which is nothing."

"But you said we don't want no runouts."

"Nobody'll run."

"This guy is."

"He's a nut, like I say. We'll get him later. We're doing all right, kid. Forget it. Sleep on it. See you tomorrow. And don't call me again unless it's important. The tappers is everywhere."

So Moss gave up and went back to his iron bed, in the room behind his mother's, to doze in the false nap between jobs. He awoke with a start at ten o'clock, cramped from oversleep, and drove rapidly across town for the last of the day. On his way home he nearly fell asleep. He staggered up the stairs and collapsed across the mattress. All night he dreamt Ben was chasing him up the slippery side of a great rock, to the brink of a deep chasm.

During the Christmas season Charlie's action normally ran between 500 and 600 bets a day, high for a drop, but the Elbow was rock-bottom slum, a policy stronghold.

Charlie wrote more slips than the average writer, but he took in, if anything, less money. The majority of the 75,000 bettors supporting Ben Erik's syndicate could take advantage of the high payoff odds which went with bets at 50 cents or more, and some of the swanky drops on Belton Avenue would write nothing in the little book. But in the Elbow a 50 cent bet was rare. Eighty per cent of Charlie's clients left an average of 20 cents apiece with him daily. The other twenty per cent were chiefly merchants, salesmen, and city employees who worked in the neighborhood during the day and lived elsewhere. Their bets averaged 70 cents. Charlie called them the carriage trade. Carriage traders bet with him, not with his subwriters, for their work was in or near the stores, where he was.

Charlie employed five subwriters at commissions of five per cent of the gross. Their profit was small, and they wrote as a favor to their customers. Between them they took in about $80 a day from 350 bettors. Charlie, with fewer slips, averaged between $85 and $90 a day — most of it big book stuff, from the carriage trade.

From the beginning of his break with the syndicate, the big book kept him awake nights. At first he thought he would lose it, because he could not afford the bargain odds Ben was offering elsewhere, and he was sure the 70-centers would want those odds and take their grift where they could get them. But they did not. To his great surprise he lost none of his regular customers. It was almost as though they did not care about winning, as though they were looking for a place to leave their change and found his drop convenient.

Then he thought they would break him. If a small bet hit,

even when he was getting started, he could stand the belt: 20 cents at 350-to-1 was only $70. He could not last if there were many such payoffs, but there were not likely to be many. With 450 slips in the little book, the chances one would hit on a given day were something less than even. The chances for a carriage trade slip were even less — one out of ten — but if one did hit, the payoff would be staggering: $525 for a 70 cent bet. Charlie did not have $525 that first day. If one big bet came in, he planned to borrow from Loretta's brother, an east side tailor, and take the risk of getting it back the following day. He had no plans for more than one.

But he needed none. From the moment of his declaration of independence, he prospered. The first day his gross was $173.80. Out of this came $3.78 in subwriters' commissions, $10 for a retired station house turnkey he had hired as combination guard and sorter, and $10 for Ferrara and three of Ferrara's friends whose beats bordered on his. The rest — $150.02 — was clean, for none of his slips hit. None hit the second day, and he cleared $174.73. The third day he had a small payoff, $52.50 for a 15-cent slip, but he took in $193.19, and when all accounts were squared he had banked $421.13 in a small tool chest he kept under a loose board in the flooring behind his counter. He celebrated by buying a new pastel sport shirt, the kind Moss Bailey wore, at Al Kelly's neighborhood dime store.

But he was a worrier, and he had to have something to worry about, so he worried about the money. It was dangerous to leave it in the drop overnight and dangerous to take it home, for Loretta might find it there, and if she did there would be questions he could not answer. In the end he compromised. He left $100 in the tool chest and carried the rest in his pocket. That was dangerous too, but it was a way out, and he took it.

Dulcy was playing in the snow by the front stoop, gathering it up in sparkling mittenfuls and showering it upon a defenseless playmate. The playmate, a little girl, was trapped in a corner between the side of the stoop and the house front, howling bitterly, and Charlie, heaving out of Peter's car, was so concerned about her plight he missed the gathering knot of neighbors across the street and the poster men beyond them, posting.

"Princess!" he protested. "Cut that out!"

She could not hear him above the thrashing of Peter's gears. He ran up behind her and grabbed her hands, and she looked up, startled. "Daddy!" she said and waited for an explanation.

"You shouldn't ought to do that, Dulce. It isn't very nice."

The other girl had stopped sobbing and was wiping the white crust from her face and blinking at them.

"Why?" Dulcy demanded, wonderingly. She could not imagine why.

"Well, for one thing, you'll lose all your friends. Nobody'll want to play with you."

"Oh." She sounded relieved. "That don't matter. I'll get new ones, where we're moving."

"Moving? What craziness!"

"Like Mommie said we are. Just now."

"She pointed innocently past him, to the far curb, and then he turned and then he saw.

Loretta was standing with Henrietta Mathias on the edge of the little crowd, her back to him. Above and to the right of her two men in mackinaws were lashing a stenciled oilcloth sign across the front of the Stephenson house. They were nearly done. Charlie could read it easily.

TO WHOM IT MAY CONCERN:

> NOTICE IS HEREBY GIVEN BY THE MUNICIPAL ZONING BOARD THAT IT WILL HOLD A PUBLIC HEARING ON TUES. DEC. 27 AT TEN A.M. IN ROOM 424 CITY HALL ON APPEAL NO. 341-49 FOR A PERMIT TO HOUSE 4 OR MORE FAMILIES ON THESE PREMISES.

He felt a sinking inside.

"So it don't matter, does it Daddy? Does it? Does it?" She

looked up at him brightly, waiting for permission to shower her
victim again. The little girl in the trap looked fearfully from her
to Charlie.

"Go inside, kid," he said dully.

"Can she come?" Dulcy forgot her game and shifted to the
new situation.

"Sure. Both of you."

He crossed the sidewalk. As the children pattered gleefully up
the steps, Loretta turned and came to meet him. Her eyes were
wet and swollen. Henrietta, walking slowly toward her house,
was openly weeping.

"Isn't it awful?" Loretta choked. "It's just awful!"

He nodded dumbly.

"What does it mean? Oh, I don't understand! Henrietta says
we're through!"

"Sure."

They stood on the curb, facing one another in the brittle cold,
silent as the shock sunk in. Charlie was tired, and as he stood
there, haggard, a vague feeling of irresponsibility, almost of excitement, crept in under the weariness, after the shock.

"Does Mrs. Carter know?" he asked suddenly.

"Oh!" She drew a quick hand to her throat. "The poor woman.
Who's going to tell her?"

"I will. Now."

He left her wobbling her head, still confused, and went down
the sidewalk with a rapid, restless step.

Lucy was a long time answering the bell. A moment after he
rang he thought he saw a drape move upstairs, but when no one
came he decided he must be mistaken. He rang again and was
about to leave when the door swung open and she stood in its
shadow, smiling.

"Why Mr. Bond! What a nice surprise! Come in."

She was less surprised than Charlie. He stared at her costume:
crimson velvet slacks, ballet slippers, and a flowing silk blouse
stained with a hundred shades of oil paint and stretched low and

tight across her full breasts. Her hair hung in loose hanks upon all but bare shoulders.

"*Do* come in!" she laughed. "I'm getting *cold!*" She trembled with a mock shiver as he hurried in, apologizing.

"I guess I should have called. I didn't think."

"Nonsense," With a peck of her fingers she took him by the hand. "Come with me. I want to show you something."

She led him down a long hall, through an archway hung with heavy drapes and into a large and unbelievably cluttered room. There were easels everywhere, holding canvases smeared with the gayest oils and what appeared to be complete contempt for form. Strewn about on chairs and little tables were messy palettes, brushes, knives, and open tubes of paint. Charlie thought it must be a storeroom for artists' equipment. An artist might have thought it a storeroom for painters' mistakes. But it was not a storeroom at all.

"My studio!" Lucy gasped, tightening her fingers about his. "I don't often let people see this."

"Some place," Charlie said, more loudly than was necessary. He looked around the room and tried to keep his eyes from her throat and couldn't. When he looked up she was smiling.

"My painting blouse." She indicated it with her free hand. "I call it my coat of many colors."

"Say," he said, still more loudly, "that's real clever!"

She glanced away. "Most people don't understand. About my work."

"Oh, I think I do!"

"I think you do," she said throatily, taking a little step toward him and smiling up at him again. "I'm sure you do." The air was thick with perfume.

Charlie felt himself reddening. He withdrew his hand and cleared his throat. "I got something, it's not very pleasant, I'm afraid. I came here to tell you about."

"Oh, I'm sure it isn't *too* bad." He started to speak and she cut him off. "Let's go over here and sit down."

They moved along a path between easels, to an alcove hidden from the door by a wide canvas curtain. Against the curtain was a long, brocaded sofa. Before it stood a low coffee table blistered with cigarette burns.

"There is where I rest. Where I plan my work."

"It's real nice, quiet and everything."

"Very. When Kenny's in the house I simply *hide* here. He's staying at his aunt's tonight, on Belton Avenue. A party, or something."

"Say, that's a break, having her near."

"Yes. Now," she ordered, "You sit there and I'll be back in a jiffy. I'm going to stir us up a couple of martinis."

"Oh, don't ——"

"Not a word, now. Take off your things. I'll be right back."

She vanished behind the curtain and Charlie sat, trying to plan how he would tell her. He thought he would have time to think it through. He had seen a martini mixed once and remembered it took several minutes. He was therefore startled when Lucy reappeared almost immediately, carrying a tray with two brimming goblets. She leaned over to rest the tray on the coffee table and he took a sharp breath.

"Now," she said, perching beside him and handing him one. "Cheers!"

He sipped tentatively. It was ice cold. It burned in his throat like a thousand tiny razor blades, and he was about to put it back on the tray when he saw Lucy had drunk half hers. He gulped vigorously and with a mighty effort kept the gulp down.

"Mrs. Mathias was telling me your office is on Striker Street."

"Ye — es," he said cautiously. "It's down there."

"Do you know Leonard Victor?"

"Leonard Victor." He was thoughtful. "No, I'm afraid not."

"Oh, dear!" She frowned sadly. "Every time I meet someone who works on Striker Street I ask if they know Leonard. They never do. I thought you might."

They laughed mechanically. Striker Street was five miles long, lined with places of business.

The gin was reaching Charlie. He stretched and looked around and saw something gleaming on the far arm of the sofa. "What's that?" he asked, leaning forward.

Lucy turned. "Oh!" she giggled. "That." A patch of brocade was covered with gold paint. "Sometimes I have such an urge I can't wait to get to the easel. I just do whatever's near. I did that once." She sighed. "I suppose I ought to finish the whole couch, but somehow I just never do. It's so sad."

They laughed again. Lucy lifted her cocktail and finished it with one powerful swallow. Charlie drank his reluctantly, with rapid little sips, wincing. He did not remember that the other martini was as large as this.

"Now then," she said, brushing her hair back from her shoulders, "what was it you had to tell me?"

"Oh." He sat up. "It's sort of hard to say. It's pretty gloomy news."

"Gloomy?" she cocked her head. "How?"

"It's about, you know, Patecka."

"Patecka!" Her hand darted to her cheek.

He nodded. "You might say we got taken by Redsedski. Seems like the Stephensons sold, anyway."

She started, theatrically. "No. No!"

"I'm afraid yes, Mrs. Carter." He puckered miserably. "I saw the sign, the zoning sign. They just put it up."

Both Lucy's hands were on her cheeks now, and she was shaking her head and staring at him, wide-eyed. "It can't be true," she whispered huskily. Charlie started to contradict her. "It can't!" she cried. "It *can't!*" He shifted uncomfortably and studied the coffee table and noticed a small square of green on one leg.

She began to tremble. The fluttering started in her fingers and crept up her arms, and when it reached her shoulders she broke down spectacularly, shaking with great sobs, the tears running swiftly down her cheeks and spotting her blouse.

"Jees," he said wretchedly. "I'm awful sorry."

He forgot he was losing as much as she.

"Oh!" She lifted her face dramatically and threw her quivering hands toward him. "I'm ruined!" she wailed, "ruined! ruined!"

"Now, now," he stuttered. "There, there."

He reached out to pat one of her hands, and as he did she threw herself across the couch with a little moan, into his lap, into his unprepared arms. He felt her breasts flatten against his thin chest and her strong hands clutching his shoulder blades and smelled her tossing hair.

"Oh, Charlie!" she wept, racking them both with fresh sobs, "help me!"

"Now, now, There, there."

She laid her wet cheek against his new shirt, staining it with mascara. He stroked her hair with an uncertain hand, and as he did she leaned heavily against him and they sprawled full length along the seat.

"Help me," she whispered, stroking his stroking hand, "help me."

He dressed awkwardly and painfully — awkwardly, for he was still deep in his coma, and painfully, because Lucy was sitting in the corner of the couch with her bare legs folded under her, combing her tangled hair lazily and watching him.

He had thought she would dress, too. He thought she ought to. But she had not. From the gorgeous jungle of her studio she had brought a brief smock and drawn it on casually, smiling at his furtive glances. It was worse than nothing, for it covered nothing. If she had buttoned it, it would have helped, but she had deliberately drawn it back and tucked the edges under her arms and settled in the pose of a peaceful cat.

He shoved his shirttail between his bony legs and buttoned his trousers hurriedly, avoiding her eyes.

"Going so soon?" Her voice rippled like a muscle. "We've only had one drink."

Up went the comb, and back, in a long and telling stroke.

He buckled his belt rapidly. "I got to go home," he stammered.

Then he tasted the acid in his mouth and remembered. "Jees! I haven't even had supper yet!"

"You ate here. Your wife won't mind. We talked about the Stephenson house and decided what we would do."

"Say!" he brightened. "That's right." He looked around for his hat. Lucy stretched a naked arm behind the couch and produced it, but when he reached for it she crumpled it coyly under her chin.

"But we haven't," she said.

His hand dropped. "Haven't what?"

"Talked. Or decided."

"What?" Charlie said stupidly.

"About the Stephenson house."

"Oh! The Stephenson house." He nodded, knowingly, and then stopped with a jolt. "What about it?"

She rose and padded out into the studio. He hoped she would bring clothes, but in a moment she returned with matches and cigarettes.

"Here." She sat and tossed him a cigarette. He caught it clumsily. "Sit down. Relax." She lit hers and dropped the matches on the table and inhaled quickly. "We've got a lot to talk about."

He fumbled with the matches and watched, fascinated, as she blew twin blue ropes of smoke through her nose. Charlie had never seen a woman do that. He had never thought he would see Lucy Carter do it. Or drink a cocktail, for that matter. Or hear her call him by his first name. Then he remembered and sat down.

She unfolded her legs and thrust them out straight before her. Her toes brushed the edge of his trousers pocket, and he looked around desperately for another place to sit. There was none. "Honest, Lucy." He puffed frantically. "Honestly, I got to go. Loretta is probably crazy wondering where I am."

"Call her and tell her you're staying to supper, comforting me."

"But I been here, I don't know how long."

"Comforting me," she continued, smoking languidly and cradling her elbow in her free hand, "and discussing the Stephenson house."

"But what is there to discuss?" he protested. "It's finished!"

She shook her head vigorously and killed the cigarette on the tabletop. He watched her with growing uneasiness, wishing she would either button the smock or take it off. "That's what they think," she said, waving her arm in a careless sweep. "The rest of the block. *We* know differently."

He gulped and nodded, wondering if he should squash his cigarette on the coffee table as she had. There seemed to be no other place.

"We know we can beat Patecka," Lucy said slowly. "After all, the zoning board hasn't acted yet."

"Well." He worried the back of his neck with a moist hand. "That's all settled, isn't it?"

"Settled?" She was arch. "Settled?"

"I mean fixed. That's what I thought."

"It *can* be fixed, Charlie."

"I mean, I heard they always go Patecka's way. Always approve it."

"It can go another way. Our way."

"It can?"

"Yes, darling. It can."

"Jees. That would be terrific." His cigarette was very short, and he extinguished it hurriedly in the table varnish, singeing his fingers. "How?"

"I have a friend very close to one of the members."

"Say! That's a break." He wondered if it really were.

"The board can be bought, Charlie."

"Bought?"

"With money."

"Oh," he said weakly. "Sure."

She drew one leg up and hugged it, resting her chin on her knee. "Don't you think you'd better call Loretta, darling?" she asked softly. "She might worry."

"I think — I guess I ought to, yes."

"The phone's in the front hall. I'll go find us another hair of that *wonderful* dog!"

She danced out, laughing.

Charlie stumbled through the studio, feeling bad about Loretta and worse about himself. For a moment he had been a man, consoling a real woman, giving her the real business. And now it turned out she had been giving him the business, and he had bought and he would pay. He would. He knew himself well enough to know he would. He had her, and she, she and Patecka, had him.

When he returned the glasses were filled, and beside them a tall pitcher was brimming and cold without ice. Lucy was sitting in the exact center of the couch, applying lipstick. He noticed with relief that her smock was buttoned.

But as he sat beside her she swung her legs to the far end of the seat and laid her head in his lap. "What did she say?" she asked.

"She said all right. She's pretty upset, about everything."

"Of course." She drew one of the goblets from the table and handed it to him unspilled. "Now. Let me tell you what *I* think."

Loretta and Henrietta were in the front room, going over the awful details once more, when Charlie entered the front hall, unaware of the time and only vaguely aware of the hall.

"That you, hon?"

"Home at last," he muttered with magnificent control. He edged down the carpet on tiptoe, bracing himself against the walls. Outside the portieres, under the light from Loretta's bridge lamp, he ruefully inspected his rumpled clothing.

"How's Mrs. Carter?" Loretta called.

"She is very unhappy." He drew his lips back and clipped each syllable carefully. "She does not know what she is going to do."

"Who does?" Henrietta moaned.

"What're you doing out there?" Loretta demanded. "Come in here."

"I am going to bed. I feel sick."

"It's enough to make anybody sick," Henrietta declared, beginning once again her review of Stephenson's fraud. "They certainly had *me* fooled. *I* never suspected for one minute. Did you?" Loretta had not. "Of course not. Nobody did. How could they? And all that money for Redsedski! No wonder he acted funny taking it! Well, we're cooked now. It just goes to show. You never can tell . . ."

Charlie went up the stairs slowly, holding the banister with both hands. He rested twice, once at the landing and once at the top, gathering himself for the great effort. In the bedroom he closed the door and leaned against it, breathing heavily. For an instant, before he concentrated on the problem of undressing, he had a vision of Lucy as he had left her, sitting tailor fashion on the floor with her head lolling against the sofa, clutching the empty pitcher to her stark and faintly bruised bosom, giggling foolishly and watching him with her terribly bright eyes as he stared with final regret at the bills strewn along the tabletop — enough, she had said, to buy his share of the first board member, but only the first. Charlie wondered fuzzily how many there were, and how much they would cost, and whether he was being taken.

Then he put all that aside and began the long fumble with his coat, his suit, his shirt, his shoes and socks, and his underwear. He hung everything but the underwear in the closet, and wadded that into a little bundle and thrust it in his coat pocket. Naked now and in order, he pulled on his pajamas, tottered across the room, fell on the bed, and crawled under the cold flat sheets. He squinted at the clock: 10:30. Early to bed. He switched out the light and turned his head into the pillow with a grunt.

At one o'clock he was awake and thirsty. He left Loretta sleeping and drank two glasses of water in the bathroom. At two o'clock he was awake and sick. He lay on his back for several minutes, feeling the little black pool form in his stomach, and then went into the bathroom again. He was there fifteen minutes, and when he came back he could not sleep. He was up at three o'clock and again at four. Each time he was violently ill, each time he sneaked back to bed in elaborate quiet, with alarmed little glances at his wife. At last, toward five o'clock, he slipped into a deep sleep. He was snoring when the alarm rang.

The sun rose.

The dawn shadows withered away and the first men, the early arrivals, drifted up the street and leaned against the brick building, smoking, silent and beaten by the early hour. Across the cobblestones, parked bumper to bumper, were twelve green packer trucks, each with the legend "Help Make This the Cleanest City in the Nation" lettered in white on its side. This was the West Garage fleet. These were the men of West Garage, the grimy, slogging infantrymen of the Bureau of Sanitation.

The sidewalk filled quickly, like a parade ground before roll call, and soon there was no space left at the wall. The latecomers sat on the curb, their shoulders hunched forward, watching the cold silver sunlight wash up the street. Some milled about uncertainly, waiting for orders. One in a peaked cap straddled the fire hydrant at the corner and glowered. "Same old crappo," he muttered to a light-skinned black on the curb. "Always late startin'. Always."

"Yuh," spat Lou Dunton. "They doan care."

Every morning the same litany.

Snake lit a cigarette ferociously. "Soon as I get mysef a spare buck I'm gonna get me a little tool shop, know what I mean?"

"Yuh," Lou spat again. "In business by yoursef, oney way to be."

"As if you get a spare buck here."

"Yuh." He sprayed the drain at his feet. "Never get it here."

Every morning. The same chant.

Up the walk in his overcoat and overshoes and funny hat, with his long, flat-footed stride, came Sam. They nodded curtly and he nodded back, a duty nod, for he was bad company in the morning until he had that slip under his sweatband.

Lou looked up curiously. "Got um all picked?"

"Uh-huh."

"New system?" Snake sneered.

Sam ignored him. He did not mind Lou, for Lou played the numbers now and then and understood. But Snake never played; he only laughed.

The garage had no door: the entrance was like a cave. It went back, a pit of darkness. In the pit was the office where the drivers met each morning for assignment. Voices floated from there now, and a knot of men moved into the pale light, a wedge of authority led by a dark, bareheaded man in an outsized brown sweater.

The bareheaded man headed for a space on the curb, and three blacks who had been sitting there scampered away quickly. Mr. Casey was superintendent of West Garage. Where Mr. Casey chose to stand he stood.

Under his bleary eye the crews gathered by their drivers, and when the gathering was done he spoke.

"I got reports," he reported, "some of you been getting careless. Nothing serious, but I don't want to hear nothing else like that. We been eighteen days without a truck run over a can. First truck run over a can gets double duty, day after Christmas." He paused and the men waited with respect. "Now don't be careless, boys." He paused again and then added, "One other thing. Way I get it, there's a lot of policy around here. Now I know nobody here gets mixed up in anything like that." They shook their heads vigorously. "But I got my orders, any man gets caught in policy, out he goes. Understand?" More nodding. Casey thought for a moment and then snapped, "That's all." He went back into the cave alone.

Sam saw Snake leering. He ran up to Joe, who was walking away swiftly. "What's he talkin' about, boss?" he asked anxiously. Joe kept walking toward the truck, and Sam followed. "What's he mean?" he persisted.

"Means just what he says, I guess."

Joe swung into the cab and slammed the door, avoiding Sam's eyes. He had been badly scared. This was the only job he had ever had. He would not know how to get another.

"But boss! I got a zinger today, boss!"

Joe switched on the ignition. "Better lay off, Sam. Bad business, policy, I'm through with it. Anyway, we can't stop at West Concord no more."

Sam was stunned. "Jest today," he pleaded. But Joe shook his head.

It was Sam's day to ride in the cab, and he climbed in arguing while Lou and Snake mounted the steep steps in the back and braced themselves against the sloping tailgate. He argued all the way out Crone Street, as the truck rumbled toward the suburbs. Ordinarily his position would have been strong, for Joe played the numbers as heavily as he. But last week he had borrowed from him, and he had nothing but his everlasting hope of winning to pay him back. He mentioned this once, timidly. Joe dismissed it lightly. "A few bucks, a buck here, a buck there, square it," he said.

The argument reached a peak at West Concord and Horrigan, where Sam usually jumped out to bet for them both. Then it died. Sam sunk back listlessly. "Mebbe I find a place at lunch," he said.

"I wouldn't, Sam. I really wouldn't. Mr. Casey's all against it. You heard him."

He turned down a side street and then into an alley. Garages and back yards faced the alley, and behind each yard stood a cluster of galvanized iron cans, loaded for collection.

The truck stopped. Sam leapt out. Snake and Lou sprang from the tailgate and the three of them swarmed over the beaten snow of the alley, dragging the cans to the truck as it drifted forward and dumping them inside. Snake and Lou worked the sides, heaving their garbage into square openings in the body. The hopper was Sam's. He filled it quickly and then shoved the lever beside it, watching the hydraulic gate sweep the withered orange peels and broken eggshells into the bowels of the packer. The motor growled as the trash was ground forward. Then the gate moved back and its lid flew up suddenly.

The lid could be dangerous. If it hit you it could split your face open. Most of the men did not like it, but Sam did. He liked to stand very close, letting it fan his face as it snapped by.

"Golly damn," Lou panted in the fifth alley, wiping his face. "Hardly started and I'm wore out already. Spell me, Sam."

"Spell yoursef," Sam muttered. "I'm wore out, too."

Lou looked at him in surprise and turned reluctantly to another yard. "You wait," he said lamely. "You jest wait."

He tired easily, and usually Sam would cover his side for him while he rested, for he was strong and did not mind the work. But this morning Sam was ugly. The number he wanted kept racing through his mind, and the quarter tugged at his pocket, and he was tortured by the thought that the number might come in and leave him with his quarter and his lost chance.

Snake watched, his red eyes cunning under his greasy visor. "Hey Sam," he called across the truck. "What's the number today, Sam?"

Joe stuck his grizzled head out the window. "How many times I got to tell you to leave him alone?"

Snake's lip curled. "You want I should tell Casey who's a big policy man I know?"

The head darted back.

"Tell me, Sam," Snake taunted. "Tell me that number."

Lou joined in, bitter. "Yah, yah, yah," he chanted with his short breath. "Gimme the hot dope, hipgee, whatsa word today?" He stopped, exhausted, and Snake began again.

"Wotta man! Sits back, thinks hard, says now we take *this* one today, and *that* one tomorrow. Just like that, no strain, no pain. Only trouble is, this one don't come in, that one don't come in, they don't none of them never come in."

He laughed brutally, stuffing a wad of paper into the side port.

Sam bulled his way from can to can, dogged and silent. A housewife, late with her trash, raced through her yard, arms bulging with wastebaskets. But he did not wait for her. He dumped her nearly empty can and went on, and when she called to him to come back, he turned his back contemptuously. She stalked back angrily and slammed her kitchen door. Joe watched her in his rear-view mirror and hoped she would not make a complaint. He wished now he had stopped on West Concord.

Snake was glad he had not, for Sam had never been so easy. "Hey Lou!" he cried, holding up limp wrists, posing as an elf. "Look! I got a winner, thunk it up all by myself!"

Lou's laughter was forced. He was completely winded. Joe thrust his head out the window again and glared at Snake. "All right, bright boy, look sharp now, we got plenty to do."

Sam was furious. He ran at a loaded twenty gallon can, tackled it with his shoulder, and half carried, half dragged it across the filthy snow to the truck, scattering banana skins and broken bones along the way. Lou paused, puffing, and hailed Snake.

"Hey!" he panted gleefully. "Look! We doan have to be careful, we thinkers."

"Sure," Snake snorted. "Like I say, we thunk up a winner. Only thing is, we got no slip on it."

A dirty cloud blotted out the sun, shadows vanished, and in the dull light they moved across the street to the next alley. Sam walked behind the others, his chest quivering and his face curiously tight, as though the muscles in his face were controlled by a drawstring someone had pulled.

He was wrestling with the wedged top of the huge iron can when Snake, leaning against the tailgate and squeezing a pimple in the cleft of his chin, decided upon a new attack.

"Think what you could do with all that dough, Sammy," he called. "Hey, Sammy! Sammy! SAMMY! Just think ——"

He ducked in time. The can top, wrenched free with sudden strength, left Sam's hand spinning viciously toward his head. It missed narrowly and crashed against the truck side with a sharp ring and then fell to a patch of ice and lay there, clattering loudly.

Joe yanked the emergency brake and jumped out. Snake crouched where he had dropped, and Lou stood motionless on the far side. The three of them stared at Sam, dazed, and he, with the topless can before him like a barricade, looked back with flat hatred.

"Doan ever call me that," he said so low they could scarcely hear him, "unlessen you want to get yoursef killed."

227

The alley was very still. Somewhere a window slid up and a woman looked out quickly and then vanished. Joe and Lou looked numbly from Sam to Snake and back to Sam again.

Snake smiled weakly. The pimple on his chin was bleeding a little, and he brushed the blood away with his slimy hand. Another drop oozed out, bright and beady and smooth. He rose from his haunches, sweating in the cold air.

"Sure. Okay. You bet." In the bags of his grimy pants his knees were shaking. "You bet," he repeated and wet his lips. The bead of blood broke, staining a bristle of beard.

"Ride up front," Joe told him. "We'll take this one slow." Sam stepped out from behind his barricade, and Joe added, "It don't matter. We got plenty of time."

Lou turned up the alley with a frightened step, and Sam picked up the can and heaved it into the hopper with a swift, powerful motion, and they worked across the suburb in silence.

SAMMY!
  Down the corridor of years
SAMMY!
  People are laughing
SAMMY!
  Watch . . . that . . . STICK!

Every morning was the same: fighting his way to school through flailing arms, his eyes squeezed shut and his stomach a knot of cold and twisted flesh.

They were always waiting for him on the narrow corner by the drugstore, where the sidewalk was crossed with their hopscotch lines and the rusty old telephone pole sagged.

And the trembling would begin when he left his front door coughing and holding his brown paper lunch bag before him like a shield — the trembling that shook him past the A & P and Harry's Pool Parlor, until he slumped forward, starting his run, when he heard the first cry:

"Here he comes!"

"Swat him, Eve! Swat him!"

"Lou*ise!* Slam him!"

"Sissy Sammy! Sissy Sammy!"

Through an ambush of bookbags and forked sticks he ran, head down, smelling their grape chewing gum and their young sweat, watching their brown legs twinkle under short calico skirts, staggering under the thudding blows until he reached the school steps sick and aching and ashamed.

Hate um Hate um Hate um . . .

A little boy, building a hate. Building it every morning. Polishing it and setting it before him as he lay nude in the corner of his mother's bed after the ritual of her caressing fingers was done and she lay asleep. Watching it grow and shaping it until it bent to reach around corners like a twisted poker, touching everyone near him with its hot poison — his teachers, the neighborhood tradesmen, the people in the flat downstairs, the father he never knew.

Sam was a bastard, the first and last child of Hattie Crawford, a charwoman with a hideous birthmark that covered her face. The birthmark had ruined Hattie's life. Her family never accepted her and pushed her out before she was sixteen, and the janitor in the office building where she worked would not have her around during the day. She worked nights and lived alone. She knew almost nothing of men until her twentieth year. Then a watchman raped her at work. Because of her ignorance the pregnancy was undiscovered until its fourth month. By then the man had disappeared. She bore Sam in a free clinic and nursed him nights in the office building between scrubbings.

Her devotion to him was absolute. She gave him her total self, caring for him through an endless series of childhood diseases, saving him tenderly — and destroying what she saved. For Sam's fatherlessness was central. If there had been a father there would have been love, not for him, but for Hattie, and, through her, for others. Without a father, without the shading and the framing he would have brought, Sam's love lost its channel and was bent in a strange direction, over twisted slopes, into a wild and hopeless country. It died there, dried by the eternal sun of his mother. It left a rut, a scar ugly and incurable on the face of Sam's life.

Without a father, without a capacity for love, without an inkling of what real love was, he grew from a frail, shy childhood into an unbalanced boyhood and was lost. Hattie, who never grasped his essential problem or even that there was one, thought him an ideal son, dutiful and supremely affectionate. The neighbors, unaware that an everlastingly obedient child is a tragedy, agreed.

Desperately, unconsciously, Sam tried to fill the awful void with fantastic dreams.

On a shelf above the kitchen sink Hattie kept a tin bank for pennies, and when the bank was full they would ride to Rogers Park on the next sunny Sunday. Sam liked the pond best. He would stand before the black guardrail, his hand in hers, reverently watching the graceful geese.

"Looka the big one, Sam."

"Uh-huh."

"Looka them wings."

"Clean, Ma."

"Clean an white an pretty."

He would stare until his mind was a dizzy blur of soft white feathers, and riding home, dozing on the trolley seat, resting in that gentle blur, he would hear, far away and hardly there at all, the broken peal of wild church bells. Afterwards, lying in bed and waiting for Monday, his head would ache. Sometimes his nose would bleed.

And in the morning:

"Harder, Sal, harder!"

"Use your *feet!* Your *feet!*"

"SAAAMMIEEEE! SISSY SAAAMMIEEEE!"

Adolescence deepened the flaw. All other loves could be simulated in the strange dream chambers of his mind, but not love of another sex, for he did not know what that was. The lost frame, the absence of all shade, were telling now; he knew only the sun, the dazzling white light, and in a world where the thin line of shadow was everything, he faltered and went down.

Sam could have been broken in many ways. He could have been completely destroyed as a functioning animal, and if he had been thrown with boys this would probably have happened. But he was struck down, not by boys but by girls exploring their own flowering with the savagery of the early teens, baiting this frail whelp other boys scorned, this wasted, scared mite whose fondlings with his mother could not, in a congested block where families slept summer nights on fire escapes, be kept secret. The heckling schoolhouse gauntlet of short-skirted figures lashing at his groin determined the pattern of his hostility. In those months the instrument of his perversion was fashioned.

Hattie began to worry about him. He was so puny and ill and so sunken in his dreams he seemed lost from her. Then, in his fifteenth year, she did lose him for ten months; a school doctor examined him and ordered him hospitalized with tuberculosis. He came back strong and healthy, his sickness behind him, and in another year he was a young brute. The girls had forgotten and were interested. But Sam had not forgotten. In his stump of a mind he remembered fiercely. On a street, in a schoolroom, at a movie — but especially on a street — short skirts and thin legs brought back the trembling, the knot of cold flesh in his belly.

Through the middle teens his hatred lay on the floor of his consciousness like firedamp in a mine shaft, too concentrated to admit outside force. By his eighteenth year it had thinned to almost classic consistency.

That June he went to work as a hospital orderly. He was a model worker and, to his mother, a model son. Each month he brought her his pitiful salary, and she planned a home for them in the city. For nearly a year there was no trouble. Then one evening the following spring a policeman leaving the hospital's emergency room heard a child shrieking. He crossed the street and found that Sam had pinned a little black girl against a fence and was slapping her with the edges of his rigid, knifelike hands. The child's clothing was torn. Sam's eyes were glazed and he was breathing heavily. At the station house he remembered nothing. He was charged with simple assault and sentenced to two years in the House of Correction.

After a month the balance of the sentence was suspended and he was put on probation. The hospital would not take him back. He hung around the emergency room, jobless, draining his mother's slender hoard and begging the nurses to give him work. They could not do it. The director had forbidden it. But they liked him, for he was a willing worker, and in time they found him a job.

One fierce summer afternoon when July was melting into August a black doctor brought an old man, a diabetic, to the hospital in a coma. The man needed long custodial care, and there were no beds for black people there. As soon as the patient was well enough to move, the resident explained, they must go elsewhere. The black hospital was crowded, and so the doctor decided to take the old man into his own home. He would need help there, the nurses reminded him. They suggested Sam.

So Sam was hired. The doctor, whose name was Finch, had a large practice but seldom collected his fees. He supported his family with a small truck farm behind the house. He also maintained a large chicken house, and it seemed to Sam he ate more chicken his first month with the Finches than in all his life until then.

In a small, listing shack behind the chicken house he lived with a bed, a creaking old chair, and a dresser with a cracked mirror. He seldom went home. In the beginning the separation from his mother was almost unbearable, but he liked the work, and the doctor liked him. So did the doctor's daughter, a high-breasted girl who was janitor in the neighborhood school.

Pellie Finch set her sights on Sam the day he arrived. He was unpacking his cardboard suitcase when she came in, barefooted and disturbing in a long cotton shirt. Half the shirt's buttons were unbuttoned, and when she sat in the creaking chair he could see one chocolate breast.

"You sholey doan have much baggage, Sam," she laughed. "Not hardly enough clothes there to keep you warm when it get cold."

He tried to look away.

"Guess you won't need much if it stay this hot." She sprawled in the chair and feigned a yawn, forcing the shirt open wider.

He fumbled frantically with the suitcase.

She rose and pranced out. Five minutes later he followed her to the house and went to the bathroom.

At supper her mother scolded her over the cold chicken. "Seems as though you girls doan wear nothin' any more. It's a scandal."

Pellie hung her head. A moment later, when her mother was not looking, she grinned at Sam across the table, her even teeth flashing in the kitchen light.

That night she came to him in the shack. She wore spiked heels and a silk dress even shorter than the fashion then, and she smelled of cheap perfume.

"Fella lahk you," she said, curling up in the chair, "must a had a lot of fun with them white nurses in that place."

He squatted on the bed, carefully sharpening his razor, a fetish with him since he first shaved. "They wasn't too bad," he lied.

"Down where I wuhk they's a white man, a teacher, an we wrassle sometimes." She laughed coarsely. "I doan wrassle good."

He shifted his trembling legs. "I'm a pretty good wrassler."

She swung her legs over the chair arm, forcing her skirt back, and rolled her eyes. There was an awful silence. He could not move.

Then she walked over to the bed and leaned over until he could smell her strong sweat. "C'mon," she said huskily. "Let's wrassle, Sam."

They twisted for an hour in the late August twilight until exhaustion overcame them and they fell back gasping. But nothing happened. Pellie undressed herself and half undressed him,

233

but each time she flattened her belly against his he broke away. She left, disgusted, without a word.

The following evening he drew her to the back porch. "Wrassle?" he whispered excitedly.

She looked at him with contempt.

"No fun. You always win."

"Mebbe I won't try so hahd."

They were in the shack five hours.

She was the first woman to throw naked sex at him and it overwhelmed him. It; not her. As a person, Pellie scarcely existed for him. She brought him sex, not the love he needed. If there had been even a vein of tenderness in her approach he would have been unmoved, as the colorblind are unmoved by twilight.

In three months she told him she was pregnant.

With the next breath, she announced they would be married, and, with the one after that, that they would live at home. Sam did not argue. Nor did the Finches argue. Sam moved into the house from his shack. He still ate chicken six days a week and still worked as orderly. He even helped the doctor when Pellie's baby was born.

The baby was a girl.

The doctor told Sam he must not expect anything from Pellie for a few weeks — "till she gets healed."

Sam's face crinkled. "Not nothin' at all?"

"No, Sam." Dr. Finch suffered from palsy. He gestured oddly with his shaking hands. "Not for a while."

The Finches, and especially Pellie, were outraged three months later when Mary Whyte, a small, worried widow living in the next block, swore out a bastardy warrant naming Sam.

"Doan tell me it's so!" Pellie shouted. "I doan believe it!"

Sam went about his work with the doctor — whose palsy rapidly became so bad it nearly destroyed his paying practice — and ignored her questions as he ignored her baby. When Mrs. Whyte's bastardy case came up he admitted paternity and was ordered to pay five dollars a week for the support of the child.

The following week he enlisted in the army.

"But you're a pa!" Pellie yelled.

"It's a war," he mumbled. "Draft get me."

The draft would not have reached him for another year, but their marriage was ruined. Pellie did not know why. Sam did not. He only knew that since the arrival of their infant daughter a link, a bond, a meaning had been lost. He had to get away.

He was assigned to a salvage company in a nearby camp and could have come home every week end if he wished. He chose not to. In the three years which followed Pellie saw him but once. In 1943 he spent a wild seventy-two-hour pass with her. The fruit of this was a second baby girl. Pellie had to write his commanding officer to increase the allotment.

When she wrote she missed him, he replied he was busy with the war.

She was therefore surprised when military policemen called on her early in 1945 and reported he was absent without leave.

He was found hiding in his mother's flat, court-martialed, and confined for six months.

He came home with a blue discharge.

To their two daughters, Pellie had added a third. "Never mind how she come here, she here, same as yore little boy, he there with Miz Whyte."

And they were relentlessly little girls, all three, playing with dolls, strutting about in their mother's clothes, chasing two kittens Dr. Finch had brought them.

Sam wanted to rest. He thought it his right. "Jest lemme lay down, take it easy for a few weeks."

But he had never paid Mary Whyte her support allowance, and his army immunity was gone, and he had no money. She complained to the State's Attorney. The matter of his delinquency brought him to Criminal Court, where he was ordered to pay her the five dollars a week and two and a half more on his arrears or go to jail.

The doctor could not hire him again. He had abandoned his

practice and retired. "I know," he agreed, his head wobbling wildly as he tried to nod it. "The law say I got to take you back. But I got no money, Sam, no more'n you."

Pellie went to work as a maid. She received four dollars a day and carfare and took the money to Mary Whyte herself, for she did not trust Sam. "I wonder," she laughed bitterly, "if I got had worsen her."

Sam himself found nothing. He really did not try. He lay each day on the concave bed in their disorderly room, reading comic books while the children toddled in and out, shouting at one another and teasing the kittens. He seethed. And waited. For trouble.

It came. But the day was a Wednesday. Pellie's day off, and since she had arranged to take the children to a clinic, there was only the old doctor downstairs, gently rocking in his starched shirt and choker collar and reading the paper, when Sam was awakened by the kittens fighting on the bed.

He snapped out of his strange dream and lunged across the mattress and missed them and kept going. The doctor heard a crash, a thud, and then a volley of tiny explosions he knew was Pellie's perfume bottles smashing to the floor. He started up the stairs, running a trembling hand along the banister and peering up curiously. Then he saw and stopped.

Sam was crouched in the upper hall with his back to the stairwell. He had stalked the kittens to a corner. They were huddled by a table, trapped, and he could have plucked them to him, but he was waiting, silent and tense, gently swaying on the balls of his feet and weaving his arms in sinister, rhythmic patterns, slowly closing in. The doctor couldn't see his hands and didn't want to. He quietly backed down the stairwell and sat on the peeling imitation leather sofa his patients had once used. He was an old man. He knew his mind was failing. He didn't understand what he had seen, and he wasn't really sure he had seen it. He felt dizzy and closed his eyes, and as he did the racket began again upstairs.

There was a sharp scrape, the kittens screamed, and suddenly

236

pictures and vases were falling and smashing, chairs were splintering, dresser drawers were being flung about in a rising crescendo of noise. The doctor sat on the couch, listening to the din and squeezing his eyes shut and shaking his head, frightened and confused.

Pellie was long at the clinic. She always was. It was free to the poor and open only for them, and no one really cared whether it ran well or not. When she returned with the children, Sam was gone.

Her father was still on the sofa in the front hall. He hadn't moved. "Gone," he said shakily as she came in. "Ten, mebbe fifteen minutes ago."

Sam had thrown his clothes into his army barracks bag, scooted past the couch, and vanished out the back door, shaking his head when the doctor started to speak and breaking into a flat-footed run, disappearing into the back yard among the startled chickens.

Pellie sank to the sofa, furiously chewing her lip. Then she threw her arms around the old man's neck and wept. The children milled about, trying to climb into her lap and bumping into one another. The tears were wilting the old man's collar. He told her to wait and went upstairs for a handkerchief.

In Pellie's room he found the kittens dead, hanging above the wreckage, suspended from the chandelier by her only pair of nylons.

Six weeks later the police picked Sam up and charged him with desertion. The doctor would not have had him in the house again even if he had agreed to return, and Pellie divorced him. The court awarded her twelve dollars a week. To pay it Sam lied about his war record and got a job with the city.

The following week he became a steady player of the numbers game.

And the month after that he met Lottie and married her.

She knew about Pellie and Mary Whyte, but she accepted the past as she had her father's illness, as a condition life laid down for the Lotties of the world, within which happiness must be found. And he, quiet again and outwardly normal, remained faithful to her, devoted to the children that came, a stable, loyal worker in the West Garage crew.

Lottie's only real regret was that he would not abandon policy. If she had understood him she would have forgotten that, for the even level of his new life lay delicately suspended between two pins, and one was the racket clocking his emotions, giving them one day at a time, holding his child's mind in an endless seesaw of elation and despair.

The other was Lottie. Because he was a child for whom sex was only a game, he needed a very special kind of wife who would mother him when the game was over and he, childlike, was tired and wanted only comfort and security. And Lottie, who had grown up ruling a house of men, was unconsciously that — the only adult in their home, the only parent. Sam loved his children, but not with a father's love. He would play with Peter Paul by the hour, giggling delightedly; yet if the little boy misbehaved, he could not correct him; he would complain resentfully to Lottie, and she would settle it. His son adored him, but he really thought of him as another, larger child. And he was right. That was what Sam was. He was a very large child with the tempered muscles of a brute and a restless savagery in his heart and an old, childhood hatred burning deep within him.

It was Lou's day to help with the noon load, but Sam went in his place. That was Joe's idea. When the truck was full he opened his door and peered back.

"Hey Sam! Wanna ride over to the fire with me?" He winked with one whole side of his face.

"Might as well, I guess. Whatsa time?"

"Quarter of twelve."

There would be time.

They left the others in a neighborhood firehouse and drove back toward West Concord. Sam felt better now. He was like a child going to a party. "I got a feelin'," he confided. "Today's a day for me."

"Hunches are good sometimes," Joe said cautiously.

He could not deny Sam his play, for the thought that the number might come in terrified him. But he was thankful the day's trash was light, for he did not want to be with Sam, nor did he want Snake around, when Sam learned he had lost.

The slope of Crone Street was bound with ice, and he edged down it carefully. A black boy in a stocking cap was sliding ahead of them. Joe swore under his breath.

Sam chuckled. "Buy that boy a real sled if'n I see him tomorrow."

"You want to go by Charlie's?"

Sam thought. Charlie, noticing he was late, might ask for an explanation, and it was not considered lucky to talk to writers of personal matters. "Lemme off here, I know a place."

Three minutes later he ducked off the sidewalk and ran down the stairs of a basement shoeshine parlor. Inside, a huge black woman in a gray sweat suit was nailing steel taps in work boots. "Yessah," she said without looking up.

"I got action," he said, grinning broadly and brandishing his quarter.

"You get no action here, Bo." She went on hammering.

He looked grave. "I ain't foolin'. I got two bits say number ——"

"I doan care what your two bits say, ain't you read the papers?"

"Papers!" Contemptuously. "What I wanta read a paper for?"

"Numbers is hot, boy. We is outa business." She dropped the finished boot into a wooden bin and picked up another. "You get no action here."

Sam was angry. "I'll tell Mr. Bond on you and yo' no action. He a mean man when he get mad."

She laughed heavily. "Boy, you jest doan know nothin', not nothin'. Mr. Bond, he ain't with a bank no more, he ain't got nothin' for to be mean *with*." She pounded the new tap viciously.

Sam gaped. "He doan take bets no more?"

"He take bets, but not for no bank. Bank man tole me, so I *know*. He in business for hisself. We is *outa* business."

"Jest the same, I'm gonna tell him."

"Go on," she said scornfully. "Tell him."

He slammed the door and half ran down the street, trying to make sense out of what she had said. There was none that he could see, and he gave it up. To Sam, Charlie was the bank and the bank Charlie.

It was a short distance. The Consolidated plant's noon whistle was just ending as he turned into the sour smell of West Concord and trotted into Charlie's drop.

The store had changed. The pinball machine was gone, the shelves were stocked with several thousand cans of tomatoes, all the same brand, and under a sickly light Charlie, the complete grocer, was grimly cordial in a new white apron.

"Good morning, good morning." He spread his hands on the worn linoleum and drummed his fingers, waiting. "You're a little late today, I see."

Sam stared about in awe. The tomato cans fascinated him. He had never seen so many in one place. The woman had been right, then. Something had happened to Mr. Bond. Sam wondered if it were something unlucky. He teetered on his heels, confused.

Charlie scowled. "Something I can do for you?"

Everyone who had come in that morning had noticed the cans, and it was beginning to annoy him. He had come down West Concord that morning with a wretched headache and bought them on an impulse, with the thought of improving his front. He had tried to get an assortment, but he needed a grocer's license to buy wholesale, and the A & P man had only these to spare.

He wondered uneasily if the Elbow were talking about him. "Something you want?" he said again, almost threateningly.

Sam tore his eyes from the shelves and gulped. "I hear you in a little trouble, Mr. Bond," he said, really worried now about his chances.

"No trouble, no trouble at all." But there was. Moss Bailey had been in the Elbow the day before, and of Charlie's subwriters only Ollie was left, and he would have deserted too, if Annie had not been in the bar when Moss gave the order.

"Well ——" Sam hesitated.

"Same business," Charlie said temptingly. "You want action or no?"

"I guess." He slapped the coin on the counter.

Charlie produced a K-book. "Quarter on what?"

Sam wet his lips with a rolling tongue. This was the best part. "I b'lieve, I jest b'lieve I'll take eight-six-eight. It come in today, my system say."

"Oh?" Systems always interested Charlie. Underneath he was convinced there really was a system to the racket, that someday someone would find it and ruin him.

"Yessah. Bible system, best they is."

Charlie scribbled the slip, his interest gone. He was no less credulous than his customers, but his superstitions were different. He thought of the racket breaker not as a magician but as a mathematical wizard — a certified public accountant, perhaps.

"Name?"

Sam told him, watching the fast writing hand with admiration.

Charlie tore out the carbon, pushed it across the linoleum, and slipped the original under the counter. At that moment the door opened and an old man came in. Sam looked up suspiciously.

"This is the sergeant," Charlie said and tried to remember Sam's name, the name he had just written, to introduce him. He could not. He never could; they were faces and hands, faces and hands that came and paid and went away. "I don't think you met the sergeant."

"Hullo." Sam was wary.

The old man nodded and went behind the counter. He was small and bald, with a thin sunken chest and a big paunch, and under his coat, on the blouse of his woolen slack suit, he wore a cheap new badge marked Special Officer.

The sergeant had never been a sergeant, or even a patrolman, but he had been on the force thirty years as a turnkey. His name was Winkler. Charlie had hired Winkler at the suggestion of Joe Ferrara. Ferrara pointed out that he had to spend most of his time checking parked cars, and that with no bank behind him,

Charlie would need full-time protection. Besides, Winkler could sort slips.

It was about all he could do. Charlie regarded the old man with faint disdain as he came around the counter, the pale light flickering along the pink and wrinkled skin of his neck. He wondered whether Winkler and Ferrara were relatives.

Sam tucked the slip in his sweatband carefully and pulled the hat on, tugging at the brim with both hands. It was too small, but he thought it lucky. He had found it in a trash collection the day his first son was born.

"Well, much obliged," he said doubtfully, not at all sure he approved of the new arrangement. "Number come in same time?"

"Same time."

"Okay."

He ducked out, still clutching the brim, and started to hurry down the narrow sidewalk.

Then he saw Lottie coming toward him. She was holding the baby in one arm and a bag of groceries in the other, pushing Peter Paul before her.

He ran back into the store. "I got to stay here," he stammered. "Jest for a sec, boss."

Charlie looked up, alarmed. "What's the matter?"

Winkler had backed against the wall of cans. When he saw Sam coming through the door he had tried to tear off his badge and hide it, but his fingers were shaking, and so he had only torn his blouse. The badge hung away from the tear, and he cupped it in his twisted fingers. He was very white.

"Nothin', boss, nothin' at all." Sam froze against the jamb until Lottie had passed. Then he looked over his shoulder at Charlie, cowering behind the counter, and grinned toothily. "Much obliged," he said and ran out again.

Charlie turned slowly and looked full at Winkler. "Protection!" he spat, his voice hoarse with contempt.

The old man smiled apologetically.

Joe was waiting in the cab, smoking his pipe. "Where you

been?" he demanded, opening the door. "I been here almost ten minutes."

"Little trouble," Sam said, sliding in.

Joe looked at him quickly. "No law trouble? Nothin' like that?"

"No. Everything okay now."

There was a loose feeling in the air, and Sam peered up at the sky. "Look mighty lahk snow," he said.

Joe shook his head. "Snowed too much already."

Joe had miscalculated twice. Before three o'clock the air was thick with a sticky snow which formed a glare ice in the alleys and slowed the crew until all hope of a short day had vanished. So Sam was still working when word of the day's number reached them. The winner was 729.

The news came from a small radio in a Hope Street bar and grill. They had stopped there to get warm, and the man at the cash register, a grizzled veteran of policy, jerked out a pencil when the Gulf results were announced. "Christ," he said, brushing the pad aside when the fourth race reported. "I wasn't even close."

"Me neither," Sam said quietly, turning his hands over the radiator. "Nowhere near."

Joe looked at him with surprise. When the cashier switched the radio on Snake and Lou had gone out, anticipating a scene. Joe anticipated one, too, and had stayed only because he thought Sam might throw tables about, or smash the radio, or otherwise bring the police. He had come perilously close before, and Joe, with Casey's warning before him, shrank from trouble.

But there was no trouble, nor even a whimper of complaint. Sam buttoned his coat calmly, pulled his hat down as far as it would go, and asked Joe if he were ready. "Got five blocks left, gettin' dark fast."

"Sure." At the door Joe's curiosity was too much. "Didn't you sort of feel like you had one? A zinger?"

Sam shook his head. "Not after that woman, the one I went

to first, beat me around. Seems lahk I knew right then it was no use. Shoulda pulled out then. Signs was all bad."

Joe nodded in solemn agreement. "They was, for a fact."

The darkness gathered swiftly as the last snow floated thinly down, and they finished by street light. With the night it grew colder. The chill cut their tired, lumbering feet as they crammed the last load into the packer.

When they were late, as they were tonight, Joe dropped two of them off on his way to the incinerator. One stayed to help him dump. It was Lou's turn to stay, but Snake volunteered in his place. He was still afraid of Sam. He did not want to ride the tailgate with him.

" 'Spect another bad night tonight," Lou said.

" 'Spect so," Sam murmured.

"Golly, I'm cold."

They folded their arms against their chests as the cruel air swept along the side of the truck and banked against the rear. Lou lived near the waterfront, where the winds were strongest, and he had no army blankets, as Sam had, to protect his family at night. His wife had been quilting endlessly since their marriage, but the quilts were never warm enough. The older Lou grew the less warm they became.

The Elbow was deserted when Joe slowed and Sam jumped off. He warmed his hands for a moment in the exhaust, and then the truck rolled away, jiggling Lou's huddled figure. Sam swung up the shabby street, stamping his feet vigorously.

He worried about the house. It was something to worry about. When he moved in with Lottie and Peter Paul it was Unfit for Human Habitation, and it was scarcely better now. His great hope was that after New Year's Day, when the junkman downstairs moved out, they could reclaim it and make it really fit, a real home, with a door and a kitchen. He caught that hope from Lottie. Hers was so strong it was infectious.

When he bought it, Sam had no idea it was Unfit. A blue card announcing the fact was posted on the front of the house two weeks after he moved in. The card was signed by the Commissioner of Health. It said Sam's house was dangerous and specified certain housing irregularities.

Sam knew all about the irregularities. He had already found the stair treads were rotted and the wiring shot. But even if he had known of them when Sanders first approached him, he would have gone ahead anyway. To Sam it was very simple then. He had to have a house, and Sanders knew of a house to be had.

Tom Sanders was a cheerful young black promoter with political connections who lived over, and worked in, a Thawe Street poolroom. Sanders always promoted himself. Everyone knew that. But now and then he promoted others, too, not because he liked them, but because it was good business. He was so intelligent and so much better informed than anyone else in the Elbow they never knew, until the promotion was over, how they had made out. It was a chance they took. Usually, it was a chance they had to take.

Sam had to take it. He was living in one room east of the Elbow then, sharing a leaky Victorian toilet with seven other families. It was hard enough with Peter Paul, but with Lottie's second pregnancy it became impossible. Through her sixth month she waddled over the mean streets, trying to find something else, and when the nurse at the clinic ordered her to rest, Sam went out nights, knocking on the scarred doors, begging space.

There was little, and none he could afford. His payments to Pellie and Mary Whyte had him strapped. He thought of reneging again and would have but for Lottie. She felt strongly about his obligations to his other women and would not hear of it.

Sanders's appearance in their room therefore seemed a miracle. He smiled genially, explained he had heard of their trouble, and knew of a house about to be vacated.

"A house!" Lottie cried. "A whole *house!* Oh, Sam!" She held Peter Paul between her swollen legs and stroked his hair.

Sam shook his head. "You got the wrong party, mister. We can't afford this. A house for us is much too much."

But Sanders kept smiling. "I b'lieve you're payin' thirty a month heah, an' ——"

"How you find that out?" Sam was astonished.

"Well, I jest heard that, an' the payments on this mortgage, for this place, is just thirty-two a month."

Sam was suspicious. "What them payments? Is they same as rent?"

"Betteren rent, cause you're buyin'. You get to own when you're all paid."

It sounded fantastic.

"Course, they's a down payment you have to make."

"How much?"

"Two hundred dollar."

Sam did not have two hundred. He barely had two. Lottie had nothing either, but she told Sanders to come back the following evening. She said she would have the money then. And she did. She borrowed it from her old employer, who remembered her and trusted her.

Two evenings later Sam went with Sanders to the house. In the narrow living room he was introduced to Mr. and Mrs. Gladding, the sellers. The Gladdings were nervous. The house was dark. A fuse had blown out, Sanders explained, and they were just out of spare fuses, so they would sign by lamplight.

"Mebbe I jest ought to look around a little, see what's what," Sam suggested.

Sanders was indignant. "I could've sold this place to a dozen, two dozen other people. I jest held it for you."

"Well, mebbe I ought to look."

"Ask the Gladdings. Ask them what kind of house this is."

"It's really a very fine ole house," said Mrs. Gladding, her voice quavering. "We really like it fine." Mr. Gladding coughed and said nothing.

Sam persisted, and so Sanders took him on a tour by flashlight. The flashlight kept going out, and Sam saw very little. He didn't care. The inspection was for Lottie's friend. As a condition of the loan she had promised him she would have Sam look the place over before buying.

Back in the living room Sanders fingered a greasy, typewritten contract. The paper had seen hard service and was braced with Scotch tape in the back, along the folds, where it had torn. He made a few mysterious notes on it while Sam counted out the $200 for the Gladdings.

"That pays them back, for their down payment," Sanders explained easily. Everyone nodded, pretending he understood. Sam did not know, and the Gladdings did not tell him, that in the five years since they had sat where he now sat, signing by lamplight because a fuse had unfortunately blown that afternoon, they had paid over $2000 in mortgage installments. They held no hope of getting that back. There was no reason for any.

At the bottom of the last sheet Sanders wrote, "I hereby assign the within contract to Samuel Crawford, witness my hand and seal," and the date.

The Gladdings signed. Sam signed another paper. Both were returned to Sanders's pocket. He looked at them brightly, blew out two of the three lamps, and rose. "That's all," he said.

That was all there was. The house was Sam's, although there was no notary present, although Sam had not even seen the contract of sale. Later he wished he had seen it. Half the monthly payments were to go toward interest, and after deductions for unspecified "expenses" the balance, "if any," was to go toward the principal. In practice, he would be credited with $8 a month toward the principal, with no reduction in interest payments. In 35 years he would own the house. It was now 125 years old.

If he missed one month's payment by one day, he lost everything. That was in the contract, too.

On the street outside, Sanders explained this. "The law say that, you got to do it."

It seemed reasonable to Sam. He jerked his head toward the house. "That why they gettin' out?"

"In a way," Sanders said evasively and walked away.

"Myohmy." Sam shook his head. "Too bad, too bad."

It was too bad. The house the Gladdings were selling was all they had, and they needed a house as badly as Sam and Lottie, for they had children, too. But they had to get out. They were in debt to Sanders for the $200 Sam had given them, and so they had been helpless when the crisis came.

Two weeks before the sale a Health Department sanitarian had visited them. He told them they must repair the roofing, the windows, the walls, the floors, and the spouting, eliminate rat infestation and improve drainage. He ordered the outside toilet destroyed and a new one built inside.

The Gladdings had not known an outside toilet was illegal. Sam still did not know it. The improvements would cost $500, and they did not have that much money. Neither did Sam.

He moved on the evening of the day they left, carrying the battered old furniture on his back across West Concord one piece at a time, coming back finally for Peter Paul and his crib. The rooms were small and cluttered, but Lottie was a determined housekeeper, even in her handicapped condition. She quickly fashioned order out of the jungle of split pipes, sagging ceilings, and spatulate floor boards, and, with nickels and dimes wrung from her thin budget, bought plumbing fixtures and plaster. She borrowed tools and in two weeks had repaired all leaks, secured all beams, and holed up all rats on the first floor. She was starting on the second the day the notice to vacate was tacked on the front door.

She did not see it go up. She worked all day on the upstairs bedrooms repairing a condemned house and did not know it until Sam came home and saw the blue card.

"Whatsat?" he cried, rushing up the stairs. "Whatsat out there?" He thought he must have misunderstood.

Lottie came downstairs and went over it with him, word by word, until all doubt was gone. They could not stay, the sign said. They had to go.

Fifteen minutes later he found Sanders at his pool table.

"You come heah," he shouted, grabbing him by the arm and pulling. "Come with me. Explain somethin' to me."

Sanders was calm and persuasive. He nodded reassuringly and promised they would not be evicted. The following evening the Health Department sanitarian, a shabbily dressed, apologetic little man, called and made clear what the law required.

"Good, good," he murmured approvingly when Lottie showed him what she had done. "Very, very good. But the ah ——"

The privy could not stay in the back yard.

"It makes no difference to me," he said, throwing up his hands as though surprised it did not. "I don't care. But that's what you got to do. Do it any way you want, only it's got to be done."

Only, Sam thought, fingering his worn hat and staring at the slanting old outhouse. Only.

The next afternoon he came home and found a dark, agitated man in a hand-painted necktie and alligator shoes waiting on his front stoop.

"I'm Herbert Stine. Her-bert *Stine!*" he said impressively, as a drill sergeant barks For-ward *March!* "I hear you're in a little trouble, eh? Not so good, eh?"

He made it sound dreadful. Sam nodded guiltily.

As it happened, as it just happened, Stine was in a position to help. Nothing underhanded now, he was on the level, make no mistake about that. Sam scratched his head. He had never doubted Herbert Stine. He had never even heard of him before.

Stine knew about the privy. He would be delighted to see that it was torn out and the proper plumbing installed. In exchange he would write a new mortgage on the property. This would raise the monthly payments to $44 a month — over half Sam's income after sending Pellie and Mary Whyte their money.

"I doan know," Sam said, wagging his head. "That's a awful lot of dough for a poor man lahk me."

Stine shrugged. "So you lose your house, so what's that to me? Nothing is what it is."

Sam signed, and a few days later two workmen appeared to

build the new toilet. They arrived as he was leaving for West Garage, and he eyed them with disdain. One was short and scrawny, with an arm withered and strapped to his chest in a leather support. The other, very fat, waddled in a striped sweater and a ragged black coat. They did not look efficient. He was therefore astonished when he came home that evening and found they had finished.

"They's all done," Lottie said, meeting him at the door with an uncertain smile. "Left here 'bout an hour ago."

Beaverboard walls had been thrown against the rear of the house, and a cracked porcelain stool sat on a raised plywood floor.

"Ummm," Sam grunted, fingering the cracks where the walls met. "Could've done that good mysef."

"We're legal now," said Lottie.

He eyed the old privy wistfully. "Lahk that better," he said. "More warmer out there, I bet."

"Better legal," she said cheerfully.

Herbert Stine came after supper, looked the toilet over, and expressed enthusiastic approval. Then he asked Sam to sign a paper declaring the work had been done to his satisfaction.

Sam did, and after Stine had left Lottie painfully figured out her new budget. On $11 a week she could manage.

Then the sanitarian called again.

He apologized. And inspected. And returned his terrible verdict: the house was still condemned. The new toilet, like the old, was outside the law. The pipes were exposed, and the beaverboard would not do.

Sam ran frantically to Herbert Stine, who exhibited the signed paper, sympathetically damned bureaucrats who told people how to run their own homes, and explained that he was very busy.

"Busy!" Sam sobbed at home, wobbling his head in his long dark hands. "Busy! Busy!"

Lottie did not understand. Hadn't they paid their $200 and signed the mortgage right?

Yes, he said, yes.

And hadn't they made their payments, like they were supposed to?

Yes, they had.

And when that city man came and said, Fix That John, they had it fixed, didn't they?

Yes, yes.

And paid for it?

Yes, yes, yes.

Then what was wrong?

The law. It must be the law.

So they waited dumbly, and soon Sanders came again and told them he knew of a prospective tenant for the first floor, a junkman who would rent for a few months, long enough for Sam to pay Stine for new walls and inside piping.

And the man came and moved his vast array of junk into the rooms Lottie had painfully repaired, while the scrawny man and the fat man erected a bulging brick wall for the toilet and Lottie waited for her baby.

And the Crawfords came and went from their new house over the shack roof, over the rusty automobile doors and the dying catalpa tree, because the door at the top of the stairs was padlocked.

Andy Hallam and his junk were in the tenth and last month of their tenancy that bitter night when Sam loped in from the Elbow, over the hutch and the rusty bridge and into his cramped home.

He was downstairs, working late. They would hear him rattling around among his shadeless bridge lamps and tarnished hardware, and now and then, in the room under the kitchen, there was a dull scrape as he moved furniture.

Lottie was worried. "What he doin' here, so late?"

"His business," Sam said without looking up from his Bible.

"Well, I doan lahk it."

Sam read on. He had memorized the Bible references from Fink Kerby's *Black Combination* for all December and was now checking the lesson for tomorrow, fixing the new number in his mind. Lottie did not know that. She thought he had given up policy, and she was greatly impressed with this religious bent.

There was a heavy bump below, and she went to the window and peered down. "Well, I'll be *dogged!*"

"Whatsat?"

"Come here."

Under the catalpa tree, among the chill shadows by the shack, Hallam was unloading a large, listing handcart. He had been at it for some time, but the cart was still heavy with junk. It loomed in the kitchen light, ugly and huge.

Sam returned to his chair, pondering. Lottie followed him with troubled eyes.

"He suppose to be outa here, gone, in two weeks."

He nodded. "I know."

"What's he bringin' more stuff in here for?"

He shook his head. "I doan know."

They sat in the uneasy silence, wondering. The cheap clock over the stove rattled out the time, second upon tin second, as Lottie waited.

He rose. "Mebbe I ought to go see."

"Mebbe you ought."

But as Sam went for his overcoat they heard Hallam's foot upon the stair, and in a moment his key squeaked in the padlock. He knocked.

Lottie opened the door. He stood on the top step, blinking in the feeble light, a short redhead in dirty khaki, with a freckled face and boils on the back of his neck.

"Can I come in?"

Lottie stood aside. Sam watched blankly, holding his overcoat. Hallam looked around for a chair and saw there were only the two, for Sam and Lottie, and Peter Paul's little stool. He hesitated for an awkward moment and then dropped to his haunches and sat against the wall, still blinking at them.

"Real cold out tonight, workin'." His voice was strident and faintly nasty, like a burlesque comedian's.

"We saw," said Lottie, sitting down. Sam sat too, and they faced one another across the cracked linoleum.

The clock over the stove ticked.

Hallam cleared his throat.

"So cold out," he began uncertainly. Then, picking up courage with the sound of his own voice, he added into the hostile silence, "It's so cold everybody ought to stay indoors as much as they can, don't you think?"

"Uh-huh." Lottie twisted her toes in her sneakers angrily. "That's why we didn't know, couldn't understand, why you was workin' out there with that cart."

Hallam started to reply and sneezed suddenly. He pulled a small roll of toilet paper from a pocket and blew his nose on it, then tore off the soiled strip and stuffed it into another pocket.

"I was comin' to that," he said, inhaling sharply. "I was just goin' to tell you about that."

"I want you should," said Lottie, biting her words.

She hated Hallam. Before they moved she thought she would be happy here. Then, before they were even settled, he had moved in and locked her and her children on the upper floor. She watched him narrowly. Her jailer.

Sam was bewildered. He swung his head absently from Lottie to Hallam and back to Lottie again.

Hallam sniffed again. "What I got to tell you, you'll understand in a minute. I got to make a living, you know, sellin' this stuff, an' I don't see how I can, you know, move right out, this month."

That was it, then. Lottie leaned forward.

"Like I was sayin'," Hallam went on, studying the wall, "it's real cold, a cold winter, and with no place to go I don't see where I can leave and get me another place before warm weather anyway."

She set her thin jaw. "You find a place. You jest get one."

He shrugged helplessly. "Where can I go?"

"Where can you go?" she said tensely, curling her toes until the sneakers buckled underneath. "You can go where you're goin', that's where."

He bowed his head. "Not when it's so cold."

She sprang up, furious. "Cold! What you know 'bout it bein' cold? We find this place here, coldest weather I ever see, move in when it lahk that. I doan see it bother you so much out back tonight, movin' new stuff in to get rid of, in this cold you talk 'bout. Cold. Huh!"

Sam nodded fuzzily. "Most freeze first night we come here."

Hallam unwound his legs and slumped against the wall. He had been through this before. "I don't see why you're so anxious to get me out. I pay my rent regular. My money's good."

Lottie snorted. "We live in a house, we want to live in all it, not locked upstairs." Her voice shook. The more she thought about it, the angrier she became.

"Well, I don't look at it that way." He chuckled. "It's your house, I'm downstairs, maybe *I'm* locked down *there*." He laughed by himself. Sam was still struggling to understand. Lottie sat rigidly.

"If you want to know, really want to know," he went on, "I'm doin' you a favor, I think. I take care of that floor good. It's better now than when I came. I'm the only guy, and you can ask anybody, the only guy when he gets through the landlord thanks him for his improvements."

"Oney improvement we want is you out." She was trembling.

"And when I go, with that extra rent you can fix up this floor real nice. Like I say, my money's good money. Sometimes I think it's maybe too good. Sometimes I wonder what I'll say if the income-tax people send an auditor around to look at my overhead when I haven't hardly got a ceiling over my head."

Sam frowned, wondering what an auditor was.

Lottie drew back in her chair. "No use arguin'," she said.

"I'm not arguin'," he argued.

"You got to go," she said hoarsely, a thread of hysteria running through her voice. "You jest got to."

He stared at her truculently. "Well, I ain't. That's the way it is," he said as evenly as his coarse, burlesque clown's voice would permit.

"Jest a sec." Sam had caught up now. "You sayin' you ain't gonna leave here when you suppose, is that what you sayin'?"

"No place to go. Not my fault."

"Not your fault!" Sam's voice rose. "Look here, man. You find a place, like she say, go somewheres else. We put you out, ever bitta your stuff, soon as this month over."

Lottie nodded smartly. Hallam looked from one to the other. "You can't do it," he said finally.

"Can't do what?" they said together.

"Can't put me out. In the snow like that."

Sam sneered. "The hell we can't. We put you out so fast you won't know where you is at. This is our house, an' we say go, you *go*."

"The law says you can't do it. I talked to Sanders just yesterday, told him my problem, what it was. He said you can't put me out without I got a place for my business to go."

Sam laughed derisively. "Can't be no law lahk that, in a man's own house."

"Is one. Sanders said so."

"Sanders doan know nothin'," Lottie scoffed. But the edge of doubt crept into her voice. There were some strange laws around. She had found that out.

"He knows this."

Lottie sat very straight in her straight chair. "You go down them stairs," she said. "Go down and lock yo' door. An' when you gone we find out what law that is, who own this house."

Sam rose, his hands heavy in front of him, awkward and lethal. "Go on," he said. "Do what she say."

Hallam looked from one to the other. Then he unfolded his legs and stood slowly to let them know he was leaving, not because of them, but because he chose. He paused and leered. "I got some more stuff to unload."

Sam started across the kitchen and Lottie drew back, but Hallam scampered over the threshold, slammed the door, and flung the lock through the hasp. Sam grabbed the knob and shook it and then turned away. They heard him downstairs, thrashing around in his junk.

"Go see Sanders," she said. "See what he say."

He was not gone long. Sanders was in his poolroom. He almost seemed to be waiting for him.

Sam came back over the automobile doors, his overshoes thumping irregularly as he avoided the ice on the metal. When he swung through the window Lottie saw his head was low.

"Couldn't find him?"

He unbuttoned his coat carefully, as though each button were a separate and difficult operation.

"He wasn't there?"

Sam sat down. "He say we can't put him out for a hundred an' twenty days."

"In our own house?" she cried. It sounded forever.

"He say that."

Sam reached for his Bible and turned to the verse for the next day. Lottie watched him vacantly for several moments. Then she went to the window and looked down.

Hallam was unloading an enormous iron urinal. He wrapped two lengths of rope around the ends and swung it to his back, then trudged across the narrow yard and disappeared through the back door, the door of the house's real kitchen.

The side of the shack was banked with rotting leaves, and as Lottie stood motionless by the sill a low wind tore one loose and sent it rolling, end over end, across the flat sheeting of the snow and away, down the alley.

The back door slammed and Hallam came out again. She watched him pull a legless armchair from the junk-cart. Then she opened the window, took a capped bottle from the ledge, pulling the stained shade to the sill.

In the front room the baby awoke from a funny dream and giggled.

*   *   *

Now the breath of Christmas sweetened the winter air, and in the Elbow there was panic. The outer slum exulted. Bing Crosby sang carols over P.A. systems in the shopping belt, Funk's hair straightener was a dollar a bottle, the Bijou advertised *Gilda* for its Xmas Eve Midnite Frolick, George Swinton hung Sherwin-Williams paint cans on a tree of wrought iron in the window behind his steel grill, plastic evergreen ropes decked the front of Ollie's Famous Bar, Stein's Super Market wore silver bells on each price card, a neon cross flashed in the toy department of Al Kelly's Five-to-a-Dollar Store, the high tenement windows above the arc lights bristled with skinny wreaths and cardboard holly, and there were some Christmas trees. Greeting card counters were crowded, ornament departments packed, toy stores jammed.

But panic swept the alleys behind the street. There was no money there. And money was necessary. Every billboard, every plate-glass window hawked gaiety at a price, and in the mean lanes behind the bank of stores everyone was broke. They were bankrupt, but they had to buy. They had to. There was no choice. The season bent them ruthlessly.

Their children scribbled letters to Santa Claus and wriggled out back doors, over tarpaper roofs, to drop them in little street-corner chimneys guarded by shivering scarecrows in tawdry red cheesecloth and rabbit fur.

"Hey Harry, lookit this. Here's a kid wants a stove, I think it is, only he can't spell it."

"Crissake. Throw it away. No stoves."

Or:

"This one wants a, you know what? A — wait a minute, I got it here. 'A big fur coat' for his old lady. Fur. F-i-r, like that. Name an' everything."

"Crazy. Get rid of it. Toys, the man said."

Lettered painfully, bearing down on the stubby pencils. Moistening the points with their lips, following the blue lines down the ruled paper. Going over the words twice. To be sure Santa would see.

Fathers sat numbly by kitchen stoves, holding their black hands close and going over the wretched business again and again, trying to find a way while mothers clattered dishes loudly.

"If you hadn't throwed it away, mebbe . . ."

"Wasn't throwed away!" Savagely. "Wasn't! Wasn't!" With burning doubt inside.

Peace on earth. Under the red and green lights, where the General Electric train whooshed through the dark little tunnel and the crowds milled, begging the salesgirls' attention. For fifty cents. For a dollar. For a dollar fifty.

"Miss! Miss!"

"Wait a sec, I only got two hands."

"Miss, this top I got yesterday, it broke."

"No return, hon. It's a rule."

Good will toward men. Between the gay tin horns and the chaste plaster models of the Virgin, the magic sets and Superatomic Gats and Cutie Pie Dollies, among the swarming shoppers, under the droning voice of Bing.

> *Away in a manger, no crib for his bed*
> *The little Lord Jesus lay down his sweet head*
> *The stars in the sky looked down where he lay*
> *The little Lord Jesus asleep in the hay.*

"Honest to God, Louise, my legs are like scrap iron."

"It ain't started yet, chile."

"It's the smell I can't stand."

"That Nigra smell. You never get used to it."

Up, up, up went the policy game, skyrocketing while the worn silver and the crumpled bills lay in stacks before the writers and the pickup men lugged the sacks of money countyward and the sorters worked late with the slips in the big barn.

December 9: 459.

December 10: 154.

December 11: 827.

While the panic grew in the brick hovels and the sad-eyed rooming houses, and the cash registers rang out, and the ragged waifs toddled over the hill, clutching important mail, down to the stores where the scarecrow Santas shuddered in the wind and sneaked quick nips to keep warm.

"Look, kid. I told yuh. I'm a helper. You know, a helper?"

"My Mama say that." In a little voice.

"She got the word. Just toys here. Now your letter, it ought to be mailed. You know, in a mailbox."

"No stamp." Shaking the scared head.

"Here. Here's three cents. Over there in the drugstore you can get one."

"Hey Harry! You're gettin' soft."

"Yeah. I'm gettin' crocked, that's why."

Reaching up to the slot marked "Letters" and pushing it twice to make sure it had gone. Trudging home in thin short pants and long woolen stockings. Wondering if Santa would remember this year and come. Knowing fiercely that he would. Trusting Santa's helper. Believing Bing.

Seven hundred letters in the dead-letter office.

The stars in the sky looked down where he lay.

Thirteen days of agony until Christmas.

Under a sky dappled with cold clouds Sam stood, a crooked figure against cluttered yards, dreaming.

One win would do it. One would be enough. A single triumph towering rich and green among the black stumps of failure would wipe them away and bring peace.

Like dammed water fighting toward a spillway . . .

— Or steam crawling under a boiler hood, feeling with long gauze fingers for the pressure vent . . .

— His tormented mind cherished this tip and that, this system and that, following them with blind faith until they vanished in a rasp of race results, leaving him lost for one dreadful moment, until he found another false trail to hold him with its twistings for one more day.

To hold him from what? What if he missed a day, or two days, or a week? What then? And what if he won? What then? What balance, what peace could he find over the spillway, outside the vent, in a place he had never known?

. . . Questions unasked and unanswered and unanswerable. Questions beyond him who knew only the power of the drive and his helplessness before it. That within him there was this vacuum, this yearning, this terrible craving for one win, one time, one day.

It was never a racket to Sam, never even a gamble. Policy was his religion. His daily defeats were as irrelevant as the unrealized prayers of a priest. Sam knew the ways of policy were mysterious. But he never doubted they were sublime.

There were other players as faithful as he, but not in the same way. They dreamed of automobiles and television sets and years of golden wealth. Sam's plans stopped at that night's celebration. Not that he wanted to celebrate: it was part of the ritual of victory. He expected it of himself. Others wanted to win for the winnings, but Sam wanted to win to win.

— To find the spillway . . .

— And the vent . . .

To have it all over, forever finished.

He hoped it would be soon: then, with the eternal flash of faith, the never-failing hunch, he knew it would. Tomorrow. It would come tomorrow.

A vision leapt up of Charlie Bond, staggering over the rusty doors with the payoff. Inside him something went loose and silly.

"You all right?" Lou Denton asked anxiously.

Sam awoke and swung a can into the waiting hopper. "Yep. Real fine."

They crossed to the next alley.

Through the waning afternoon they worked in silence, finishing in a dead end not far from the Elbow. Sam swung up on the tailgate beside Snake.

Since the attack their whole relationship had changed. Snake was essentially a coward, and once his cowardice was tagged and hung up for all to see he quickly sought terms. For the past week he had been seeking them with Sam.

Through the haze of his dream Sam heard him talking now of money.

"Course, you got this policy down, I guess, you been at it a long time, but a beginner like me does real good in craps."

"Craps?" Sam asked vaguely, pressing his back against the truck body to stop the shaking.

"Yeah. Last night, just for the hell of it, I went along. Game floats, you know, all over town. You got to know somebody. Anyway, I went along. Shot real good, cleared sixty bucks in two hours, bang, bang, bang, like that."

"Sixty bucks!" Sam stared at him, his long jaw sagging. *Sixty bucks!*

"I most died. I kept thinkin' I'd quit, but I kept goin', and pretty soon there I was." He braced himself against the hopper lever and slowly, keeping his balance, drew out a bulging wallet. "See?"

Sam saw. And thought. He thought so long Snake decided he had lost interest. He was slipping the wallet back in his pocket, disappointed, when Sam spoke again.

"How you find this heah game?"

Snake grinned. He had been saving this all day. "Place you find everythin' good in this town. The club."

Sam frowned. "What club that?"

"Why, the club. The Central Democratic Club."

"Oh." He remembered now. Sanders had taken him there with Fink Kerby. It was just before the fall elections, and the place was swarming with people eating roast oysters and drinking beer while a little man with a faint mustache made a speech no one heard. Sanders had some kind of job with the club. He promoted something there. Sam had wondered that night what it was. He wondered again now.

"Game right in the club?" he asked.

"Naw. They take you there from there." He watched, pleased, as the interest grew in Sam's face. "It's really a big deal."

"How much it cost?"

"Well, you ought to have fifty bucks anyway. A guy I know lent me mine."

Then, with a snap of his teeth, he shut up, suddenly aware of the trap around him. But he was too late. Two blocks later he heard Sam's wistful voice beside him.

"Hey Snake."

"Yeah." He felt it coming.

"Can you lemme have some a that dough you got? Jest till tomorrow."

"I can't." Snake thought fast.

"Why you can't?"

"I — I owe it. To the guy gimme fifty."

"I thought you made it clear, you said."

"In a way ——" He was floundering.

"I give it back. I'm lucky."

"Well ——" He was lost. "How much you need?"

"Jest fifty, lahk you had."

Snake had to give in or challenge Sam's luck, and he could not risk that. He leaned against the lever and eased the wallet out again, wondering, with a stab at hope, if Sam might win as he had won. The hope vanished as he handed the bills across the tailgate. That kind of luck came only to green gamblers, and Sam was no beginner.

"Much obliged," Sam said, taking off his hat carefully. He pulled that day's dead slip from his sweatband and threw it away, slipping the money in its place. Then he screwed the hat back on his sloped forehead.

Snake watched the money vanish, feeling ill. "Ain't you afraid you'll lose it, up there?"

Sam grinned and tapped the soiled crown. "That's my lucky hat," he laughed. "Nothin' bad ever happen with that hat on."

Snake wished he were as sure. He leaned back glumly and watched the pavement roll out from under the truck tail and felt like a chump.

When they returned from the incinerator, the Elbow was noisy with seasonal activity. Beyond Ollie's bar workmen were unloading curbstone counters and bazaar awnings on West Concord, and as Joe cut across Thawe Street Sam saw two patrolmen rigging festive cord over a tiny stage in the stationhouse yard. He had an impression of false starlight and a doll lying in a straw crib and wondered what it was.

At Horrigan Street he jumped easily from the truck. Snake's wave was halfhearted, but Sam didn't notice. He swung jauntily toward the Unique, certain now his worries were over. As he passed Swinton's he saw a late bulb burning in Charlie Bond's store. He chuckled to himself. This time he would win, this one time.

Lottie and Emma Kerby were babbling in the kitchen. They were so excited Sam walked between them and into the bedroom without a greeting. He didn't mind. His own excitement was great, and he was afraid Lottie would see it if she were watching.

He tried to settle down, but the more he thought of Snake's story and what it could mean, the more excited he became. He sat on the bed, clenching and unclenching his fists in the darkness as the chorus swelled in the kitchen.

Then Emma was gone and the other room was quiet.

Lottie busied herself at the stove for several minutes. Then she called: "Sam? You there, Sam?"

He came into the light with an affected slump and sat carefully in the rocker. "What's all this noise? What's goin' on?" His voice was strident with control.

She rattled pans, deep in her own thoughts. "Ladies' fair, for Christmas, tomorrow."

"What ladies? Where?"

"In the Elbow, white ladies sellin' things. Doin' it to get acquainted, seem lahk."

That afternoon a patrolman had come through the alleys, shouting at the women. At first they thought he was looking for someone in trouble, and none of them would come out, but he perched on a fence and called persuasively, and suddenly everyone was outside, milling around on the cobblestones, listening and jabbering among themselves. The policeman was an old Erik man, and he had come only to cover himself at the station house.

He had, however, conveniently suppressed news of the bazaar's real purpose, relayed through Big Ed Sylvester's lieutenants.

Lottie's hands were shaking, and she smoothed the broad of her skirt with them. She was upset. Sam did not understand why.

"He say these ladies, live in fine houses, havin' their fair here to be friendly."

"Lahk a rummage sale?"

"Better."

Sam shook his head. "Doan sound right to me."

She looked at him hotly. "I doan care how it sound, I think it's right nice."

"Doan know why they comin' down here." He looked around the room dismally. "Not much to see," he said. Then he wished he hadn't. It was the very thing he wished he had not said. She began to cry.

"I mean, I mean, not much nowheres," he stammered. But the tears streaked down her dark face and dropped from her chin, moistening the collar of her thin dress. She lifted her skirt and dabbed at them. Underneath her petticoat was a retailored army field jacket binding her spindly legs. They stuck out awkwardly, straight sticks in funnels of cheap cotton.

Sam tried again. "This place," he began, peering about with exaggerated approval, "look real nice. Clean and comfortable. I lahk it fine."

The sobs died slowly. "Do the best I can, with half a house an' him stayin' downstairs."

He nodded eagerly. "Sholey do, an' it's a real good best."

"Miz Kerby, she say it was so bad before, with all them rats in here, an' they all gone now, no rats at all."

"Why yes, honey, an' when we get him out, get the whole house, we'll be all set." He looked up cautiously. She was better now.

She blinked to clear away the last tears and took a final peck at her cheeks. Then she swept a vigorous glance across the room. "This is the worst room. This floor is jest terrible." She prodded the rotten linoleum with a contemptuous sneaker. "Tha faucet, that sink, they doan belong here." She skipped from corner to corner, over the yards of peeling wallpaper, and at last her eyes, most rueful and most sad, came to the naked windows. "What I really need, most of all," she said softly, "is somethin' to show for Christmas, somethin' you can see outside, make it nice an' homey. Yes." She smiled gently. "That would be jest fine."

You'll get it tomorrow, Sam thought fiercely. The best. The best there is.

"I got to see Sanders about the law again, tonight."

"Yes," she said, studying the bare glass. "Yes indeed."

Tom Sanders spat viciously in the cuspidor and lifted two fresh cues from the rack, balancing them, one in each hand, trying to decide. Then he put one back and brandished the other, sliding it along the bridge of his left hand.

"Okay, Whipeye," he called. "Set 'em up."

Whipeye brushed the blue chalk from his hands. "All set, big boy. Set an' still rollin'." He was a swarthy, peppery little Armenian with a nervous twitch in his cheek. Tonight he felt good and was good. He had taken three games straight.

"We'll see who's gonna roll," Sanders said sourly. He had not wanted to play again. He hated to lose and this was not his night. But he had beaten Whipeye so many other times he could not quit.

The balls lay shiny on the green field. Whipeye crouched over the far end, sighting down his stick. Then he jerked it back and let go with a swift, straight stroke.

Wham went the cue ball, thudding into the triangle, and *plop, plop, plop* went three others, dropping into the leather thong pockets.

"Cripes," Sanders muttered.

"Things is tough all over," Whipeye snickered, swinging into position and putting the five ball away with another *plop*.

Things *were* tough all over, Sanders thought, and getting tougher. The racket was all right, but it was different. People were walking around with tight, scared looks, running away if you asked a simple question. A promoter could hardly promote even a game of pool any more. Business had never been better, and the heat had never been hotter. Sanders had never heard of such heat. The gestapo was everywhere, asking nosey questions, spying. Say something friendly, flash a roll, and they were all over you, pulling you in for a sweat job. Without his rent cuts and his share of Gormley's craps project, Sanders would be holding a pan, he figured, or on his own like that scab Bond.

Plop, plop, plop, went the three, ten, and four balls.

Sanders was worried. He was especially worried about Gormley. Ordinarily he did not mind cheating on the big boss. His whole relationship with him, indeed, had been a cheat, for he was paid as a precinct executive, and since the ward was the most solidly organized in the Seventh, he had never added more than one vote, his own. So whenever the ward captain had dreamed something up Sanders had been glad to go along with it. Until now. Now he was worried. With Joe Murdock's writers out of action and Murdock off somewhere, in the sweat-box probably, the new game was swamped. The word was getting around. It might even get to the big boss.

The nine ball teetered on the edge of the corner pocket and spun to one side. "Okay," Whipeye said. "Take it away."

There wasn't much to take. Eight balls sprawled across the baize, none easy. Sanders lifted his cue reluctantly and leaned over, wondering which one to take and where to put it. Then out of the corner of his sighting eye, he saw the shadow come through the doorway and felt the crooked fingers plucking at his sleeve.

"Hullo," Sam grinned. "Can I see you for a minute?"

Sanders relaxed. Usually Sam annoyed him, but he was glad to turn from the game. "Sure. What's on your mind?"

"Frienda mine, he tell me 'bout a crap ——"

"Wait a minute." He put down his cue. Whipeye, working the overhead score beads, was listening. "Let's go in the back."

They walked down the aisle between tables. Whipeye watched them, his cheek twitching with curiosity.

"Okay," Sanders whispered at the last table. "What did this friend tell you?"

"He tell me a crap game, lots a dough, is somewheres 'round here. Say they know all about it at the Central Club. I thought mebbe you could hep me, fix me up."

Cripes. Was there *anybody* who didn't know?

He looked at Sam dubiously. "Big dough is right. I doan think you got that kind."

Sam took his hat off ceremoniously and pulled the sweatband down. The bills lay moist against the leather. "That's a kind a dough *I* got," he said proudly.

"Well. Mebbe. For the little game, mebbe."

Sam's eyes rolled. He had never heard of a game too big for $50. "They's two kinds?"

"Yeah. Stick around. I'll be right with you."

Sanders told Whipeye he had to go — he had a deal on, and it couldn't wait. Whipeye protested he had as much as won this one. Sanders conceded and paid him off. He was glad to get away.

"C'mon," he said to Sam. "My car's outside."

Sam had never ridden in the Buick before. He had seen it parked before the poolroom or before houses whose tenants were renting or buying through Sanders, and once, when Fink Kerby nearly sideswiped it on their way to the Valley, he had caught a glimpse of the red leather cushions and the glittering dashboard. Now he sat inside, actually inside, on the cushions, under the yellow canvas top.

He fingered the chrome glove compartment timidly. "This sholey is nice."

"What?"

"It's a real nice automobile."

"Gotta trade it in, get me a new model."

Sam pondered this. He decided Sanders couldn't be serious. No one gave up a car like this unless the installment people came

267

and took it. Maybe they were after him and he was just saying that to cover up. But that could not be. Sanders was a promoter, a really good promoter, and people didn't take things away from him. It was just the other way around.

He gave up and watched the blocks speed past. On Crone Street they stopped speeding and then stopped altogether. One of God's Wagons had broken down, blocking their lane, and the cars on the inside would not let them pass.

God's Wagons were Chryslers with P.A. systems built on the roofs. They had been equipped by the Gospelists, a religious sect which had come out of the South the summer before and was sweeping the Elbow. On the back of the crippled Wagon's speaker box was the legend:

OH LORD!
PROTECT AMERICA
CONVERT RUSSIA
SAVE US ALL

Sam squinted at it. " 'Pears to me they ain't ever gonna move," he said. "They's stuck."

"Frig the bastards," Sanders grunted, trying to edge into the inside lane.

Sam shook his head solemnly. "Doan do to cross God," he said. "He just doan 'preciate it."

Sanders wrenched the wheel and the Buick slid out of the jam and down the street. He sat back and snickered. "You mean, the way Charlie Bond is crossin' God? No, you're right, he doan 'preciate it, God doan."

Sam was puzzled. "Is Mr. Bond in trouble with God?"

"Yeah. A God that doan lahk his writers to scab, that's the God that's after Charlie."

Sam turned from Sanders and pulled a small alphabetized magazine from his pocket. Under "D" he read "Danger is luck." He folded it thoughtfully and slipped it back in his pocket.

The Central Democratic Club was a brick corner building with a FormStone front. The yard behind it was a parking lot for ward captains, but the only captain who came regularly was Gormley, and so the precinct executives had taken it over. Sanders sped down the short drive and zipped on his emergency brake at the last moment. The car skidded to a stop beside the rear door.

"My-oh-my," Sam chuckled. "You sholey can make it talk."

Sanders locked the doors and got out swaggering.

The back room of the club was for pool. In front of it was the bar and, facing the street, the reading room, for show. The meeting hall and the cardroom were upstairs. The pool tables were deserted. Sanders led Sam into the bar, a long room with mirrored walls and black glass tables. A drunken old man in a black suit was alone there; perched on a leatherette stool with his head between his hands and his elbows on the bar.

"Evenin', Mr. Cross," Sanders said respectfully. "You seen Junior?"

The old man wrinkled his lips in an emblem of contempt and looked away. At that moment the bartender, a husky young black in shirtsleeves, came in from a side kitchen. "He's listenin'," he said softly. "Doan talk while he's listenin'."

Sam cocked his head but heard nothing. Then he saw Mr. Cross was jiggling slightly. His head was bald and fringed with fine white hair and it jiggled with the rest of him, like the bouncing ball in a musical short. He was perilously close to falling from the stool. The bartender stood behind him, alert.

Sam followed Sanders into the reading room, craning his neck. The oyster roast had been held in the parking lot. He had not been inside before.

He jerked his head back toward the bar. "Whosat?" he whispered.

"Ole man Cross. The bank's law man."

Junior was not here, either. The room was empty. They found him in the second-floor bathroom, and they heard him before they saw him. Sanders had been wondering aloud where he might be when his voice rasped through the door marked Men.

"Don't mention my name in here," the voice ordered and then fell silent. They looked around to see where it might have come from, and in a moment Junior's homburg-capped head peered out, followed by Junior.

Sam had expected a young man. Junior was nearly fifty, with a square, beefy face and the suspicious eyes of a teller. But no teller ever dressed as Junior did. Under his homburg, which was yellow and tilted forward, he wore a maroon silk shirt, a thick tweed sport coat, green slacks and huaraches. He was tucking the shirt in his pants and chewing the stump of a dead cigar.

"It's you," he said accusingly, running a ferocious eye over Sanders.

"This is a boy of mine," Sanders said, indicating Sam with a jerk of his thumb. "Wants a little action."

Sam smiled brightly.

Junior inspected him narrowly. "Okay," he said finally. "I'll take a chanct."

Sam giggled. "Ain't no more'n I'm takin', mister. I'm right lucky tonight."

Junior grunted skeptically and they went down the stairs. Sam trailed, feeling his way along the unfamiliar banister. At the bottom he passed a face he knew, going up.

"Whosat?" he asked Sanders.

"Gormley."

"The big boss?"

"Big as you'll ever see, boy."

From the bar came a sharp cackle of laughter, then sounds of a tussle, then loud swearing. Junior snickered. "That Cross. First fall tonight."

Sam laughed politely without understanding.

"You ready?" Junior asked.

"Yep."

Sanders had disappeared.

Five minutes later Sam was lost. From that moment he was in a world of strange streets, among strange people who spoke a strange language and did not even seem to be aware of him until they were ready for him, ready to put him through the strange routine devised for the Sams of the Seventh.

The only one he knew was Junior. He didn't know him very well and didn't get to know him better in the cab. Junior opened the door, thrust him in the back seat, and then climbed in the front and started a running conversation with the driver on the Gulf races.

Three blocks from the club they stopped at a drugstore. Junior went inside, to a telephone booth, and whispered something to the cabbie when he came back. They seemed to know each other.

From the back Sam watched the dark streets, wondering where they were. He pressed his face against the frosted glass and tried to see the signs but could not. Once he leaned forward and asked.

"Where we goin'?"

"Niggah heben, seben 'leben," Junior drawled. The cabbie burst into coarse laughter. Sam slid back on the seat, confused and hurt.

They drew up before a hotel and Junior opened his door. Sam started to get out.

"Wait a minute." The driver held out a hand. "That's a buck ten an' a quarter tip."

Sam looked blank. Junior prodded him with a fat thumb. "Pay the man, boy."

Sam took off his hat, pulled out a $10 bill, and pushed it through the window.

"Christ," the cabbie spat. "That all you got?"

"Yep." He grinned proudly.

The driver fished in his pocket and handed Sam a wad of crumpled bills and some change. Sam counted it laboriously. There was $8.35 in all. He was still looking for the rest of it when the cab slid away and vanished in traffic.

"Hey!" Sam called. "Hey!"

A policeman across the street looked over, suddenly interested. Junior grabbed Sam by the arm and drew him from the curb. "C'mon, you wanna get us in trouble?"

271

"But ——"

"C'mon."

The policeman kept watching, fascinated by Junior's costume. They walked hurriedly, and as they did a slick young man in army officer's pink trousers, an Eisenhower jacket, and bright red mittens joined them. Sam was in the middle. At first he did not know the young man was with them.

Then Junior spoke to him. "You been out tonight?"

The young man shook his head and pointed to a cab with its flag up. "There's one. Let's get it."

Sam was glad they were leaving this place. The sidewalk was broad and crowded with well-dressed people, and he felt self-conscious.

They squeezed into the back seat, Sam still in the middle, and the young man gave an unfamiliar address. The driver boldly swept through a U-turn under the policeman's eye and headed east and then south, toward the waterfront. Sam listened to the meter and fumbled with his trousers each time it clicked. His hand kept brushing Junior's slacks. At the third brush Junior turned irritably.

"What're you tryin' to do?" he demanded.

"Nothin'," Sam said meekly.

He was sorting the coins in his pocket. He wanted to be ready with the right fare. He had not counted on this extra expense and did not want to risk another short change. At least, he thought, this would be the last ride.

It was. But when he handed the driver the money, with a quarter tip carefully added, Junior prodded him again. "Double it," he snapped.

Sam slumped.

"Double it!"

Then he noticed the young man was still in the cab, looking at him coldly. "I got to get back, don't I?" he said with heavy scorn.

"Yessah," Sam said miserably, in automatic deference to the pink pants, "I guess so." He paid, wondering if they would le him in the game at all with so much of his roll gone. Snake hadn't told him about this.

The cab disappeared with the steerer and three dollars of Sam's hoard. He was left with Junior on the dark and windy street, standing on a bus stop before a sprawling warehouse. The warehouse gate was ajar. Junior led him inside, up a flight of steps, through a door, down a long, drafty corridor, past a lookout man in denim, and into a freight elevator.

Upstairs the game had just begun. In an inside room on the third floor two housemen stood with bowls of fresh dice beside them, working wooden rakes over long tables under twin droplights. Already each game had a score of players.

Sam was dazzled by the money. It lay stacked in bins before the croupiers, and in smaller piles before the players, green with authority. He noticed there was very little talk. Everyone else was looking at the money too, with the same quiet respect, with the same aching greed.

A husky man in shirtsleeves and a ragged straw hat nodded to Junior at the door, and they went to the smaller table. "Start here," Junior said. "The kind of dough you got don't say nothin' with the big guys."

He left and Sam stood clumsily by himself, away from the table, holding his old hat in both hands, still watching the money. There was so much of it, and it lay so loose. He wished he could be alone with it for a few minutes, not to steal it, just to be with it.

"Eighter, eighter, Ada from Decatur." A lanky black was rubbing the dice feverishly. "Hah!" He let go, and they bounced against the wooden board on the far side and then lay still.

"Crap," drawled the houseman, raking in the bills.

The man grunted, swore, and nervous laughter rippled around the table.

Sam drew closer, studying the table. He had shot crap before, at the hospital and in the army, but never this kind. In the middle of the felt pad covering the tabletop was a white rectangle marked

"Field Numbers," with betting squares inside. On either side of the bounceboard were combination-bet squares paying three-to-two, six-to-one, and seven-to-two, depending on the combination, and the action was heaviest there as the dice passed from player to player and the shooters chanted and the houseman raked and the onlookers bet For and Against in blocks along the table edge.

Most of the men at the little table were blacks, shabbily dressed and strange and timid like Sam. Even the houseman seemed poor. He was a pale young man with a thin, ragged beard. He looked like a painting of Christ.

The big table was different. The bettors there were flashily dressed. Most of them were white, and they knew one another. They handled the bills easily and razzed their croupier, a ruddy old man with black garters around his shirtsleeves and a black string tie. They smoked cigars, and, now and then, glanced curiously at the small game, where the players shot and swore and looked back enviously, hoping to win enough to join them. The little book, watching the big.

One of the men from the big table had fallen from grace and was trying to get back. He had missed seventeen passes in a row, trying for a six when it was his roll and betting against the hot men when it was theirs. His cash had dwindled rapidly, until he could not afford to lose again at those stakes. Then he had come over here, where the action was smaller. He stood against a corner, a corduroy hat cocked back, sweating, still trying for a six and still missing. Now and then he looked at the cardboard sign above his old cronies. It read:

$$\$50 \text{ MINIMUM } \$50$$

The small game had no sign, but only a big-bladed electric fan hanging motionless from the white steel ceiling. There was a minimum, however, as Sam discovered when he crept out of the shadows with Snake's money in his hand, ready and confident.

"Gimme them squares," he grinned at the bearded youth. "I'm hot."

The boy looked at him flatly. "Keep your shirt on, doc. It'll come around."

It came around quickly. The houseman swept up pile after pile of shooters' bets and presently raked the dice away from a loser and flipped them before Sam.

"Okay. What's on your mind?"

Sam ran his tongue over the back of his teeth. "Want new bones."

The boy shrugged and tossed him a fresh pair. "They come with the joint."

Sam pressed a five-dollar bill on the table edge and laid it carefully on the five square. He reached for the new dice. The rake flicked them out of reach. He looked up dumbly.

"Uh-uh." The youth wagged a finger. "It takes a sawbuck here."

Sam puckered, debating. That changed it. He had better try an even number, six or eight. He tried to decide. The man in the cocked corduroy hat had been working for a six and had lost every time. Maybe that was good. Maybe it was bad. Sam had never run into that before. He did not know.

"C'mon, c'mon, c'mon," said the houseman, drumming his fingers along the bounceboard top.

Sam still did not know, but he was afraid they would pass him by if he waited to look it up in his little magazine. He pushed a ten-dollar bill on the six and picked up the dice.

"Wait a minute." The boy was smirking, tapping the fin with his rake. "You wanna bet six *and* five?" Several players tittered. The croupier at the big table called over impatiently. "Let's go, over there."

Sam put the offending bill away hurriedly. Then he rolled the dice between his hands, talking to them. "Li'l sixer, fixer, mixer . . . Li'l sixer, fixer, mixer . . . yah!"

With a twist of his wrist he sent them tumbling across the felt. They ricocheted against the bounceboard and stopped. Two fours.

"Crap," said the houseman, sticking a crumpled cigarette in his beard and raking in the $10. He lit the cigarette with a lighter and shoved the dice in front of the next man.

The outcast from the big game was smug. Someone else could miss a six.

Sam watched the game go from him, stunned and confused. Since Snake had handed him the money that afternoon he had not believed he would miss one pass, had known he would win with the dead certainty which rolled up to him and washed over him like a great tide each time he lost.

He turned and walked to the door, where Junior was talking to the hood in the ragged straw hat. "I lost," he said.

Junior rose. "Let's go."

Sam shook his head. "Still got some."

"I thought ——"

"Lost one pass."

Junior swore. "For Crissake." He sank down and turned his back.

The game swept up to the man in the corduroy hat and stopped. His luck had turned. He could not lose. Six times he turned up six, increasing his stakes each time. Hunched over, dazed by the switch in his fortunes, he rubbed the dice before each pass until the skin on his palms was raw. Then he let them go with a gasp which could be heard at the big table.

When he crapped out with $50 on the baize he had won $1,200.

He gathered it up in a thick wad and backed away. "So long, small-timers," he jeered and crossed the room.

"Easy go, easy come," said the bearded boy, passing the dice along.

Sam put his magazine away and stepped into the place the man had left. He moved in on a hunch. That end of the table must be hot.

When the game came to him he put $20 on six and hunched, as the other man had, rubbing the dice hard. He glanced down the table. The smart money was against him. He smiled confidently and flipped his wrist.

The dice came up seven.

"What'll you have, Jackson?" the houseman asked the next man, a bowlegged black with glasses. The game had left Sam again.

Left him again in that vacuum. With the tide rolling away. Left him numb and disbelieving. With $15.35.

That round was uneven. The black with glasses made his point twice, and a redhead in overalls made $40 on one pass and lost $15 on the next. The others crapped out with the first throw.

Sam's heart was pounding when the houseman flung the dice at him the third time. He had watched the play carefully, and this time he was sure. Six had come up twice and was due once more. He felt it was due. He would win on six. He felt it.

The tense faces turned toward him and he grinned. "Watch me," he chuckled. "Watch Mr. Lucky."

They watched with eyes glittering in the bright light, watched him drop $15.35 on square six.

"Looks like six's big night," the houseman murmured.

Legs spread apart, head thrown back, Sam whispered. Eyes rolling, dice cupped in his hands, breathing in the cup, he chanted low:

"Sixer, fixer, mixer. . . . Gimme a roll . . . *sixer . . . fixer . . . mixer . . . YAH!*"

The dice shot across the table, clinked against the board, bounced back, and rolled together, tiny acrobats, to a sudden stop. Sam leaned forward, leering foolishly.

Four, said the dice.

"Crap," said the houseman.

He raked in the money.

The game was shifting to the next man when Sam sprang after it.

He flung himself across the felt, hands open and clawing, trying to get it before the houseman dropped it in his bin. And when he could not reach it he climbed on the table and scrambled over the baize on his hands and knees, slipping, like a dog on ice.

The boy shouted for help, and the frightened players backed away as Sam lunged across the table screaming: "Fake! Fake! Fake!"

The hood at the door ran over and grabbed his thrashing legs, yanked powerfully until he tore him loose, and pitched him to the floor. Sam struggled for a footing and the hood kicked him in the point of the groin.

"Ahhhhhhh!" the players gasped.

"Fake!" Sam wrenched from his twisted stomach. "Fa-ake!"

The big game had stopped. The ruddy old man in the string tie looked over the heads of the backing players and spoke crisply to the hood. "Hit him again, Abe."

Sam's hands were cupping his groin as they had cupped the dice. Abe kicked them, driving the bent fingers into the shrunken sack.

"Ahhhhhhh!"

— *Sissy Sammy! Sissy Sammy!*

"Fa-a-a ——"

— *Hate um   Hate um   Hate um . . .*

He was vomiting.

Junior fell on his chest and beat him with the back of his fists, his homburg tilting forward over his wet forehead until he could not see, while his fists drummed back and forth, back and forth, battering the drooling mouth and the white and terrified eyes until Sam's struggle ebbed and left only his scream of pain.

The old man looked over from the big table. "Got him?"

Junior rose, mopping his brow. "Yeah."

"He's all right," said Abe.

"Get him out."

They carried him down the freight elevator and put him in the back of a station wagon. He gibbered incoherently for the first two blocks. Then he quieted down, whimpering and wiping his bloody nose on his overcoat.

Junior asked him where he lived.

"El-bow." A spasm shook him.

They pulled into Horrigan Street and pushed him out in front of the Unique. He was on his knees as they drove off.

He stood slowly, teetering.

His nose had stopped bleeding and the blood was clotting on his face, but the pain was still flashing through his belly, and the fingers of his left hand were swollen and hurt. He groped and found his hat and put it on drunkenly. It pitched to one side and hung rakishly.

For several minutes he staggered around in the darkness, bumping into buildings. Then he limped out to West Concord and saw the station house flagpole black against the night sky and headed for it, reeling down Thawe Street in a cloud of pain. He approached the old stone steps, hollowed by generations of the troubled, and saw the little stage under the false starlight in the yard and wondered again what it was.

Under the frosted wires the arc lights burned weakly, trailing a shadow in the dirty snow behind him. It was a slanting shadow, lame and jerking, with arms hung loosely. The mouth sagged open, a dent in the face, and the overcoat dragged unbuttoned, and the head lolled, wobbling the cocked hat. He took the steps one at a time.

An hour later Lottie heard the scuffling on the automobile doors and put her small, worried face to the window.

"Here he come," she breathed.

Peter Paul stopped crying and began to clap his hands and sing:

All around the cobbler's bench,
The monkey chased the weasel.

He should have been in bed. But Lottie had thought Sam would be with Sanders a half hour at most and had promised him his father would tuck him in.

" 'All around the cobbler's bench' . . . Papa!"

279

"SAM!"

First the swollen hand. Then the torn, scabbed face. And finally the bent and limping frame.

He leaned against the window, eyes closed. His hat was gone. In his right hand he held a naked plaster doll with a crushed head. He held it like a bowling ball, with his fingers wrapped around the neck and his thumb in the crease.

"You're hurt!"

He nodded dumbly.

She was frightened. She put her hand on his arm and when he flinched asked tenderly, "What happen? What happen, Sam?"

He wet his thickening lips. "Hit me. They — hit me."

"Yes," she said softly, as though that explained it.

Peter Paul stood behind the kitchen chair in his homemade knit pajamas, holding the slats with both hands and peering through them at his father.

"Papa!" he said again in a small voice, but they did not hear him. He let go with one hand and frowned, puzzled.

"You set down," Lottie said, "an' rest. I'm goin' over Miz Kerby, get some bandages."

Sam sunk into the rocker while she put on her coat. "Now jest rest easy," she said. "Doan move none."

She went out the window and slammed it behind her, scampering over the doors and holding her jacket together in front with one hand. She had forgotten Peter Paul.

He was standing beside the chair with his little spaniel eyes on his father, hoping Sam would laugh and wiggle his fingers in his ears so he could laugh too.

Sam did not notice him. For a time he did nothing but lean back and breathe deeply, holding the doll tightly. Then he felt his nose dripping again and put the crook of his sleeve over it to stop the blood.

The child giggled. "Do it again!" He stamped his bare foot. "Do it again, Papa!" He held his breath expectantly.

Sam lowered his arm slowly, letting the blood drip in his lap, and looked over with red little eyes. "Do what?" he asked harshly.

Peter Paul's father had never looked at him like that before. No one had. He was too small to know what the look meant. But he knew it was not meant to be funny. He was confused, but he still wanted to play. He had waited so long.

"That." He giggled again, uncertainly. "What you jest did."

Sam put the doll aside and leaned forward. The lines around his eyes were tired and ugly. He swept his sleeve across his nose savagely, tearing off a scab. The blood dripped faster.

"That what you mean? Want Papa to do *that*?"

His voice was cutting. The child held the chair slats with both hands and shook his head, fighting the tears. No, Papa.

"What, then? Huh? Huh? Huh?"

"Doan know." Shaking the kinked hair. "Doan know."

Sam stood menacingly. "Doan know, but you want Papa to do it. That make sense. It sholey do. You little bitty thing, tellin' Papa what to do. Huh. I knowed you when you was jest a greasy lumpa meat, is all, an' I make you that again if you doan look out, see?"

Peter Paul's face tightened to cry. He looked for a place to hide but there was none. He could not get under the chair, or under the kitchen table, and Sam was between him and the door to the bedroom. So he looked up at his father for one last pleading moment and then buried his face in his pajama sleeve and wept.

He was only there a moment. Then he heard the swift step and felt Sam's gentle hands lift him from the floor and carry him back to the rocker, caressing him while he rocked him with a soft croon.

They were both asleep when Lottie came in with the bandages. She had never seen Sam look so peaceful, and after waking them and leading them to bed she decided to wait and dress his eye in the morning.

But there was no time then. At dawn Sam was under arrest.

The cops came before breakfast. There were two of them, old and out of shape, and it was still dark, and so they edged across the unfamiliar bridge slowly, crawling along the ice and swearing and calling warnings to each other.

"Hey Herb, watch the tree limb, it don't look safe."

"Watch yourself," the first man puffed, cramming Sam's crushed hat into his hip pocket. "That door ain't anchored so good."

They were nearing retirement and bitter at still being patrolmen, and they took it out on each other. The leader, Herb, was florid and slightly alcoholic. The other, a thin man with a small gray face and rimless glasses, was called Slim. Usually the lieutenant kept them in the station house and sent them out on routine calls. This was different. This was not routine. But there had been no one else around, and so he told them to be careful and call for help if they needed it.

"Herb." Slim was plaintive. "This don't look like the place to me, Herb."

"This is it, all right."

They had roused a woman at the other end of the alley and come across the back yards with her confusing directions, Herb insisting this was the house and Slim not sure.

The window flew open. Lottie's scared face peered out.

"Hey!" Herb panted.

She slammed the window shut and vanished. He scrambled over the last door and rapped sharply on the window. "Hey!" he yelled. "C'mon, open up." He squinted and saw Peter Paul inside, cowering in a corner. Then he tried the window. It stuck. "Stay there," he called to Slim. "If I say get, get."

"Yuh," Slim said sullenly. He had not wanted to go first, but now he wished he had. The night wind was cutting.

Lottie had run into the bedroom, where Sam was slowly dressing, moving his sore and beaten body carefully and wincing. "Police," she whispered urgently. "It's the *police, comin'!*"

He sank to the bed, studying the shoe in his hand and avoiding her eyes. She shook his arm. "Police!" He shook her off and held the shoe closer, as though it were unfamiliar, this old shoe he had worn for three years. "*Police, Sam! Jest outside!*" Herb was banging on the window now.

She looked at Sam wildly and fled back into the kitchen and flung up the sash. Herb thrust his indignant face in and glared. "About time. Where is he?"

"Where who?"

"Him."

"Him?" She smiled foolishly and waved a bony arm at Peter Paul, who watched, fascinated. "That the him you want? That li'l boy?"

Herb's eyes swept the room, flickered past the child, and spied the broken doll on the floor behind him. "There it is!" he shouted and bounded across the linoleum and picked it up.

"Mine!" Peter Paul cried, reaching with both hands. "My toy!" He had found it upon waking and decided it was a present from his father.

Herb tucked the doll under his arm and looked at Lottie grimly. "I got a warrant," he said. "You gonna tell me where he is or am I gonna find him?"

"Him?" Lottie said again distractedly, trying to think who he could mean.

There was a step in the other room and Sam came to the doorway dressed. "You want me?" he asked mildly.

Herb pulled the hat from his pocket. "This yours?"

Sam nodded sluggishly.

"How about," brandishing the doll, "*this?*"

"Mine!" Peter Paul cried again, stamping his foot.

Sam nodded.

"Okay." Herb crooked his finger. "Some people I know want to talk to you."

Peter Paul looked to Lottie for help, and she looked at the policeman. "He done nothin'," she said, quivering.

Herb grunted. "He done plenty."

There was a tapping at the window, and they turned and saw Slim's face pressed against the warped pane. He was twisting his neck to see inside and fogging the glass with his breath so he could not.

*   *   *

283

It was the strangest case in Paul Gormley's magistracy. He found the charge on the docket before court and called the reporters in. "We don't get good numbers raids, maybe," he chuckled, "but we get some weird babies. This is just what you want."

It was just what they wanted, but they had to wait for it. Paul had found during his first term that if he began arranging cases to suit people, even himself, the pressure from petty lawyers and cops became unbearable, and so he told them regretfully they would have to wait until Sam came up on the docket.

There were no other stories worth covering, and so they lingered outside, questioning Herb and Slim.

"It was just a small struggle," Herb said with a shrug.

"Practically none at all," Slim agreed.

Herb glared. "I wouldn't say that," he told the oldest reporter, a tall man in a bow tie. "Slim, here, was outside, on the lookout."

"How'd you find the doll?" The reporter looked at Sam curiously. He stood between the two policemen, looking over the heads of the people who came and went down the passageway to the courtroom. His coat was open and his shoes were wet. He had wanted to go into the bedroom for his overshoes, but Herb had not permitted it. Afterwards Lottie had come to the window with them, but by then they were over the shack roof and gone.

"He had it hid," Herb said with another shrug. "I found it with his kid's toys, in a corner."

"That's a good touch," one of the younger reporters said approvingly. He made a note of it.

The captain strode up, his mustache bristling and his blunt shoes swinging along the dusty floor like weapons. He had started in this station house as a patrolman, and when the Department shake-up brought him back from East Bay he had been very proud. But his plans, like Seaver's, had been thwarted, and he was in a sour mood this morning; headquarters had blandly assigned six of his men to cover, of all things, a society bazaar on West Concord, and there was this incredible business with Sam. He scowled at him. "You're good for a month, anyway," he snapped.

"And a sermon, if I know Gormley," a reporter added.

Sam blinked at the name, remembering hazily, and said nothing.

"When's he come up, Hardy?" the older man with the bow tie asked.

"Case after next."

"After the bag?"

"That's it."

"We better go in."

They filed through the door and took up stations behind the recording lieutenant. The room was long and narrow and crowded with blacks straining to hear. Most of them were witnesses or friends of defendants, and when testimony was disputed they would mutter and argue among themselves until Paul rapped his gavel or Lieutenant Nuggio told them to shut up.

The bench ran the width of the room, and a brass rail ran with it, along the top. Traditionally only policemen and members of the bar were permitted to lean on it, but Paul was an informal magistrate, and when he was on the bench anyone within leaning distance leaned.

"Ruby Jones!" the lieutenant bawled.

In the back of the courtroom a small group of spectators stood hip-to-hip reading racing forms and looking like a Christmas-card choir. There was a sudden tossing behind them and Ollie Wetlek appeared, glanced around belligerently, and walked down the aisle to the rail. A thickset patrolman in a shapeless squad cap joined him.

Paul smoothed his mustache and smiled at Ollie. "Are you Ruby Jones?" he asked.

Ollie shook his head humorlessly. "Just a witness."

"She's over here," a lumpy, coarse woman called from the side door.

Ruby Jones minced forward crookedly, smirking at the dirty floor and fumbling with her belt. It needed to be fumbled with. It was a rope, a common clothesline rope tied with a great knot on the side to hold up baggy trousers, and it kept slipping. Above, where her flannel shirt parted tentatively, her navel puckered gray and drawn. Her hair was long and tangled, like a man's after a deep sleep, and the mottled skin of her neck was caked with grease. Her hands were scarred and filthy, and now they left her belt and clutched the railing.

Paul looked down disdainfully. Her shirt was half unbuttoned, and from the bench he could see her shrunken dugs. "Matron," he said dryly. "Will you please — ah — *arrange* the defendant; I want to try her, not undress her."

His voice trailed off and the spectators tittered. The matron prodded her with a rough elbow, and Ruby Jones hitched up her trousers, buttoned her shirt, and smirked again. Paul looked away. The smirk faded and her mouth hung open stupidly. Ollie studied the wall behind the bench.

"You are Ruby Jones?" Paul asked, officially this time. She nodded. "You are charged with being drunk in a public place to wit the premises at 754 West Concord Street, being the property known as Ollie's Famous Bar. How do you plead, guilty or not guilty?"

"Guilty," she croaked.

"Guilty," Paul repeated, looking at her sharply. Her voice was almost masculine. "Do you wish to be tried in this court or before a jury?"

She gave no sign, and he took off his glasses, polishing them fatuously. "That means," he said briskly, "do you want to go downtown and stay in jail for a couple of weeks while they pick twelve jurors, or do you want this settled right here, now?"

Her head drooped and from under the cap of hair came a murmur he took as assent.

"Will all the witnesses in this case raise their right hands? Do you solemnly swear that all the evidence you are about to give is the truth, the whole truth, and nothing but the truth? All right, let's hear the officer."

The thickset cop had been walking his beat on West Concord shortly before midnight when he heard loud voices at the door of Ollie's bar. He investigated and found Ollie and this woman —

he jerked his head, signifying Ruby Jones — arguing over whether he should serve her another drink. Ollie had pressed no charges, but she — another jerk — had been unable to walk, so she was brought to the station house and booked.

Paul nodded without listening, and, when the cop had finished, asked Ruby if she wanted to say anything.

"I told you guilty," was all she wanted to say.

"You got anything to add?" he asked Ollie.

Ollie was uncomfortable. He was biting his lip and doing things with his hands along the brass. "Well." He paused. "It didn't, that is I don't think it did, really happen like the officer said it did."

"No?" Paul had perfected the skeptical shrug. "How did it happen, then?"

"Well." He bit hard. "This Miss Jones, she was celebrating, and ——"

"Celebrating?" Wryly. "What was she celebrating?"

"Well, she just got back, your honor, from a trip abroad."

Laughter in the courtroom.

"And where, Miss Jones," Paul asked, with a leer for the spectators, "was this trip abroad?"

" 'Rico." Her voice was barely there.

"I see." Paul winked broadly at Nuggio. "Puerto Rico is abroad now." The lieutenant winked back, glad the magistrate was in a good mood and hoping it was not too good. Light fines and suspensions upset him. They made him feel he was not earning his pay.

"After celebrating," Ollie went on miserably, "she was maybe a little tight, but I wouldn't really say she couldn't walk. I mean, she looked to me like she was walking okay."

The squat cop snorted. "You should've carried her two blocks. Dead weight."

Ollie started to say something and decided against it.

"Nothing else?" Paul asked. "Very well. Ruby!" Her head snapped up. "Do you have a record downtown?"

She shook her head hopefully.

"I don't mean just being drunk. Shoplifting? Disorderly?"

No, nothing like that.

"Ever peddle your tail?"

A faint flush touched her wasted cheeks; then she answered with a slow, final shake.

"All right, I'm going to give you a break. I'm going to fine you twenty dollars and costs." He paused, rolling his tongue along his upper lip, watching the shoulders slump. When they had stopped he added, "But I'm going to suspend that fine. If you come in here again I'll charge you with leading a dissolute course of life. Now for Crissake take a bath."

The spectators laughed hugely. Ollie turned from the rail, but Ruby did not move. The matron winked and nudged her. "That's all, hon," she jeered. "Keep dry, now."

Ruby leaned back and turned and went down the aisle clutching Ollie's arm and smiling foolishly at the floor, going out with him past the knot of racing fans, out past the booking desk and into the street. With a prim step and a timid smirk. Ruby Jones.

Paul chatted with the reporters. "That guy's getting a cheap shack job," he told them. "Any time you're hard up, be a defense witness."

They laughed and wrote it down. It would be good for the office. Lieutenant Nuggio looked sad. Drunkenness was usually good for at least ten dollars and costs. You never knew with Eri men.

Sam was limping into the courtroom with Herb and Slim behind him. The reporters stopped laughing and began to write rapidly.

Paul settled back, watching the witnesses assemble. They stretched before him, a solid line. For a cheap larceny it was very unusual. The spectators buzzed and shifted on the benches.

There was first Captain Hardy, standing on a little side step reserved for him, tense in suppressed anger, an avenger in a gold badge. Then, on the prosecution side, came a desk sergeant, the station-house switchboard clerk, three patrolmen, and the broker doll. The doll was the most important witness. The last patrolman held it tenderly.

For the defense there was only Sam. Behind him Herb and Slim stood with folded arms.

The lieutenant glanced respectfully at the captain. Hardy nodded shortly.

"Sam Crawford," Nuggio whispered. "That's page forty-five, your honor."

"Samuel Crawford, you are charged with the larceny of one doll, value unknown, being a reasonable facsimile of the Saviour. How do you plead, guilty or not guilty?"

Sam beamed. "Hullo, Mr. Gormley." He wet his cracked lips. "Remember me?"

Paul sat up and eyed him closely. "Yes," he said quickly. "Please answer the question. Guilty or not guilty."

"Not guilty," Sam said cautiously.

"Do you wish to be tried in this court or before a jury?"

Sam shook his head and Paul mechanically explained the constitutional right of choice, running through his memory swiftly and picking up Sam from the night before, with Junior and Sanders. There had been some trouble at the game. Higgins, the head croupier, had had him roughed up. Higgins would. That was his way. But why was he *here?*

Sam knew what a jury trial was, but he hesitated before turning it down. He did not want them to know he had been in court before. He was afraid they might call downtown and get his record.

But it did not matter. They had him. They would have had him even without the doll. The witnesses were sworn and the desk sergeant testified first.

"Judge, it's I'd say close to ten o'clock last night, this man comes into the station all beat up, limping like he is now and says he wants help. So I ask him what happened and he don't know. Don't have any idea even. Just wants us to do something, only what he don't know. Well, I talk to him a while, you know, to try and find out what it is, because he's in bad shape, but he

289

won't say. Just says he wants us to get the guy put it to him. Only he don't know where he got beat up, or who did it, or how, or even when. Finally I'm a little sore. I got work to do. So I tell him to beat it.

"Then I notice something funny. In his eyes. A funny look, like he's asleep and dreaming with his eyes open. Not daydreaming. Not that. I can't explain it. But he's wandering all over the station with this look, this funny look, and then I ask Joe here, Officer Hatfield, to put him out. That's the last I hear of him until Red Sepp comes running in and tells me he seen ——"

"Thank you, Sergeant. Officer Sepp will testify for himself."

"Yessir."

Paul was on edge. It could be Seaver had heard about Higgins and wanted Sam downtown to find out what he knew. It could be. Or Sam's arrest could have been a fluke. It could be the fluke that would ruin him, because once Sam was in that cell block, Paul had no control over him. The thing would have to be fixed right here. Now.

Two of the patrolmen beside the sergeant verified his testimony, identifying Sam. Then it was Hardy's turn. While the reporters scribbled furiously, he explained what Sam had done.

In the days when he was sergeant here, the captain said, the station house had erected its replica of the manger every year in the open yard beside the cell block, on the paved walk which ran from the station garage to the community toilet.

It was a form of worship, as carol singing is, as Christmas trees are. It was for the whole neighborhood. The station was very proud of it. The captain was proud. The men were.

Hardy had built the manger roof himself and brought the first load of hay from the Department stable in a squad car. And the three Christmases which followed, until his transfer to East Bay, he had led the others in adding to it, giving it a sky of blue plaster, a star of wrought tinfoil, little farm animals with real horsehair and sheepskin from Al Kelly's toy department, and models of Joseph and the Virgin.

"We had a hijacker here one whole December. He was a real good carver. Before they took him downtown he did both."

The centerpiece, however, was not carved, nor had they bought it. It was a doll left in a cell on the women's side by a homeless little girl the Christmas that the manger first went up. They treasured it as a symbol of the season.

"When you come right down to it, it was the only sacred thing there."

During the war the display had fallen into disuse, and Hardy had resurrected it this year. He paused, straining for words, held up a trembling hand and looked at Paul. "I guess you seen it this morning."

Paul nodded. He hadn't, but he could not let the captain know that. The old man was certainly broken up. Cops.

"That's all I got to say." Hardy leaned back, wiping his eyes.

An embarrassing silence followed. Patrolman Sepp spoke mercifully into it.

He had been in the toilet, alone, when he heard the first wood splintering. He rushed into the yard and found Sam destroying the manger. The plaster sky was shattered, the tinsel star lay on a snowbank by the garage, and the little animals and models of Mary and Joseph were strewn about. Sam was tearing the boards from the little roof when he saw Sepp. He picked up the doll and fled. Sepp chased him down Thawe Street, losing ground in the long block between the station house and West Concord. Sam skidded to a stop at the corner, took a grip on the doll's legs, and swung from his heels, smashing the head against a lamppole. Sepp raced up, but when he arrived Sam had vanished with the broken doll, and there was only his hat, pitched crown first into a drift.

Herb held the hat out. Paul glanced at it quickly and looked away. "You're sure this is the man?" he asked in a troubled tone.

Sepp looked Sam over. "Sure I'm sure. There was a light here."

Herb and Slim told their story with flourishes, and then Sam's turn came. Paul spoke to him gently, telling him his rights and asking him how he happened to be in the station house the night before.

"Whatsat?" Sam was wary. He had been preoccupied throughout the testimony and really hadn't heard it all.

Paul looked down at the docket and up at Sam again. He wondered how large a fine Sam could afford. The larger the fine, the larger the chance he was taking. With the reporters here, flat dismissal was impossible. And, he reflected bitterly, he had brought them in.

He asked about the beating.

"I got hurt," Sam said carefully and stopped. His trouble was bad enough. He didn't want to make it worse.

"Yes, I'm sure you did. I know you don't want to go into details, but could you just tell us — ah — when it happened?"

"Doan know when."

"Well." Paul wasn't getting much help. "I suppose your mind isn't very clear about last night."

Hardy shuffled his weaponlike shoes. "It's never clear when they're boiled."

Paul looked at him sharply. "Please. You presented your case, Captain. Let the defendant give us his."

"Okay, okay." Hardy and Nuggio exchanged a glance. Erik men.

The ball was Sam's. Paul had cleared the field and handed it to him and told him to run. He could not lose unless he dropped it. He dropped it.

"Lahk they say, I done it."

The captain snorted triumphantly and the lieutenant held his pen a quarter inch above the Disposition column.

Paul was furious. But he was in this too. So he picked up the ball and humbly handed it across the rail again. "But I imagine you were a little confused, weren't you?"

This time Sam chose not to take it. He eyed Paul suspiciously and decided it was safest not to say nothing. He was swept by a strong desire to wrench the doll from Sepp and beat what was left of the head against the bench. The desire was running over him like a tide when Paul broke in and dammed it.

"I'm sorry, Sam," he said in an elegiac tone, carefully shredding a cigarette butt in the ashtray before him. "Really, I'm sorry, because I think there must be something else here, something you haven't told us. But unless you ——"

This time Sam understood. He grabbed and ran.

"Lahk I say, I must've done it, Jedge, cause they's too many saw me. But Jedge, your honor, I wasn't mysef. Right after they, or he, or whoever it was beat me up, I jest blacked out. That's what happened, for a fact."

Paul folded his hands with a little sigh. "I thought so. What you need is treatment, not punishment. You're guilty of being sick, that's the big thing you're guilty of."

"*Sick!*" Hardy choked, his face scalded red. The lieutenant withdrew his pen with a shrinking motion. It seemed to him the world was treating him very badly today.

Paul looked at them coldly. He knew they disliked him, and if it had not been for the press he would have thrown this one in their faces. He heard the reporters behind him, writing, and went on.

"However, in view of the remarkable character of this crime — and whatever the reason for it, it was a crime — I can't let you go. I'm going to have to fine you fifteen dollars and costs."

The spectators babbled.

Captain Hardy stood transfixed.

Lieutenant Nuggio wet his lips.

Sam stood apart, looking curiously heavy. "Doan have it," he said flatly. "No money."

Paul leaned back and felt his moist undershirt against the chair. He had done his best. "Next case," he called wearily.

The reporters left. Herb punched Sam's hat into his hands and shoved him toward the cell block. The lieutenant closed the grim lips of the docket and slumped forward on a rebellious elbow, certain the Department was going bankrupt.

*   *   *

Sam was in jail less than two hours. It was a terrifying time, with the captain pacing the concrete corridor, denouncing Sam and Paul and Ben Erik and threatening to see justice done despite them. But at eleven o'clock it was over.

Lottie brought the fifteen dollars.

She got it from Tom Sanders.

He came over the automobile doors two hours after Sam had been taken away, and with him he brought a roll, an apology, and the fear Sam had spilled the story of the crap game to the cops.

Junior had given him the details of the beating over the phone the night before, and early that morning word had come that Sam was wanted for a disturbance at the station house. So Sanders had put two and two together and come here with his roll, his apology, and the wrong answer.

He had hoped to beat the cops. When he found Sam had been taken he was very upset. He sat and held his shaking hands. "I doan get it," he said. "I doan get what they want him for."

He thought Lottie knew and he would find out from her.

She thought he knew.

"They didn't say," she murmured, changing the baby's diaper on the kitchen table. "It was most peculiar."

"I left him early last night, real early. I guess I should've seen him home. I jest doan know what happened."

She pinned the pins without replying. Sanders never deceived her. If there was trouble, and he was around, he was the trouble. *She* knew *that*.

He counted his roll. He knew how much was there, but he had to do something with his hands. "Wonder what he'd be doin' in a station," he murmured, watching her.

Still she said nothing. Not yet. She was not ready yet. She took the changed baby back to his crib and closed the door on his outraged shriek, carried a bucket of soiled diapers to the sink and filled it with water and then sat down.

"Now," she said. "Tell me what happen last night."

Sanders was stunned. "Why Miz Crawford! How would I know?"

"You know," she said positively. "Now you tell me."

He shook his head. "You got me wrong, you sholey have."

"Mebbe. Mebbe only Sam know, Sam an' them police he tellin' it to."

A shadow crossed his face and she knew that was it. She went after him with a barrage of questions, tracking him, cutting him off, hemming in his lie until she could almost see it crouching there on the kitchen floor between them.

But Sanders had been a promoter too long. He dodged her until she was exhausted and they sat in the stalemate without speaking.

Emma Kerby saw them there when she tapped on the window.

Lottie turned her back on Sanders insolently and opened the sash. "How do, Miz Kerby, come in."

Emma swung over the sill and stood tentatively. "Much obliged."

"You know Mr. Sanders, he our landlord."

"How do," Emma said mechanically. Sanders waved an indifferent hand.

"I oney got a minute," Emma said. She tilted her head sadly. "My li'l boy Albert, he been in court, he see Sam."

Sanders sat up. Lottie clenched her fists. "What'd they do?"

"They fine him fifteen dollar. Oney he broke, so they put him in jail."

Sanders stood. "What'd they say he did?"

Emma shook her head. "Doan know. Albert couldn't understand. He oney a li'l boy."

Lottie squared her narrow shoulders. "Miz Kerby, can you take my boys for a spell?"

"Why yes. Bring um over in ten minutes, Miz Crawford, I'll be ready." She left.

Lottie turned to Sanders with an outstretched hand. "Gimme fifteen dollar."

He reached for his money. He was afraid, as Paul had been,

of what Sam might say downtown. He might have said too much already. He gave her $20. In that roll it was the smallest bill he could find.

With court costs, the city's bill against Sam Crawford came to $16.45. The lieutenant sullenly handed Lottie the change and went for him.

From the slatted bamboo door of his office Hardy watched her silently. He stood leaning against the door jamb with folded arms, glaring, and slowly Lottie became aware of him. She took a firmer grip on Sam's overshoes and wondered if they really were going to let him go. Perhaps not. Perhaps they would arrest her, too, and if they did, who would take care of the children? Lottie had never been in a police station before. She did not know about such things.

The captain cleared his throat noisily. "Always find the money, don't you?" he called across the empty room.

She nodded timidly and looked away, hugging the overshoes and fumbling self-consciously with the garters under her home-made petticoat. The garters were old and their elasticity gone, and her stockings had slipped and wrinkled in little pouches below her knees. Hardy watched for several minutes and then laughed shortly.

"Ain't we proud," he sneered. Abruptly he flung out his arms and wheeled into the office, slamming the slatted door.

Lottie waited, trembling, until Nuggio brought Sam out. They shuffled down the old corridor, and Sam grinned when he saw her.

"You sholey come fast. Who tole you?"

She thrust the overshoes at him and took him by the hand. "C'mon," she said. "Let's get outa here."

Nuggio gloomily watched them leave. Sam trailed her sheepishly, awaiting the inevitable question. It came on the sidewalk. "Now," she said, stopping and turning. "Put on them shoes, here, an' tell me what this all about."

He pulled them on as slowly as he could and then straightened, staring over her head. "Wished I had them this mornin'."

"Uh-huh. Now tell me what happen."

"It was nothin', nothin' at all."

"Nothin'! You call that money nothin'?" She put a hand on either side of his face and turned it down, as you would turn a child's face up. "It was the numbers," she said. "Now tell me right, Sam Crawford. It was that."

In the vise of her fingers he nodded, lying.

"I thought so. I jest knew it. *Numbers!*"

She spun away and headed home, lecturing indignantly while he hobbled behind in shame, one foot on the curb and the other in the gutter, his head down and his shoulders slack.

They reached West Concord and stopped: the street was almost impassable. It swarmed with shoppers spilling off the narrow sidewalks and out across the cobblestones, defying traffic, dragging children through holes in the crowd and hurrying, hurrying toward a great arch of red and green lights beyond Ollie's bar and then reappearing on the shoving walks with bundles, hurrying, hurrying home.

The noise was deafening. Sam looked up, puzzled. "Whatsat?" he shouted.

"Fair," Lottie shouted back. "Ladies' fair."

He started into the street, but she plucked his sleeve and drew him back. "You go on," she cried: "Take them kids from Emma till I get back."

He protested, "Joe, he turn me in sick, lose a whole day," but she shook her head emphatically. "Go on, till I get there. I oney be a little time." Sam shrugged and plunged into the mob, disappearing immediately, and when he had gone Lottie opened her change purse, counted what was left of Sanders's bill, and headed decisively for the bow of red and green, sticklike legs swinging in sagging stockings.

The lighted arch had been Alma's inspiration. Beneath it she sat in a camp chair, wrapped in a steamer blanket, sulking. The bazaar was an enormous success, and there was a certain irony in the gathering of Elbow money for Wallace Gillette's campaign. But Alma's sense of justice was unsubtle, and for her the sale was pointless unless the Elbow knew its purpose. She had briefed the club carefully, and each member had memorized a short speech for customers, but the noise and the press of business had made all that impossible. So she sat. And sulked.

Before her squads of Valley women hurried along the frail curbside counters, dealing out tinsel and seals and wrapping tissue and grabbing change with rapid, nervous pecks of manicured fingers. There was a short lull; Madelaine rushed back, white hair tousled and earmuffs askew, and snatched a pile of gray cardboard boxes from under a little awning. "These are the very last ornaments," she said excitedly. "They'll be gone in another half hour. Isn't it wonderful?"

"*Every*thing will be gone," Alma moaned, shaking her head.

Madelaine paused, surprised. She could not imagine what was wrong. The enthusiasm of the crowds had exceeded every expectation, and despite her own premonitions there had been no incident, not even the glimpse of a familiar face. She started to say something, changed her mind, returned quickly to the counter and found Lottie there, wedged between a bill-waving black woman in a belted mackinaw and a policeman. She was clutching her change purse and twitching eagerly.

Madelaine cocked her head hospitably. "Made up your mind?"

Lottie frowned in indecision. There was so much to choose from — stars of silver wire, evergreen garlands with frosted tips, tin Santas climbing down tin chimneys, strings of lights, ornaments of all sizes and colors.

"You have a tree?"

"No, ma'am." Lottie puckered thoughtfully. "Jest a window."

"Oh! I have the very thing," Madelaine said confidently and drew from under the counter a great oval wreath, nearly three feet long, spangled with red and silver balls.

Lottie gasped with delight. "Lahk that *fine!*"

"Splendid. It's five dollars."

298

"Oh ——" Eyes fell and looked away. A heavy man in a knit cap appeared beside the policeman, shoving with a strategic shoulder, and Lottie was fast disappearing when Madelaine cried, "Wait a minute!" The man retired momentarily and she surged back.

"What were you thinking of paying?"

"About" — Lottie held up the change purse — "jest about four an' a half."

Madelaine peered at the price tag and ripped it off. "That's it. I made a mistake."

Lottie was retiring, beaming, holding the wreath against her woolen jacket, when Madelaine called, "You have very good taste!" But she was sliding behind the knit cap again, and all Madelaine saw was a rapid, timid little glance before the wall of customers closed tight. She wondered if she had heard her and, if she had, whether she understood.

Lottie had not heard, but she understood, and as she trudged through the crowds and into the winding alleys her understanding rang within her. She did not even notice that her right garter had given up and the old stocking was shriveling down her thigh, gathering in loose wrinkles around her knee. On Christmas her window would be dressed, her home would wear a bright new gown — she knew that, she understood that, she heard that beating swift and hard and warm under the old jacket as she headed up the shack, over the automobile doors.

A brittle wind was rising along the floor of the warren, carrying Bing Crosby across the Elbow. Downstairs Andy Hallam rummaged among his junk. The Consolidated whistle shrieked noon.

Wallace was in the library. Madelaine recognized his Packard in the drive, and as Sarah opened the front door she saw him, sitting behind the desk in his hat and overcoat, smoking one of her husband's imported cigarettes. Cameron was on the threshold, waiting. He beckoned gravely. "Maddy, would you come in here a minute?"

She crossed the foyer uncertainly, wondering what they wanted.

Ordinarily this door was shut to her. She would rather not have seen anyone for an hour or two, for she wanted to shower and change her clothes. But her husband was motioning. She went in.

"Wally!" she scolded. "Take off your hat!"

He smiled wearily, preparing for the eternal effort. "I can't. You don't heat your house." But he doffed it and put it in his lap.

The desktop before him was littered with scrap paper covered with meaningless lists of numbers. Madelaine glanced over, trying to read them as she took off her own hat and hung her coat over a chair, but Cameron stepped in front of her, deliberately blotting them out.

She gave him a furtive little smile and arranged herself in a leather chair, folding her hands and waiting.

He seemed disturbed. "How was the sale?" he asked absently.

"Oh, we sold everything, and ——" She saw he really wasn't interested and changed pitch. "Those women! They said there was nothing at all to this Erik business."

Wallace leered mysteriously at Cameron and he, with equally mysterious pique, demanded, "Who, may I ask, are *they?*"

"Oh, two of the ladies. Just two."

Cameron glanced triumphantly at his brother-in-law.

Madelaine knew this silent language intuitively. There had been an argument, it had been settled, and now they were exchanging potshots in the wake. She even knew who had won. Wallace had. Otherwise he would not be smoking one of her husband's detestable cigarettes.

"Wally's going away," Cameron announced, attempting to be casual. "Going on a trip."

"Oh? How nice." But there was more to it than that. He was always going away.

Wallace leaned back contentedly in the swivel chair. "I think it's very nice."

She was right, then. Wallace *had* won. "Where are you going?"

They exchanged a narrow look. "It's a secret," Cameron said.

"In fact, it's such a secret we don't want anyone to know he's away. It's very important they shouldn't."

"Well." She looked at her brother doubtfully. "I hope you have a nice time."

"Oh, I will. It's very pretty, where I'm going." He grinned. "In fact, you might say the scenery's suitable for framing." Cameron cleared his throat noisily, and Wallace added soberly, "I'll be leaving in about an hour. I'll be back tomor ——"

"Oh, Wally, what a shame!"

"—— row. I'm not supposed ——"

"Just when I had plans!"

"—— to be gone at all," he finished desperately.

Madelaine was distraught. She had invited a half dozen members of the club for cocktails, to meet him. "Can't you wait a day?" she asked hopefully.

"Afraid not."

"Oh, dear." She twisted her hands.

Cameron coughed. "The *important* thing," he said sarcastically, "is he's supposed to be here. If anybody calls here and asks for him, say he's out, or busy and can't be disturbed. Don't, for God's sakes, let anybody know he's not in town."

"But what will I tell those people?" She fretted, lost in her special problem.

"What people?" Wallace asked.

"Why, I told you Sunday. You never listen. The people I've asked this afternoon to see you."

"*What!*" they exploded together.

"Just as he's getting to be a celebrity," she said petulantly, "he goes away."

Cameron crouched above her chair. "You've asked people here? Today? To see Wally?"

"Yes. And I think it's just mean."

"Oh fine," he groaned.

"Is something wrong?" she asked innocently.

"Something wrong?" He appealed to Wallace. "Oh, my God!"

She looked at her brother. "What *is* he talking about?"

But Wallace was deep in thought, his hands pressed together, worrying the cleft of his chin. They waited while he thrust his lower lip out farther and farther, thinking it through.

Then he said with decision: "I'm sick."

"You're what?" Madelaine asked.

"Sick," he repeated. "Upstairs."

Cameron nodded slowly. "It'll do," he said.

"Oh, dear," she cried in exasperation. "I give up."

"While I'm gone I'm sick. That's what you tell people. Tell your guests they can't come." She started and he raised his voice. "They can't come because there's sickness in the house. Me. I'm the sickness."

"Well." She was still baffled. "If it's really necessary ——"

"It is. Very."

She rose, defeated. "Is that all?"

They nodded solemnly and she took her hat and coat and went out, tiptoeing, as though that would help the conspiracy she was abetting but did not understand.

Cameron closed the door after her with relief. "I don't think that'll be a problem," he said, coming back to the desk and perching on the mass of paper. "If it works, he'll be too busy to wonder how it happened."

"It'll work."

The sheet immediately before Wallace bore one number, circled and underscored. He had drawn the figures with great vigor, pressing hard on the pencil shank. Halfway through the lead had broken, and he had finished with the stub.

The number was 555.

He picked up the paper and read reverently: "Five, five, five."

"It would be funny if we got mixed up," Cameron chuckled.

"What would be even funnier would be if I got caught." Wallace was nettled by Cameron's nervous flippancy. "You've got Henderson's number there? I told him you'd call first thing tomorrow."

Cameron fumbled in the pile of scrap paper, drew one slip

out, studied it gloomily, nodded, and then put it in his vest pocket, patting the cloth. "You really think he can do it?" he asked.

"I'm positive. So is he."

"And we can depend on him?"

"Of course! He's a businessman."

"What I can't figure is this. He's ruining his business. If it works, he's out of a market. Who'll buy Black Whatever-its-name-is then?"

"*Black Combination*." Wallace hesitated. Henderson was planning a string of scratch sheets aimed at the bookie trade, and to Cameron the book was very like policy. He decided to dodge. "In a way, we're buying him out."

"We're paying enough, God knows."

"It's worth it."

"If it works."

He has to have that last word, Wallace thought, fingering his hat angrily. He glanced at his watch. "I'm going to have to leave soon. It's a long drive."

They went over the details. Cameron thought Wallace should leave him an address, or at least a number, where he could be reached.

But Wallace thought otherwise. "It's dangerous and unnecessary. There mustn't be any way they can trace me later."

Cameron argued. "You called him down there, person to person."

"I had to. You know that."

The telephone rang. Cameron listened a moment and then cupped his hand over the mouthpiece. "Here's Helen." Wallace's secretary was across the state border, at the Hayestown Airport. "She's got the passenger list."

"Let me talk to her." He took the receiver. "Helen? Read me the whole thing."

Cameron took Henderson's number from his vest pocket, read it several times, tucked it back jerkily, fingered the vest buttons, one by one, and, when he had finished, started over again.

"Thanks. So long." Wallace hung up and took a deep breath. "We're safe. I don't know one."

He stood and put on his hat. On the portico they shook hands clammily. "You'll hear in the morning. From a pay station. I'll say on, or off, and that's all. Right?"

"Right."

Cameron patted his vest again roughly. The great doubt still crouched on his shoulders. "Take care of yourself, now," he said loudly and added in a hoarse whisper, "I wish there were some way we could do it legally."

"There isn't," Wallace said tersely. "You know there isn't."

"It's such a risk. If only somebody else could go!"

"Well, somebody can't. He just won't deal with anybody else."

Cameron frowned, still troubled, and Wallace left without another word, stamping out to the Packard. He wants this as badly as I do, he thought furiously, but he can't stand getting his hands dirty.

On the highway he turned west, driving swiftly through the hazy afternoon. By nightfall he was in Hayestown, and there he began shedding his identity, piece by piece.

The Packard was parked in an all-night garage near the airport at six o'clock. An hour later he took off on a westbound flight. He was in Louisville at 10 P.M. In a public toilet there he changed quickly to a rakish checkered suit and a broad Stetson. His homburg and his business suit were checked in a dime locker. He kept his overcoat, draping it over his arm.

Then he applied with crossed fingers for a reservation on the next flight south. He had taken a chance, waiting until he was here, but applying in Hayestown would have been even riskier.

Behind the chrome counter a girl in a cute cap checked Operations. "We can give you a seat on the 11:20," she told him. "Name, please?"

"Clark."

She smiled professionally. "Going to the races, Mr. Clark?"

The conspicuous fan relaxed in his cheap suit. "I've missed half the meet already."

The girl murmured her regrets, weighed his valise, and turned to another traveler. Wallace faded discreetly into the lounge.

In another hour he was again airborne, the Stetson tilted at a careless angle, studying a racing form. Over Tennessee he fell asleep. Even there he lost a little of himself, for when the flight put down at 1:30 A.M., his face was dark with a thin crust of beard.

In the airport lobby he dialed a suburban number.

"Yes?" said a guarded voice.

"Joe Clark, from Chi."

"Okay, pal. Gimme half an hour."

Wallace wore dark glasses in the cab. He despised them, but his caution was stronger than his distaste, and he did not take them off until the taxi drew up before the palm-frocked façade of Philip's Health Service and the driver, reaching across the plastic seat cover, opened the door.

"Don't get cooked," he grinned.

Wallace tipped exactly ten per cent and sauntered inside.

Behind a wire screen a moon-faced clerk in a bent eyeshade was playing solitaire. "Dirty, mister?" he said without looking up.

Wallace flushed and checked himself. "I want the large room. I have friends coming."

It was one of those antique baths with cubicles and had been chosen for that. Registering at a hotel would have been difficult.

"They come the right place," the man said. "We make boy scouts out of old men."

Wallace paid and left his bag. The clerk rang a bell, and a muscular man in a T-shirt appeared and led him back. "Swim or hot room first, mister?"

"I think I'll take a plunge, thanks."

"Sound off when you want me."

He left, and Wallace undressed, slipped into the rope mules provided, and clattered out to the deserted pool. A sign behind the diving board told why Philip's customers should enjoy themselves.

Every Member an Individual Case
NEVER CLOSED
Physical Conditioning at Its Finest
OVERNIGHT ACCOMMODATIONS
Ask Your Physician About Our Service

He paddled around in the shallow end, relaxing in the warm water, and dried himself on one of a pile of large, thirsty towels stacked by the door. He was sawing the moisture away from his crotch when he found, with some confusion, that he was being watched. A man in a pongee shirt was peering through an opening in the tile wall opposite.

"Are you a lifeguard?"

The man nodded solemnly.

"Well, please tell the boiler I'm ready to be boiled."

The pongee shirt disappeared and presently the man in the T-shirt reappeared, whacking his hands together and beckoning.

Wallace was sprawled on a slab, groaning under a merciless thumping, when the eyeshade was thrust into the rubbing room twenty minutes later. "Guy in your party come, Mr. Clark," said the clerk. "He's waiting in your room."

"Sure." Wallace grunted and rose with an effort. "I better shower." He was glad of the chance to get away.

In his cubicle he shook hands with an athletic, sportily dressed man of middle years. "How've you been?"

"Pretty well, pal. What's the time?"

Wallace took his watch from a hook under his clothing. "Two-twenty," he said.

The old sport undressed quickly. "They'll be here in ten minutes. I'll cut my rub short."

At 2:30 they began to arrive, dripping through the assembly

line of dry heat, flailing hands, and showers, and drifting into the cubicle. By three o'clock the talks were in progress. There were five talkers: Wallace, his contact, and three others. All were stripped, toweled, and sweating in the hundred-and-twenty-degree steam.

"The fives are best," the oldest of the strangers agreed. "Any other would be tough except zero, and I guess that's out."

"That's out," Wallace echoed.

The man shifted on his stool. He was a lumpy, florid diabetic in his late forties, with gray hair parted precisely in the middle and swept back. The towel was gathered in a thick knot just below his navel, and his legs were pocked with insulin needle jabs.

"Peggotty's the place man," said the old sport. "He and Rorsch won't have any trouble."

Rorsch, a melancholy young man with bony knees and an isolated hank of hair in the hollow of his chest, looked up quickly. "We'll have as much trouble as anybody else if the stewards catch wise."

"Sure." Peggotty tugged at the towel with manicured fingers and repeated: "As much as anybody."

"Nuts," snapped the third man. "I'm where the trouble is."

"Farris handles the show," explained the sport.

Wallace nodded, trying to separate them in his mind. Until now he had thought of them as one man.

"It's me and Quinlan got the rough ride," Farris went on. "The straight and place are a cinch." He stared indignantly at Peggotty and Rorsch. "They know that."

"Well, we'll settle that later," Wallace said amiably. Farris lapsed into an angry silence. He was blond, in his early thirties, with milky skin blotched by the steam.

They went through the mutuel routine, arranging signals, and when that was done Wallace broached the payoff. He made each a flat offer: $5,000 apiece for Peggotty and Rorsch and $8,000 for Farris. They haggled hopefully for a few minutes and then gave in. It was nearly 4 A.M.

"I'll call Quinlan," said the sport.

"He's got to be called?" Wallace was distressed. "I've got to get this settled and get back.

"He lives near. He wouldn't come until we got the rest taken care of. He can afford to be choosy, you know."

"You want us any more?" Farris asked.

"No." Wallace wiped the sweat from his face. "I guess we're straight. You'll get half your money Tuesday."

"*Half!*" said Rorsch and Farris together.

"The other half after the races."

"It's all right," said the sport. "He'll make it good."

They looked at each other doubtfully and then shrugged together. Wallace turned the steam down and they left for the showers with stealthy glances at the door and muted goodbyes.

Quinlan, Wallace's last and best buy, arrived within the half hour. He was bespectacled and shriveled, with fine black hair and no chin, and naked he looked gnomish. Despite the heat and the informality he would not remove his glasses, and they clouded, giving him an opaque stare, like Daddy Warbucks'.

Quinlan had talked things over with the old sport. He knew just how it could be done and insisted on telling how, sparing them nothing, not even his technique for speedy operation of a Peerless adding machine. He spoke in a drone, with a slight lisp. His voice was sedative, almost narcotic, and Wallace was dozing when a sinister drop in the monotone awoke him with a start. Quinlan wanted $15,000.

"I — we — hadn't planned on that much," Wallace stammered.

Quinlan removed his glasses. His eyes were flat and winking mildly. No one said anything.

"But I guess we can manage it."

It was Cameron's money and Wallace was tired.

They went over the details. Quinlan was to get $10,000 Tuesday and the rest within twelve hours after the races. It was to be in small bills, none over $20. They were to be wrapped so and delivered so. Quinlan was a professional. He remembered everything.

"You're positive nothing can go wrong," Wallace said at last. He was haggard from lack of sleep and the nagging worry something unforeseen could ruin him.

"It's all right, I assure you," Quinlan assured him. "It happens now and then," he replaced his glasses, "by mistake. It's never been noticed."

"It's okay, pal," said the sport.

He and Quinlan left together. Wallace followed shortly, lingering under the lazy shower and dressing slowly. The man in the eyeshade was gone, and the new clerk eyed him curiously. His suit, for all its tawdriness, was heavy for the Gulf. He averted his eyes as he passed the counter and damned himself for not bringing seersucker.

Outside it was dawn. He lugged his suitcase six blocks to the Greyhound Terminal, where the nearest telephone was, and arrived giddy from the strain and sniffling a little. The sharp change and the bath had been too much. He was picking up a cold. Madelaine, he reflected sardonically, would not be lying to her friends after all.

In the booth he leaned against the glass door, sluggishly shaking the quarters in his fist, waiting for the operator to put through the station call.

Cameron answered with the first ring. Since Wallace's departure he had scarcely left the desk and was himself groggy from lack of sleep. He could not have slept if he had wanted to, for Henderson had called every hour, demanding to know if there was any news.

"Ah — yes," he croaked. "That you — ah — down there?"

"This is me. I'm fine and dandy."

The connection was bad, and Wallace's clogged head did not help. Cameron was cautious. "You sound sick."

"I got a cold."

"What about the trip? What do you hear?"

"It's *on*." Wallace squeezed his eyes in a spasm of fatigue. "The trip is *on*."

"On, you say?" Excitement sharpened Cameron's voice. "You say it's *on*?"

"That's right." He spelled it. "O–N."

"Got you. Thanks very much. Goodbye."

"So long."

They hung up, two exhausted old men ready for bed. Wallace's sleep was restricted by the next flight to Louisville. Cameron's, when he uncradled his bedside phone after calling Henderson, seemed limitless. Actually his rest was shorter than Wallace's, for at 10:15 he was awakened by Helen, arguing loudly with Sarah and demanding to see him. He staggered heavily down the stairs, fumbling with his bathrobe, blinking and scraping his fat tongue with his teeth.

Helen had heard the first radio bulletin. She shouted the news at him, and he grabbed the balustrade and spun around and ran back to his bedroom and dressed frantically, his mind awake now and racing.

On the eighth day of Seaver's failure he had returned to headquarters in a towering rage, whipped past a protesting Griesel, and flung open the commissioner's door. He was a little man, driven by ambition, and the disappointment of the past week had been almost more than he could bear.

"I don't have to take this crap," he cried. "I know what they're doing. I'm gonna hold 'em at the drop while the papers come."

Zipski was standing at a wall map of the city with his hands locked behind his back. He did not turn around. "Come here." He put his finger on Belton Avenue. "You been operating in there."

"All this week. And if I'd held 'em ——"

"Never mind. How long between when your spotters leave there and come in for the papers?"

"Fifteen minutes, maybe twenty."

"All right." He glanced at his desk clock. "Every drop in the

Seventh's working overtime right now. Send out three men to spot a place. Only instead of all three coming in, tell one to stay. I want to know what happens when the spotters leave."

By early afternoon they had the third man's report. The other two had left for headquarters at noon. At 12:32 a four-door Pontiac came racing down the street and skidded to a stop in front of the drop, and a white man with bifocals and a pocked face climbed out hurriedly and rushed inside. Five minutes later he and the writer ran to the sidewalk carrying a canvas bag. They locked the front door, threw the bag in the back of the car, and drove away, turning the first corner on two wheels. The vice squad arrived twenty minutes later.

Seaver seethed. "That just proves what I been saying. If we could hold 'em there till the papers come, we'd get 'em all."

Zipski rapped his pipe on the desktop. "You don't see anything else?"

"Well," he said grudgingly. "They know we're coming."

"You're getting bright. And who tells 'em?"

"How should I know?"

"You're going to find out."

The following morning Zipski sent Seaver out alone, with instructions to telephone Holloway when he had seen enough for a warrant. Holloway went out in plain clothes and replaced him. Seaver came in to swear out the papers. His clerk dropped the warrant carbon in the wire basket as he left to drive directly to the drop.

Holloway greeted him on the sidewalk. "They just left. The writer and a flunkie. Ten minutes ago."

"Well," Seaver said grimly. "It's you or me. How about splitting the payoff?"

Holloway did not laugh. He gave the brim of the unfamiliar porkpie a tug and climbed into the police car with a sick heart. For the first time he knew, beyond all hope of denial, that there was a renegade cop.

That night Zipski decided on a blanket tap of all trunk lines leaving the headquarters building. The men were briefed the following morning, and in the afternoon the bleeders were clipped in and the earphones switched on.

There were thirty bleeders, one to a trunk. Seaver had only twenty men. Zipski assigned him a dozen patrolmen from Traffic.

The trunks ran out of the main room in the Communications suite, through a small, unused room, and into the wall. The thirty policemen sat in this vacant room, on the floor, with their equipment in the center, a vast tangle of rubber tubes and monitoring boxes. They leaned against the wall with their clipboards on their knees, recording all numbers called and anything which seemed significant. Most of the time they listened to the endless chatter of administrative routine. Occasionally one would overhear a personal call and tell the others about it and be silenced by Seaver.

"I think Eckhart's got a nurse knocked up over St. Mary's ax-room," a slope-shouldered sergeant chuckled. "Wait a minute. Yuh, she's three months gone, wants him to marry her."

Weary laughter from the others.

And from Seaver: "Shut up, Wood. You're listening for another kinda leak."

A deafening roar.

"That ain't bad, Cap."

"I mean it, now. The telephone people is very strict."

Actually, the telephone company rules did not permit tapping at all, and technically Zipski was using the equipment for service observing, checking on the time required to place a call in the building. The company knew what he was doing and winked at it. It drew the line, however, at pay phones, which had their own trunks. There were four of these in the building, all on the first floor. Zipski could have tapped them from the outside but decided against it. Instead he posted men in plain clothes inside the booths for a half hour after every warrant swearing. They were told to become involved in long conversations and to note anyone who looked inside urgently.

Zipski's greatest problem was security, and it nearly beat him. He could control the conspicuous activity behind Communications, for the little room had a separate entrance, and the men were told to come and go one at a time during slack periods, when a dummy vice squad was out keeping up appearances. But he could not stop thirty men from talking, however often he told them every man in the Department was under suspicion until the leak was dammed.

On the afternoon of the day the tap began, Gregg met Sergeant Wood at a water cooler on the third floor. "How's the big campaign?" he jeered. Seaver's squad had become a Department joke. "How many you got now?"

The sergeant sulked.

Gregg drank and straightened, wiping his mouth and smirking. "How many? Just them two? Myself, I think *they* was framed."

"All right, all right," the sergeant snapped, playing with the fountain knob. "You'll see who we're gonna frame, and I wouldn't look very far if I was you, either."

He meant nothing, but Gregg went back down the corridor brooding, and when he reached his office he phoned Paul. The dummy squad was out, the taps were off, and so no one picked up the call.

"I got nothing I can put my finger on," he whispered, watching the stenographers in the next room through the open door, "but I'm worried. It's a hunch I got. Something one of Seaver's boys said."

"What was it?"

"Something about framing somebody. It didn't make much sense, but the way he said it, it worried me."

"Anything else?"

"Well, Bull told me an hour ago they got some new raiders, men off the beat."

If Paul had been altogether loyal to Ben, this would have been enough for him. It happened that his law partner had had business at the telephone company the day before and had seen Morelock leaving the office of an executive there. This, with the news that

Seaver had been given more men, should have aroused his suspicions, and it did.

But Ben, like Zipski, had his traitor, Paul. Since Murdock's recall from his run Paul had built his first floating crap game into a chain, absorbing the numbers players there, and the chain was prospering. If the leak were shut off and the syndicate closed down, even for a day, Murdock would be free of his telephones. Free, he would go back to his writers, who would tell him of the crap games. He would report to Ben, and Ben, his overconfidence gone with Bull's tips, would move against Paul's cozy racket.

So he squelched his doubts. "Nobody's been bothering Bull, have they?"

"Bull? You know Bull, nobody hardly sees him. He's part of the furniture."

"I guess you're right."

They hung up on their one chance.

Bull went about his business contentedly, assuming that every day the conspiracy worked was that much more insurance against discovery. He had reported the new raiders to Gregg from duty, not concern, and when he came downstairs and found all the booths occupied, he was incurious. He returned to the second floor.

At the moment he entered an empty office there and closed the door, the leader of the dummy squad dropped in to see Seaver before leaving. "Going out, Cap," he said.

Seaver lit a cigarette and looked around for an ashtray. "Call the old man and tell him what you find."

"As if he didn't know."

The raid was set for a vacant store in the 100 block of Crone Street: the address was scrawled across the top of the listeners' clipboards.

Three floors down, Bull dialed "9." The dial tone broke flatly and he spelled out the number. F. O. 2. 7. 6. 0.

In the tapping room a patrolman shifted his cramped legs and wrote it down. F. O. 2. 7. 6. 0.

Seaver found a discarded Dixie cup and pulled it toward him. "See you later," he said to the dummy squad leader.

The door closed.

Joe Murdock took the receiver from the hook in his bedroom. "Black's Delicatessen."

The patrolman shifted his legs again and snickered. "Christ, they're ordering food now."

"Would you please send a loaf of bread and a quart of milk to 109 Crone Street?"

"Hey!" The cop clenched his clipboard.

"Okay," Joe said. The line went dead.

Seaver stood quickly, the cigarette slanting from his open mouth. "What you got?"

The policeman took off his earphones and told him.

"Whose voice was it?"

"I don't know. It sounded old."

"You got the number?"

"Right here. Fort 2760."

"Come on. Fleming! Take over that trunk."

Zipski listened, clutching his pipe and taking notes. When they were through he told the patrolman to bring the men from the pay stations. They were back in less than three minutes, panting from the stairs.

The man from the last booth was a rookie, young and excited and terrified of Zipski. Three people had wanted the booth while he was in it.

"There was Whitey, the colored man, you know, he's a janitor," he stammered, "and an old woman, she had a case in traffic court, I think. Anyway she come from there. And then there was that old man from Records. The one they call Bull."

Zipski frowned, trying to place him. "Bull?"

No one said anything. Then Seaver blurted, "Bull Hoover," with sudden vehemence.

Zipski's frown deepened. "Bull Hoover?"

"In the Record room." Seaver spat. "Where I am."

"Oh. I remember him now." He knocked the heel out of the

pipe. "Let's see." He reached for the tobacco pouch drawer. "He files warrant carbons, don't he?"

Seaver nodded, twisting furiously in his chair. "You got the guy."

The next day was Thursday.

Gregg was caught. If he had been given a few minutes to himself, if the word had come from Griesel, over the Department exchange, he could have warned Bull and called Paul. But it did not come that way.

Shortly after 8 A.M. Seaver put his head in the office door. "Conference in the old man's office. Right away."

Gregg followed him down the long corridor. His morning meal lay in his stomach, a cold wad. "What's up?" he asked on the elevator.

"You'll find out."

Gregg wondered if it were the abuse of the sergeant at the water cooler. He had heard the old man was very sensitive about the failure of Seaver's squad. He hoped it was only that. He did not see how they could nail him. Nevertheless he rode up with an odd feeling of going down.

Then, as they stepped out on the fourth floor, his natural optimism welled within him. Maybe the commissioner had some special assignment for him. It was probably only that.

He was right. Zipski shook his hand and waved him to a chair. "You're stuck in that office so solid I never see you any more," he said, puffing vigorously on his pipe. "About time we got you out on the street once in a while, Gregg."

"Yessir." The old man was in fine spirits. He wondered why, and as he wondered, as the first doubt crept into his mind, Seaver said it, and he knew.

"Hoover works directly under Lieutenant Gregg, sir."

"I know."

Gregg sat rigid, the sweat forming in the hollows of his body. "Something about Hoover, sir?" he asked in harsh falsetto.

"Quite something. I don't know that you can have been expected to know about it, but I thought you might worry, so I asked you to help us clean up this mess. Your man Hoover is a felon. We have evidence."

Gregg's chest was tight. "Whatever it is, I'd like to help."

"I thought so."

Seaver cut in. "About Hoover, sir, I'd like to be on that detail."

"I gathered you would. Lieutenant Gregg will go after the contact, with Morelock."

Griesel ushered in Holloway and then Morelock. When they were seated the patrolmen came in and stood. Zipski went over the instructions carefully. Then Morelock and Gregg left with their men and their warrant, and the others took up stations in the building.

On the way out to the squad cars, Gregg made a stab at escape. "I got to go to the can," he told Morelock. "Why don't I meet you in the garage?"

The inspector shook his head. "I'd go myself, but we got to hurry. This is a Nigra neighborhood. We can use the alley."

At 8:30 A.M. Bull came to work.

In his wallet was five hundred dollars of Ben Erik's money.

He had kept it all in an old lunch box under a loose board in his attic and on Gregg's advice had sworn not to touch it until the heat was off. But a new heat was driving him the other way, and he had talked himself into spending a piece of it on his wife, for a necklace, on this ninth shopping day before Christmas. The stores were open late, and he thought he would walk up to Stuart Street after work and buy a real necklace, a five-hundred-dollar necklace.

Records was deserted. He hung his blue overcoat on the three-pronged rack by the door, capped it with his hat, and put the brown paper bag with the two peanut butter and jam sandwiches in it on the shelf above.

He began his routine.

First the warrant basket. Nothing there. Then the Out box by Seaver's desk. Empty. Then down into the building, through

Communications and Missing Persons and Permits, picking up the slips and flimsies that bureau heads had assigned to the files. In Administration he glanced into Gregg's office and saw he was gone and his cap and coat gone with him. For a moment he wondered idly where Gregg might be, and then his wonder turned to the missing coat with its heavy nap and bright new buttons, and the high-peaked cap swooping above the glittering visor. He thought of his own shabby uniform, dull where it ought to be shiny and shiny where it ought not to be, and decided he would order a new outfit the moment the heat was off. Perhaps sooner.

Holloway's basket was crammed, as usual. Bull snatched up the sheaf of papers and shoved them under his arm carelessly, wrinkling those on the outside with deliberate spite. Holloway was Gregg's superior. It was Holloway who had rejected Bull's repeated applications for transfer, as though, Bull reflected bitterly, walking a beat were any harder on varicose veins than stairs.

After Administration came Personnel and then Traffic, his last stop and his busiest. A stenographer loaded his free arm with dossiers and he started back, bracing himself for the long climb. He observed with approval that the pay stations by the candy and gum Vendomats were empty.

Up the steel stairs he headed, puffing. The electric clock over the water cooler on the first landing read 9:03.

Morelock and Gregg stood before the chalk-scarred wall, Morelock relieving himself and Gregg pretending to, carrying the gesture through. He stood exposed for half a minute, thrusting his hip forward to shield himself from the inspector. Then Morelock turned and Gregg turned with him.

"How much time we got?" he asked.

"Depends. Twenty-five, thirty minutes."

Gregg shivered. "Cold."

"You're kidding."

They walked down a narrow alley, between high board fences, feeling the dry snow rustle underfoot. They were safe here. The fences were so high no one could see them from the windows on either side. At each end of the alley a patrolman was stationed, to intercept anyone who happened by and hold him until the raid was over. On so cold a day it was unlikely anyone would. They had been there fifteen minutes and no one had.

Joe Murdock's house was east of them. Two patrolmen were watching it through chinks in the board fence. As Gregg and Morelock passed them a husky rat came racing along the fence-top, head low, tail straight. One of the patrolmen squealed and jumped back. The other grinned and winked at Gregg. "East Bay," he whispered scornfully. "They don't have no rats there." The squealer settled back into position, red with shame.

Morelock turned up his wrist and glanced at his watch: 9:21. "Let's go over it once more," he said.

They checked the men for the last time, the inspector brisk and confident, Gregg haunted, as he had been since leaving headquarters, by the fear of what Paul would say and Ben do. Nothing would satisfy them, he thought miserably. They would never believe the truth. And beyond this first terror there was another, shapeless still but huge. Somewhere in Ben Erik's tottering organization a record of him must exist. The somewhere could be in this house. And even if it were not there, Gregg knew where Zipski could soon find it. It lay on the surface of Bull Hoover's mind, ready to be torn free.

He felt his breakfast still churning in his belly.

There were four men in front, four in the alley behind, and one in the radio car on the side street. The four in front were hidden between buildings opposite Murdock's house. In the rear were the two lookouts and the patrolmen at the fence.

The radio car was the raid's link with Zipski, and as Morelock and Gregg approached, the driver gave them a sign. They hurried over. "Warrant's out," he said urgently. "He just got it."

Morelock jerked his thumb toward the house front. "Get across the street," he told Gregg. "Move fast."

Gregg circled the block in a dog trot. As he approached the

street he heard a bus gusting exhaust and wondered idiotically what would happen if he broke for it, and jumped aboard, and rode to the end of the line.

As Bull came back into Records, breathing heavily, he heard footsteps behind him. He did not turn. He never did. It was one reason he had always been inconspicuous. But as he drew up at the little table where he sorted his papers, he saw three policemen walk on past him, toward Seaver's desk. One was Meise, Seaver's clerk. The other two were new raiders.

The taller of these was a sergeant, and as Bull stacked the first flimsies from Permits on the corner of his bench he saw this sergeant sit at Seaver's desk and arrange penciled notes, preparing to dictate a warrant. Meise was waiting before a typewriter stand nearby, shuffling half-sheets and carbon paper. The other man, a patrolman, looked on.

Apart from his treason, Bull envied these men. If he could have been one of them he would have gladly returned Ben's money. Sometimes, dreaming away the winter evenings by his kitchen stove, he would lay aside his back copies of *True Detective* and give himself to the wistful hope that Holloway would change his mind and send him to a beat. Holloway would be doing the Department a favor, he told himself, for he would be a good cop, and the vice squad's troubles would vanish.

He could not hear the sergeant dictate. He could have moved to the cabinets by the typewriter and heard, but the warrant would come to him soon enough. He bent over the papers from Missing Persons, sorting.

Once he had asked Holloway for an interview. The talk had been postponed for months, and when it came at last Holloway told him he was too valuable in Records. Then Bull did something very foolish, and Holloway almost equally so. Bull asked if he might be permitted to carry a gun, and Holloway laughed. Later he tried to explain away his laughter, but it was no good. Bull knew why he laughed. It was a laughter he never forgot.

He had always believed the ban on sidearms for clerks was a

slur on their manliness, because he thought a gun made a man. He cringed before men with guns. He cringed now as the tall sergeant approached him, holster swinging, warrant carbon extended. "For the record," the sergeant said without looking up.

"Thanks." Bull grinned, bowing. "Thanks very much."

The sergeant and the patrolman went out, and a moment later Meise followed. Bull took the carbon to its file, glancing down swiftly as he slid it in. The address was 478 North Brandt Street. The time of oath had been left blank, but he did not notice that.

As he came down the stairs he saw Meise standing before the bulletin board on the fourth floor, studying a week-old notice. He spoke and Meise spoke and he headed for the next landing.

When he had gone, Meise skipped into an empty office, picked up a phone, and dialed extension 111.

It was 9:25 A.M.

Joe Murdock flung his arm across the dresser, sweeping the cards with it, until they lay strewn along the mirror edge like leaves against a fence bottom and the dresser top was bare.

Except for the two phones.

They sat on either side of him, crouched on the varnish, mute and awful. For over a week now he had waited before them, their slave, through game after weary game of solitaire. He did not dare leave the bedroom for more than a half minute at the most, and then he had to station his wife by the dresser, for with its silencer the ring would not be heard beyond the threshold.

She came in with coffee, prim in a starched apron. "Any news, sweetie?" she asked softly.

He shook his head and reached for a cigarette, his ninth of the morning. Alice Murdock knew nothing of her husband's business. She asked questions infrequently, and then only to be polite, for she did not care to know. It was enough for her that they lived in a decent neighborhood and were without needs. She went out quietly.

He drank the coffee in swift gulps, staring at himself in the mirror and wishing once more he had told the serviceman to install the telephone elsewhere. At the time this place seemed best. He had not noticed the mirror then.

The chair scraped roughly as he pushed it back. He went to the window and looked out bleakly at the windswept yards and the fence beyond. As he watched, a well-muscled rat scooted along the fencetop and someone, a tardy child, he guessed, cried out. The rat disappeared behind an abandoned brick privy and Joe turned away, vowing to have his section destroyed and replaced with Page fencing. There was a nest somewhere in the neighborhood, and the wood attracted them. With the children they could be dangerous.

The clock on the bedside table ticked solemnly. It read 9:24. A little fast. Make it 9:20, or 9:21. Time for the day's first raid.

Joe wished the last raid had gone and he could quit his vigil. He wanted to call Ben but could not tie up these phones until all the drops were closed. Alice could not call the barn for him. She knew Ben Erik only through the newspapers, and Joe could not give her his new number. Ben's county phone was almost as restricted as these two. Like them it was unlisted and billed at a separate address, to avoid suspicion from the mailman.

Joe wanted to talk to Ben for two reasons. The first was Joe's children. Until now he had diverted them by advancing the ritual of Christmas, but after next week they would be home from school every day on vacation. Home, they would become curious about his strange business in the bedroom, and being children, they might spread their curiosity around the neighborhood. Joe thought he ought to take a furnished room for the phones. It would be more difficult, for his wife would not be there to serve him lunch, and less comfortable, for she could not bring him coffee or watch the phone while he went to the toilet. But it would be safer.

The second reason was Paul Gormley. The evening before one of Joe's writers had called with a strange story. The run, he said, was swarming with floating crap games which were soaking up his old customers. The games were operated by a former bookie named Higgins. Two days before, when Paul was in the territory, paying off the writer in a bar, Higgins had appeared and addressed Paul by his first name. Paul had ordered him away with some heat. Higgins had left growling, "One more crack, you get yourself a new boy."

Joe hesitated to bother Ben. Getting the daily number was always a headache when the races were in the south. With the county location Ben's service from the Marsh Sports Daily had deteriorated alarmingly. But if what his writer had hinted was true, and Joe suspected it was, Ben ought to know about it. After the writer left he had called the barn without success — Ben had slipped into town to see Jody, Otto reported. He planned to try again this afternoon.

He slid the chair to the dresser and began to shuffle the cards dismally. He was one game down. Maybe he would get it back this time. He didn't much care. But it was something to do. He fingered the top card, ready to deal.

Just then the incoming phone rang softly.

Bull had come down the stairs jauntily and impatiently elbowed his way through the crowd of traffic violators and police court witnesses. When he found all four telephone booths occupied again, he was confounded. He recognized Flesch, the rookie, in the end booth. Calling his girl again when he's supposed to be on duty, he thought wrathfully. One of Holloway's pets. He considered asking Flesch how long he would be and decided he had better not.

He halted by the Vendomats in indecision. The cubicle he had used the day before would be risky. Gregg's office was too far away.

Then he saw the press room. It led off a landing halfway up the north staircase. The reporters would be in police court. He wondered why he had not thought of it before.

Back through the mobbed corridor he went, a bowed and blinking figure in faded blue, muttering and shoving toward the stairs.

Zipski rapped his pipe on the radiator.

It was the only sound in that tense nest. Thirty listeners sprawled over the floor in grotesque attitudes, arms and legs thrust wherever they would fit, heads bent gently forward, as though in prayer. Waiting. And listening.

Three feet from Zipski a sergeant stood by a recording machine. The needle sat ready on a virgin disk of green. From its base two wires ran, through the sergeant's fingers, ending in dangling clamps.

Zipski rapped on the radiator.

At the door a lieutenant in earphones knelt, clutching a hand microphone. Now he looked toward the radiator and caught the commissioner's eye.

"Inspector Morelock reports no activity in the house, sir."

Zipski rapped his pipe.

The door opened, and over the lieutenant's shoulder a patrolman pressed a tight face. "Going into the press room, sir," he whispered at the radiator.

Zipski rapped.

"*I got it!*" A listener by the window flung out his hands. "*Gimme the wires!*"

The sergeant tossed him the clamps. The men on each side of him dropped their own phones and closed the thin steel jaws on the coiled trunk cable at his feet. The room leaned swiftly toward the window, and the green disc spun slowly, cutting grooves.

But Zipski only rapped.

The press room was a dead end, irrelevant to the rest of the building. From the balcony before it steps led down to the first floor and up to the second. There was no other exit, for wide and dusty windows lined the street side.

Three desks, one to a newspaper, faced three walls. Against the fourth, where the windows were, a rococo Victorian couch leaked stuffing and a police radio croaked routine calls. Someone had twisted the volume knob to the far right, and as Bull came into the empty room, the voice of the dispatcher filled it:

"Car 9, go to 1310 Douglass, take a report, Car 9, go to ——"

Bull turned the knob down, and the dispatcher finished with a sepulchral whisper, "—— 1310 Douglass, take a report."

He sat at the desk on the east wall and reached for the telephone. Then he stopped in confusion. The place where the dial should be was smooth. This was a direct line, linking the press room with the newspaper's city desk. Bull pushed it aside, annoyed, and cast around. On the floor he found another phone, with a dial, and he picked it up and set it before him, grunting with satisfaction.

He dialed 9. Then: F-O-2-7-6-0.

Outside, on the street floor, Holloway started the long climb to the balcony. At the stair foot stood Seaver, his body shielding his drawn pistol from the corridor crowd. Flesch guarded the little door at the end of the balcony, where the stairs went up again, disappearing through the ceiling on their way to the second floor.

Joe Murdock's phone was ringing.

Holloway was climbing.

Joe answered. "Black's Delicatessen."

Holloway was on the landing. He waited by the jamb, listening.

"Would you please send a loaf of bread," Bull purred; "and a quart of milk," shaping his lips carefully, "to 478 North Brandt Street."

A pause.

Then Joe excited: "You sure you got that right?"

"Huh?"

"That 478 North Brandt, that right?"

Bull frowned indignantly. "It was on the warrant."

"But that's *here!* It's *here!*"

The masks were down.

Holloway loomed in the doorway, a blue cloud speckled with brass. "All right, Hoover. Come on. Let's go."

The receiver crawled slowly away from Bull's ear and slipped over his wrinkled cheek. When it reached the hump of his jaw the line went dead, and as it left his face altogether and fell, with his hand, to the desktop, he grinned weakly. Then he remembered. "Goodbye," he said to the dead line.

"Come on, old man."

Bull forced the grin wider. "How're you, Inspector?" he said, very politely, returning the receiver to its hook and patting it gently. *There*, he patted. *There, there.* "How are you today?"

"Come *on!*" Holloway started toward him, fists clenched, and just then the police radio by the leaking couch broke in. "Car 14. Go to 478 North Brandt, report to Inspector Morelock. Be careful. Car 14. Go to ——"

Holloway was beside it. He flipped it off and then reached out with a massive paw and sent Bull spinning against the desk. The desk edge dug into Bull's flabby buttocks, but he did not bounce. He bent over backwards. He was still grinning. The crest of his naked skull was brilliant with sweat. He was fighting tears.

"I ——" he choked. "I." It was all he wanted to say.

"Out the door!" Holloway roared, shoving him roughly toward it. Bull went.

On the balcony he made his break. Seaver's gun did it. When he reached the balcony and looked down and saw that barrel pointed at him, he spun sharply and raced toward Flesch, his tongue buckled flat over his teeth and his cheeks streaming. Holloway pounded after him.

How he got past Flesch no one knew. Holloway, who was less than six feet away, swore he went through the rookie's legs. Flesch said he ducked under an arm. Seaver, starting up the stairs with Bull's first twist, thought he went right through him.

In his panic Bull did not even know where he was going. He lunged forward, pumping the steps after him, and burst into the second-floor hall. Behind him he heard the cadence of Holloway's breath and the sound of many feet.

Down the hall he fled, past a string of offices. Two patrolmen sprang in front of him. Holloway reached out to grab him. A metal door appeared on the right, and Bull shot through it. Half a step behind him came the inspector, and then Seaver and Flesch, trailing.

They were in the ladies' room. It was deserted. The gates of the three booths hung open.

Bull jumped in the third, locked it, and crawled up on the stool, his thin shanks folded under him and his arms locked over his paunch like those of a halfback charging. He was past sobbing. The little wind still in him oozed out in soft bleats.

"All right," Holloway panted. "Let's go. Over the top."

Bull waited for the men with the guns.

Morelock was closing in. With the first sign from the radio car his men swarmed over the high board fence, ducking and running across the snowbanked yard and up the back porch, hammering on the door and shouting.

Gregg stood on the front stoop with his thumb hard against the doorbell and his free hand motioning his men to the windows. All along the street doors were opening and dark faces appearing. In less than a minute the street was jammed. The mob surged up to the curb and stopped, waiting for blood in hungry silence.

"Police!" Gregg cried.

"Police!" yelled the men on the back porch. "Police!" No answer from the house.

Morelock shoved Joe's fence gate aside and strode over the snow. "Break 'em in!" he bellowed, scanning the empty windows. "All together!"

In front, Gregg's door gave easily.

The momentum of his rush carried him across the living-room floor. He crashed into a little table covered with Christmas cards, and as it collapsed he thrust the heel of his hand against the wall and spun, bracing himself in the tiny wreckage.

Behind him the four patrolmen were tumbling through the smashed door, fanning out with drawn pistols.

Before him Alice Murdock crouched on all fours under a bushy Christmas tree, trembling, watching him with terrified eyes. She had thrown herself there when Joe locked the doors and had not moved since. A sprig of evergreen was jammed in one nostril, but she did not turn her head. She did not seem aware of it. She looked like a trapped animal.

327

Upstairs a toilet was flushing.

One of the patrolmen broke for the stairs.

"Hold it!" Gregg shouted. The man turned, astonished. "Watch her," he ordered and went up himself.

As he reached the second floor he heard the back door fall in. Then the toilet flushed again. He headed down the hall, toward the sound, slowing his step.

Joe was kneeling before the bowl with one hand on the toilet chain and the other clutching a final batch of papers. He was about to plunge them in when he looked up and saw Gregg standing on the threshold, fingering his revolver.

He sat back on his haunches, defeat in his face.

They stared blankly at each other across the narrow distance, listening to the toilet suck up strength.

Then Gregg heard Morelock thumping up the stairs.

"Get rid of it," he whispered, gesturing wildly with his gun. "Get rid of it!"

Joe crammed the papers into the pool at the hopper bottom and pulled the chain. The water gushed quickly and the last slip dipped and disappeared, leaving a great bell-shaped bubble to break at the pool surface. Gregg, with Morelock almost on top of him, stuck his gun in Joe's stomach, forcing him back, and groped for the papers. Too late.

"Get 'em?" Morelock puffed.

Gregg shook his head dismally, still groping.

The inspector swore.

Joe raised his hands slowly, flicking his eyes from Gregg to Morelock and back to Gregg again, moistening his lips with a tight tongue.

Below them the second radio car had arrived. Murdock was taken downstairs and handcuffed to his wife, and Gregg led them through the crowd and into the back seat.

"Burke!" he called. "Davis!" Two patrolmen shuffled forward heavily in wrinkled overcoats and baggy trousers. "Get in with 'em."

Morelock came down the stoop grimly. "Don't look like a

damned thing here. I'm leaving Nugent and Wiscowski for a good look."

"Want me to stay?" Gregg asked.

"Good idea."

The inspector crawled into the front seat and slammed the door. The car nosed out through the mob and was gone.

Gregg went over the house carefully. He left it a chaos of uprooted bedding and emptied drawers. Even the presents under the Christmas tree were torn open and left among shredded seals and red tissue paper. But there was nothing there.

While the others were waiting for the squad car to take them back, he slipped out to a corner drugstore and made a telephone call.

When he returned the car was ready.

Under his arm was a carton of Lucky Strikes.

In his pocket was a package of single-edged razor blades.

Cameron was reknotting his bow tie for the third time, muttering in exasperation, when the telephone rang. It rang simultaneously on all three extensions, and simultaneously he, Helen, and Madelaine answered: he in his bedroom, Helen in the foyer, and Madelaine in the study.

"Hello," they said together.

Henderson, bewildered by the chorus, fell silent. Then he stammered, "Mr. Cameron? You there?"

"I've got this," Cameron barked into the receiver, and Helen and Madelaine hung up. "Henderson? Heard the news?"

Henderson hadn't. "I just wanted to tell you we're out on the street. Like I told you we'd be."

"Out. Out." He tried to remember and gave up. "Wait a minute." He switched off the bedside radio. "Out where?"

"You know, the *deal*." Henderson's voice was edged with suspicion. You never knew who was going to welch. "The book. It came off the presses an hour ago. Send you one if you want."

"Oh yes, yes, of course. I get you now." He really had forgotten. His mind was still numb. "Yes, please do."

"What's this news you're talking about?"

"Well, I'll tell you, Henderson, I haven't got time to explain right now, I really haven't. Turn on your radio, you'll get it."

"Nothing about our friend?"

"No, nothing like that."

"Heard anything else from him?"

"No, no, not a word. Nothing. Look, can you call me back?"

"Sure." Henderson's voice was curt. "Can and will."

"Okay. Goodbye."

He was back at the mirror, wrestling desperately with the tie, when the phone rang again. He decided to let it go, and then the failure of his new knot changed his mind. He wrenched the tie off, flung it across the bed, and snapped up the receiver.

Madelaine was talking to a stranger. "I'm awfully sorry, but he really is too sick. The doctor said he's recovering, but he can't come now. If you can call later ——"

"How about Mr. Cameron?" the stranger asked. "I tried at the track. They said he was here."

"Hello?" Cameron broke in. "I'll take this, Maddy." She hung up. "This is Jarvis Cameron."

"Oh, Mr. Cameron?" The stranger was a reporter, calling, he carefully explained, on a deadline. "I'm sorry to hear about Senator Gillette, but we got word ——"

"I think I know the word."

"The commissioner's statement?"

"Yes."

"We'd really like a comment from the Senator."

"Impossible. Call Sylvester."

"Well, we have. We've got something from him, but we'd like ——"

"Sorry, my boy. The Senator can't talk. He'll be better tonight. Try then. Goodbye."

He slammed the receiver down and returned to his dresser, fuming. It was rotten luck, having Wallace away at a time like this. He had just begun to shape the smaller grievance, Wallace's

330

refusal to leave a number where he might be reached, when he fell upon the full indictment.

"Damn!" he groaned, twisting the knot into a hard ball.

Wallace's whole trip was unnecessary; the bribing of Henderson, a foolish waste. It was as he had suspected. The entire plan — Wallace's, he reminded himself, not his — was an absurd risk. Erik's organization was dead, and they were delivering it a useless and expensive kick.

Once more the phone rang.

It was Big Ed, exultant.

"Cameron? Say, you heard about it?"

Cameron, glumly thinking of the loss, answered that he had.

"Say, what's the matter with you? It's tremendous! Most tremendous thing could've happened!"

So it was, Cameron agreed. Tremendous.

"How's Wally?" Big Ed asked guardedly.

"I — I think he'll be all right later today. About suppertime."

Ed paused, reluctant to hang up. "Christ," he chortled, "I'd give my roll to see old Ben right now."

"Think he suspects anything? About — you know."

"He's too busy. That's the beauty of this thing."

"Well. Wouldn't surprise me if he took the gaspipe before then."

"Ben? You don't know Ben. This is just the time to watch him. This is when he gets dangerous. I mean dangerous."

Cameron rang off and went back to the mirror, wondering what Erik had left to be dangerous with. He studied his tie, decided it would not do, and unraveled it and started again, slowly, methodically, suddenly realizing he had no reason to hurry and wondering why he had thought he had.

Henry Loomis heard it first.

Ben had gone down from the loft to use Otto's shower, leaving the radio by his cot turned on. Henry was bowed over his books in the cubicle beyond, trying to concentrate among the squawking of the soap operas and wishing he had nerve to switch it off, when the announcer interrupted to bring him the special announcement.

Through the roar of the shower Ben heard him shouting.

"Mr. Erik! Mr. Erik! We're in, I think, real trouble!"

Ben twisted the faucets to the right and stepped out, a glistening ape.

"What's eating you?" He fumbled for a towel.

"Murdock! He's been arrested! And a cop, a clerk cop ——"

He trailed off. Ben had stopped in the middle of a wipe and was staring at him.

"Go ahead." Ben dropped his eyes and went ahead, drying himself with long, deliberate sweeps. "The clerk cop what?"

"They say he gave Murdock dope. From the inside," Henry finished feebly.

"Anything else?" Ben reached for his shorts.

"That's all he said."

"Good." He dressed quickly and efficiently in the cold room. "Ready for your sorters, Henry?"

Henry shook his head, deciding wretchedly the bulletin had not been important after all.

"Better get ready, then."

Henry left, and within a minute Ben had slipped on his coat and followed him to the loft. He sat on the bed crosslegged, thinking, while Henry, in the next room, went over his figures uneasily, knowing he was there and wondering why he was so quiet.

Then Paul was on the phone, jabbering defeat.

Ben listened calmly until Paul mentioned Gregg's call.

"He went over the whole place? Find anything? Good, good. What did you tell him?" He listened, smiling. "It might work. It could work."

Paul wanted instructions.

"Stay right where you are. Keep in touch with Gregg. I wan

a report from him every night after work. Not by phone. Meet him some place, then come out here. Starting tonight."

Ben meant to keep the syndicate *going?*

"Absolutely. I'll tell you about it tonight."

Paul asked if Ben were out of his mind.

Another smile. "Maybe. That just could be. See you tonight."

Outside Otto was driving up with the stunned pickup men. Only Hugh Slade, thinking of his wife's wrath when she learned something had been kept from her, could say anything.

"We didn't even know," he fretted. "We didn't even know what was going on, how the raids was kept away."

"A lot of things I don't tell you," said Ben, moistening a cigar. "Does Costello tell Abbott everything?"

They sprawled on the old wicker furniture in the back of the barn while Otto went for the sorters. Ben dictated their orders. All drops Seaver had raided unsuccessfully were to be moved that afternoon. Beginning the next day writers were to operate for one hour only, the hours staggered by pickup runs and changed each day. Every writer was to hire a lookout to circle his block during that hour. If a stranger were seen watching a drop, it was to close at once.

"Immediately," he said firmly. "Before they get the warrant."

"How do we pay the lookouts?" asked Milt Feinblatt.

"We don't. The writers do. Out of their cut."

Izzy Friedman looked worried. "How's the dough?" he asked. "Suppose we get a big hit?"

Something inside Ben shrank. He managed a shrug. "Money's no problem. We made a lot last week."

They looked at him curiously. The last week had not been especially prosperous, and they knew how expensive it was to carry Joe Murdock's writers with no action on his run. But he stared them down. They studied their shoe tops, believing because they had to.

"Maybe we'll make a lot more this week," Moss piped, anxious to please. "*Black Combo* come out today for one number positive — first time they ever done that. Saw it about an hour ago. Business ought to be terrific."

Ben looked up with interest. "What's the number?"

"Five-five-five."

Ben nodded. "It could help."

"What about singleshooters?" Moss still carried Charlie on his conscience. "It's a good time for scabs."

"Any scabbers get rid of, I don't care how, I just care you do it, the first time the knockoffers get hot."

Moss took a deep breath. "It'll be a pleasure," he said, winking at the others.

Ben looked at Eddie Finch sourly. Eddie was lighting a fresh cigarette from his dying butt with the studied gesture they had seen Joe use so often. "How about Murdock?" he asked, looking at the wall. "What happens to him?"

"Murdock?" Ben said with an exaggerated frown. "Murdock. Let me see. Seems to me I heard that name before." He narrowed his eyes and looked straight at Eddie. "But I can't remember where."

They exchanged quick little glances of herd fear. Slade wet his lips. "Say ——" he protested.

"Say yourself," Ben snapped, staring them down again, one at a time. "I got one rule right now. Stick with me, that's my rule. Don't ask questions. Break that rule ——" He drew his fore-finger across his throat.

They sat in the uneasy stillness, fidgeting.

Then the phone rang.

Ben answered and listened with grim satisfaction. He hung up with a flourish and faced them, smiling faintly.

"I got a telegraphic mind," he said. "That was Paul."

Then he told them.

Bull Hoover had just been found in his cell with his neck sawed open, dead in a sheet of gore.

In his bloody hand lay a razor blade.

With a single edge.

Shortly before noon that day the door of the Trinity Hospital O. B. Clinic opened slowly and a bedraggled girl in insufficient clothing stepped out into the bluff wind.

The door closed and she leaned against it, blinking frowsily. On so cold a day she looked unreal: her flannel shirt was half unbuttoned, the fly of her khaki trousers was open, and below frayed cuffs the ankles in her cracked loafers were bare and blue.

Yet she did not seem to mind. For a moment she looked without seeing down the neatly shoveled concrete walk and the even snow stretching on each side to the antique wrought-iron fence. Then, rocking in the fist of the wind, she leered, almost cheerfully.

Behind her the door was trying to open. She stepped aside grudgingly and let it. A gaunt woman in a woolen suit came out carrying a blanket.

"You forgot this," she said gently, holding it out.

"I told you," the girl said sullenly. "I got no money."

The woman smiled. "I know. You don't have to pay. It's on us."

She watched her take it with rigid fingers and tuck it under a flanneled arm. Then she reached into the pocket of her suit blouse, hesitated, and with a decisive movement brought out a ten-dollar bill. "This is on us, too," she said.

The girl took it without a word, slipped it into a trouser pocket, paused, and transferred it to another pocket, fumbling with the bulky blanket.

"That one had a hole," she explained tonelessly. She turned her face from the wind and tightened the slack skin around her lips. "I didn't think it could happen," she addressed the wall. "After all this time."

Abruptly she swung down the walk, her tangled hair idling in the wind's blast.

"Take care of yourself," the woman called tenderly.

"Happy days."

The first empty cab sped by without slowing, but the driver of the second knew her, and he drew up before the hospital gate and opened the door with a long arm.

"Hi, Rube. What're you doing over here?"

She climbed in, hugging the blanket to her narrow chest. "I'm a nurse," she said thickly. "In training."

He chuckled, the chuckle dying as he recalled hearing something about her and tried to remember what it was. "I was talking to Ollie yesterday," he said vaguely, cruising toward the waterfront with his meter flag up. There was a silence and then he remembered with a start. "Say! Ollie said you might be in a certain jam."

"I am. The doc just told me."

His face deepened with concern. "Not knocked up?"

She smiled apologetically into the rear-view mirror.

"No!" He looked around sympathetically. "Tough break, kid. It's a real bad winter."

"Terrible." She glanced about nervously, suddenly embarrassed. "Take me over to Haldemann's, Hildie. I got to get some things."

He turned back to the wheel. "Sure, kid."

At the department store she pushed the bill toward him, but he shook his head. "Meter's been up the whole time. I couldn't break a sawbuck anyways."

She put it back with a shrug and picked up the blanket. "Say, Hildie, do me a favor. Don't say nothing to Steiner, at the diner. He might, you know, fire me or something." Her face was pert with anxiety. The other thing was too big to have reached her yet, but this was small enough to feel and fear.

"Not a word, Rube."

She slammed the door and he pulled away in heavy traffic, leaving her timid in the curious glances of the shopping mob.

She waited for a gap in the crowd and darted through it to the store lobby. A bank of telephone booths lined one wall of an alcove there. She slipped into one of these and drew a dime from the watch pocket of her trousers. She had lied to the woman at

336

the clinic. She hadn't been broke at all. There had been the dime and a nickel besides.

"What is it?" Fred answered roughly. The head of the social agency had just rejected his report on discrimination with a curt note, and he was feeling low.

"Freddie? It's me."

"Hey! Where've you been?"

"Oh, around. Look. I want to see you this afternoon, in about two hours. Can you come to my diner? It's the Unique."

"Well, I'm supposed to eat with Dad, but I guess he's forgotten all about it since the big news. It's pretty terrific."

"Good." She did not want to hear it. She knew all about big news. "I got to talk to you." She paused and then said huskily: "I'm pregnant, Freddie."

"You're — you're *what?*"

"I can't talk about it now. My boss Steiner'll be out. We can talk at the diner. In two hours."

"But ——"

"I'll see you, Freddie. So long."

She slid the booth door open and went out into the store.

Haldemann's was not the best or even the cheapest department store in the city. She had heard enough in her modeling days to know it as the trade knew it, as a clip joint. But it carried everything, and it was a store where a bum could shop without prejudice. Haldemann's didn't care whom it clipped.

She went to the basement. It was no season for bargains. She would wait until after Christmas for most of her wardrobe. Today she only wanted something clean, something she could live in, and sleep in, for another week. These rags had suddenly become intolerable.

She bought a cheap cotton dress — *not* very stylish, she thought, remembering Candy and how it would have horrified her — a work sweater, two pairs of anklets, and rayon underpants. The pants were a problem. She had forgotten her size. "It's been so long," she explained to the fat saleswoman.

The woman eyed her coldly and recommended a six. After

Ruby had left, climbing the stairs stiff-leggedly, she called the floorwalker over. "Pants, she wanted. She must've seen her priest."

"I heard." He nodded wisely. "She probably don't want 'em to wear at all. Probably she wants 'em to filter radiator alcohol."

He had heard that from a friend.

Outside on a bitter corner she waited for a streetcar, standing in an eddy among the shoppers, between a telephone pole and a trash can, shivering in the wind, wishing the old strong wish and pushing it away.

Across the street the gay neon of Harry's Bar & Grill beckoned. She walked around the pole. Harry's, where she saw the war end. Pushing it away. In her pocket was $2.48. Back around the pole again. Plenty for a good belt. Pushing it away.

The trolley rattled up. She took a seat in the back, on the side away from Harry's, and tried to forget. But a little girl across the aisle kept losing her transfer. She would lose it and find it and then deliberately lose it again. It was a game she was playing. Ruby thought if the little girl did not stop she would jump off the streetcar and buy a pint of Bellows with that $2.48 and kill it in the store open-throat.

But the little girl didn't stop, and Ruby didn't get off, not until she reached the Oak Street Public Baths. Her strength surprised her and pleased her. She had seen so many of her promises fail. Now, for the first time, she began to have a little faith in this one.

The bath overseer was a squat, pushed-down man with red hair and freckles. He shoved a towel and a wafer of soap across the counter without looking up. "Five cents," he murmured.

She paid not five, but twelve cents, for she bought a comb and rented another towel. "I got plenty to wash away," she told him.

She didn't have to tell him. He knew that coarse voice.

"Well, well, look who's here," he cackled, eying her and scooping up the change. "The boys must be payin' up. Last time you was broke."

She slipped the comb in her hip pocket and shuffled away without answering, feeling his curious stare at her back. He had known her in the days with Ira, when many parties ended here, and she liked him, but all the old jokes seemed stale now, and she wanted a bath.

She was in the Women's Division half an hour, dissolving the wafer in three complete soapings, and when she had rubbed herself down and combed the mop of hair straight and pulled on the new clothes, with the pants feeling strange and tight, like a girdle, she paraded out proudly.

"Reds, you got an old hair ribbon?"

He whistled shrilly. "What you doin' tonight?"

"Not what you think. Got that ribbon?"

He had it. In his Lost and Found closet Reds had everything from a British busby to a belt-of-thousand-stitches. She posed before the cracked mirror in the anteroom, one hand on the frayed ribbon and the other on a straight hip.

Reds whistled again and called his mopper. "Hey, Stoney, come here. How old you say she is?"

"I got no idea," Stoney said warily.

"C'mon, guess." He winked. "Forty? Fifty?"

She picked up her old clothes and the blanket and headed for the door. "Go on, spoil it, you red-headed son of a bitch," she said and slammed the door on his nasal laughter.

But on the curb again, waiting for another trolley, she felt decent for the first time in months. On the streetcar she dropped the dime in the fare box with the strange elation of a man lighting his last cigarette with his last match.

Outside the sky was thickening.

Inside Fred sat dawdling over his second cup of coffee. He glanced impatiently at the Pepsi-Cola clock over the mirror. Quarter to two. Fifteen minutes more.

He had arrived a half hour before, hoping she would be early, too. When he found she was not, he ordered coffee and produced a pencil and paper and began making a list. Fred was a listmaker.

339

Over the bureau in his furnished room was a pad labeled Things to Do Today. When it was blank he would draw up schedules of Ideas for the Agency, of Letters Owed, of Birthdays and Anniversaries, and these were crammed in a drawer of his desk at the office and carefully recorded on a List of Lists under the blotter. His immediate answer to any crisis was to itemize it.

This one was discreetly headed "Jan's Trouble." The first three entries had been written almost immediately. They were "Find the Father," "Borrow from Dad," and "Get Doctor." After that there was nothing. He had spent the past half hour unsuccessfully trying to think of others, and, now, at last, he swallowed the bitter pill and made the fourth and last entry: "Get Advice."

Fred thought he needed advice. The pill was bitter because he considered himself a man of the world and it had to be swallowed because he was not. He was many things which were more important, but at his age he did not consider them so. For him nothing could match experience. To deal with this he believed he had to have experience, or advice from someone with it.

He was convinced it would have to be dealt with, as convinced as she was that it would not. She had called him for help, but not the kind of help he was invoicing. She had lived her way long enough to know that no single grief was so great time could not wash it away. What she needed from him was help, not from this one trouble, but from all her troubles, from the great multiple catastrophe which had been building up all her life, and which she now at last recognized and at last feared. This one thing was in itself unimportant. It was her understanding that mattered. She did understand, or she would not have called him. For he alone could help her. For he alone loved her without pity, and it was love without pity she desperately needed.

Fred, with his lack of experience, could not know what she, with her abundance of it, did. And so he made his pathetic little list, unaware that advice, the last thing he could give, was the last thing she wanted.

Jan is going to have a baby. He weighed the dreadful fact. To Fred, illegitimacy was not real. You made jokes about it, the way you made jokes about Pat and Mike. He knew no Irishmen named Pat or Mike, and he knew no unmarried girls who had babies. He supposed there were such people, but he had never had anything to do with them and had never thought he would.

Jan is carrying a bastard. A bastard. How many times had he used that word? A thousand. Make it ten thousand. And never once thinking what it meant.

Jan is pregnant. It was the sort of thing you dreamt about after an evening with a girl in her father's club room, or a park in the Valley, or a hurried, successful fumble between nylon thighs after the last dance at the Country Club pavilion. He had dreamt about it, and he supposed the girls had, too. Doubtless Jan had, many times, he thought wryly.

Then he remembered: Jan did not dream. She never had. It was one of the marvels of his childhood. She would close her eyes at night and open them the next instant and it would be morning. So she could not have dreamt of pregnancy. Maybe that was the trouble. Maybe if she had been a girl who dreamt she would have been all right.

He pondered this.

A man in a paper bag, punching.

He finished his coffee and set the empty cup on the saucer with a frustrated clatter. Steiner hurried over, his hunchback wiggling anxiously. Customers in Brooks Brothers suits seldom came to the Unique.

"Something else, sir?"

"Well ——" He would have to order. "You got any doughnuts?"

"Yessir." The caked apron fluttered like an old flag. "Fresh baked."

"Let me have one."

"Coming right up."

The diner door opened and she came in, shivering. Steiner appraised the new outfit sharply. "Well, well," he jeered. "Princess Elizabeth come to pay us a call. Ain't that nice."

Fred looked at the pale blue skin, aghast. "Is *that* all you wear on a day like this?"

Her eyes met his in a swift look of caution, and he turned to the doughnut. It was small and shriveled and entirely black.

"You don't have to worry about her, mister," Steiner chortled. "If you carried her anti-freeze you could walk around in a bathing suit." The image delighted him. "In a bathing suit!" he said again. The twisted back bobbed with glee.

Ollie Wetlek came in and sat at the far end of the counter. Ruby slipped behind the counter and ran to wait on him. Fred watched over his doughnut, wishing she would walk.

"What'd the doc say?" Ollie whispered.

"He said it'll be a boy and look like you."

"Oh, Jesus." He thought of Hoot and his face darkened.

"Cheeseburger?"

"I guess."

"Punkie at the bar?"

Ollie nodded. His brother read water meters for the city. On Thursday, his day off, Ollie hired him at fifty cents an hour. He did not need the help, but his brother needed the money and worked hard.

Steiner made coffee before leaving, filling the cloth bag at the top of the urn with a coarse grind and then pouring three dippers of hot water through it. He left it to simmer and hung up his apron and struggled into his leather jacket and ski cap. "I'll be back, five o'clock," he told Ruby. "Keep 'em happy."

"Don't spend all your money," she said.

"Me? On Christmas?" he simpered, setting his hips. "Who would I spend it on? You know I don't know any little boys."

No one laughed, and he went out and down the street with a hurried limp.

Ruby introduced Ollie to Fred. "A good stickman and a tremendous guy."

Ollie was embarrassed. "I keep telling her to lay off," he apologized.

But not as embarrassed as Fred. "Hello, hello," he stammered.

In Fred's circle sticks were called bars and you only kidded with bartenders. "It's really a great pleasure," he lied.

They gnawed at their tasteless food, haunted by the same vague sense of guilt.

And she, watching them, was curiously pleased and bright, like a child.

"How're you feeling?" Ollie asked her, biting into the second half of his hamburger with determination.

"I got a mouth tastes like a wrestler's jock strap, but I won't wash it out, if that's what you mean."

"I mean — mean your — you know." He reddened.

"Oh, *that*. It's a pleasure by comparison."

Fred was fighting his doughnut. Ollie saw his discomfort and rolled off the stool. "I got to get back," he said. "Punk and Annie get into terrible arguments."

When he had gone Ruby came over and slumped beside her brother, resting her head on her arms and watching him gravely. "Why don't you stop," she said softly.

"Stop what?"

"Trying to eat that crap."

He smiled and put it down. "It *is* pretty bad. How long have you been working here?"

She sat up with a shrug. "How long? I don't know how long. Remember when we were kids how the movies would show years go by? Somebody would be looking out a window and it would be snowing and then the snow would melt and the sun would shine, and then the leaves would dry up and fall?"

"Sure. Sometimes they'd just show a calendar, with the pages flipping away, one right after the other."

"That's what it is for me. Winter, spring, summer, fall, rolling up in a big ball, with me inside."

"Hey! That's a new one. They never used that ball one."

"I'll write Hollywood a letter. Maybe they'll send me a check."

"But maybe they used it by now. That was a long time ago. I don't see movies much any more."

"Me neither."

"I'm a snob, I guess."

"Snob!" She grimaced. "What's a snob? Everybody's a snob some way."

"What kind of snob are you?"

"Me?" She shrugged again. "I'm nothing. Caught in the middle is what I am."

He laughed lightly. "We're all caught. The thing is not to struggle. Ever notice the strugglers get hurt the most?"

She ran a caked fingernail along his lapel. "You're a struggler, Freddie."

"Yes," he said. "I am."

"Are you happy, Freddie?" She asked it tenderly, the most profound question she knew.

"Right now," he said unevenly, "I'm pretty goddamned unhappy."

The door opened with a rush and a dark face, rough with healing scabs, peered in anxiously. "You seen Mr. Charlie Bond?"

"He must be closed, Sam," Ruby said. "You're late."

"Oh." The scarred face fell. Down the street the packer truck honked. "Got another quarter, wanted to get in the big book." He slumped against the jamb, a study in disappointment. Then the truck honked again insistently and he spun away and was gone.

Ruby swung her stool back to Fred. "It'll work out. At the clinic they said I could be a, you know, a house patient. I'll get some little pink things and ——"

"No!" he cried. It was an awl in his heart.

"What's the matter?" she asked, bewildered.

"Pink's a lousy color."

"Well, blue then."

"No color. Don't get any color at all. Get a doctor."

"I don't want a doctor."

"Well, I'll get one, then. I'll find out and get one."

She looked at him with despair. "How? In the classified ads?"

"My boss. He'll know one."

"A nice question to ask a boss."

"He's different. He won't mind."

"What'll you say? Beg pardon, my sister got crocked three weeks on a barge and got a hangover quinine won't hang in?"

"He won't mind."

"Hell he won't," she said bitterly. "If he won't I don't want any part of him. If he's the kind likes to help girls in trouble, he's probably got a little trouble of his own he likes girls to help." She shuddered. "I know that kind."

He hesitated. Then: "Who's the father, Jan?"

She shook her head. "That's out."

"Well," he said, hunching his shoulders hopelessly, "what're you going to do?"

And she, in a hopelessness greater than his, rocked back in her cheap new pants. "Nothing, that's what."

He considered his doughnut gloomily. "What we really need, when you come right down to it, all we need is a husband."

It was stupid. He regretted it immediately.

"All! We! You mean you're going to find somebody to *marry* me!" The blood scudded into her face, burning the network of tiny vessels just under the skin. "How? Smear a little Tabu on the right places and say, here's a sweet thing, only be careful, don't lie on her belly too hard, she hurt her liver in an accident, and ——"

He started, alarmed. "What's the matter with your liver?"

"—— and fix me up with big falsies and say, how'd you like to crawl in church with that?"

"Don't."

"Oh, balls."

"Don't say that."

"Oh, Freddie, don't be so stuffy."

They stared ahead, hurt. Fred was about to speak when they heard a wild scuffling and turned to see Moss Bailey dart in and slam the door and lean against it, panting. "A rat," he said gruffly. "Outside. Biggest one I ever saw."

He tilted his snap-brim back and sat before the candy case. Ruby hurried down the counter. "Coffee, Mr. Bailey?"

"Yuh."

"Anything else?"

"Nope."

"Thank you, sir."

Fred watched with concern. He hated to see her truckle. Yet, he supposed, she had done worse. He wondered what else she had done and felt the awl again, tearing. It was stupid. It should not make a difference. But it did.

She left Moss brooding over his coffee and slid back on the stool. "Mr. Bailey's one of the most important people around here," she said so Moss could hear. "He's a businessman."

"It looks like snow or somethin'," Moss said irrelevantly.

"Again?" she asked brightly.

But he did not answer. He seemed preoccupied.

Probably a slum landlord, Fred thought, or a landlord's agent. He said politely, "What business is he in?"

Down the marble counter Moss's eyes snapped meanly. "The business business," he said, putting his coffee down. "Any questions, bub?"

Fred chose not to answer. He could hear his sister's quick breath and knew she hoped he would not. Instead he said quietly, "I wish we could go back, sometimes, to the park."

She sighed. "They were happy days, Freddie."

"None like them since."

"Well." Remembering hazy yesterdays at the Tavern, at the Klub. "I don't know. The parties weren't all bad."

"Just about as bad as they could be."

"Well. I was like, more satisfied then."

"Satisfied." He hissed it. "Are you satisfied now?"

She clenched her hands across her abdomen and looked him full in the face. "Oh, Freddie! I *want* this kid! I *want* it!"

Down the counter Moss looked up curiously and then turned back to his coffee.

"Wa-want it?" That had not occurred to him.

"*Yes!*"

A score of arguments welled up, but he looked into her eyes, filling slowly, and all the arguments dissolved, washing away and leaving his mind clean. "Then you'll have it," he said, reaching for two cigarettes to celebrate the end of that. "Maybe it won't be such a bad Christmas after all."

"It'll be a swell Christmas." She inhaled deeply.

He grinned, waving out the match. "My boss says Christmas is for pagans anyway."

"You and your boss."

Moss rattled his saucer loudly. "Coffee!" he bawled.

"Yes, Mr. Bailey."

She scooted behind the counter and served him so quickly he had not finished shaping the insult when the cup was before him again and she was gone.

"You could have it at the house," Fred suggested timidly.

"No." She shook her head. "I couldn't."

Moss decided to insult from here.

"Dad's so busy with Erik he wouldn't even see you."

Moss changed his mind.

"It wouldn't be any good," she said. "It would spoil it."

"How about Uncle Wally's? He isn't even out there. He's at the Highland, tied up in all his deals."

"That voting machine! I don't trust him."

"Oh God," he said desolately. "Isn't there anyone you trust?"

"You, Freddie. I trust you."

He stared into the ruins of the doughnut.

She glanced at the juke box by the door. "Play me a song, Freddie. Something nice."

He sauntered over, fumbling in his pocket for a nickel and studying the selection. "Not much here."

Moss wheeled on the stool with a dirty grin. "That was a nice one last week," he said to Ruby. "*Daddy's Little Girl.*" Fred looked up coldly, but Moss went on, ignoring him. "Where's all baby's daddies, Rube? Gone bye bye?"

She dropped her eyes. Fred shoved a coin in the slot and punched *Joy to the World.* He returned to his stool. "Remember this?" he said softly. "The music box. With the star on top."

She nodded, smiling.

"Who's this guy?" Moss rasped nasally above the carol. "One of your pappies come back for a quickie?"

She stared at the counter, unsmiling now. Fred's fists were knots in his lap.

Moss sang off key: "Like angels that sing, a hea-venly thing ——"

"Ignore him," she whispered.

"—— and you're daddy's lit-tul girl."

"Oh, shut up!" she cried.

Fred spun toward him, patting the top of his head furiously. "We're minding our own business," he stammered. He was so excited the words came in jerks.

Ruby plucked at him. "Freddie. Don't."

Moss rolled his eyes craftily. "Oh, pardon me. I don't want to get in the way of a guy's little private tail. Not me."

Fred stood, quivering. "Shut up," he said, almost inaudibly.

Ruby ran her eyes over his back wildly. "Please, Freddie, will you for Crissake *please* ——"

"Please, Freddie," Moss mimicked in falsetto. "I got the hots for you, Freddie, *pul-eese!*"

Fred skidded across the asphalt tile. The skid beat Moss. It brought Fred in full career, and Moss could not slide off the stool in time. He saw the thin fist coming and started to duck and ducked right into it. His lips flattened against his teeth, and he tasted the new blood and half lay between stools, riding away on his shock.

"Okay," he said sluggishly. "You wait."

Fred's voice was thick. "You bother Jan again, bother her again I'll break your neck." His hands dropped, still making nervous fists.

"Okay," Moss grunted, remembering the name. "Wait."

He wobbled to a stand and rolled into a walk, then stopped, rocking dangerously, reached down, scooped up his hat, and staggered out the door. It closed with a squeak of hinges.

"He's a good customer," Ruby said flatly. "He'll tell Steiner."

"Let him."

"It's my job, Freddie."

"But you heard what he said!" he cried.

"Sure. So what?"

He threw up his hands in exasperation and dropped on the nearest stool. "I don't get it. I just don't."

"No. You don't."

She looked very tired. Her lids were low, and under them her eyes were dull and cloudy. They watched her hands, crawling up from the knees slowly in the old test and resting, spread wide, on her flabby thighs. The fingers fluttered furiously, the thumbs brushing the sheen of her clean rayon pants.

"Christ," she muttered. "I could use a tank of milk."

"But you won't. Jan, you won't!"

"No, but that isn't your fault. Go away, hero. Go get yourself a medal."

He stepped back, bewildered, waiting for her to look up. But her eyes, her beaten eyes, lingered on the flickering fingers and the bleached rayon.

In the lost silence the coffee urn perked feebly.

"I'm going," he said weakly.

"So long."

"Goodbye."

"Happy days."

Outside he hesitated, peering through the windows. She was working among the flue holes and the rat holes behind the grill, wiping grease stains from the plaster wall.

He walked toward West Concord, rubbing his bruised hand.

Moss had been right: the first icy ribbons were pelting the cracked sidewalk.

Sleet streaked from the muddy clouds staining the sky.

4·
— 555

FOUR days after Christmas, Seaver struck. All Ben's stopgaps failed. They were sound and might have worked, but his writers, grown overconfident, had followed them indifferently. Some hired no lookouts. Those who did stretched the assigned hour of operation to two hours, or three or more, swelling their commissions to meet the added expense. Under Zipski's orders the vice squad methodically charted drop locations, building a bank of warrants. On December 21 they were ready. They closed in during the busy noon hour, flushing fifteen writers and nearly $3,000 in policy slips and cash. Arraignments for the fifteen were scheduled that afternoon. Criminal Court dockets were cleared and the trials set for the following morning.

Wallace was jubilant.

"Why not?" he crowed. "It's only the beginning."

"Every time I think of that money I feel sick," Cameron said sourly.

"Smartest money you ever spent, Jay. That money'll kill policy."

"Zipski's killing it dead enough for me."

"Correction. Zipski's *crippling* it. But I doubt he'll reach Erik himself, and even if he did the fever would still be there for someone else."

Cameron was unconvinced. "What's the difference?"

"You'll see Friday. Ben thinks he's in trouble now. He don't know what trouble is. Friday he'll be lucky if he can pay his own water bill. That, Jay, will be the end, not only of Erik, but of numbers."

"You're sure Henderson has that much influence?"

"He's reprinted twice already. As he says, figure it out for yourself."

"Figure It Out for Yourself" was the featured article in each month's *Black Combination*. The Editors predicted one number for each week, day unspecified. The standing title was a challenge no one could accept, really, for to figure it out one needed access to certain occult formulas locked in the magazine's safe. The Editors claimed an impressive record of successes, and although the claim would never have survived an audit, since the first week of publication, when the predicted number had hit, "Figure It Out for Yourself" had prospered on the passionate faith of several thousand readers. This week they observed with excitement that the figuring took up the entire issue; that the number predicted was for a specific day, Friday, December 23; and that to be sure no one missed it The Editors had displayed it in red on the cover. Players who had long ago abandoned the game in disgust were saving and preparing to sink everything on 555 on the eve of Christmas Eve.

Ed Sylvester's forecast of Ben Erik's reaction could not have been more accurate: Ben was far too busy to be aware of *Black Combination*. Ordinarily he would have seen the risk and acted. He could have refused all bets on the number. There were precedents for that. But lately Ben had paid less and less attention to Henderson. In the early days of the racket he had needed him, as a promoter of policy, but since the war the syndicate had become so well established the magazine had ceased to be really vital to the business. It was returning now with a vengeance, bu Ben did not see it. Because he was so busy.

Busy meeting bail from his dwindling reserves for the unlucky fifteen. Busy explaining to the jittery pickup men that holders o evidence slips must forfeit their winnings, since Seaver would know who they were. Busy preparing a statement, for release to the newspapers through Paul Gormley, announcing that Ben jamin I. Erik was out of town and would remain there indefinitely. Busy keeping busy, keeping away despair. Busy trying to forget he was lost.

For Ben was almost through. His money was nearly gone, and in the morning he would be obliged to end all payments to Joe Murdock's writers.

Bail was no problem: he had his professional bondsmen. Bu when the fining started — and with Zipski and the State's Attorney pressing the bench it would start the next day — the formal collapse of his organization would begin. He could meet perhaps forty $100 fines, but after that the writers would go to jail. When the jailing began they would leave him, and without them the syndicate could not function.

For a moment, after the first raids were announced, Ben wa too near panic to act. Then he realized he could not shut fear from his mind. He sat down in the old barn with his cash box and Henry Loomis's books and calculated his chances. At the present rate of attrition, he estimated, he would be broke before New Year's Day. A week later he would be out of business.

There were no avenues of help left. He could not fight, for he had nothing to fight with. Murdock was in jail. Gregg was terrified and useless in his terror. Gormley was ineffectual and curiously uninterested, and the others were numbly awaiting a leadership he could not give them. He could not bargain. With every raid his prestige outside the district was crumbling. About all he had was his popularity in the Seventh, and that would disappear the day his organization closed down.

He stared blankly at his cramped handwriting on the yellow

sheet, wondering what had happened. Once he had depended, not on paper and figures, but on men like Otto. That time had passed, and Otto was now the least useful man in his organization. For over a decade Ben had thought it well past, thought that the new time was better, easier, richer, more sensible. Now he knew he had been wrong. But it was too late. Society had taken away his guns and set him up for the kill.

He pushed the page aside and sprawled full upon the cot. Under his wrinkled trouser front his belly was swollen and painful. He had not urinated for six hours. He felt old and tired and beaten.

Hope sent Moss Bailey as its emissary.

Ben heard the car in the barnyard and for a moment thought it might be Seaver, coming after him, and for a moment did not care. Then Moss's whining, persistent voice drifted up to the loft, choked off at every pause with objections from Otto. Otto's arguments died away, and then Moss was climbing the ladder, wheezing as his car had wheezed in the snow.

He came in without knocking.

"Boss, I'm sorry to bust in like this."

"Then why do it?" Ben had not spoken for an hour. He noticed how dry his voice had become.

"It's awful important, I think."

"You got followed here." Ben stated it as a fact.

"No."

"Yes. Probably yes." What's the difference, he thought. It doesn't matter.

"No, boss, honest, I come the back road. Listen, boss. You know Cameron, Gillette's brother-in-law, the one with all the dough?"

No answer for a stupid question.

"He's got a daughter," Moss said triumphantly.

"You don't say. That's the big news?"

"I know her, boss."

"Well, well, well."

"She lives in the Elbow, down West Concord, a drunk and a cheap lay. Works in a lunchcart, gets fractured every night." He waited, but Ben signified nothing. "Well," Moss continued, excitement rising in his voice, "she's knocked up with some smokie' kid. I heard her, talkin'."

"When?" Ben asked sharply, studying the rafters now with real interest.

"Couple of days ago."

"So now you tell me."

"I didn't know for sure, boss. I had a lot to check, you know, birth records and everything, to find out if she really was what thought. No doubt about it, she is."

Ben sat up slowly and looked Moss over.

He stood by the door, running his tongue over his thick lip, rocking in his square-toed sport shoes. For as long as he had been with the syndicate he had been insecure. Now he had come to salute Ben's flag just as it was fluttering down.

"She is," he repeated, his voice harsh with conviction.

Ben lit a cigar carefully. It could be. It just could be. "I'll find out if she is," he said at last.

"I'm right, boss. That's what you'll find out."

"You said you knew her."

"That's right."

Ben lay back and gripped his cigar tightly in his teeth. "Let' hear it. Everything you know."

Moss spun the web of fact and gossip, and when he was finished, Ben knew what he had. He had a weapon to fight with or bargain with, or would have soon. It would have to be very soon. He would have to move quickly and carefully, and he would need Moss.

His cigar was a stump. He dropped it on the loft floor and stepped on it. Then he leaned forward, his elbows on his knees, and told Moss what he wanted. When he started the air in the cubicle was foggy with smoke, and his breath stirred it up in little blue whirlpools drifting around his drawn face. It settled slowly a lazy blanket across the boards, and drifted out the door and down the ladder, to the long hall of the barn, where Otto stood guard.

"Set it up," he concluded. "Make it tomorrow if you can. I got to get the others ready."

Moss's face shone. "It's perfect, boss." He made a fist and socked it into his right palm. "It's a cinch."

The fist drew out the blue tangle of broken vessels in his forearm. Ben leaned over, studying them deliberately, and then looked up into Moss's working face. "It better be, kid," he said quietly.

Two hours later Moss shuffled into the Unique Lunch, whistling loudly and looking like a hair tonic advertisement.

Ruby saw him coming in the mirror behind the grill. She caught her breath and started, nearly knocking over the Pyrex urn bowl. Steiner called sharply from the sandwich board. "Watch it!"

She caught it and pushed it back among the bags of fresh coffee. Watch this, she thought.

But Moss headed for her, not Steiner. He pounced on a stool, beaming. "How's about a cupa coffee, Rube?"

She set it before him silently and he ladled in the sugar, grinning.

"Hey, Steiner," he called. "Anything in the rules about her sittin' with a customer?"

The hunchback paused in surprise and then bobbed merrily. "Not if you don't mind gettin' a dose," he cackled.

Moss patted the stool beside him. "C'mon. Buy you a cupa Joe."

She blinked and came around the counter slowly, ready to duck if he swung. "How've you been, Mr. Bailey?" she asked timidly.

"Fine!" He winked and lowered his voice. "As good as can be expected."

She saw his fat lip and glanced away. "I'm sorry."

"Forget it! I had it comin'."

He sucked at the cup rim and put it down. The coffee was too hot. "I guess I was just jealous," he said slyly.

"Jealous!" Her eyes widened. "Who're you kidding, Mr. Bailey?"

"Moss. Moss never kids about things like that. I just never saw you all dolled up before, is all." He inspected her wash dress carefully. "I see you got on the same outfit."

"The only one I got," she said wryly.

"Well, I like it. Thing is," he looked into her face, "it's just a suggestion, you know, but maybe a little lipstick, real bright, would bring your color out."

She giggled and slid back on the stool. "That's for girls, you know, go out a lot."

"Well?" he said archly.

She felt giddy. She could not remember the last time a man had bothered to flirt with her. It was strange and exciting and faintly nostalgic.

"I forgot my coffee," she said and went and drew it.

He followed her to the urn and back with cheerful eyes. His coffee was cooler now and he drank it slowly and waited, letting her thoughts grow.

"I bet it gets lonesome here," he whispered. "Every day with nobody but him to talk to."

He jerked his head toward the sandwich board, where Steiner was kneading egg salad with dirty hands.

She hesitated, wondering if he were trapping her into disloyalty. Yet she knew that could not be: if he wanted her fired, a word of the fight would do. She had lost worse jobs for less. She nodded emphatically.

Moss chuckled. "I thought so. What I was thinkin' was, you and me could get together one of these nights, have a little fun."

She searched his face, then lifted her coffee cup gravely, with both hands, and took one tiny, deliberate sip. "Sure. That would be swell."

356

"Terrific!" he whispered. She searched again. He did not look pleased. "What I figure is," he said, advancing rapidly now, "we could go to a joint I know and hoist a few, dance a little."

That was the catch, the catch there had to be. Well. It was a nice idea. "I guess I wouldn't be very good company there." She gulped the hot coffee recklessly, feeling the scalding wash. "I don't drink any more, Mr. Bailey."

"Moss." He was tense with annoyance. "You don't *what?*"

"Drink. On account of a condition I got."

"I know all about that condition. It don't mean you shouldn't have a few for the road. I don't mean get boiled."

She shook her head. "A rummy like me don't know what a few is." She said it proudly. Admitting it had taken a long time.

"If that's the way you feel, you don't have to drink anything. Not a thing. Just come, have a good time, at this joint I know."

"It wouldn't be any good, Moss."

"Look," he argued. "I think it would be good. Really swell is what I think it would be. Believe me," he tapped the counter with a rigid finger. "I want you to come. I mean it. I want you to."

If she could just believe. If she only could. She looked back over men she had known in her best days and remembered only a few who had even pretended so much. She tried, but it was no good.

"It's really swell of you, Moss. I mean it. But it wouldn't work out."

The cheer faded from his eyes and they darkened. He edged close to her. "Does Steiner know about this condition you got? He wouldn't heckle you much, would he? Not much he wouldn't."

She put her coffee down and laid her hands beside it and said nothing.

"And does he know about guys come in here, get in fights with steady customers, try to drive away business?"

She leaned forward heavily. "What Steiner don't know don't hurt him."

"Don't hurt you, you mean."

Whatever he wanted, he knew how to get it. "Yes," she said. "That's what I mean."

"Don't get me wrong. I just think we could have a good time, is all."

"Sure."

"You're gonna come?"

"Sure."

"Good!" He grinned. "Tomorrow night?"

"Sure."

"Pick you up right here? About ten?"

"Sure, Moss."

He left explaining he had an important telephone call to make, and when he was gone she washed their dirty coffee cups. Steiner was cramming the last of the egg salad into his crock and covering it with waxed paper. He swept the ragged celery leaves to the floor, wiped the wooden mixing spoon on a dish towel, and took two tins of tuna fish from a rear cupboard, preparing the last spread. "What was on his mind?" he asked, opening the cans.

"He wants me to go out with him."

"You don't say?" He dumped the tuna fish in a metal bowl and ladled a vast blob of mayonnaise on top of it. "That's a break, huh? I mean a guy like him, with all that dough."

"Yeah." She wiped down the sink and put away the cups. "If you can trust him."

"Well, that's a fact. You never know."

"I wish I knew."

He squeezed the mush together, stealing little glances at her. Lately she had been behaving oddly — sober all the time, quiet, and so clean it made him self-conscious. He preferred her as she had been, hung over in the mornings, stealing out to Ollie's every hour, loose and talkative with the men at lunch, cadging tips and spending them afternoons at Ollie's, tippling enough to leave her slightly incoherent, reeling a little and tolerant of his vilest jokes. That was the Ruby he knew and liked and judged worth the missed days and the broken plates she left when she staggered out after the supper dishes, headed for Sticktown. That was the Ruby he wanted back, and because he thought Moss Bailey would bring her back he approved. What she needs, he thought lewdly, that Bailey will give her.

She looked up quickly from the Coke machine and caught him peering at her. He jerked his head away and hurriedly dumped the tuna fish salad into a jar. It was so thin it poured.

"Steiner," she said.

"What's on your mind?"

"Can you let me have ten?"

"Ten!" He almost spilled the salad. "What for?"

"Clothes."

"You just got some clothes."

"They're dirty, I got no change. I want to be sharp tomorrow. Just some things over at Al Kelly's. You'll get it back."

"Clothes." He sniffed suspiciously. But maybe she wanted to get a little edge first. He better hold it to be sure. "Okay. I'll give it to you tomorrow."

"Thanks, Steiner. I won't forget."

After the noon rush next day he tossed her the bill and winked. "Take the afternoon off, kid. I can manage. I'll get all the snakes killed in the morning before you come in. If you come in."

"Sure, Steiner."

At Kelly's she bought first a pair of pants a size too large and a loose-waisted skirt, then a brassiere, her first in five years, and a cheap cardigan. For a long minute she hesitated between flat-heeled shoes and spiked heels and chose at last spiked heels and, with her last dollar, a cheap pair of silk stockings. The stockings meant no supper, and she had no garters.

But her landlady gave her strips of adhesive tape to hold them up.

And she spent the supper hour washing her hair.

The late editions of the evening papers on December 21 revised their banners to announce that the vice squad had seized, not fifteen, but sixteen policy writers that day.

359

The sixteenth was Charles F. Bond, 38, white, of 841 Linvale Place. He was arrested at his West Concord grocery store shortly after two o'clock in the afternoon. Arrested with him was Lewis J. Winkler, a former turnkey drawing retirement pay from the Police Department. The raid followed an anonymous telephone tip. The tipster was believed to be a disgruntled player.

Charlie and Winkler were sorting slips when the raiders came. They had broken the slips into hundreds and were beginning on the 700 pile. The two o'clock news had just announced the mutuels from the second Gulf race. Charlie had calculated the pool at $23.70 and noted with satisfaction there were very few bets in the 700's that afternoon.

The money was between his knees, in one of the tomato can cartons. Between Winkler's knees was an empty .45 caliber service revolver. Charlie had bought it in a hock shop. He had no ammunition because he did not trust Winkler's aim. In a pinch he thought the gun might frighten a thief.

The door was locked, and they were so intent they did not hear the first knock. The second was much louder, and they looked up together, startled.

"Jees!" Charlie saw the three men at the window and tightened, crumpling his slips into a wad. "Who's that?"

Winkler squinted. The figures outside were a blur to him. He thought they were blacks. "Late, late, always late," he complained. "They know we're closed up." He started to deal again into the crude bins.

Then Charlie saw Ferrara. He was standing behind the plain-clothesmen, clumsily holding a pair of handcuffs.

"Oh, God." He jumped off his stool and edged along the counter, looking around wildly and drumming his fingers on the cheap linoleum. "Trouble, trouble."

Winkler stood, straining to see. Since his first day here had been waiting for gunmen, had lain awake nights haunted by the fear of them. Now, as Charlie reached the end of the counter and the first and largest of the plainclothesmen flung his shoulder against the lock, he believed they had come, that his time to defend Charlie's property was here.

He stooped gingerly and picked up the service revolver, holding it against his quivering belly with both hands and backing away. He wanted to hold it in one hand, by the grip, pointing the muzzle toward the men, but he was shaking badly, and he thought if he tried that he would drop it. He came up against the back wall with a jolt. His eyes rolled out of control. He squeezed them shut and held the revolver tight and tried to stop the shaking.

Charlie watched his front door come down. He was afraid to open it, afraid the big cop would keep coming at him and knock him down. He did not know what to do, and so he stayed at the counter end, weak with terror, and watched the door collapse.

It gave easily. The hinges were rusted and the screws loose, and they broke with the raider's second lunge. He ran into the store and vaulted the counter and grabbed Winkler's pistol. The old man did not open his eyes. He folded his empty hands against his stomach and slid gently to a sitting position. A thin string of spittle hung from the corner of his mouth.

The other two cops sprinted after the leader. The first pinned Charlie against the wall and ran his big hands over him, looking for a weapon. The second dumped the sorting bins and spread the slips on the counter.

"Wait'll Seaver hears about this one!" he panted. "Look at this stuff!"

The leader punched out the revolver clip. "Empty," he said disappointedly. "It's still a deadly weapon."

Ferrara came in, peering around cautiously. "Find anything?" he asked.

The leader looked at him scornfully. "Jesus. You call yourself a cop."

Ferrara pretended he had not heard. He held up the handcuffs. "Want these?"

"Throw 'em here."

Winkler opened his eyes as he was being handcuffed. He looked up into the hard face of the cop and smiled pitifully. "Hello, George," he whispered.

The leader looked startled. "I'll be goddamned. Hey, Whitey, remember Baldy, the keyman?"

Charlie's searcher half turned. "Son of a bitch. How long you been writing, Baldy?" he called, searching.

"He don't write," Charlie said. "I'm the writer."

"You're the writer, huh?" The cop stood back, satisfied he was unarmed. "Looks like you wrote yourself a little bad news."

"It's a chance you take," Charlie said bravely. He wasn't thinking about jail at all. He couldn't think of that yet. At the moment he was worrying about the number coming in. If one of his customers had a hit, he wouldn't be here to pay him.

He watched the third cop stuff the slips in brown paper envelopes and write notes on the back. The man finished and shuffled the envelopes together. "Where's the cash?" he demanded.

"Under the counter," the leader said. "In that big box."

On the sidewalk outside there were many people moving around, peering in the windows and jabbering excitedly.

Charlie recognized Ollie Wetlek's worried face pressed against the glass. Ollie looked from Charlie to Ferrara and then Charlie lost him in the crowd.

"Hey, stumblebum," the leader snapped at Ferrara. "This is your beat. We'll be out in a minute. Clear us a way."

The patrolman went out and began ordering people around with violent, unnecessary gestures. He was glad of the chance to do something. Inside, the leader was cuffing Charlie to Winkler. Even in the first notch the cuff fitted loosely. Charlie's wrist was very thin.

At four o'clock they were arraigned with the others before a substitute magistrate. Paul Gormley was unexplainedly, but not unexpectedly, absent. "Sick, I guess," Captain Hardy winked at Lieutenant Nuggio.

Paul's replacement was a Sylvester man who just happened to

362

be in the captain's office when four o'clock came and Paul did not. He found *prima facie* cases quickly and set bond at $5,000 on each count. Moss Bailey stood in a corner of the courtroom with a bondsman, and when the afternoon session was over he went with him to meet bail.

Charlie and Winkler stood apart from the others in the narrow hall behind the bench. As Moss came up Charlie wet his lips. "Hi, boss!" he said and started a gesture which failed as Moss passed without speaking.

"I'll take 'em all," Moss told Nuggio. "Everybody but that guy." He pointed directly at Charlie. Charlie stared at the floor. He had not expected bail from Moss. But Moss did not have to snub him.

"How about Baldy?" Nuggio asked hopefully. He had been thinking about Winkler. It did not seem right to put an old keyman in a cell.

"Don't know him. Never saw him."

The bondsman took a gold fountain pen from his pocket and unscrewed the cap with a professional twist.

The present turnkey was a former protégé of Winkler's, and he treated him with great respect. "I got number five in good shape," he said, taking their valuables at the cell block gate. "It was redone last summer. They put in a new floor, and ——" his voice trailed off in embarrassment "— and everything."

A sergeant arrived, conspiratorial. "Touch luck, Baldy." He looked around. "That deadly weapons charge'll never stick," he added confidently.

The old man looked at him dully. He rememberd the sergeant's face but not his name. He had not been in the station house for five years. He concentrated on the name, trying to work it free from the shadow of his memory. It suddenly seemed important.

"I guess we'll be going downtown soon," Charlie said, vaguely resentful, above the cold dread he kept pushing away, of the special treatment Winkler was getting.

"First thing in the morning," the sergeant said cheerfully. "Court don't start till ten, but you got to be presented first. Got

363

a lawyer?" Charlie shook his head dumbly. He had not though
of that. "Better get one," the sergeant advised him.

He took him to a pay telephone in the station house and waite
while Charlie stood inside helplessly, wondering what to do
Then he remembered. He knew a lawyer: Lucy's friend, Wilson
But he did not know his first name, and when he turned to th
classified section of the directory he found five Wilsons listed a
attorneys. Lucy would know. He dialed her number. It rang busy
He tried again and again it was busy. The sergeant was swingin
his arms restlessly. Charlie called Loretta.

He had planned to call her anyway, after he found a lawyer
to tell her he would not be home that evening. Even as the phon
rang on the other end, he thought that through some miracle h
could survive tomorrow's trial without her knowing of it. Enoug
luck and the right lies would do it. Or so Charlie thought. Unt
Loretta answered.

"Yes?" Her voice was strained and cautious. "What is it?"

"It's me. Charlie."

"Oh!" She was frightened. "Where are you?"

"I won't be home tonight, kid. A little ——"

"Oh, I know! I know!" The sob, abruptly stifled, told him sh
knew. "It's in the papers. Al saw it." Her brother Al followed th
races. Every afternoon he bought a Sports Final on the corne
near his tailor shop.

In the papers. Charlie felt like hanging up, quitting, lettin
himself be borne along by the tide. It was so much stronger tha
he was. In the dirty glass of the telephone booth he saw himse
reflected pitilessly: little, scared and lost, lost and irredeemabl
like the policy slips in the marked envelopes.

Loretta was talking rapidly, flooding him with questions. Wa
it true? Wasn't it a mistake? How had it happened? Could sh
see him? Was he all right?

"I'm in jail," he said flatly and immediately felt purged. "
need a lawyer."

"A lawyer?" Tremulously and very faintly, the one questio
she had not asked.

"Listen. I haven't got much time. See Lucy" — he corrected himself without a pause — "Carter. Ask her the number of that lawyer, that Wilson, the one she had at the meeting that night. Have him in the courthouse, where I'll be, at ten. Got it?"

Silence.

"Honey, have you got it?"

"Yes."

"Understand?"

"Yes."

He hung up and opened the booth door, feeling very much the city's prisoner. The sergeant took him back to the turnkey, and the turnkey led him to the block, to number five, where Winkler was. The old man was sitting on the bottom bunk, slumped forward with his elbows on his knees and his bare head, withered and white, sunk upon his chest.

The lock turned loudly. "Called my wife," Charlie said. "You got anybody to call?"

Winkler grunted and waggled his head with his hands. Then Charlie remembered. Winkler lived in a boarding house run by a policeman's widow. That was what was bothering him — how she would take it, what the other boarders would think, whether he could stay there. Charlie swung up to the top bunk savoring this, drawing a wretched measure of comfort from another's misery.

Supper was cold and slimy and the night long. He lay on the hard canvas, breathing through his mouth to shut out the odor of stale urine and sweat, feeling the numbness wear off. His capacity for shock was small. He had to absorb it a little at a time, wrapping the fragments with understanding one by one and tucking them away on the narrow shelves of his mind. Through the early hours of morning he tossed, wrapping and tucking, wrapping and tucking until exhaustion crept mercifully over him and he fell asleep.

He awoke at dawn with a jerk. The night turnkey was standing in the doorway, swearing. In the corner of the bottom bunk Winkler was huddled with his blanket around his head like a shawl, crying softly. The old man had wet his bed.

*   *   *

Judge W. Stanton Rogers danced into the courtroom. He was on the bench, leaning forward attentively, before half the spectators had risen, and as they sank back to their hard wooden seats in bewildered little clumps of two and three he eyed the clerk impatiently. This was a big day for the judge. The newspapers had called for swift justice, and he meant to give them that. Twenty years before he had been appointed by a freak Republican governor. He was a young man then, marked, he thought, for greatness. But an endless succession of Democratic administrations had left him stagnating here, and he had grown bitter as he grew old. Here, today, in this courtroom, the Democrats were on trial, and he was the judge. He fingered his gavel lovingly.

Spread on a long, low table before him were copies of the indictments. Behind that was another table, small and uncluttered, for the lawyers. Then came the prisoner's bench, the short railing, and the mob of spectators. All the seats were taken, and the back of the room was crowded with standees, three deep. One of the bailiffs, an indignant little man in gartered shirtsleeves, was ordering them to leave. No one paid any attention to him, and as the gavel pounded he gave up and retired to a corner sulking.

In the empty jury box a reporter sat disappointed. There had been rumors Ben Erik would be here, but he was not, nor was big Ed Sylvester. Several of Big Ed's ward executives were in the third row, looking expectant, but the only Erik man present was Paul Gormley, poised for a quick exit in an aisle seat near the rear. The reporter noted this and sprawled in his seat of privilege.

"Silence!" the clerk crowed for the third time. The gavel pounded.

The judge leaned over the bench. "I thought there were sixteen," he whispered to the clerk. "I only count fifteen."

"The other's waiting downstairs," the clerk said quietly. "His lawyer hasn't come. Herbert Smith!" he bellowed.

Herbert Smith shuffled forward on rope soles. He was a handsome man, near forty, with dyed hair and a face flabby from dissipation. The clerk droned the oath, and on the lawyer's table a young, apple-cheeked assistant state's attorney made furious notes. Beside him sat Ben's man, Thayer Cross, stark and moral in a high collar and string tie. Cross watched the young man uneasily, wondering if he ought to be taking notes too. He had not tried a case in four years and he knew Paul was watching. But Ben had ordered only a token defense and Cross could not think of any notes to take and so he just sat there, shifting uneasily under the beamish judge.

The preliminaries were over. Herbert Smith pleaded not guilty. Seaver appeared in a side doorway, holding a sheaf of fat envelopes. The city began its case.

In the marble-walled basement, by the sheriff's office, Charlie waited through Herbert Smith's trial, and Victor Geoff's, and David Flemm's — waited for Loretta and Wilson with the station-house sergeant and a growing sense of panic. He believed he had to have a lawyer. Without one, he thought, his case would be postponed and he would be returned to the cell block to await another trial.

The sergeant had been downtown infrequently and knew little of the courts. "I don't remember anybody without a lawyer," he said, shaking his head with conviction. "No. I never saw one."

Charlie looked around in desperation. The corridor was empty. A few furtive men hurried down the broad steps, turned into the public toilet, and slunk out again with dark, suspicious glances.

"Wouldn't anybody here know?"

"I guess." But the sergeant let it drop there. He was ashamed of his ignorance. "Don't worry. Your wife'll come."

An elderly man in quiet dress descended the staircase slowly. "Let's ask him," Charlie said. "He looks like he'd know."

The man came abreast of them and the sergeant cleared his throat. "How's it going?" he asked. "In Rogers' court."

"Very quickly. He just finished the fourth."

"How're they doing?"

"A hundred apiece." The man stopped and patted his vest thoughtfully. "If you ask me ——"

367

"A hundred dollars?" Charlie cried, appalled.

"Certainly." The man looked at him curiously.

"Do they have to have lawyers, the writers up there?"

The man smiled. "They better have them today."

"But do they *have* to have them?" Charlie persisted. The sergeant turned away, embarrassed. The man looked from Charlie to the sergeant and back to Charlie again, taking in the tableau. Then he turned and walked slowly toward the toilet without answering.

"Jees." Charlie wiped his face with a soggy handkerchief. "Nobody gives you a break."

"Well ——" the sergeant began tentatively.

"Why so soon? Why bring me up so soon? I had no time at all, only one night to get ready."

"You're lucky it's numbers. Look at old Winkler with that deadly weapons rap. He's got to wait over Christmas in hock, they won't try him till next week."

Charlie started. Christmas in jail. He saw himself on the bunk over Winkler, eating the wet hash the cops called food while Dulcy opened her presents at home without him. He folded his arms high on his shoulders and buried his face in his elbows.

Voices babbled. Steps rang out. And down they came.

He looked up and saw Loretta peering about uncertainly. "Here we are!" he shouted. "Down here!"

She saw him and cried to the others. They were two: her brother Al and a short, fat man in a bright bow tie and tortoise-shell glasses, carrying a briefcase.

"Jees! What kept you?" He ran a fluttering hand along his jawbone, feeling the ragged growth a borrowed razor had missed and patting it absently. "You're late."

She looked at him oddly and put her hands on his shoulders and kissed him, lightly, on the patch of missed beard. Under it he blushed. The sergeant backed away in confusion.

Charlie gulped. "Where's Wilson?" he demanded.

"I couldn't get him," she whispered. "I'll tell you later. Al got Mr. Pervis."

Charlie stared at the bright bow tie in amazement: Call-me-George Pervis was a legend in the city. He tried to imagine what Pervis's fee would be and floundered in a surge of figures.

"Charlie," Al said proudly, drawing himself up in his seedy topcoat, "I want you should meet George Pervis."

Pervis extended an oily hand. "Call me Georgie."

They drifted toward the toilet, planning the defense, leaving Loretta with the impressed sergeant.

In the courtroom Judge Rogers was trying his sixth case. On the bench before him his gold watch lay open: he was timing himself. He noted with satisfaction he was picking up speed as he went along, setting a new record with each conviction and breaking it with the next. The clerk's records were snarled, the court stenographer's tape was a twisted knot, and Cross's voice was hoarse from shouting exceptions. Still Rogers swept forward, beady-eyed, triumphant.

The indictments lay in an untidy pile, shoved to one side of the long table, crowded by heaps of policy slips. One of Seaver's men was perched on a chair before them. His only duty was to keep the exhibits straight. Like the stenographer, like the clerk whose function he was usurping, he had fallen far behind.

"I find the defendant guilty!" the judge barked. "One hundred dollars and costs."

He glanced at his watch with satisfaction and leaned back, awaiting the new arraignment. A confused undertone rolled across the room, and one of Big Ed's men dealt from a roll of bills into the lap of another.

Paul Gormley slid gently into the aisle and pawed his way through the gang of spectators in the rear. The reporter strode swiftly after him. The courtroom murmur swelled and the gavel thumped mechanically.

From the judge's chambers a boy in an alpaca jacket appeared, caught the clerk's eye, and came across the room hurriedly. They talked for a moment in low voices, and then the clerk spoke briefly to the judge, who grinned wickedly. "After this one," he said.

Charles was being led in behind the sergeant. There was a lag and then Pervis made his entrance, strutting and trailing a hospitable hand. The courtroom regulars perked up; the reporter, who had returned to the jury box after an unsuccessful pursuit of Paul, rushed feverishly to sharpen his pencils; and Thayer Cross and the young assistant state's attorney swung around.

"Well," Cross said, wiggling his brow, "I thought you'd retired."

"Just resting," said Pervis, with an elaborate sweep of his hand. "Like you."

The assistant state's attorney nodded shortly and addressed himself again to his notes. He had never seen Pervis before and was curious, but unafraid. He had heard he had become so completely the clown no bench now considered him seriously.

Charlie sat upright among the other prisoners, enjoying the warm caress of confidence. He had waited a long time for his lawyer, and his faith was humble and blind.

"Now everybody's here," the clerk called across the exhibit table.

Pervis looked around with mock excitement. Then his face fell dramatically. "Everybody who's nobody."

The courtroom regulars tittered. Charlie smiled hesitantly.

"Be careful, Georgie," the clerk baited him. "Nobody might get sore."

"I don't care what nobody says," Pervis sang, shuffling his little feet rhythmically, "so long as they say it behind my back."

He dropped into the chair beside Cross with a thump. The regulars roared. Charlie giggled adoringly.

"All right, Georgie," the judge leered. "You'll have your chance in a few minutes."

"Damned few," Cross muttered. "What a court."

"Don't worry." Pervis nudged him. "I'll fix his clock."

"I should've known you'd get into the act. What's your client paying you, a commission?"

"In a glass house I wouldn't get my rocks off, if I was you."

"The poor man's Milton Berle."

"Call me Georgie."

In the rear corridor, behind the final mob and the last bailiff, Loretta stood, straining to see. Al had given up and turned his back dejectedly, puffing on a bent cigar, but she was still darting up, clutching her pocketbook tightly and peering over the wall of pin stripe and tweed.

"They aren't doing a single thing!" she said indignantly.

Al inhaled deeply and coughed. "I bet they're watching Georgie." He spat out the smoke and reeled a little, his eyes watering. He was unaccustomed to cigars and had bought this one as a treat after retaining Pervis. Al admired two trades above all others: racketeering and shystering. When he found his own sister's brother was in one, he had splurged on the other.

Loretta took up her watch again, hoping to find a break in the wall and slip through.

"Milton Weintraub!" the clerk bawled.

"Not Charlie?" Al was disappointed.

Loretta dropped back on her heels. She did not know whether to be relieved or not. Under the knitted suit jacket her heart was turning over rapidly, and her mouth was dry. She wondered where the wives of the other defendants were. There were no women here, and only a few inside, and none of them looked like wives.

Two of the men in front of her were discussing Charlie's case. She listened eagerly.

"Wait'll Georgie gets up there, then we'll see some real action."

"Two'll get you ten he don't get his boy off."

"You kidding? I said action. Five'll get you ten his boy gets the limit."

The other man said nothing, and Loretta felt suddenly sick. She told Al to wait there and went looking for the ladies' room.

When she came back she saw him down the length of the hall, motioning frantically. She ran up, panting.

"What's the matter?"

"Charlie! He's coming up right now!"

Milton Weintraub, not choosing to testify in his own behalf, had been fined less than one minute after Thayer Cross had waived the right to examine evidence. With Paul gone, Cross's interest had gone also. He yawned and slumped in his chair.

Pervis was on his feet, humming under his breath and dumping the contents of his briefcase on the table. They consisted largely of newspapers and several dog-eared briefs. Judge Rogers, with a chuckle, recognized an appellate decision of 1932. Pervis stacked them all neatly on the corner and turned to Charlie.

"Look, kiddo." He leaned over and put a wet hand on each shoulder. "This is a toughie, understand?"

Charlie swallowed and nodded. He had a quaint sense of being in a pit. The pit was steep and deeply graded, and perched on little shelves above him were Pervis, the sergeant, the clerk, the assistant state's attorney and, up near the top, the judge. The spectators were outside the pit, peering over the rim and exchanging sly jokes about him among themselves.

"Okay," Pervis was saying. "Signed the papers?" He indicated the indictment pile with a twist of his fat frame. "Okay. Stay with it."

"Charles F. Bond!"

Charlie stepped forward, feeling a familiar tug in his bowels. The clerk directed him to raise his right hand and he heard the oath dimly, through a curtain of chatter. Before he could say yes, or even nod his head, he was asked how he pleaded. He opened his mouth and heard Pervis plead him not guilty. He said it "Not guilty" with an affected croak and drew a small laugh.

"Take your seat," someone said. Charlie sat.

"Mr. Monroe," came a voice above the bench. "You may proceed."

The assistant state's attorney called the three raiders and Ferrara. Pervis waived cross-examination for the first three and admitted the policy slips with a casual flip of his thumb over one bundle.

But when Ferrara had testified — his testimony was inconsiderable and deeply hedged with self-justification — Pervis moved up to the bench. The judge watched him, catlike.

Pervis began: "Sergeant Ferrara ——"

Monroe was on his feet, objecting testily that the officer was a patrolman. Rogers said nothing, and Pervis went on.

"*Sergeant* Ferrara — you will be a sergeant soon; with your fine record, I'm sure it's an oversight — tell us how long you been on that beat."

"Three, four years," Ferrara stammered.

"How long have you known the defendant?"

"That long."

Charlie shifted uneasily. Ferrara was so stupid. He could give the whole thing away.

"You've known him three, four years maybe. Ever had any trouble with him?"

"Nope."

"Of course you haven't. Now tell me, Sergeant, there was a crowd in front of the defendant's store yesterday, wasn't there? During the raid."

"Sort of."

"In your seasoned opinion, Sergeant — now I want you to think carefully before answering — was or wasn't that sort of crowd a traffic menace?"

"Well — sort of."

"The sort of crowd was a sort of traffic menace." Pervis cakewalked to the snickers. He stopped before the bench and pivoted. "If the court please, your honor, that raid yesterday caused more trouble — correct me, Sergeant, if I'm wrong — more trouble in that block than in the four years the defendant's been there. Sergeant Seaver, if the court please, should be the real defendant here. That's all. Step down."

He swung into his chair with a cunning wriggle and an eye on the scribbling reporter as the laughter grew. Seaver, standing against a side wall with his men, turned scarlet under a thousand curious eyes. Monroe scratched placidly in his notebook and the judge, with a shrug, hammered for order and glanced at his watch.

Charlie watched the bench worriedly. Fun was fun. But at a time like this!

Immediately he was on the stand: the city's case was complete, and Pervis was presenting him as his only witness. As he crept under the microphone, into the chair, he looked across the dense room and saw Loretta, mouselike, squeezing between two tall men.

"Mr. Bond, you been a grocer how long?"

"I guess five years."

"Make a pretty good living?"

"Yes. No. I don't remember."

"But mostly no. You're a poor man."

"I'm a poor man," Charlie parroted. He had trouble listening. His mind wandered. He brought it back, thought it strange it should have wandered, and, in thinking, let it go again.

"You're a good man, too. Churchgoer?" He waited. "I say, you're a churchgoer?"

Charlie started. "Sure."

"Family man, too. Getting ready for Christmas."

"I got a little girl." It was out. Immediately he was angry. It had no business here. He glanced meekly toward the rear of the room and saw Loretta standing very still, cradling her pocketbook in her cramped arms.

"A little girl." Pervis rolled it off his tongue slowly. "Getting ready for Christmas." Charlie nodded dumbly.

Pervis turned to the peering bench, hands outspread. "If the court please! Don't Sergeant Seaver even believe in God?"

He made it sound faintly nasty.

The judge led with a chuckle, and the spectators followed. Pervis looked archly at the assistant state's attorney, who shook his head, waiving cross-examination; then he pirouetted and beckoned Charlie from the stand. In the back of the room the men where shaking with laughter and Loretta was fighting tears. The judge announced his verdict, but no one behind the guardrail heard it. Even the reporter had to ask what it was. Charlie was guilty. He was fined $100 and costs.

"Like the others!" he cried.

"C'mon," Pervis said urgently. "Downstairs."

"Michael Cohn!" the clerk called.

The judge looked at his watch crossly. He hoped Pervis had not given the others ideas.

The sergeant trailed them to the stairhead, where Al was waiting, and said, "We got to go to the sheriff's office."

"Where's Loretta?" Charlie asked Al.

"In the can. She's awful upset. She'll be here in a minute."

"Let's go," the sergeant said, and Pervis added, "We got to pay."

Charlie drew back, stricken: "I can't! They took my dough!"

He turned to the sergeant, supplicating. The sergeant looked at Pervis, and Pervis locked his hands behind his broad back and smiled cheerfully at a blank pillar.

Al twitched uncomfortably. "Go ahead," he muttered. "I'll loan you some I got."

He had some, but not much. The advance to Pervis had rocked him: his bank account was nearly empty. But at home, in his sock drawer, he kept a small reserve. He could draw enough for the fine now and bank the reserve tomorrow.

Charlie gave him a grateful look. "You'll get it back," he promised. He went downstairs with the others.

The sheriff's office was small, with bleak buff walls and walnut benches partitioned to prevent lying across them. In a chair by the clerk's desk Otto Lutsche sat reading a comic book. As the convicted writers came down he paid them out. When Charlie entered, Otto rose and spat and stamped out of the room. The sergeant picked up the comic book and sat in his chair.

Al was long at the bank. Waiting, Pervis and the clerk exchanged stories while Charlie fidgeted on a bench. It was one of those seats which are never comfortable for thin men, and he kept shifting position and standing and sitting down again, scratching himself and squirming.

Loretta followed Al to the threshold and waited there, red-eyed and aloof. When the fine was paid the clerk handed Charlie a blue chit, explaining, "Pick it up this time Monday."

Charlie looked at him blankly.

"The money. That they took from you."

"Oh!" He felt better.

But immediately Pervis took him aside and warned him. "Don't try any payoffs with that. Remember they got the slips, with the names."

He nodded gloomily. He was under a finger, then.

The sergeant shook his hand with inappropriate heartiness. Pervis saw them to the door while Loretta walked swiftly ahead to the streetcar stop.

"Gimme a call," he winked, "any time."

"Thank you a lot," Charlie said politely.

Al nodded enthusiastically. "Believe me, Mr. Pervis, it was ——"

"Call me Georgie."

"Georgie, it was really a real treat."

Dulcy stepped back into a cone of fading sunlight, clapping her hands. "It's *beautiful!* No — don't turn them out!"

But Charlie pulled the plug anyway, and the constellation of tiny lights went dark. "Got to, sweetie," he grunted, crawling out under the branches. "Save it for tonight."

She sulked briefly. "It was so pretty."

"It's pretty now."

They stood by the windows, admiring it. Charlie had bought the tree an hour before and together they had decorated it: first the stand, then the lights, the ornaments, and finally the glittering tinsel and the false snow.

"Wait'll Mommie sees it," she breathed.

Charlie stroked the smooth curve of her cheek. After all, it was for Loretta. Christmas was for Dulcy, but not the tree, not this year.

The child rushed forward to move an offending bulb, and he sank heavily into the Morris chair, suddenly exhausted. Through the trial — remembered now as a bad dream is remembered, in snatches, with great vacant spaces in between — through the sessions with Ollie and the players and the raising of the tree, he had swept ahead on his nerve. Now his nerve was breaking and he was stopping.

376

He leaned back drowsily, closing his eyes. Tomorrow loomed, threatening, and he opened them again quickly and stared at Dulcy, arranging tinsel. That would be a day, that tomorrow. With $50 capital and the angry winners of today spreading poison about him and the run on one number.

"Daddy, this star makes it look lopsided."

"Put it in the middle, Princess."

One number. He thought of *Black Combination* with resentment. If whoever ran it wanted to ruin himself that was all right, but he had no right to take a chance like that with the lives of others. Of course, it wouldn't hit. But what if it did? It wouldn't, though. But it could. What if it did?

"Can I put the lights on, Daddy? For just a minute?"

"Why?"

"To see how something looks."

"All right. For just a minute."

Why if it did, it did, that was all. It was over. The whole mess was over. He paid the winners back and split the surplus among them and came home broke. Monday he looked for a job, a clean job. It was as simple as that. Or almost as simple. There would be a few loose ends. Quite a few, come to think of it. Some of the winners would be sore, as some of yesterday's had been today. Some of them would not understand, as those today had not. There would be some like that. He might have to look for his new job with a split lip. That could happen.

"Turn them out now, Dulce. Mommie'll be home soon."

"Just a minute, Daddy. Just one more minute, please!"

"All right. Hurry up."

And, of course, there was Lucy's zoning board. Not hers, really, though God knew it ought to be hers, hers and his, with all the money they had poured into it. The zoning board would be lost, unless he could talk someone else in the block into pledging his share, and he could not do that, not without Loretta knowing how much he had given Lucy. And that was out. So the rezoning would go through. That would happen.

"That's enough, now."

"All right, Daddy. It's all fixed up. Don't it look nice?"

"Wonderful."

So with a split lip and no job and a house slipping from under him, he would greet the new year. With the loose ends tied, that was the way it looked if the worst came. Of course it would not happen, but it was nice to know it could be worse than that. The worst it could be would be if Loretta found out about Lucy. That, *that*, would not, could not, happen.

The front door slammed.

"Hello!" he called.

"You're home?" Loretta's voice was muffled by many packages.

"Sure. Come on in, have a look."

Dulcy stood under the tree, hands clasped, eyes shining. When her mother came through the portieres she cried: "Look! Look!"

"Well, now!" For the first time that day Loretta smiled. "Isn't that nice!" She collapsed on the divan, her lap vanishing under an avalanche of brown paper and string.

"Turn them on, Princess," he said.

She scurried under the branches and pushed the plug in, and their faces were freckled with twinkling points of light.

Isn't that *nice*," Loretta repeated, blinking theatrically.

"We thought you'd like it," he said. For a moment he felt warm and content and unworried.

The evening meal was peaceful. There was one horrible moment during coffee when Dulcey came in waving the evening paper, insensible to the brutal headlines, demanding the comic strips be read to her. But Charlie put her off with vague promises of a television set, and she went off chortling.

When she had gone, Loretta said quietly, "You're going to that same work tomorrow?"

"Tonight. Right now in fact. I got to, till I can get out, close it up."

"Oh, I see," she said automatically.

But she didn't.

*   *   *

An hour later he was walking the block between Thawe and Horrigan streets, writing the next day's numbers. He wrote from the sidewalk, for he did not dare use the grocery this soon after the raid, and he wrote on the move, halting before Swinton's and Al Kelly's and holding his K-books under the blood-red neon to see. Two garish Santa Clauses stood on the corners, ringing bells and crowing. Charlie gave each $5 and told them to watch for strangers. The night cop, a brother-in-law of Ferrara's named Piombino, stood across the street, doing tricks with his espantoon. It was understood that if Piombino dropped it and swore loudly, trouble was coming. But no trouble came.

Charlie's plan was to write nights and early mornings. He noticed in the paper that Seaver raided in the noon hour, when the drops were full, and he thought if he could close all bets by nine o'clock in the morning and get out of the Elbow, he would be safe. On arrival he passed the word along the block he would be there until Ollie Wetlek closed. He hoped he would do enough business to make it worth while and did. The men swarmed out of the alleys, clutching change and shouting, and he was mobbed. Part of the attraction was Charlie himself. His arrest was already an Elbow legend, and many were drawn by curiosity. But that was the smaller part. The larger was written on four out of every five slips in his books. In the Elbow, it was 555 by a landslide.

He stipulated Ollie's closing as his own because he was afraid to stay on the street with more than a few dollars in his pocket, and with Ollie open he could stop in there every fifteen minutes and stack his take behind the bar. At first Ollie was against this. The raid had frightened him, and he was through subwriting. But Charlie told him he would keep all the slip carbons in his own pockets, and since there was nothing incriminating in the money, Ollie agreed to help.

It was cold on the sidewalk. The Santa Clauses offered to share their bottles with him, but he declined politely. He tried to stay outside as much as possible, running into the bar and emptying his pockets of cash and running out again, absorbing all the

business he could, but toward ten o'clock he could not stand th
sting in his ears any longer, and he came inside to get warm. H
stood by the door, stamping his feet, a red-faced, shivering figur
in a large, lumpy overcoat thin in the elbows.

The room was crowded. This was Ollie's busiest hour. All th
booths were occupied, there was no room at the bar, and Ollie
uncapping beers and filling shot glasses with a furious bustle
threw an endless series of nervous glances at the Christmas tree
hoping no one would knock it over. Some of the drinkers wer
white. Ollie averaged one serious fight a week.

A scrawny, bearded old man came out of the crowd, wavin
a bill at Charlie. "Fi' fi' fi'," he cried, nodding emphatically.

"Can't do it, Manny," Charlie said. "Not in the bar. Com
on outside."

On the street he tore off the slip and exchanged it for the bil
"Where'd you get a dollar?" he asked. Manny lived in a littl
shack with a wheezing phonograph and a stack of sentiment
records. Even in the Elbow he was notorious for his povert
"You never had more'n a dime before."

The old man leered and swung away with a grotesque ste
"I'm not telling, you're not knowing." He disappeared into th
bar.

Charlie headed toward two obvious clients in front of Stein
Super Market, troubled in his prosperity. So many of his regul
customers had multiplied their normal antes by so much, ar
nearly all were playing the one number. Both men in front
Stein's left heavy bets on 555. His chapped hands shook as h
wrote it.

They went off punching one another playfully, and he lean
against the window, tightening his chest to fight the cold. I
was about to walk down to the Unique on the chance it was st
open when a taxi cut sharply out of an alley where taxis seldo
went. As it flashed under the arc light he saw Steiner's waitre
sitting by the rear window, laughing. He caught a fleeting glimp
of the man beyond. It looked like Moss, and he shrank into th
cold shadows at the store edge. Probably Moss was still sore

him. He crossed the street, instinctively seeking Piombino's protection, and gave him his tip now to insure it.

"Many thanks!" Piombino said, twisting his night stick in a double flip and brandishing it at the end. Then he lapsed into a morose silence and Charlie felt uneasy again.

Twenty minutes later the lights in Ollie's bar winked on and off and the crowd surged into the street noisily. Ollie followed shortly and crossed with a bulging shopping bag under his arm. He handed it to Charlie.

"Whew!" he moaned. "Some business. I'm dead."

"I saw one of your best friends in a taxicab, no less," Charlie said, tucking the bag under his coat. "The girl, you know, Ruby."

Ollie frowned. "She's going out with that pal of yours I don't trust. That Bailey guy."

"No friend of mine," Charlie said lightly. He wondered what Ollie's interest in Ruby was. You never knew about those things.

"I'll see you to Striker," the cop said. "Everybody in the Elbow knows you're loaded."

Ollie grunted goodnight and Charlie and Piombino walked to the streetcar, Piombino striding ahead with his holster unsnapped and Charlie, slowed by the weight of the shopping bag, struggling to keep up with him.

At home he noted gratefully that the newspaper had vanished. Loretta was reading a magazine in bed, and when he came in she smiled and held up her face to be kissed. He could not remember when she had done that before.

He gave her the money for Al, undressed quickly, and turned out the light. Abruptly he sat up and turned it on again, remembering. "You were going to tell me about Wilson, the lawyer, why you couldn't get him."

She paused, thinking, and then yawned a forced yawn. "Mrs. Carter wasn't home."

He sank back satisfied and was almost immediately asleep. Loretta lay awake a long time before switching the light off. And after that she lay a still longer time in the darkness, going over the part she had not told him.

She had not called her brother the night before until after three unsuccessful visits to the Carter home. Each time she had stood on the stoop, ringing and waiting. She had gone back twice because she knew Lucy was there. The evening paper had been taken in.

Tonight, running home with her packages down the block of watching houses, she had met Henrietta Mathias. Henrietta was seething with information. That morning she had seen Lucy, and Charlie's plight had come up.

"I don't feel sorry for him," Lucy had said. "After all, it isn't be-kind-to-dumb-animals week, is it, Mrs. Mathias?"

Henrietta had retold this with gestures and elaborate sympathy. Then she had turned and cut across the street, bobbing and clucking and looking quickly up and down the empty street.

She kept falling down. It's the heels, she thought defensively. I'm not used to the heels. And the sawdust's slippery here, and there's a loose board somewhere. There, in front of the bar. Ought to fix that, nail it down and get some clean sawdust. Don't matter to me, I don't mind, but somebody else, that did, could sue. Make it this time. Easy, easy. Go slow. Steer wide. Watch that — *Oh! They're laughing!* Quick, now. Upsy Daisy, Lazy Mazie. But they keep laughing! Well. Long as they don't, he don't get mad. Long as it's a joke. But why can't I just sit down? No place to sit. Why not? Isn't. Well. Don't they have a girl, can't she get the drinks? Out. Out where, it's her job, isn't it her job? Oh. Oh, that's all right then. Jesus. I couldn't even make it to the *men's* room, and it's nearer, if they gave me a medal. Goddam these heels. That sawdust, and that board. Couldn't be the stuff. Only had one, maybe two. Make it three and be safe. Only three or four and what's that, nothing. It's maybe the way I am, I can take it any more. Well. Like Moss said, I got one party coming. Or going. Only why do *I* have to get the drinks? Where's that girl, I never even *saw* her. And why don't they fix that board, that one, whichever one it is, I can't see with the sawdust. Back now, careful now. No spilly the drinky. Careful, careful. Wis

hey wouldn't watch. Careful —— *OH!* Oh, *again!* I'm *wet!* But
hey're laughing. Well. Long as they don't get sore.

She swayed toward the table, her eyes flat and unseeing, step-
ing with exaggerated caution, waving the empty tray like a tam-
ourine. But she could not make it. She could not stand. She
ept falling down.

Moss looked down at the soft, disheveled pile and jeered.
"Loose?" he asked.

She lifted her mottled face without understanding.

"You loose?"

Then she remembered. "Asa goose." As he had taught her.
"Loose asa goose."

He roared. Otto roared. The dark man with the curly mustache
oared.

Only the black was silent. He sat quietly in the corner of the
ooth beside Moss, biting his fingernails and looking away. He
as not drinking tonight. He was being paid not to drink.

"Moss." The voice from the floor was thick with pleading.

"What'll you have, goose."

"Coupla fingers?"

"You just got a whole fist."

"Spilled it. Moss."

He motioned to the bartender, and she wondered why he had
ot done that before, the times she had to go. The man came
ver quickly.

He was bowlegged and little and all of a color, blue. He wore
blue sport shirt, blue suede shoes, and navy slacks, and his eyes
atched his pale, cyanotic face. He knew Moss. They whispered
nd he went away and came back carrying a small beer glass,
rimming brown with a bead but no foam. He bent over and
anded it to her carefully.

She cupped it with both hands, disappointed. Beer.

"Go ahead," Moss said quietly. "On me."

She sipped, felt the dark wash in her throat, and then suddenly
nd impulsively bolted the rest. It wasn't beer, and she wished
e had some more.

The bartender took the empty glass from her, put it on th
table, and methodically produced a bottle from behind his slac
and put that down too. She looked up thirstily. Moss silent
poured five fingers and handed them down.

"One more for us, Greek," he told the man. "This'll hol
her."

She sat tailor fashion, with her back braced against the boot
side and her face in the little glass, sucking up the whisky wi
rapid little sips. Sitting so, her skirt crept high on her thighs ar
stretched taut across them. Moss could see the strips of adhesiv
tape holding up her cheap new stockings, lined now with a doze
runs, and across the aisle and toward the rear a young man wh
had wandered in with a party of friends could see the thin be
of rayon beyond, damp from the spilled drinks and stained wi
the grime of the sawdust floor.

Ruby did not see the young man. She was barely consciou
of Moss and his friends, the men who had arrived and taken h
seat, above her. Except for them and the loose board fretting
her mind, she was unaware of the rest of the room. She tilte
the glass back, holding the last dark draught against the roof
her mouth, savoring it and then letting it go. It gurgled noisi
and was gone. She lifted the tumbler wordlessly and wordless
Moss filled it.

But the young man saw her. He was one of four, two me
and two women, sitting in the only other occupied booth. T
women were in slacks and head scarves. They were drinking be
and whispering to one another and looking at the men and t
tering. The back of the other young man was to Ruby. He w
telling a long story sonorously, and no one was listening. H
friend kept throwing furtive little glances down the aisle, first
Moss and then up the ruined stockings, past the adhesive stri
over the stained rayon.

The watcher was himself watched by the bartender. The Gre
shuffled nervously behind his bar and hoped there would be
trouble. He had offered to close the bar for Moss, and that h
been the plan, but at the last moment Moss had decided a s

picious policeman might look in. So the Greek shuffled and watched the young man, who watched Ruby, and she squattered on the floor, sinking deeper into her stupor while Moss poured from above.

The Greek's Bar was six blocks from the waterfront. It was too far from Striker Street to be respectable and too far from Sticktown to be disreputable and had never prospered. He had done his best, but his compromises all turned out badly. The walls were pine-paneled to eye level — sailors looked in and turned away. The brass bar rail had been replaced by a copper-lined gutter — partying sportsmen spat in it and left. In despair the Greek had installed a massive, 100-record juke box to lure the best of both. The worst came, the waifs of organized and disorganized society drifted in to listen and cadge what they could. He struck back with three signs now posted above the bar mirror, warning customers not to stand in the doorway, not to solicit drinks, and not to look for credit from him. He had kept the juke box. It was divided into five panels of twenty records each, entitled "Hit Tunes," "Old Favorites," "Waltzes and Polkas," "Foxtrots and Rhumbas," and "Classical Selections." All the Classical Selections were in Greek.

Toward this juke box the curious young man moved now, a dime jutting conspicuously from his fingers. He slowed as he passed Ruby, who was rocking now to some inner rhythm and cradling the half-empty glass to her spotted sweater. He smiled, she looked at him blankly, and he passed on.

In his booth the girls in slacks were preparing to go to the ladies' room. The other man was still telling his interminable joke — a shaggy dog story, he had explained at the beginning — but they were ignoring him, clutching their pocketbooks and waiting, poised on the edge of their seats. He finished and slumped back, chuckling.

"Is that *all*?" one of the girls asked, astonished.

He nodded mirthfully.

"Oh, *Harry!*" "Honestly!"

They cackled and rose.

The young man at the juke box was long making his selections and when he came back, a Hit Tune thumping behind him, hi booth was empty. He waved the Greek over and ordered anothe round, lit a cigarette and returned to his watch.

Ruby staggered to her feet. "Drinkin' too mush," she mum bled, groping for the booth side and trying to focus on Moss.

He looked up from an intense conversation with the black "Well?"

Her head wobbled. She meant it to shake. "Hafta ——" sh swallowed painfully and went on with a gasp "—— go ona wagon watcha diet." No one said anything, and after another swallov she explained again, "Diet," and beamed proudly.

Moss sipped his drink thoughtfully and then glanced up sud denly. She had been watching his head, and when it jerked u she lurched away, frightened, and caught herself. "What's th matter?" he demanded. "Aren't you havin' a good time?"

She beamed again and waved an erratic hand. "Havin' wor nerful time!" She had forgotten already.

He grinned and, shifting toward her, ran a hand up one leg under the billowing skirt. "Somethin' tells me you got what takes." He winked at the others.

She anchored her legs apart and held out her glass. "More, she said dully. He filled it and she drank. "Happy days," sh said. He filled it again and again she drank. The dark man wit the mustache, the black, and Otto looked over one another shoulders.

"Loose?" he whispered.

"Aza gooze."

The Hit Tunes switched on the spinning post and the new on thumped even more loudly.

The door to the ladies' room swung open and the girls fro the other booth came out chattering. At the same time the men room gave forth the shaggy dog storyteller. He drew up besid one of the girls and patted her buttocks. She swaggered unco sciously.

The other girl paused at the edge of their table, watching Rul with open curiosity. Then she slid in with a muffled giggle and whispered to the storyteller and his girl. Their faces darted out, gaped, and darted back with a snickered chorus. The young man ignored them, staring relentlessly on.

On signal from Moss the Greek hurried over and put a fresh bottle on the table. Moss eyed the remains of his third drink speculatively. "I'll have just one more," he said. He looked up into Otto's disapproving frown. "I don't want none," Otto said. The dark man nodded and Otto shifted his frown to him.

Moss glanced down with satisfaction at the slump of Ruby's shoulders and, as he turned back to the table, saw the young man for the first time. He stiffened, glowered, and then realized the starer was intent and did not see him.

"Greek," Moss called loudly. "Get the lady a chair."

Then the young man shifted quickly and frantically engaged the girl beside him in conversation. The Greek arrived with the chair and helped Ruby into it. She perched precariously on the edge, leaning heavily on her elbows, with the heels of her hands flattened against her cheekbones, staring bleakly at the drink Moss had set before her. He reached over and primly pulled the folds of her skirt over her knees and turned and muttered something to the black. The man nodded listlessly. His legs were cramped and he wanted to get out and walk but did not dare. He was afraid Moss might not like it.

From the sidewalk outside came a lusty shout. Everyone but Ruby peered around at the door, and as they did it swung open to admit a sharp puff of night air and seven Cuban merchant seamen, preposterous in Panama hats. They stood in a huddled group, eyed the room menacingly, and then wheeled slowly toward the bar. In their midst a captive figure bobbed erratically, and as they approached the copper gutter and strung out along it, the figure broke free.

Free, he nearly collapsed from lack of support and saved himself by a heroic lunge at the bar. He was a gaunt, red-eyed little man lost in an ancient army overcoat and a ragged stocking cap. He was Hoot Vogel.

"Whasis place?" he inquired.

"This place my place," the Greek said with a servile little smile. He was afraid these people would make trouble.

Hoot's reply was incoherent, and the seaman on his left nudged him violently. His legs buckled, and the man on the other side caught him.

"Wanna drink?" they demanded together. He nodded excitedly and the Greek poured whisky for everyone. The Cubans sipped theirs morosely, but their hostage gulped his and, turning with elaborate grace, inspected the premises foggily. He focused on Ruby. Moss watched narrowly. The Greek held his breath.

With a shuffling, faltering step Hoot edged across the open floor. Five feet away he halted, weaving. "Rube!" he croaked.

Down the aisle the young man and his friends glanced up, and from the bar the Cubans squinted. Moss was tense.

"Rube!"

With great effort she rocked back in the chair and looked around. "Hoot," she grunted. "Hullo, Hoot."

His mouth worked strenuously but brought forth only a thin spume of saliva which broke and dropped on the coarse weave of his coat. His eyes winked rapidly. She lifted one chapped hand to her breast and rested it there, and they stared at one another stupidly, with growing confusion.

Moss looked rapidly from Hoot to the Cubans, back to Hoot, back to the Cubans, wondering whether to risk a scene. They saved him the choice. One of them stepped away from the bar and crammed his absurd hat over his brow. It was a signal: the others followed.

"Hey!" the first Cuban snapped. "Wanna drink?"

Hoot hesitated, torn.

"C'mon or stay, don't matter," the seaman said and headed for the door. His comrades gathered about him, forming a new wedge for a new bar.

"You better go," Moss said darkly, jerking his thumb.

Hoot danced feebly on one foot and then the other. The door

opened, the night air swept in, and he blurted, "So long, Rube," and fled, dragging his overcoat and clutching at his wretched cap.

She turned to her drink without a sign. Her mouth hung open. Her eyes were stitched with a drawing thread.

The giant juke sobbed erotically. The Greek, celebrating the peace, had fed it a quarter.

They were in the car, moving down Striker Street under an arch of evergreen and neon. Otto was driving, the black was beside him, and in the back, wedged between the dark mustachioed man and Moss, Ruby was singing.

"Ahhh wanna get-cha, ona slow boat to Chi-na, all by myself, all a-lone . . ."

Her voice trailed off brokenly as she lost the lyric. For a moment there was only the smooth moan of the motor and, beyond it, the distant, subtle noises of the downtown traffic.

Then Moss snorted. "Could've been better, could've been worse."

"Worse how?" asked the dark man.

"Could've been a fight with the spics over that smokie."

"Witnesses," said the man meaningfully and sunk into his overcoat as they stopped at a light.

Moss held his watch to the window. It shone red and then green and then red again under a glaring sign advertising 28 BURLESK CUTIES 28, and it read three minutes to midnight. He felt a twitch coming in his gut and grabbed the arm rest and rode with it. Half an hour, he promised himself. Half an hour.

"I tried to get her off alone. You saw me. She had to dance. Dance!"

"Some dancer," the man said and chuckled.

She stirred. "Wanna dance. Wanna dance, dance, dance."

"You'll dance," said the man.

"Lousy party."

"You'll dance all right," he said.

Otto cut over to a one-way street, where the lights were timed, and they rolled swiftly out of the cabaret district, past the darkened office buildings and department stores and into the dirty edge of the Seventh.

"Smell that air!" Moss jeered. No one laughed.

The black lit a cigarette nervously, and in a moment the car was blue with smoke. Ruby started to slump forward and would have fallen against the front seat if Otto had not suddenly turned the car into a side street, throwing her back.

The street was narrow and lined on both sides with cars, all prewar and badly parked, and Otto crept carefully for two blocks. In the third block he turned off his lights and gunned forward, and in the sixth he slowed. Immediately ahead, under an arc light at the base of a triangular block, two policemen were waiting with upturned collars and averted faces. Otto stopped beside them and the dark man opened his door. The men came forward straightening.

"Give us twenty minutes," said the dark man. "Not no more than twenty." The policemen nodded together. "Remember," he told them, "second floor, chalked door, walk in. Okay?" They nodded again and stepped back and he slammed the door.

Moss studied his watch under the feeble light. Twenty minutes would be just right.

Otto took a sharp right, a sharp left, and stopped at one end of a short block of sagging houses. There were no street lamps and the only light issued weakly from behind an occasional streaked window. The air was smart with the odor of burning kerosene. They were behind the Elbow.

Ruby sat up slowly. "Whasis?"

Doors slammed. She was alone in the car. Blurred shadows were moving around jerkily on the narrow sidewalk, and she peered out at them, trying to see. She slid toward the door, and as she did her feet kicked something over. It rang dully against the floor board. She reached down thirstily.

The door swung wide. It was Otto.

"C'mon," he whispered, holding out his arms to help her.

"Bring the bottle," Moss called softly from the darkness.

"Hell witha bottle," she panted, straining toward Otto. "Bring ne."

Suddenly they were all there, reaching for her. Arms tugged nd lifted. What was going on?

The cold air cut her face and swept up her dress. She vished they had waited a moment longer while she took one nore pull.

They were going up stairs, past a door, across a hall and up nore stairs. Far away at the end of a winding cave a naked bulb inked strangely. Their hands were rough, they were puffing. Vhat *was* going on?

A landing. More stairs. Another landing. No — another hall. , doorway. The hands were letting her down. On the floor? No, n a bed. Not her bed. Too soft. Were they going away? Were ey gone?

The light sprang up and they were above her, peering down a little circle, like faces over a bear pit in a zoo. Overhead the alls were stained and peeling, and the ceiling hung in gay strips. 'he room was unfurnished. There was only the bed.

Moss pushed the bottle toward her, uncapped. She grabbed it agerly, swallowing before it was in her mouth, and the warm rength spread throbbing through her. She pushed it away and eld it against her chin and watched the black undress.

He *was* undressing!

His coat and trousers and shoes lay in a pile in the corner, ad he was unbuttoning his shirt with swift flicks of his fingers. ow it was off, and now his undershirt was off too. Into the pile ey went. He was slipping off his undershorts.

What was going *on!*

In a ragged frame of plaster and loose wallpaper she saw him ouching in the corner, naked and black and big. She tried to ove and then hands were on her again, fingers under her skirt, aring away the adhesive tape and the shredded stockings, rough uckles under the cardigan, pulling it over her head, thumbs ding along her ribs, fumbling with her brassiere. Then a sharp tug from all the fingers, all the knuckles, all the thumbs, and her loose pants slid over her hips and knees and heels and she lay stripped and shivering.

What was ——

A spray flecked across her belly and she smelled it above her own smell. It cut across her thighs and the frantic thought struck her they might throw it all away. She looked around wildly and saw Moss, an uncorked pint in his fist, shooting it across the bed, criss-cross, criss-cross, marking great X's with it, tying her to the sheet with rancid strings of cheap whiskey.

What was going ——

Another hand plunged down with the fifth, her fifth, thrusting it violently against her gums. She tasted blood and sucked at the warm neck, thought she was going to be sick, sucked again and suddenly was sick, pumping with tired muscles over her slimy chin, into the sheet. Someone swore. The bottle was in her mouth again. She sucked.

What was going on!

The bed creaked rustily, and in the mad moment before the light went out she saw the black, shining and huge, looming overhead. Then all was darkness. Steps rattled away, vanished and were followed by other, slower steps approaching heavily. The light went on again. Voices again babbled. Again rough hands dug at her, pawed her, rolled her over . . .

In the sick light she thrashed feebly.

The lieutenant looked down wearily. With his alpaca coat and mussed gray hair and steel-rimmed spectacles he looked like a clerk and was.

"Name," he grunted. She sagged between the two policemen. "Know her name?"

"Name's Jones," said one of the cops. "Least that's what she used here last week."

The lieutenant wrote it in the great brass-bound docket.

"Sex, female. Age?" He squinted. "How old, sister?"

"Thirty-five's safe," said the same cop.

"Color white, nationality U.S. Occupation?"

"She's a whore, Ed."

"I guess." Ed shuddered. "Married or single. Hey, sister!"

"She's out. Make it single. She's single."

"Read and write, yes. Place of arrest?"

"405 Syke Lane."

"Time of arrest?"

"Twelve-thirty."

"Umm. Charge her dissolute course, drunk and disorderly, resisting arrest, disturbing, striking officer. Suit you?"

They grinned and nodded.

"Harry, call the matron," the lieutenant told a patrolman across the stairs. "Put her over there. Bring me the nigger."

They carried her across the dusty floor, lifting her by the elbows, and lowered her into a straight chair. She watched the black booked. He had dressed hurriedly as she was being dressed, and was nearly as disheveled as she. But he was better equipped to cope with the lieutenant. No one had to answer his questions for him.

His docketing was nearly finished when the matron arrived. She had just come on duty and was cheerful. "Hi, Sweetie," she called, coming down the stairs.

Ruby attempted a smile. It was grotesque. The woman laughed harshly. "Hear you been working the black market. Ba-a-ad business!" She laughed again.

Ruby did not understand. She tried to look quizzical, but her control was poor, and she merely appeared sad. The matron slapped her lustily on the back and caught her before she fell. "Forget it. It's an occupational hazard. Your friend'll fix you up."

Ruby stopped struggling with her confusion and tried to concentrate. She *did* have a friend. Who was he, her friend?

The booking of the black was completed, and the patrolmen were extending it with unnecessary questions, to the annoyance of the lieutenant, when the double doors facing on the street broke open and a violent man in a dirty bow tie entered carrying a Speed Graphic. "Preston, the *Star*," he barked.

The lieutenant looked up mildly. "What's on your mind?" he demanded.

"Hear you got a case of interracial tail."

"That's right. Her," the lieutenant pointed, "and him."

"I want a shot."

"Didn't know your paper used things like that."

The patrolmen helped by leading the black to Ruby, and he cooperated by coming readily and even leering on request. The matron was discreetly in the background. She had learned to judge lens angles and knew just where to stand to get in.

Ruby never knew what happened. By the time she was aware of the figures clustering around her the first bulb had flashed. She blinked and saw the violent man violently shifting plates, felt the black's hand drop to her neck and thinking it was a policeman was about to look up at him when the photographer said brusquely, "Okay, Sexy, smile. C'mon, c'mon, *smile!*"

Again the grotesque effort.

The bulb exploded.

The double doors collided violently and the photographer was gone.

A moment later they opened and Tom Sanders entered, glanced furtively around the room, and approached the lieutenant, whispering. The lieutenant listed and asked, "The girl too?" Sanders shook his head. "Hey Nick," the lieutenant called. "Bail for the nigger."

"Not for her?" asked the matron, dismayed. She had a magazine serial upstairs and had no intention of looking after a drunk if she could help it. They could be so messy.

"Take her up," the lieutenant ordered.

"Ollie," Ruby croaked.

"That's it," the matron said excitedly.

"That's what?"

"Ollie Wetlek, runs a bar down the street. He'll bail her out." She went to the phone booth.

The two patrolmen fuddled and looked up, worried. "We don

think that's such a good idea, Ed," said one. "Not in her condition," said the other.

"What d'you mean?" the matron asked indignantly from the
booth.

"Of course it's a good idea," the lieutenant snapped. He had
been with Big Ed for thirty years and was opposed to all Erik
cops on principle. "She's got her rights, same as the nigger."

Ollie was dressed five minutes after the matron called. Ten
minutes later he was in the station house, peeling off bills. By
then, Ruby had been without a drink for over an hour. The fog
was clearing: she knew where she was, where she had been, and
roughly what had happened. When he had met her bail and
came to get her she waved weakly and tried to wink. Her eyes
fluttered wildly. He thought he had never seen her look so bad.
The vomit on her chest had soaked through the sweater, and
some of it was in her hair. Her dress was torn and she was shaking.

The matron handed her over with a coarse laugh, and they
went out.

On the street she hesitated, and he hesitate with her. "Les
open up the bar," she mumbled. "Wanna stiff one."

He saw one of the arresting cops in the window, watching.
Too late, Rube. Better turn in."

"Don't wanna turn in. Turned in, dint work. Wanna ——"
he faltered, and he caught her. "—— big drink," she finished,
rawing herself up stiffly like a figure in a posture chart.

He glanced uneasily at the window. The cop was still there.
Rube, I can't. I'd lose my license."

"Hell witha license. Do I getta belt or don't I? Answer me that
ne simpa queshion."

Now there were two cops in the window. "No," he said. "I
st can't."

"Okay." She jiggled with scorn. "Don't mind me. Got lotsa
iends, good joes'll fix me up." She wheeled elaborately and
aggered away.

"Rube!" he called. "Come here!"

But she did not come. She tried to hurry and fell, but before he could reach her she was up again, crawling ahead. At West Concord she hobbled to the middle of the intersection, paused listed toward the left and then followed the list, shambling toward the waterfront.

He followed her to the edge of the District, trying to reason with her. Finally he ran in front of her and caught her by the shoulders. They shrank in his hands. "Rube!" he blurted. "You got no right!"

She stood motionless until his hands dropped. "Go 'way," she said thickly. "Calla cop. Copsis pretty tough on guys bother pregnant girl, so beat it."

He stood helplessly aside and watched her weave down the chipped cobblestones, like a beaten dog limping home, headed for the piers.

Four hours later Charlie Bond dismounted a Striker Street trolley and plodded through the bitter dawn to his writing station outside Ollie's darkened bar. He was still frowzy with sleep, unreconciled to the new day, when Joe Ferrara appeared across the street and hailed him.

"Say, Mr. Bond, you're a real early bird today."

Charlie yawned desperately. For two nights now he had been awakened rudely, once by the turnkey and once by the alarm. He waved with forced cheer.

"I didn't know you got up this time."

"Every morning," Ferrara bragged. "Life on the force ain't easy." He crossed the cobblestones, dug into his tunic pocket and brought out two new dollar bills.

Charlie was amazed. "Never thought you'd go for the racket."

"I got a hunch," Ferrara said sheepishly. "On five-five-five."

Charlie's heart dropped. It was like a run on a bank. Last night and now today. "You and fifty million Frenchmen."

"Just a hunch I got," Ferrara repeated, pocketing the slip and shifting uneasily. He was afraid Charlie would bring up the trial. But it was the last thing Charlie wanted to talk about.

396

"How's Winkler?" He felt he ought to ask. "Still feeling lousy?"

"Oh, ain't you heard about Winkler? He had a heart attack."

"Jees, no! Serious?"

Ferrara nodded impressively. "Took him to the hospital in a municipal ambulance yesterday morning, right after you left. They said he looked terrible."

Charlie plucked guiltily at his overcoat collar. He wondered if the cops blamed him. "Poor sergeant," he said sentimentally.

"Sergeant?" Ferrara sniffed. "He was never no sergeant."

"In a manner of speaking, I mean."

"In a manner of nothing. He was a keyman."

He strode off, really offended, as the first wave of policy cusomers came out of Horrigan Street, lunch baskets in hand.

For the next two hours Charlie was swamped. He wrote and grabbed change, working feverishly with both hands until he thought he would drop. Still they came. By eight o'clock he had taken in almost $200. With the bank of the evening before, his pool for that one day was over $400, nearly $300 of it on the one number. He calculated the big and little books as he wrote: if 555 came in, his winners would be entitled to $165,000. It was fantastic, a bad dream better left undreamt.

At 8:30 he slipped away to the Unique for a cup of coffee. Steiner was scrambling himself a mess of eggs and whistling.

"I saw that girl of yours last night in a cab," Charlie said, ladling in sugar.

Steiner giggled happily. "Don't see her here, do you? She's plastered, if I know her, absolutely dead blind."

Charlie blinked. "You say it like it was good."

"Sure it's good, it's what she needs a lot of in one end. In the other end what she needs she gets when she's that way." He winked obscenely. "I know."

"Well," Charlie said uncertainly. "It takes all kinds."

"Takes all kinds for her," Steiner snickered.

Back on West Concord Charlie was surprised to see Ollie Vetlek pacing the sidewalk before his bar, blowing gusts of frosty air and shaking his head in a pantomime of misery.

"Couldn't sleep?" Charlie asked agreeably.

Ollie turned, hollow-eyed. "She isn't there. I'm out my dough and I should've let her stay there. For her own good."

"Who? Where?"

"Ruby, in jail."

"She was in jail?"

Ollie looked at him wretchedly. Charlie was about to ask pointedly about Ollie's family when a fresh wave of men turned ou¹ of the alleys and he was lost in a shower of silver. When they were gone, Ollie had gone, too.

He was himself ready to leave a half hour later when he hear¹ a cry and saw Sam Crawford running toward him from a bloc¹ away. He waited, shivering. "Well, you're the last one," he sai¹ decisively as Sam came up. "Positively the last."

Sam rocked, gulping air, too breathless to talk.

"I thought you'd be here last night," Charlie said. "An oldtime¹ like you."

"Didn't know . . . just heard . . . thought you was in jail . . was goin' somewheres else," Sam gasped.

"You been going somewhere else?" Charlie asked sharply. "¹ I known that I wouldn't've waited."

"Better luck with you, boss." Sam yanked off his filthy clot¹ gloves and poked a sheaf of bills at him. "Play with you ever¹ time I can. My lucky man."

"Eight bucks!" The largest bet until then had been three "Where'd you get that?"

"Saved it," Sam lied. "For a big deal lahk this."

"Guess you want triple five."

"Sholey."

Charlie handed him the slip carbon and tucked the frayed bil¹ under his bulging coat and left. Sam watched him plod towa¹ Striker Street and, when he had gone half a block, called in¹ pulsively, "Big day, man!" Charlie gave him a sour look over h¹ shoulder and then moved on, waddling like a horse with sadd¹ bags.

The truck was waiting in the alley. Sam trotted toward it, clucking excitedly. Everyone in the crew had something on the number, but none as much as he. The evening before he had pried open Andy Hallam's back window, carried two dozen bushel baskets of scrap iron to a junkyard three blocks away, and peddled them there. He intended to pay Hallam back that evening. He did not doubt he could. The others in the crew were hopeful, but Sam was sure, dead sure.

Zipski was uneasy. He knew very little of Henderson. Morelock had never kept a steady finger on the pulse of the syndicate, and Seaver had been too busy for details. But when a copy of the *Black Combination* finally reached the commissioner's desk, and he saw today was the day, he was troubled.

He switched on the intercom. "Get me Seaver." Then he remembered. Seaver would be out on a raid. "Wait a minute. Forget that. Is my car in service or out?"

"Just came back this morning, sir. This time they said it's really fixed."

"Get it. And find out where Seaver is."

The Lincoln met him on a windswept Belton Avenue street corner. He was with a party of raiders, bundling slips while a writer, an elderly man in a leather jacket, stood handcuffed and shivering against the squad car. Zipski's driver cut in behind them and Zipski rolled down the window. Seaver handed his bundle to a sergeant and stepped over.

"We're really going places now," he said. "If this keeps up we'll need nets."

"Fine." Zipski drew the magazine from under this laprobe. "What do you know about this?"

"Practically nothing. Matter of fact, I just saw it the other day. I sent a man out to talk to the guy that runs it, but his office is closed and his wife said he was out of town. Why?"

"I don't like it."

"Not much we can do. The lottery law don't cover it. But I

don't think it's anything. The way I look at it, we're putting him out of business, too. He just lives off Erik, and he's cashing in before it's too late."

"I still don't like it. Keep in touch with his wife and bring him in when he gets back."

"Right."

Seaver turned away, and Zipski signaled his driver to return downtown. He settled back, thoughtfully chewing his unlit pipe. As they swept down the narrow streets he glanced at the clock in the dashboard, wondering why it had stopped at exactly ten o'clock. Then, with a vague feeling of alarm, he realized it hadn't stopped at all, but was running, on time.

It was the largest day's take in the history of the syndicate. By 11:15, when Otto picked up Eddie Finch at the mouth of a snowbound alley with the last slips, the gross was nearly $67,000 and that was under the play, for nineteen writers, Seaver's catch that morning, were not reporting. Over $38,000 was on the one number, and this, together with the tremendous size of the bank, produced sharply mixed feelings in the abandoned barn where Ben, bearded and twitching, was playing his last and best card. Nothing but money could stop him now. He had been sure of that since eight o'clock that morning, when he called the Cameron home and asked for Wallace Gillette.

"Good morning, Senator," he had said cheerfully.

"Who's this?"

"Erik. I kind of thought you'd be out there."

"Where are you?"

Ben laughed scornfully. "Did you get my picture?"

Moss had thrust the envelope in the Cameron mail slot, rung the bell three times, and then waited in his car until the portico light went on.

Wallace was silent. Then: "Where is she?"

"Never mind." So they don't know either. Good. "I know where she was when that picture was taken. Cameron there?"

"He won't talk to you. You know that."

400

Ben laughed again. "I just wondered if he'd seen the docket, is all."

"Listen," Wallace said hoarsely. "Have you read the law on blackmail?"

"Blackmail?" Ben tried to sound insulted. "Who said anything about blackmail? All I'm saying is I got this picture and some other things, and I'm going to sit back and see what happens and try to make up my mind what I should do with them. As a citizen."

"Wait a minute." Wallace put down the phone and Ben could hear muffled voices arguing. Then he came back and said, "Where can we reach you?"

"You can't. I'll reach you, later today. I or somebody. Goodbye, Senator." Wallace started to talk again, but Ben said, "That's all, Senator," and hung up briskly.

As the morning waned, his cheerfulness had dissolved in increasing uneasiness as reports of the fever in the District reached him, and when the pickup men came in with the loaded sacks, he really began to worry. He had not thought it would be that bad. If Cameron could call off Seaver, he would need only an average payoff today to see him through. But the payoff would not be average. It would be abnormally small or impossibly high. If the number hit, it would entitle the holders of winning slips to better than $25,000,000. Ben did not figure it out, for he knew how ridiculous it was, but Henry did and presented it to him, neatly figured on a machinetape sheet.

"Like the national debt," Henry grinned.

"I don't want to see it." Ben broke into a sweat and turned away. "What am I, Rockefeller?"

"It's got no chance, Mr. Erik. Only a thousand to one."

He had made the calculation, not from any thought the number might come in, but as a mathematical exercise. Staggering sums fascinated Henry.

No chance, Ben thought, watching the sorters. Only a thousand to one. He dismissed the nagging fear, and it came back. Again he dismissed it, and again it came back. Only a jerk would worry with odds like that, he told himself angrily, and still it came back. A deep frown settled into his face. He pulled at one ear nervously.

The piles of slips were enormous and would have been unmanageable if Henry had not told the sorters to first weed out all the 555's. They had been bundled in old grain sacks and stacked under the blackboard. The sorters had just begun on the others. It was very cold in their end of the barn. They could see their breath, and their hands were stiff. The old woman, Gladys, was having trouble. Henry, trying to help her, was only confusing her.

Outside a car crumpled snow. Otto swung the door wide, and Paul came in, pink and squinting. "How's business?" he called. "I hear it's big." Ben nodded curtly, and Paul unbuttoned his coat. "Just saw Thorpe downtown. Every day he gets wilder."

"Wilder how?"

"Crazy wild. He thinks triple five's coming in. I guess he saw it written on the side of a pink elephant."

"Don't joke," Ben said sortly. It struck him that lately Paul had been taking the syndicate's problems altogether too lightly. "I been trying to get layoffs for the last hour long distance. No luck."

Paul shrugged. "You're worried?" Ben ignored him, and he said, with some pique, "You wanted to talk. About what?"

Ben jerked his head. "Upstairs."

Paul still did not even know Cameron had a daughter. Ben had kept all that from him.

The pickup men were in Henry's room, exchanging slips of paper. They looked up guiltily as Ben put his head in. "What's going on?" he demanded.

"It's a pool," Milt Feinblatt said sheepishly. "On the first number."

"Anybody got five?"

"Me," Hugh Slade said defiantly. "I have."

In his cubicle with Paul, Ben shook his head sadly. "They never learn. Everybody bets but me."

"*Argue?*" Cameron shouted. "Who's arguing? It's past that. Anything I've got he wants, he can have. Anything and everything." He flung out his arms to show how little that was.

"You're doing just what he wants," Wallace said coolly. "You couldn't do it any better."

Cameron rushed to the bar and frantically mixed a drink. "Good. Swell. The better I do it, the better I like it. Anything he wants makes me happy. I give up, understand?"

Wallace did not. According to his lights, if two people were on bad terms, the misfortunes of one did not precipitate the collapse of the other. Yet on his arrival he had found Cameron sitting dazed, studying the sordid tableau in the glossy print and running his finger over and over the girl's unretouched face, as though to wipe away the horror there. The Senator shook his head hopelessly. The entire relationship was beyond him. There was no room in his world for children.

"Give it a little time," he said cautiously.

Cameron gagged. "*Time!*" he spluttered. "Time for *what?* For her to be tortured, killed? *Time*, my God!"

I don't think it's that serious," Wallace said mildly. "I'm sure it isn't." He studied the shiny photograph once more. "I realize just as much as you do how important this is."

He did: in halftone, three columns wide, it could be disastrous. Cameron splashed another bolt of whisky into the glass and flushed it with soda. "Wait'll Maddy sees that. See how much time *she* wants to give."

Wallace opened a drawer in the desk and slipped it in. "I don't think she ought to ever see it," he said. "Not ever."

"Listen." Cameron sank into a chair. "We've got to call Zipski off, call everything off."

"I doubt if that could be done now, even if we wanted to." He glanced at his watch. "It's too late."

Cameron gasped. He had completely forgotten. He was on his feet immediately. "Get them on the phone! Stop it! He'll go crazy, do anything!"

But Wallace did not look up from the watch face. "Too late, Jay. It's already started."

And fifteen hundred miles away, on the lush Gulf shore, it had.

The horses ran below, but the money ran in the calculating room, high in the grandstand above the main bettering ring, surrounded by chattering tote machines and winking lights. The totes, vast and electronic, banked one long wall, clicking softly as the betting surged and falling silent in the moment before the horses thundered out across the turf. They were precise and incorruptible, the one flawless link in the mutuel chain. No seller could punch a two-dollar ticket from his window in the ring without it registering in the machines above. When the machines stopped, locked by the warning buzz in the starting gate, the ticket sellers stopped too, their punchers frozen by the totes.

From the tote wall a tangle of tiny rubber cables led to three electric signs on the opposite wall. The signs carried the dollar totals in the straight, place, and show pools. They would carry them by individual horses when necessary: beneath each was a control board thick with numbered keys, and when the number of a given horse was pressed, the sign above flashed the money bet on that horse, in that pool, at that time. The bottom key on each pool board controlled totals. On the straight board this was held down by a rubber band, so that the changing sign above, shifting with the betting tide, always registered the running total of straight money.

The pools were serviced by the three calculating men, Farris, Peggotty, and Rorsch, and the signs were for them. They sat at little desks covered with blank forms and pencils, ready to list horse-by-horse bets, when the totes stopped the ticket sales, and to figure the mutuel payoffs after each race, when the stewards had announced the winners. That Friday afternoon all three were working for Wallace Gillette. The fourth man in the room on Wallace's payroll was Quinlan, the State Auditor.

The horses ran below, under the critical eyes of ten thousand spectators, but the big money ran under the eyes of Herbert Quinlan. From his desk and stool by the totes he ruled the mutuels. There were six other men assigned to the calculating room, but none was important. One was an electronics mechanic hired by the tote company to repair its equipment in an emergency. Three were telephone men who relayed the race results up from the infield and, when the odds calculators had figured the mutuels and Quinlan had given the word, called the figures down to the payoff divisions. The fifth was the track auditor, a doddering old man who was entirely dependent on Quinlan's books and kept none of his own. He was usually absent, watching the races. There was a mutuel manager, but he had other duties and was seldom there.

Because Ben Erik used total mutuel prices for his daily number, all the calculating men had to be in on Wallace's fix, although the heavy work was to be done by Farris, in the show pool, and covered by Quinlan on the official sheets. Between the announcement of the winning horses and the posting of the payoffs — in that brief moment — Peggotty and Rorsch were to whisper their calculations to Farris, and he, juggling his three sets of figures, was to make sure the number to the right of the decimal point in the total price pool was a five. Quinlan could pass this fraud and still balance his books by manipulating the breakage, the odd cents left over each calculation and kept by the track, which paid off only in tens of cents. It was Quinlan's prayer that breakage would be high and his doctoring therefore easy. If this adjustment to five were down more often than up — if he could use odd pennies from the ignorant winners below and not from the track to make it — he could show respectable breakage in his weekly report. Only a major investigation would unearth the truth, and a policy wholesaler fifteen hundred miles away was in no position to call for that.

Shortly before two o'clock, as the straight pool for the second race climbed past the $40,000 mark, Quinlan slid off his stool and shuffled over to the show table. Farris looked up nervously.

"Hello, fella," Quinlan lisped. "Standing the gaff?"

"Little tired."

"Tough night, eh?"

Farris looked around quickly and whispered, "Tougher day."

Quinlan rubbed the loose flesh frame of his mouth and passed down the line, nodding significantly at Rorsch and Peggotty. All three spun to watch him shuffle back. It was cool for the tropics, but they were sweating.

The straight money had passed $50,000; it was post time. Curiously, the room had no clock. Quinlan drew a white gold wafer from his pocket and glanced down. It was just 2 P.M.

One of the telephones rang and one of the telephone men answered. "There they go," he drawled. Quinlan smiled agreeably, and Farris, Peggotty, and Rorsch leaned over their sheets.

They operated the control keys swiftly, holding the number of each horse down just long enough to record the money bet on him. When the totals were down and the state's percentage had been subtracted, Quinlan came over and slipped carbons out from under their long forms, returning quietly to his desk.

Two of the telephone men were listening intently with headsets. A full minute passed. Then one said, "It's up," and the other said, "Seven horse, Three horse, and Two horse," and the calculating began.

For Rorsch and Peggotty it was no more complicated this day than any other. Rorsch took the total money bet on horse Seven, subtracted it from the win pool, and divided it into what was left. Peggotty split the place pool in half and divided the money on horse Seven into one half and the bet on horse Three into the other.

Farris's show pool was $15,541. From this he subtracted show money on the three winners, split the remainder into three pools, divided the winning bets into them, and scribbled the results, $2.74, $3.29, and $2.79, one under another. Cutting these to $2.70, $3.20, and $2.70, the legitimate payoffs before juggling breakage would be $290.54 on his table. "Good," he muttered

The others were ready.

"Six-forty," Rorsch whispered. Farris wrote it down.

"Four-twenty, four even," Peggotty muttered. Farris wrote it. He added his own and the sheet read:

WIN	PLACE	SHOW
$6.40	$4.20	$2.70
	4.00	3.20
		2.70

$6.40 + $8.20 + $8.60 = $23.20 — Total Mutuel Prices

He underscored the 2 to the right of the last decimal point. Sweat was streaming from his forehead now, forming beads in his eyebrows and stinging when he blinked. He bit his lip, added a dime to each of his three figures, prayed Quinlan would make it right, and scribbled a new page:

WIN	PLACE	SHOW
$6.40	$4.20	$2.80
	4.00	3.30
		2.80

$6.40 + $8.20 + $8.90 = $23.50 — Total Mutuel Prices

Then he kicked Peggotty and Peggotty kicked Rorsch.

"In the straight," Rorsch called out, "Number Seven is six-forty."

Then Peggotty: "In the place, Number Seven is four-twenty, Number Three is four even."

And Farris: "In the show, Number Seven is two-*eighty*, Number Three is three-*thirty*, Number Two is two-*eighty*."

The telephone men repeated the numbers after them, chanting them out to the payoff divisions and the operators behind the big board in the infield. But the infield board could not light up and the divisions could not pay. Not yet. Not until the State Auditor approved.

Quinlan had been working all three pools on his adding machine while the calculators figured in longhand. He was very fast and was nearly done when they were. As Farris added dimes to each of his three mutuels, Quinlan had added them to his, following the pattern set up that night in the bath with the old sport. And as Farris called out his figures, Quinlan looked down at his machinetape, saw the total price pool of $28.50, eyed the five approvingly, and sang out: "Okay. Let 'er rip."

The telephone men jabbered, the board lit up below, the divisions paid.

Then, between races, Quinlan worked on the record, the important record for the stewards' weekly meeting. Farris's work had cost the track $401.20. Less show breakage, this was $110.66. Breakage from the win pool was $204.63 — from the place, $329.91. He took $70 from each of these, wiping out the loss in the show and giving it a passable $30 breakage.

By then the telephoners were listening for word of the third race. Quinlan slipped out his watch and saw it was 2:30 P.M.

"There it is," the man with the drawl called.

The calculators copied the horse-by-horse bets, working the keys.

Subtracted the state's take.

Lifted up the carbons for Quinlan's cool hands.

And sat tight, waiting.

"They're in," one of the telephone men barked. "It's the Nine horse, the Four horse, and the Five horse."

This time Farris's pool was $13,285. He subtracted the winner's bets, split the $9,195 left into three pieces of $3,065, went into long division, and came out with $2.48, $2.17, and $2.12. Breakage was still holding.

Rorsch and Peggotty whispered urgently. Farris listened and wrote: $7.50 in the straight, $3.30 and $4.30 in the place. Total mutuel prices, with the show: $21.70. He cut his first two payoffs to $2.30 and $2.00. Adjusted mutuel: $21.50. This time the track would make money.

"In the straight, Number Nine is seven-fifty."

"In the place, Number Nine is three-thirty, Number Four is four-thirty."

"In the show, Number Nine is two-*thirty*, Number Four is two *even*, Number Five is two-ten."

Quinlan finished with him. "Let 'er go."

Up went the infield board, out went the cash from the paying windows.

Peggotty lit a cigarette from a guttering match. "Toughest five grand I ever made," he murmured.

"Shut up," Farris growled. "Who's doing all the work?"

Rorsch looked at him coldly. "It's taking you long enough."

"Long enough!" Farris stammered. "*Long enough!*"

His voice was shrill, and the telephoners looked over with amused interest. Quinlan slid off his stool and scampered over. "What's the matter, boys? Somebody had a deuce on that race?"

"Get this guy," Farris sneered, jerking his head at Rorsch. "I got the whole ——"

He stopped suddenly. Quinlan had laid a deceptively limp hand on the back of his neck and was squeezing the tendons in a tightening vise. Farris's face twisted. He was about to cry out when Quinlan let go.

"It's only a job, boys," he lisped pleasantly. "Isn't it, Stan?"

They turned and saw Stan Michaels, the mutuel manager, standing in the hall outside. He was on his way to the payoff ring, and in his arms he cradled a dozen thick bundles of bills.

"How much you got out, Stan?" Quinlan asked.

"Quarter million, now. Double's next. How about bringing in Virgin for me?"

"One animal's like another to us, Stan. We don't even know their names. They're just numbers to us, Stan, you know that."

"Well, pray for Number Six, I got a fin there," Stan said and disappeared down the stairs on the far side.

Quinlan went back to his desk humming softly. He did not look back at the calculators, and they, bunched tensely like jockeys in a turn, stared sightlessly at the calculating sheets for the fourth race.

Below, the horses broke.

"Out even," the first telephoner said excitedly. He had a piece of this one.

As half the daily double, the fourth race drew a heavy bet. The straight pool was over $70,000. The place was $25,000, the

409

show $16,000. The telephoner yelped encouragement to his horse as the calculators set up their sheets.

"Hell!" he sobbed at the finish.

"That's it," snapped the man beside him. "Three horse, Seven horse, and Four horse."

Farris cut, divided, and listed the three mutuels: $2.71, $2.72, and $2.88. Poor breakage. He hoped the adjustment to five would be down. If it were up, Quinlan would have to strain.

The muttering came from his left.

Rorsch: "Eight-thirty."

Peggotty: "Four-forty, three-eighty."

Farris added rapidly: $8.30, $4.40, $3.80, $2.70, $2.70 and $2.80 were $24.70. He wiped his forehead on his sleeve and sighed gratefully. The adjustment would be down, then. He wiggled his pencil briefly on a slip of scratch paper and stepped on Peggotty's shoe.

"In the straight, Number Three is eight-thirty."

"In the place, Number Three is four-forty, Number Seven is three-eighty."

"In the show ——" Farris paused, frightened at the sudden thought his addition might be wrong, then plunged ahead "— in the show, Number Three is two-*sixty*, Number Seven is two-*sixty*, Number Four is two-eighty."

He sank back quivering, waiting for Quinlan. Twice the carriage of the Peerless Adder snapped back with a muted click. Then Farris heard the gentle lisp: "Okay, fellas, That's it."

The total price pool for the fourth race stood at $24.50.

The telephoners signaled the payoff.

The third five was in.

Farris sucked air. "It's made," he said thickly.

Peggotty and Rorsch fumbled for their shirt pockets with one motion and lit cigarettes.

Quinlan finished adjusting breakage. He cut up the surplus from the fourth and distributed it expertly, plugging a few suspicious holes still left in the second race, and made out fresh reports for all three races. The true records were folded and slipped into a pocket. He was clean.

There were five minutes left before the fifth race. Quinlan slipped off his stool and strolled toward the door. "Got to get a drink," he said and disappeared into the hall.

Down the stairs he went, past the money-room guard and the washroom, to a palm-lined promenade looking out on the main betting ring. He peered down, spotted the lithe figure of the old sport leaning against a post near a program stand, caught his eye, nodded abruptly, and passed on. The sport ducked behind the post and vanished into the crowd.

A half hour later, in another part of the city, he sat jauntily in a telephone booth, dropping quarters in the coin box and listening to them bong. He waited patiently while the long-distance phone buzzed faintly on the other end. No one answered. He waited a few minutes and tried again.

Still there was no answer. The telephone was ringing in an empty house.

The chain began with Ollie and ended with Madelaine. When Ollie found Ruby had jumped bail, he checked with her landlady and Steiner and then called his brother Punkie and told him to come run the bar until he returned. He went down to the waterfront alone, looking for her. Ollie did not tell Steiner what had happened, but his brother, dropping into the Unique for a cup of coffee, did, and Steiner told Fred. Fred came to the diner at noon to make peace with his sister. He ordered a bowl of soup and waited and, when she did not appear, asked Steiner when she would be in. Steiner told him what he had heard from Punkie and broke into wild laughter. Fred threw the soup in his face and called his mother.

By early afternoon Ollie, Fred, Madelaine, and Sarah, her maid, were roaming the piers, inquiring in flophouses and cheap bars and hardware stores, searching.

Theirs was the unofficial party. The official party was headed by the official head of the family. It was larger and more efficient, though scarcely more devoted.

Wallace had persuaded Cameron to go to Zipski. Cameron had refused at first, but Wallace insisted the important thing was to find the girl, that it was pointless to deal with Erik, or even discuss a deal, until they had talked to her and put her in proper care, and Cameron, incapable of wrangling in his grief, agreed. They were in his Packard, passing through the outskirts of the business district, when Wallace spun the wheel and turned down a side street. "I'm going to stop at the Knights of Columbus," he said.

"Why?" Cameron demanded.

"Big Ed's office is there. We may catch him in."

"I don't see ——"

"He's in this too, Jay. He may be useful with Zipski."

But he was not in. A powerful constituent was under suit, his secretary explained, and Big Ed was in court as a character witness. Wallace instructed her to reach him at once and direct him to Zipski's office. "Say it's urgent," he told her and strode out to the waiting car.

"We don't need him," Cameron said shortly.

"I'm inclined to think we will."

Zipski was in telephone conference, and Griesel explained they would have to wait. Cameron snorted and threw himself angrily into a chair. "Tell him who's here," he ordered. "We're in a hurry."

Griesel set his mouth primly. "You know the commissioner," he explained to Wallace. "You know how he is when he's busy. He'd be indignant if I went in there now."

Wallace nodded understandingly. Cameron twitched.

The light on Griesel's switchboard box went out and he flipped on the intercom. Zipski would see them now. Wallace escorted Cameron through the door solicitously, as a Samaritan would a cripple.

The commissioner listened attentively and, when they were finished, asked to see the picture. Cameron delivered it up re-

412

luctantly. Zipski glanced at the glossy face briefly and then looked closely at the back.

"Wonder how he got this," he murmured.

"Newspaper photographer, I imagine, don't you?" Wallace said with some surprise.

Zipski tapped it on his desk. "This wasn't taken by a newspaperman. They use lighter paper and stamp their names on the back."

Cameron was confused, Wallace intent. "You think it was a frame-up?"

"Does the girl have a record?"

"Of course not!" Cameron exploded.

"We don't know," Wallace said.

Zipski checked Records, then called the station house and talked with Captain Hardy. He hung up and folded his hands. "There's nothing on Janice Cameron ——"

"There!" Cameron said triumphantly.

"— but she wasn't booked as Janice Cameron. She was booked as Ruby Jones, and we know Ruby."

"Never heard that name," said Cameron.

"The girl in the picture is Jan," Wallace said.

Zipski drummed the print on the desktop. "The name is unimportant. It's the same girl. It's possible she was framed" — he waved the picture — "very possible with this. But with her sheet . . ." He shook his head. "Damned little we can do. Nothing, in fact."

"But it's blackmail!" Wallace cried.

"Blackmail?" Zipski asked archly. "Did he ask for money?"

"You know what he asked."

"If he suggested pressure on me, Senator, I don't pressure."

Cameron shifted his slack face from one to the other. "Can't we settle all this later? I mean, the important thing is to find her, isn't it?"

"It is," Zipski agreed. "We have a bureau of missing persons."

Wallace was indignant. "Oh, come on!"

Cameron stood. "I want more than that, Commissioner." He

413

hammered the desk with a fat fist. "I want every available man you have tracing that girl."

Zipski gave him a gray look. "You're giving orders, Mr. Cameron?"

"Damn it," Wallace snapped, "don't you want to get Erik?"

Zipski tossed the picture on the desk and stood, leaning on stiff fingers. "Let's get this straight. The Police Department serves a million people in this town. When a law's broken, or we think it's broken, we go to work. Policy is against the law, so we break it up. Legally, without trying to *get* this guy or that guy."

"My daughter ——"

"Your daughter may be missing. She's entitled to our protection. We have a bureau to help her. I suggest you apply there." He turned to the window.

Cameron sprang up, scarlet, grabbed the picture, and spun toward the door. Wallace rose with him, swearing softly. They were on a threshold when Zipski spoke.

"I had a call just before you arrived," he said in a queer voice. "A neighborhood disturbance in Three Forks. Seems the first two numbers for today are in, both fives. Any guesses on what the third one will be — *gentlemen?*"

Cameron started back spluttering, but Wallace caught him by the elbow and guided him through the outer office, to the hall beyond. "Damned prig," he said between his teeth.

"I'm going to hire Pinkerton's," Cameron said hotly. "Hire every damned man they got."

They were on their way out of the building when they met Big Ed coming in through a revolving door. He turned them back.

"Don't tell me," he said easily. "I know."

For a month he had been quietly tapping their phones, and an hour after Ben's call that morning he had had a report of it. He had checked the hospitals, Trinity among them, and he knew. He really knew.

Cameron started to recite his grievances against Zipski, but Big

414

Ed interrupted. "The Police Department can handle this," he winked, "without the commissioner's help."

He took them to Morelock's office. Morelock held the telephone and dictated the orders as Big Ed dictated them to him. Within ten minutes a dozen patrolmen had left for the waterfront.

"Well!" Cameron said admiringly. "I can see we found the right man."

"Perhaps," said Wallace, "the commissioner's retirement should be speeded up."

"Zipski." Sylvester drew his forefinger across his throat and hissed it: "Zip-*skee*." Morelock joined respectfully in his harsh laughter. "I got an appointment at four," Big Ed said, studying his watch, "but I want to talk to Hardy, see what he can find out."

Wallace had an engagement — he didn't really, but he disliked trailing in Big Ed's glory — and left them on the street. Morelock's car was waiting. He rode in the front. In the back Big Ed worked his rough charm on Cameron, sympathizing with him and making elaborate promises of retribution. In the presence of grief he was his oily best. "I'm a father myself," he said huskily. "I know what you're going through." Cameron nodded grimly, and Big Ed went on. "Horsewhipping's too good for him. Take my word for it, we'll give him what he deserves."

"If only I knew where she was." Cameron's eyes were damp.

"I don't want to worry you, I really don't." Big Ed's voice dropped subtly. "But I don't like the looks of that man with her, in the picture."

Cameron blinked rapidly.

"Like I say, I wouldn't get too upset, but you know Nigras, how they are."

Cameron buried his face in his beefy hands, and Big Ed relaxed, fingering a tiny mole on his neck. For some time he had known the usefulness of his zoning board to Cameron was about to end, and he had been searching for another service worth the same fee. For the moment, his policemen would do.

They crossed Winecoff Street, entering the fringe of the Seventh, and were immediately caught in an enormous traffic jam.

Morelock peered out. "What the hell."

The block ahead was swarming with blacks running crazily from curb to curb, shouting and waving their arms, beaming at the honking drivers and crowing.

Big Ed rolled down his window. The sour smell of the slum rolled in. "Something's happened," he said, craning his thick neck. "See if we can pass these guys."

But they could not. Doors were opening all along the block, and people were rushing out and threading their way between the cars, calling to one another. Cameron lifted his head and looked out.

"Where do they all come from?" he asked, aghast.

Broken glass tinkled on the right. They turned and saw a squat black man, sweating in shirtsleeves despite the cold, smashing an armload of glassware at the base of a hydrant.

"Hey!" Morelock yelled. "Cut that out!"

They caught a fleeting glimpse of his ecstatic face as he flung another empty jar to the pavement.

In a corner house ahead a window opened abruptly and without warning a grinning woman dropped a lighted kerosene stove. It fell to the gutter, narrowly missing a small boy, and rolled up harmlessly in a smoky bonfire, coating the windshields of the first cars in the jam with a skin of soot.

"They're crazy!" Cameron cried.

"My God." Big Ed sat up. "I know what it is."

He opened the door and climbed out. A ragged waif approached, yelping, and he tried to stop him, but the child raced by, ignoring him. An old woman was hopping around in a little circle over a street drain. Big Ed went over and took her by the arm. Her eyes stopped rolling for a moment and she stuttered something and then shook him off, twisting in her strange jig. He returned, nodding gravely.

"That's it, all right," he said, slamming the door behind him.

The fourth just reported from the Gulf. We made it. Everybody's winner."

Cameron gaped. "It makes *that* much difference?"

Morelock snorted. "This is nothing. Wait'll tonight, when they really find out."

Big Ed sighed. "Hell to pay. Real hell." But he did not seem concerned. "No point trying to get through this," he told Cameron. "You better wait for the reports in Morelock's office." He snapped his fingers at the driver. "Turn around."

They pivoted in a tight U-turn and headed back toward headquarters. As the dancing mob flew past, someone a block away lit a string of firecrackers. Muffled by the distance and the closed windows it sounded like machine-gun fire.

On the old wicker furniture the pickup men crumpled where they had dropped when the teleflash speaker over the blackboard announced the last mutuels. The announcer had signed off scratchily long ago, but no one had moved. The sorters sat at their desks with folded hands, looking like an overage grammar-school class on good behavior, and behind them Harry Loomis stood stiffly, ready to hiss transgressors into silence. From time to time he glanced timidly toward the front of the room, wondering which of the sprawlers would move first, and they, absurdly solemn in their bright shirts and suede shoes, watched Paul for a signal. He knew Ben best, he would know when it was best to ask Ben what they should do.

But there was no signal. Paul did not know this Ben. He could only watch as they watched, and as he did he realized with a sudden sense of shame that Ben was about to collapse.

He sat very straight on the edge of his chair, his hands on his knees and his elbows rigid, staring intently at nothing. The more earnestly he stared the less he saw, for his eyes were blurred from pain, and the people in the room, framing the nothingness he stared at, were bent and distorted by the blur, like figures in a warped mirror. Then the teardrops formed gracefully on his lids

417

and rolled gently down his drawn cheeks, and new blurs form
where they had been.

Paul cleared his throat extravagantly. "Ben," he said softly.

The pickup men leaned gravely toward the straight figu
Henry drew himself up, and the sorters brightened. Ben shift
formally. He had reached that hideous point where correctne
even as exaggerated, hysterical correctness, is important. "Y
Paul."

"We got to do something, Ben." He pointed to the sacks
slips.

Ben considered them. His jaw waggled and he straightened
with an erratic hand. "Paul," he said, sounding every consona
"I got to take a leak, Paul."

In the outraged silence Gladys snickered nervously. Her
glared and she stopped.

"We'll wait here, Ben," Paul said kindly. "Go on upstairs.

"But I can't, Paul. Not all day I haven't been able to."

"The pickup men have to leave."

"Not once," Ben insisted stridently, "all day."

Milt Feinblatt and Izzy Friedman looked at the floor, emb
rassed. Eddie Finch studied the bags of slips sadly. Moss Bai
looked bored. Only Hugh Slade still watched the taut figure w
eager, vicious eyes.

A full minute passed and no one moved. Then Paul smooth
his little mustache with a precise stroke of his forefinger. "List
Ben. We've absolutely got to get going, one way or the oth
right now."

"Pardon me." Ben rose, shifting forward on his hands, a
staggered toward the loft stairs in a faint crouch.

"Ben!"

But Ben ignored him. He was leaving them all, raising
knees high, like a runner in a dream, balancing himself with
arms. At the bottom of the ladder he paused, turned and focu
on Moss. "That was a real good job," he said haltingly. "Gett
that glossy was real good."

Moss's lip wrinkled in a sneer. For any triumph of his own he
[h]d contempt.

Ben went up the ladder weaving. Twice he nearly fell, but no
[on]e looked. When he was gone they relaxed. The room rustled
[wi]th little stretching movements. Paul stood, rubbing his hands
[to]gether briskly.

"Let's face it, boys. Numbers is dead. Anybody tries to write
[th]e District after today is committing suicide."

Henry was stunned. "Couldn't we try another place? Say East
[Cit]y?"

Paul shook his head, almost gaily. "Somehow we been had.
[Ho]w, I don't know. But believe me, policy'll be poison in this
[tow]n from here in. No, we can't pull out of this one. We,
[pe]rsonally can, but numbers can't."

Eddie Finch nodded glumly. "I don't even see how we can
[pu]ll out."

Paul frowned judiciously. "I wouldn't say that, Eddie. There's
[oth]er gimmicks."

Milt and Izzy exchanged a swift look, and Milt said, "You got
[an]y in mind?"

"Well — maybe. Depends. I been thinking about it."

Hugh Slade had been wetting his lips nervously, waiting to
[spe]ak. "I need more than ideas," he said shrilly. "I got respon-
[sib]ilities."

"This is a little more than an idea." Paul smiled meaningfully.
[Q]uite a little more."

Moss nodded enthusiastically. "A new gimmick's what we need,"
[he] agreed.

Milt looked at Paul narrowly. "What about Ben?" he asked
[qui]etly.

"Anybody can see Ben's a sick man," Paul said sharply. "What
[he] needs is treatment."

"The treatment?" Milt inquired lightly.

[T]he others turned on him angrily. "That isn't the point," Eddie
[gro]wled.

419

"You want a job or not?" Moss snapped.

"I got a family," Slade almost shouted.

Milt showed his hands with a little smirk. "Am I protestin₁ I only asked."

"He only asked," Izzy echoed. "He didn't object or anything

Henry had been waiting anxiously. "What about the ba₁ today, Mr. Gormley?" He could not bear to leave his books ope₁

Paul shrugged. "What can we do? If we try to pay the winne₁ back we get killed."

"Killed dead," said Izzy.

Henry nodded, crestfallen, and Moss asked, "Don't you thi₁ we ought to get out now, warn our writers? I mean, tell them clear out now, absolutely no payoffs today."

"Good idea. I'll get in touch with everybody here tonight tomorrow on this other thing."

They rose with relief and moved toward the front of the bar where Otto, unaware that the number was even in, stood watc The sorters still sat at their desks, awaiting dismissal. Paul w about to speak to them when slippered feet shuffled along t₁ loft hall above and Ben's voice came down weakly. "Paul? Wou₁ you please come up here a minute, Paul?"

Paul winked at Moss, and Moss winked back, and Paul calle₁ "Take it easy, Ben. I'll be right up."

The slippers shuffled apologetically back down the narrow ha₁

"It was like beer," Slade was saying to Milk as they walk₁ past the abandoned cow stalls. "Too good. It had to end."

"He was good with beer and good with policy. In his day y₁ couldn't beat him, you got to give him that."

"That's a fact, he *was* good."

They spoke as though Ben were dead.

The crew was working a suburb, where policy was only newspaper bugbear, and they thought they could not know ₁ number until their return to the incinerator. So they finished ₁ route in a frenzy of can-heaving and lid-slamming and raced b₁ through the miles of terraced streets and neat brick homes reach the District, where the grift was. Sam was poised on the back, ready to leap from the tailgate when they reached a likely bar, but that was unnecessary, for when they came to where Hooker Place narrowed into Hooker Avenue they heard the din and they knew.

"Hip-gee!" Sam yelled, spinning his new hat away in a great sailing arc and bursting into wild laughter.

"Rich!" came Lou Dunton's muffled shout from within the cab. "I'm rich!"

Joe yelled something incoherent, and the truck lurched from curb to curb before he righted it.

Beside Sam, Snake grinned broadly. "This beats a crap game. I got eight hundred bucks for one."

"Eight hundred!" Sam whooped, "I got six thousand!"

"You was right," Snake cried admiringly above the roar of the motor. "You knew."

"HmmmMMmn!" Sam screamed, imitating a siren as they tore past an old man cartwheeling in the gutter, "Hmmmmm-MMMMmmn!" Snake joined in the falsetto and they shrieked together: "HmmmmmmmMMMMMMmmmmmmmMMMMM-nmmmn!"

"My-oh-my," Sam panted. "Never seen so many people."

Windows were open everywhere, filled with singing people, and ropes of plastic evergreen had been flung out, spangling the tenement fronts. Across the face of one building an American flag flapped angrily in the wind. The crowds thickened, and Joe slowed and finally stopped completely before a towering barricade of broken furniture.

"Movin' the ole stuff out," explained a man in a red bandanna.

Joe nodded understandingly, as though this were perfectly reasonable. He backed to turn in an alley, and as he did Sam jumped from the tailgate and ran up to him.

"Got to get home, Joe. Got to be there when the man come."

"Sure," Joe agreed.

"Me too," said Lou.

"Sure. Tell Snake he can go too. I'll take it in by myself."

421

He pulled into the alley alone as they scattered, running.

Sam ran all the way to the Elbow. As he came out on West Concord he saw a score of black men milling around in front of Ollie's and growling among themselves. Charlie Bond and Joe Ferrara were in the middle of the mob. Charlie was talking excitedly. The crowd was heckling him.

"Losers, I bet," Sam muttered. "Ought to take it betteren that." He walked over to see.

Ferrara was off duty, and his overcoat was unbuttoned to show that, but he had his stick and was waving it warningly at the crowd. "Take it easy, now. Just stay back there."

Charlie was pale. His back was against the brass guardrail protecting Ollie's window, and his hands were curled against his chest. He was pleading: "It just can't be done right now, I just don't right now have it, not here, right this minute. You don't ——"

The rest was lost in the throaty derision of the mob. "Roll it up and shove it," one man called, and the others took up the chant, swaying rhythmically and dangerously as they sang out, "Roll it up and sho*vit, roll it up and shovit . . .*"

"Whatsa matter?" Sam asked one of the men on the edge of the crowd.

"He say he doan pay."

"Mebbe you doan have a right number."

The man glared. "I got fi' fi' fi'," he said indignantly and waved a slip at Sam.

"I got a eight-buck piece a that," Sam grinned. "Six thousand bucks is what I got comin'."

"Man, you got hooked right." The man jerked his head toward Charlie. "He say no payoff."

Sam moved uneasily among the men, trying to catch Charlie' eye. He was sure there was something wrong, that these were losers. He should have looked at that man's slip. It couldn't be the same.

"Tomorrow," Charlie begged. "It was such a big hit. I didn' hardly expect ——"

"Frig that!" someone shouted. "Frig you!"

The crowd was swelling. A dozen had come since Sam and were on the outside, pushing. Charlie was bent against the rail. A hand reached out and pawed at him, missed him but caught the brim of his hat, tipping it over his face. He took it off and held it over his breast with both hands, like a patriot watching the flag come down. His face shone moistly in the late afternoon sunlight.

Punkie Wetlek opened the door. Annie's seamed face leered in the darkness behind him. "Hey Ferrara!" he called. "How 'bout getting these guys outa here?"

"Shut up," one of the men growled. "We'll take care a you, too, man."

"Aw right, aw right," Ferrara snapped, jiggling his stick. "Let's start moving."

Suddenly the crowd shifted toward him and he was pinned against Charlie. "Quit shoving!" he yelled. He tried to use his stick, but his arms were wedged against him. "Quit it!" The pressure was building up as the mob closed in, a black vise of hatred. "Cut it out!" he screamed. He felt Charlie's hands digging into his back, Charlie's face crushed against the back of his neck. He tried to scream again, and as he did a mackinawed arm struck his open mouth and stuck there.

Sam was ground forward in the press of many bodies. He was gasping, trying to free himself, and shrieking with the others. Because he was tall he could see Charlie, or as much of him as anyone could see. He was flattened against the rail behind Ferrara, a few feet from Punkie, and only one ear and the outline of a shoulder jutted from the wedge — an edge of meat, like the Spam in a Spam sandwich. He had slumped a little. His face was between the policeman's shoulder blades. He wasn't moving, and Sam was beginning to wonder if he was hurt when the screaming mass shifted again and lurched forward and ripped Ferrara away from him. His head bobbed up, Punkie Wetlek jumped aside, and he disappeared through the open door, into the bar.

423

"There he go!" shouted someone near the head of the wedge.

The mass wavered for a stunned moment and then broke afte
him. Wood splintered: the door was being torn away. Glass splintered: Punkie had been thrown through the frame. Sam thrashe
in the loosening grip of the mob, wheeled and started toward
Horrigan Street, and as he did he nearly tripped over a soft lump
below. He looked down and saw between the flashing of man
feet Ferrara, blood spurting from his battered face, staining hi
open tunic.

Sam headed for the alleys behind the bar, without knowin
why he wanted Charlie, or what he would do with him if h
found him. At the corner he pivoted without slowing, brushin
past a cringing Santa Claus, and ducked behind the Unique, int
the jungle of divisional fences. He leapt over a pile of empt
Miracle Whip jars at the very moment Charlie shot hatless fro
Ollie's back door, darted behind a sagging brick privy, and van
ished up a swaying catwalk. Sam knew where the catwalk le
He doubled back, pumping with his long legs. Behind him h
heard an enraged yelp as the mob spewed out of the rear of th
bar and found no Charlie. Somewhere a police whistle blew.

In the next alley he braked to a stop, peering about rapidl
At the end of the block several children were playing before
snowbanked fence. He made out the bareheaded figure frantical
threading his way among them and yelled: "Hey!"

But Charlie valuted the fence and was gone. Sam yelled "Hey
again and bolted after him.

Through the Elbow they ran, Sam gaining as Charlie's le
failed, while the women cheered from behind lines of froze
wash and the shivering children scattered. Charlie was trying
reach Striker Street. The goal helped: with safety six blocks aw
he kept going despite the stitch in his chest, the wrenching stra
in his knees, until three turns and two fences later, with Sam
hands fumbling inches from his shoulders, he broke out into th
dazzling neon of the street and collapsed by a trolly stop, sobbin
Several people looked at him curiously. A waiting woman dre
away.

Sam was above him, sweat-streaked and racked with gasps, leaning against the trolley pole with both hands and looking down stupidly. His eyes were wet and he was trembling. "They . . . chase . . . you," he panted. As though he had not.

The dregs of Charlie's effort rose warmly in his throat, suffocating speech. He wagged his head. "Tomorrow," he said at last. "Can't now." The whiz of his breath slowed. He rose to one foot and then the other, supporting himself on the pole. Sam stood several feet away, watching him and smiling.

"Big day for me, Mr. Bond."

From six blocks away a streetcar was approaching. Charlie saw and plunged one shaking hand into his coat. "How much you owe me?"

"Eight dollar, I got six grand comin'." His eyes shone. He moistened his lips happily.

Charlie plucked apart a knot of bills and held out a batch of them. "Here's what you give me." He hesitated. He could not go on lying forever. "That's all there is," he said.

Sam took them automatically with one hand and held the other out expectantly.

Charlie shook his head. "That's all, understand? I got no more for you. You get back what you gave, that's all."

But Sam did not understand. He pushed the empty hand forward with a jerk. It stabbed Charlie in the chest, and he stepped back guiltily.

"No more. You give me eight I give you eight. Okay?"

Sam frowned. "Doan lahk to be made wait. Want it now."

"Not tomorrow, not ever. No payoff, see? I haven't got it. No payoff ever."

Sam stared at the sheaf of one-dollar bills. The trolley rolled and its door opened. Charlie fled up the single step, disappearing among the standees. The conductor was about to close the door when a woman, buxom with ribboned packages, called urgently from behind Sam. The streetcar waited for her, and as she pranced out to it he jumped off the curb and followed her in and inside. The conductor swore over his crumpled bill but

425

changed it and slammed the door shut. "Move to the rear of th
car, please!" he called wearily.

Sam saw Charlie swinging from a strap across the aisle. Th
conductor ordered everyone to the rear again and Charlie obe
diently edged past a man talking to one of the sitters. Sam di
not budge. He remained near the front, letting the new passenger
work past him, keeping his eye on Charlie and his knees tense
ready to duck if Charlie looked in his direction.

But Charlie did not. He studied the car advertising until th
trolley approached Linvale Place; then he tugged the bell cor
and pushed his way toward the rear exit. Sam slid to the front
jumped out quickly, and stepped behind a safety pylon, watchin
Charlie obliquely. Charlie crossed with the traffic. Sam waite
and crossed against it, trailing him by half a block, dodging behin
telephone posts and mailboxes. Charlie turned up his stoop. San
crossed the street, saw the vacant Stephenson house, and heade
for it; Charlie let himself in. Sam darted up the Stephenson
steps. The front door had been removed by carpenters, and h
stepped inside warily. There was no one there. The carpenter
had gone. In the stripped living room he sat on the floor, restin
his chin on a sill and watching the speckled bow of red and gree
light in Charlie's window with savage, flickering eyes.

The afternoon waned, the brutal cold numbed his feet an
hands and stung his eyes. But he did not move. Motionless h
waited, a shivering specter crouching in the shell of the old house

In half an hour Charlie's door opened and he came down th
steps. The specter swung forward and saw him hurry down th
block to the huge old house on the corner and stand on the stoop
ringing urgently — saw a drape upstairs drawn back and the fac
of a darkhaired woman peer down furtively — saw Charlie rin
again and yet again — saw him pound loudly on the door an
finally abandon hope and return down the sidewalk, stampin
angrily.

He vanished into the house and reappeared shortly with Dulcy
She was pink and excited in a tightly buttoned little blue co

nd leggings, and she ran ahead of him, down a block to Belton Avenue, left a block to the drugstore.

Behind them crept Sam, twisting to loosen his clothes where hey were stuck with frozen sweat.

Mathias's Pharmacy was in a basement, approached from the treet by a short flight of concrete steps. The steps were icy, and Charlie called a sharp warning to Dulcy: "Be careful, Princess! Go down careful!"

She went down one at a time, holding her arms high above her head to show how careful she was. George Mathias was vaiting on a customer at the liquor counter. When he saw her e whistled. "Look at *that*! All dressed up so nice there's nothing eft for Santa Claus to give!"

She looked down shyly. The customer, a young woman in aloshes, smiled indulgently and left with a square package, passg Charlie on the steps.

He winked at Mathias and shook his head severely at Dulcy. So cold I can't keep my house warm, but she's got to have ice ream. How about that?"

"Ice cream, Daddy."

They moved toward the fountain with her, laughing. They did ot notice a dark figure slip down the icy steps and slide into the lephone booth by the door.

Dulcy reached gravely for her cone and moved to the toy ounter, licking methodically. Mathias ran a damp rag along the ounter. "You shouldn't go out without a hat on a day like this, harlie."

"It's very healthy, they tell me," Charlie said defensively.

"Uh-uh. I'm a pharmacist, I know." He kept wiping although e counter was clean. "I been listening to the radio," he said at st, putting the rag down and scratching his broad waistline eculatively. "Bad business today, Charlie?"

"Very bad. In fact fatal."

"So? Getting out?"

"After today I got to. I got nowheres near enough to pay."

"You're smart. When I heard you was in the racket I was amazed, really shocked. You're better out." He leaned over the Coke machine confidentially and whispered, "What about Ben Erik? I guess he's washed up, too."

"Well, I don't know," Charlie said doubtfully. "Fact is, I don't even know if the big man *is* Ben Erik. Whoever it is, I bet he's rich."

They argued. One of Mathias's customers, a Hearst reporter, had convinced him that Ben was a power, not only in the city but in Washington.

"Like I say, I don't know who's boss," Charlie said shortly. He wanted to forget it all.

But Mathias persisted. He was secretly delighted to find he knew a real writer, secretly disappointed that Charlie was quitting. "It reaches right up to the top," he said owlishly, looking around carefully and adding, with a grim nod, "look at Yalta."

"Maybe so," Charlie said hurriedly. "Look, you got any heavy little brown envelopes, the kind hold change? In your stationery stuff."

"I got just the thing." Mathias moved to the front of the store. The door of the telephone booth closed quietly as he searched among the boxes of vellum and opened again as he returned waving a package. "This what you mean?"

"That's it." Charlie reached for his wallet.

"What's that for?"

Charlie frowned. He wished Loretta and Henrietta weren't such good friends. "I got to pay back today's bet to them that should've won. It's only fair. I'm going to send 'em down to a guy has a bar there, on West Concord."

Mathias was cynical. "If it was me, I'd keep it. With the blockbust, and everything, things is tough enough. And you don't even have a job."

Charlie winced. He had thought of that too.

"What're you going to do?" Mathias asked instantly.

"Well. I used to slice up chickens, you know, fryers, for

428

market downtown. I was real good at it. I thought I might go back to that."

"Jobs never been tighter," Mathias said gloomily. He rang up the stationery sale on his antique register. "I don't say they will be, but they might be, full."

"It's hard times," Charlie mumbled wretchedly. He saw his mortgage foreclosed and his wife and child starving and counted his change.

Then Dulcy piped from the notions counter, "Daddy, this would look *beau*tiful in my new dolly house I'm going to get it," and waved a tiny crib at him. He laughed. "Come on, kid. Santa's coming tomorrow night, you can wait."

"Oh, I just *can't!*"

He scooped her up delightedly and trotted up the steps, ignoring the ice.

The door swung shut. Immediately the door of the telephone booth opened and Sam came out. Mathias was pouring a gallon of simple syrup into a porcelain crock as he approached the fountain.

"You got sandwiches?"

"Sure," Mathias boomed with false heartiness, "just the thing." Since Patecka had begun operating in this section an increasing number of blacks had been drifting into the store. Some were easy to deal with, but he did not like the look of this one. "Live round here?" he said casually, indicating a stack of waxed paper packages on the fountain counter.

Sam ignored him and picked four packages. "Got any knives?"

"Knives?" He forced a smile. "What kind you want?"

"Lahk huntin' knives."

"What you want that for?" he asked aggressively. But the light Sam's eyes was so peculiar he added with a feeble chuckle, "Hunting, I guess."

"Some wuhk I got to do. You got one?"

It happened Mathias had, not one, but an even dozen. He had bought them from a traveling wholesaler the year before and

429

had not sold one. This, indeed, was his first request. So he fough
the shrinking in his stomach and nodded. "Just the thing." He
compensated for his qualms by charging Sam double.

Even so the sale worried him, and after Sam had left he called
Henrietta. "There's a Nigra hanging around, babe. No, it don'
look like nothing. Just better make sure everything's, you know
locked tight."

Henrietta called Loretta at once, less to warn her than to tall
to her. Ever since she had heard that the number had come in
and crushed policy, she had wanted to ask her how badly Charli
had been hurt. But they could only talk for a moment, for Dulc
had run ahead of her father, sliding on the gutter ice, and wa
at the front door, ringing insistently. Loretta hung up and wen
to let her in.

Charlie waved from the middle of the block. "What a skate
we got! She's a regular Sonja Henie!"

On the corner Sam stood in the twilight light, bent slightl
against the wind, watching Loretta gather Dulcy up and carr
her inside. His shoulders and Charlie's were crooked with th
same hunch, and he was bareheaded as Charlie was. From be
hind they looked oddly alike.

Somewhere behind the Elbow the Gospel Tabernacle bell peale
with a sharp, angry stroke, and Lottie, listening, shivered in he
frayed robe and held the baby's hands to the stove, warming ther
as she warmed his bottle.

Early in the evening she had brought her new wreath fron
under the bed, and now it hung over the bare window frame,
cheerful border for her anxious face. She had planned to save
for Christmas Eve, but when Emma Kerby called over that th
drops were not paying off she had taken it out to solace Sam o
his return. She knew he had bet. He had not told her, but sh
knew: with the rising excitement in the neighborhood he did n
have to tell her. At first she had dreaded his step. Then, as sh
fed the baby and peered out at the deep shadows beyond the de
tree, beyond the automobile doors, she prayed for it.

But it did not come. She put the child to bed.

Peter Paul was asleep, groggy from a late supper. Lottie sat in the still kitchen and listened to the shouting on West Concord, wondering if Sam were among the angry mobs. From time to time the separate yells gathered into a great roar and she shuddered. Once she fell asleep. The baby's whimpering awoke her. She had no idea of the time and with him awake could not go into the bedroom to find out. The kitchen windows were ruddy with a strange red light. She went to see. Far off, thirty blocks or more, a billowing fire threw sparks into the sky. The crowds were still baying, and above their clamor sirens shrieked.

The Central Democratic Club was burning.

The rioting began at twilight, as dusk thickened in the mean streets, reached a peak at midnight, and tapered off through the early morning hours, ending shortly before dawn, when the last drunks were jailed. It was at midnight that the club was burned. The fire was the most spectacular result of the Seventh's disillusionment, and until another and far more tragic episode swept it into the back of the public consciousness, it claimed the stunned city's attention the following morning. But it was after all only one incident. There were others as brutal and as damaging. The sacking of Ollie Wetlek's bar was one. It sent Ollie's brother and Joe Ferrara to the hospital, lost Ferrara his job, since he was off duty at the time and suspected by Captain Hardy of taking bribes from Charlie — and cost Ollie nearly $1,000 in repairs he could ill afford. The attack on Hugh Slade was another.

When Paul Gormley sent the pickup men to warn their writers, he thought they were safe, for the syndicate always paid off in winners' homes. When a player's number came in he went home and waited there while the organization checked his address with his precinct executive and came to pay him. Paul thought the writers and the pickup men could use this lag to get away, and so did they. If everyone with a bet on 555 that day had been a regular syndicate customer this would have worked, but many were not. Many of the new players did not know they were

431

supposed to go home, and so they went to the drops and demanded their money. Several writers were caught this way, as Charlie had been. Most of them lied their way out or got away as he had. Hugh Slade did neither, and because the crowd attacking him found out he was a pickup man he suffered that much more.

The crowd heard it from one of Slade's new writers. Slade was in the man's drop, explaining hurriedly why there would be no payoffs, when three winners came in jubilantly. The writer shrugged and referred them to Slade, identifying him. Even then he might have escaped if he had not lost his head, but the drop was a shoeshine parlor, very narrow, with a little door, and he became panicky and broke for it. They caught him easily and pulled him, hysterical, behind the counter. Several other winners had arrived meanwhile. They stripped him, beat him, smeared his bleeding body with great gobs of shoe polish, and then tossed the raw, discolored, unconscious piece of meat into the street and spat on it. A doctor arriving in the neighborhood a half hour later on an emergency call found him and took him to a hospital. There, under sedatives, he talked wildly of the syndicate. An intern called Seaver, charges were entered against Slade's name, and the whole thing got in the newspapers. The trial was set a month away, for he was expected to be in the hospital at least that long. His skull was fractured, and one leg was broken. His priest came to comfort him.

Hugh Slade, Punkie Wetlek, and Joe Ferrara were the most seriously injured victims of the mob, although the outpatient departments of three hospitals were jammed all night with lesser complaints, one of them from the wife of a writer whose home address was known to his customers: two blacks intercepted her as she left for the grocery store, bloodied her nose, tore off her coat and dress and pushed her down an open storm drain. Her husband, who watched all this fearfully from behind drawn curtains, refused to come to the hospital to pick her up, and she was returned home in an ambulance.

The mob's most telling work was done, however, not on peo

le, but on property. The rioters wanted people, but the writers, knowing the syndicate was bankrupt, got out of the District. So they smashed. And splintered. And burned. By ten o'clock, when tight-lipped Zipski personally toured the waterfront, ordering details of East Bay police to abandon an unauthorized search and reinforce Hardy's men, the reinforcements found whole blocks aglow with street bonfires of furniture and clothing and equipment found in sacked drops. From the charred noninflammables they could tell what the front for this or that drop had been. Dressers smoldered by smashed tailor shops. Wire mannequins lay twisted near gaping dress shops. Before a gutted novelty store a weird mass of noisemakers, rubber cigars, and plastic wigs steamed foully among a thousand sputtering and popping gauze images of the Virgin.

No buildings were burned in the Elbow, for the wildest rioter knew there would be no stopping a fire begun there. Indeed, the plan to burn the Central Democratic Club sprang, not from the mob, but from a white man who had never bet the numbers and looked upon the riots as a godsend. He was a minor Republican politician who had run unsuccessfully against Ben's candidates for fifteen years, and when he went down into the alleys and saw the temper of the men he made a speech identifying Ben as their real enemy and the club as a symbol of Ben. He told them they were fools to leave the club standing and even suggested how it might be destroyed: with bottles of gasoline, capped by flaming wicks, thrown through the windows. Until then no one had thought of laying the treachery to Ben. Policy slips had never been written in the club, and the rioters knew it only from the free oyster roasts. But they were looking for a scapegoat and this man gave them one. They surged up West Concord, a howling mass of three thousand, and surrounded the building. Several precinct executives tried to head them off, but they were either thrown aside or absorbed in the mob. The police came late and in thin ranks. At the last moment they threw a volley of tear gas into the black, screaming swarm, but by then the crowd was around the club, the bombs were lit, and a dozen arms were

cocked, ready to throw. In five minutes all three floors we
roaring. The firemen arrived in fifteen minutes. Before they cou
bull their way through the wall of flailing arms and find th
hydrants, the roof had dropped into the cellar. Fortunately or
of the precinct executives had run ahead and warned the clu
and so there was no one inside.

These were the direct results of the syndicate's collapse. Th
indirect results were less distinct, but they were there, for everyon
who had bet the big number and won and discovered he ha
won nothing was ruptured, and only a lucky few could strik
back at the agents of their misery. The others loaded up o
Madeira and looked for what was left, found there was nothir
left but extensions of themselves and went after them. They wer
the pitiful ones — the wife beaters and the child beaters, th
drunken ship caulkers in Three Forks who raked one anothe
with open razors, the little knot of yelling plasterers who thre
themselves on the community Christmas tree in front of the blac
Y.M.C.A. and pulled it down on themselves. As Friday wane
and died and slid over midnight into Christmas Eve every statio
house in the city was crammed with them, shouting and snarlir
and retching vilely on the vile cell floors. For all of them, th
night was an endless personal horror stretching into the blea
days ahead, as far as their tired minds could reach, and stretchir
on from there, forever, to the end of their tired, bleak lives.

Charlie could not sleep. The night was full of noises, strang
creakings and sighing under the eaves and on the street belov
He thrashed from one side to the other, turned his pillow ov
and buried his head under it, and cupped his hands over h
warm loins. Still he could not sleep. He was exhausted, his who
body ached from the strain of his flight through the alleys. Y
when he gave up and sat on the edge of the bed his eyes fle
open, undrowsy and alert.

He stood and looked down at Loretta. She lay on her side, h
knees drawn up and one arm thrust under the pillow. She stirre
Her mouth twitched and then was still.

He scratched himself absently. A sudden gust of icy air rustled his pajama blouse and he shivered and plodded out, closing the door after him, and tiptoed down the hall, past Dulcy's room.

"Daddy!"

He put his head in the door, a finger to his lips. "Go to sleep," he said quietly.

"What're you doing, Daddy?"

He smiled: she was positive he was up on some secret mission of Christmas. "Just getting a drink of water. Go to sleep, princess."

She wanted a drink, too. He brought it from the bathroom and stood over her while she forced it down, proof of her thirst, and handed it back after a last, tight-lipped gulp. " 'Night, Daddy," she gasped and held her face up to be kissed and then turned it into the pillow.

A patch of square moonlight lay across the bed, and as he closed the door he saw her lying wide-eyed in it. A little girl, awake two nights before Christmas, dreaming of fantastic toys.

He fumbled his way down the banister and groped for the switch at the bottom. Behind the portieres the living room sprang into light, commonplace and shabby around the splendid tree. He sprawled in the Morris chair, opened the coffee-table drawer, found one stale cigarette squashed in a package, lit it, inhaled once, choked out the acrid smoke, and killed it in a clean tray.

"Some Christmas," he muttered desolately and rose.

He studied the green fingers of the sparkling tree, walked across the room to the closet by the arch, opened it, and took down the parcels from the upper shelf, feeling them and holding them up to the light. In the very back, hiding under a mantle of green paper, was one too large for wrapping: an enormous split doll's house, furnished with tiny chairs and beds and a bathroom with spigots that turned. Smiling faintly he pulled the mantle aside, felt the midget chairs, twisted the little knobs, and then replaced the green paper and the parcels.

He closed the door, snapped out the light, and climbed the darkened stairwell. Outside Dulcy's door he paused, wiggling his toes in the draft. She was still awake, moving under the bedclothes. He wanted to speak to her again but decided against it and in bed again, snuggled against Loretta, he quickly fell into a deep sleep.

Across the numb street, Sam saw the light go out. He sank back on his haunches, his eyes widened and cleared, and again he swept the knife along his thigh in long, slow strokes.

It was a good knife and Sam liked it. But it was not sharp enough. He wanted it to cut with a flick, without pressure, so he ran it back and forth, back and forth, listening to the harsh lisp of steel on twill. He counted the whets backward from one hundred and when he reached zero tried the blade on the palm of his left hand, slicing lightly at first and then harder until he drew blood. When it came he sucked it away hungrily and started stroking again. His left palm was raw with soft, running clots.

He was in his ninth hour of occupancy of the Stephenson house and in all that time had been entirely without warmth. He had lost all feeling in his feet, his face was a frozen mask, and only the knife had kept his aching hands awake. Now and again a convulsive shudder racked his chest and his chin wobbled miserably. But he did not rise or even shift. He remained locked in his crouch, watching the shadow-freckled block intently.

The moon vanished behind a ragged, scudding cloud. Across the low tar belly of the street, above the brick shelf of sidewalk, the wall of yardless houses was washed in ghostly starlight. Between the dim lampposts on each corner but one beam of light shone, a tiny shaft in an upper window of the big corner house. Deep into the black morning it gleamed on the stone window sill, and Sam watched it, sharpening his blade and testing it, sharpening and testing until the floor below him darkened with a broad, sticky stain.

Toward three o'clock the front door of the corner house opened, a cone of light appeared on the steps, and a small, gray man hurried out carrying a briefcase. Behind him the door swung shut, drawn by an unseen hand, and as he turned the corner, pinching the crown of his hat, the house went dark.

Sam had outwaited the block.

He slid the knife into his fatigues and from his shirt drew the drugstore sandwiches. He ate slowly, skinning back his stiff lips and gripping with his teeth and pulling the bread away with clawed hands. When he had finished he wadded the strips of waxed paper into a greasy ball, stood and tossed them lightly through an open door behind him, into the vacant dining room.

Almost immediately, before he could turn away, there was a soft rush, a mass scurrying — the sound of many tiny feet racing across the old wood. He slipped his knife out and crept forward on the balls of his feet. Flitting across the bare boards, crossing and recrossing and snapping at the paper with famished fury were a score of lean, hungry shadows — rats drawn by the naked house.

He retreated warily, kicked the door shut with his foot and withdrew to his bitter post by the window, folding his frozen legs under him and bunching down, stroking the knife along the taut will of his thigh. His jaw went slack and his eyes glazed.

Somewhere in the city slept a thirteen-year-old boy whose short cut to a Boy Scout patrol meeting would spoil his holiday — somewhere an ambulance driver with a duck tunic soon to be stained beyond repair. Somewhere, in the anesthesia of fatigue, was an intern who would lose a professional bet. Somewhere a reporter about to beat the town lay beside his new wife, a rewrite man who would earn his pay tossed fitfully, a copyreader who would risk libel dreamt of promotion. Somewhere the even breath of a psychiatrist rippled his thick mustache. He would write a letter, urging steps. Somewhere a manufacturer lay swaddled in an electric blanket. He would offer a reward and deplore. Somewhere a tailor snored stridently. He would close his shop in mourning. Somewhere slept a judge who would issue a warrant, a clerk who would record it, a captain who would carry it. Somewhere justice slept — to awake alert and righteous and vengeful.

But Sam did not sleep. He sat open-eyed in the cruel night, building a hate. Building it: drawing it together, shaping it, then buffing it raw, picking at it, tearing at it, keeping it festering, angry, ready, and just under the critical mass.

Everywhere in the sleeping city were those who would call him a monster. *Fiendish* was a word they would use, and *degenerate*. Sam was those. Vile. Depraved. Perverted. Bestial. He was everything they said he was.

He was more.

He was a God-seeker who had found God dead.

Who had found him loose and rotting in a slaughterhouse of fraud.

Who had found . . .

— The spillway . . .

— And the vent . . .

And was toppling down a bottomless pit without any sides.

He was a man without choice.

For the spark of discovery was flaring through the fine dust of his ego. The sheet of flame had begun its advance across the layers of firedamp.

And there was no stopping it.

Because once established, the velocity of an explosive wave is constant, unaffected thereafter by environment, wholly dependent upon the nature of the fuel.

So Sam crouched in the dead center of ground zero as the wind figured through the vacant house and the ruthless chill drew taut the brown bag of his scrotum.

So he sat, numb as the bleak street, waiting out the last hour of all the loveless nights of his life rolled into one.

The sun was a pale stain in the dark East Bay sky, casting thin shadows in the gutters, etching the house fronts in shades of gray. One by one the households stirred: alarms rang, bare feet flinched over cold bedroom floors, toilets flushed throatily, hands fumbled with underwear, socks and stockings, shirts and blouses, skirts and trousers. Switches were turned in upper halls, in stairwells, in front rooms. The sidewalks outside were crossed and recrossed with bands of light as each family announced to the dim morning that it knew, it was up and about, it would be ready.

An hour before, a boy in ear muffs and ski boots had come this way on a wheezing motor scooter, and by the front door of each subscriber lay a copy of the morning paper neatly folded three ways.

Charlie padded down the foyer in mules and reached out and drew his in, unfolding it with his back to the door.

"Jees! Guess I wasn't the only guy had troubles yesterday."

Loretta put an inquiring head around the kitchen door. Behind her breakfast cackled noisily.

"Look at this!" He held the front page before him like a sandwich board.

The club fire was pictured at its height. Under a heavy black line was the story of the riots. A separate column dealt with the beating of Hugh Slade. There was a picture of Hugh, taken when he was much younger, a portrait of conscious rectitude.

"Goodness!" Loretta said and hurried back to her stove.

He read the stories carefully, breathing rapidly when he came to the description of the scuffle in front of Ollie's bar. He ran a frantic eye down the type, then relaxed with a grateful sigh. The newspaper, afraid of libeling Ferrara, had not mentioned Charlie at all.

Dulcy came downstairs dressed.

"Well Princess! Thought you'd be asleep for hours. Don't you know it's a holiday?"

"For you, too," Loretta called above the spluttering pans. "You should've stayed in bed. I was planning a nice brunch for you." Womanlike she had become solicitous, almost patronizing, since the trial.

"Couldn't sleep," Dulcy explained to her father.

"Want to check on a job," he explained to her mother.

Actually it was Charlie who could not sleep and Dulcy who wanted to check. She had heard the rustling of the tissue paper the night before and was suspicious. She peered behind the evergreen, half hopeful of finding something, half afraid she would.

Charlie chuckled. "Tomorrow, Princess. Not today."

"I was looking for something I left," she said defensively.

"Sure you were." He tossed the paper aside. "C'mon. I think Mommie's ready for us."

The pans were quiet and he could hear the coffee percolating.

They were sipping it when the chimes rang. Dulcy had bolted her cereal and was systematically exploring the living room, and she answered it. A moment later she ran in with Kenny Carter.

"Mommie, I want to go out."

Loretta paused, remembering Henrietta's warning of the stranger in the neighborhood. "Oh, I don't think so, dear."

"*Mommie!*" Dulcy stamped her foot. Kenny drew back inconspicuously. He was a respectful child.

"Go into the parlor, both of you," Loretta ordered.

They retreated with hopeful eyes on Charlie, and when they were gone he suggested they might as well play outside. Loretta, reluctant to worry him, agreed hesitantly. "Kids suffer the day before Christmas, I guess," she said.

"Sure they do."

He had a plan. An almost certain way to see Lucy would be to return Kenny when the children were through playing. The more Charlie thought about it, the more convinced he was that he had been easy.

Dulcy greeted the announcement with gay squeals, Kenny with the grave announcement he had brought his tricycle and hoped she could have hers.

"Can I, please, Daddy?"

Charlie looked out. The sidewalk ice was nearly gone, except in front of the Stephenson house, which the neighbors had religiously avoided since the arrival of the workmen.

"Sure, kid, I'll put it out."

He carried it down the stoop, nearly tripping over the unobtrusive Kenny, while Loretta supervised the donning of Dulcy's blue snowsuit and rubber boots.

"Come back in a couple of hours," he told them at the door.

"There might be, just might be a surprise for both of you." He winked, and they grinned, and he went inside whistling.

"You're going job hunting?" Loretta called from the dishes.

"In a while." He settled on the sofa and reached for the paper. 'Want to see what's what in the Help Wanted first." But instead he read the riot story through again from the beginning, wondering if Hugh Slade knew Moss Bailey.

Outside, the children had mounted their tricycles and were in addled conference. Dulcy had suggested they ride six blocks north to the old Valley Line tracks, where there was snow.

Kenny was doubtful. "I'm not supposed to go there."

"Nobody'll know."

"You aren't supposed to either."

"Oh, don't be sissy."

They argued with the fierce recrimination of the very young. Suddenly Dulcy pumped her knees and sprinted recklessly down the walk and away. Kenny hesitated for a moment, then hurried after her, calling indignantly, demanding she wait. Dr. Hegel, coming up the walk with his shabby black bag, dodged aside and cheerfully waved them on.

Neither he nor they saw the shadow quiver in the vacant window opposite and withdraw quickly to the rear of the house, where an alley ran parallel to the street.

Down Linvale Place they sped, pausing at the intersections to throw sharp little glances either way and then rushing on, over the low curbs and down the brick paving, helmeted heads bowed, leggings driving the pedals furiously.

Behind them, across the street, the shadow flickered from house to house.

In the fifth block they pivoted and followed a side street to its dead end, a hundred yards away. Below lay the ravine. Fifty years before, when the rich wintered in town houses and summered in the Valley, businessmen had commuted along this siding, where rusted rails and stripped switches now lay in ancient disorder. A quarter-mile away, at the ravine head, the main line of the Union

Railroad appeared briefly, but here there was only old iron and abandoned slag and snow. The snow looked deep to Kenny.

"We could get stuck."

His mother often reminded him of his frailty.

Dulcy gave him a scornful look and plunged ahead, down the gently sloping draw emptying into the gorge. Again he followed.

They parked by a switchbar of obsolete type and ran around in the snow tramping patterns with their boots. The east hill of the ravine blotted out the feeble sun. It was darker down here, colder.

"Want to go home," Kenny insisted.

"Poof!"

"Not supposed to be here."

To entertain him she pyramided a little snowdrift with cupped mittens and began reshaping it into a castle, explaining what she was doing with animated little gestures and breathless chatter. He watched, bored, noting with prim satisfaction that the snow was dry and would not stay put.

The ravine was darkening, the chill deepening.

"Hurry up."

"Towers are hardest," she puffed.

He pondered whether to go back without her and decided he ought not: there was the surprise, he could not get it without her. So he stood arms akimbo by her bowed figure working on drawbridge and moat, turret and walls, busy in a child's world of her own, kneeling in the snow, biting her lip, while the shadow came down from the shoulder of the hill, with her mittened thumb running along the powdery parapet, making it stay put, while the shadow came down half stumbling, with her breath a sheen of frost on the darkening air, while his shadow unseen came wobbling in the knees, head cast low and arms swinging in great arcs, into the forgotten gorge.

And his breath came hhhhhhhh hhhhhhhh hhhhhhhh and straight as the sharp edge of darkness through the tricycle tracks he strode his left hand a fist leaking blood his eyes half shut his open overshoes flopping clickclack clickclack while section one of the Union Limited from New York roared by the ravine mouth and straight as the last sharp edge over the carpet of snow to the old switchbar where the blue snowsuit squatted in the bunched snow sheeting and the tricycles sat crooked by the slag (and there was someone else, a boy) and his overshoes flopped outward and outward and his breath came hhhhhhh hhhhhhh hhhhhhh hhhhhhh and the blue snowsuit (and the someone else) heard the crunch of broken snow and sensed, felt, saw the shadow on the castle and looked up together, pink cheeks shining in the weak winter light, eyes unwise and trusting saw eyes small and cloudy and red — sensed, felt, heard, and saw and shrank back frightened as the black paw drenched crimson wet clawed out and caught the thin blue shoulders in an icy embrace and the steel gleamed cruelly in the shivering air and his breath came hhhhh hhhhh hhhhh hhhhh hhhhh and (HE'S NOT SUPPOSED TO DO THAT) the blue snowsuit with a long sighing scream ricocheting against the walls of the empty canyon flattened against the stained green twill and they wove sideways and sideways and red eyes snapped beadlike and the cruel gleam flashed dizzily and (HE'S NOT HE'S NOT) and something tore (NOT SUPPOSED) and something cracked (SUPPOSED TO DO THAT) and the fountain sobbed foaming in the blue and the stained green and his breath came hhh hhh hhh hhh hhh hhh and the wet steel swung up to tremendous height of dripping wavered crazily as the flopping overshoes thrashed in the reddening snow and a long scream broke in a gargling suck with a hard whoosh into pulpy mush (NOT SUPPOSED TO NOT SUPPOSED TO fleeing wild-eyed up the draw) while the fount sobbed dazzling bright on the blue and the stained green then on the blue and the churned snow screaming and fighting screaming and fighting for breath to scream again and along the wasted slag by the old tarred ties he ran swaying oddly shedding a sodden coat and a clotted blade disappearing around a bend AND AND AND among the dead and twisted iron tracks doubled up in shredded sticky rags she crept to the switchbar and dropped the crushed sack left against it whimpering weakly staring down at her spurting breast with glazed astonished eyes . . .

(A passenger on section two of the Union Limited peered down
the dark ravine and thought he saw a figure lurch in the snow.
But as he looked the gorge flashed past. He could not be sure
and so he said nothing.)

Between Jake's Wharf, where the river mist crept over the foot
of Sloane Square, and the shaggy stone front of the Public Comfort Station on Shadway Street, lay Sticktown. Here, where the
cobblestones were flecked with gull dung and the shore lined
with derelict barges, were over fifty sticks. Or taverns, or bars.
But no cocktail lounges, no cafés. In the plushest stick the floor
was covered with sawdust, and all the toilets were interracial,
bisexual, and chain-flushed. Here, in squalor, lived the barnacles, the beached seamen of the old fleet, and the dogfish, the
sweet-water stiffs with perpetual thirsts who begged towline from
the barnacles and slept it off in the barges, where the mist was
thick and the finger of the river very near.

Sloane Square was the focus of Sticktown, or rather the focoid,
for there was nothing in it, absolutely nothing. During the monu-
ment craze of the 1880's a city councilman had proposed a shaft
in memory of lost merchantmen, but the neighborhood was already sinking rapidly, and the motion died in committee. Since
then the square had seen no improvements and little mainte-
nance. Its cobblestones had begun to crumble before the turn of
the century and were now scarred with great ruts filled with frozen
rainwater.

The wharf and the sunken barges bordered one side of the
square. Each of the other three was built around a public insti-
tution — the Port Mission for Seamen on the north, the Mari-
time Union Hall on the west, and, on the south, the Anchorage,
a dormitory for barnacles with small pensions. Massed between
the mission, the hall, and the dormitory were clumps of ram-
shackle, sad-faced buildings with street floors occupied by cramped
sticks of exotic name — the Cave of Bagdad, the Star of East
Bay — and second floors housing sinister little furnished rooms.
There were a few lunchcarts advertising ten-cent Hoboken Brew.

but they were unpopular and constantly bankrupt. Stickmen never went bankrupt, for although no one came to the square by choice, many had to come — the old fleet because the Anchorage was there, the new because the hiring hall was. And because seamen of all ages were free spenders, the dogfish came, to beg line and jakestep in and out of the sticks and, now and then, into the greasy, littered waters of the river.

When the gestapo fished one out, there was a moment of respectful silence among the dogfish. The twitching faces stilled for a moment and the blear eyes looked out thoughtfully at the shattered stones and the fading mission sign. Then, after a pensive scratch or two, everybody took a swift belt and the party rallied once more. Nothing could stop the party for long, not tragedy, nor poverty, nor even the East Bay gestapo in their nifty blue suits.

"Ossifer, if I had a uniform like that, know what I'd do with it? I'd parlay it, see? Hock it for a roll, somethin' I could *use*."

The trembling fingers on the arm, the tailwag in the wet eyes. And from the cop the beat it, crumb bum, stare.

"Salesman, you got to be told how many times I'm no touch? On your way or it's the bucket."

"But I got responsibilities!" The Salesman, whose full name was The Angel Salesman, lifted a face like a skinned orange. "I got a girl." With faint pride.

"Horse?"

"A *new* girl," he croaked.

"Sell your plasma."

"They won't take it, you know that."

"Peddle your statue."

The Salesman started indignantly. "I'm tryin'!" He pointed across the square, where a winged figure of stone sat on a little handcart under a lamppost. "No takers!"

The policeman shrugged and turned away.

"Ossifer ——"

"Go pound sand," the cop said and left.

The Salesman crossed, glowering, to his waiting handcart. He was a short man with broad shoulders and almost no neck, and he always walked erectly, with a jaunt which looked military but was neurotic. Fifteen years before he had lost his wife and erected the marble Angel over her grave. Since then his life had turned in cycles of shame, marked by periodic pawning of the statue. Shortly after the war he had gone to work scavenging empty gallon jugs and selling them to a cider maker for a nickel each. But, it was winter now, the cider season was past, and the Salesman had responsibilities. So he was peddling his Angel once more — or trying to, since all the hock shops had closed when Jake abandoned his ferry service — and feeling very bad about it. His eyes were damp as he pulled the loaded wagon up Front Street, by the water's edge.

The air was coarse with a salt chill as he left the square and approached the rotting barges, where the river wore a scum of black twigs. This was Sticktown residential, a land unique. Among the barges men lived alone by their own law. Only a corpse brought the gestapo here.

In one of a row of condemned frame houses lining the street a window screeched open and a mite of a man thrust out a head of scraggly white hair. He yelled directly at the trudging figure: "Salesman's sellin' his stature! Salesman's sellin' his stature!"

There was no one else in sight, and the Salesman did not look up. The mite cast around frantically, wailed down the scale — "His stature Salesman's sellin' " — and the window dropped with a sharp yelp. The plodding figure marched grimly on, thin shanks swinging in perfect cadence. Behind him the Angel sat rigid and chaste.

He skirted the bow of the beached *Franklin J. Smith* and entered the cove where the derelicts were thickest. Just ahead against an olive sky crossed with snowy spars, he made out a profile perched on a familiar hull. He waved his free hand and pushed feverishly on.

She sat cross-legged on the barge roof, smoking one of his cigars. The Salesman's cigars, like the Salesman, were short stubby, and carefully tamped. Inside the filler was mongrel: cigarette tobacco torn from street butts and dried salvage from An chorage spittoons, salted with Bull Durham. Every Sunday the Salesman rolled the week's accumulations in discarded wrapping paper and stored the rude stogies in his quarters below, and there, in his absence, she had found them.

The thirty-six hours since she had left Ollie Wetlek on the edge of the Elbow had deformed her almost beyond recognition. The essential structure was still there, but dropsy had blown everything up. Her body was a tube. One eye was closed, the other bulged. Her neck swelled turgidly, and her mouth was a drawn slit curving downward in a tremendous frown. Into this frown she poked the soggy end of the cigar, puffing until red streaks laced her swollen throat while one hand reached stiffly for a large jar beside her brimming with a milky broth and the other stroked a patchwork of distended veins on her left calf. Both legs were mottled and bare and puckered against the cold. Her stockings were gone, her spiked heels broken. Her sweater and skirt, a different color now, were stretched taut against the column of her trunk, and over her sloped shoulders a camouflaged shelter-half hung.

Out came the cigar, in went the broth. She coughed and turned and looked out with the one popeye at the river boiling under the twigs.

She sang to herself, rocking with the rhythm.

> There were rats, rats, bigis Caddylacks
> In th' store, in th' store . . .

Her voice was like a file. She oiled it from the jar, gagged again, and finished her song.

> . . . rats, rats, bigis Caddylacks
> In th' quar-ter-ma-ster's store.

The Salesman entered through a rent in the hull and came up the barge ladder, panting. "Nobody wants it," he said angrily, stamping on the dirty snow floor of the deck. She began the chorus again, ignoring him for the twigs.

447

"A whole hunneret dollars it cost." He lifted his blooming face challengingly.

She wasn't listening. With that ghastly eye she stared over the misty river, where the icy waves formed a fine, tossing froth beyond the blunt prow of the barge. She lifted the jar and gulped its dregs, sealed chapped lips over a white line of poison, and put the glass down empty. Far away where the fog closed down on the waters they were black and steady.

The Salesman was pacing the deck, undecided. It was Christmas Eve, and he had to do something. He stopped in mid-stride. "Mig's got some port we could have," he said hopefully.

She peered sideways into the empty jar and straightened with a belch. "Not strong enough to kill wha's in th' bottom."

The river churned, slapping little waves against the prow.

He paced, stopped, paced and stopped again. "Wiggie's gotta juga th' cure I might get."

She folded blue claws over the broad of her belly and swayed

. . . rats, rats, bigis alley cats
In th' flour, in th' flour . . .

He shrugged and disappeared down the open hatch, reappeared carrying a half-empty bottle and poured the lees into her jar.

"I'll try Striker, oughta be somebody."

He leaned over in farewell and they fumbled awkwardly for a moment. "Gemme some stuff," she said huskily, twisting away

The Salesman straightened, disappointed, squared his shoulders and went down the hatch. On the street below he picked up the cart handle and stepped off with his left foot. Behind him the Angel fixed his back with stern stone eyes.

Ruby heard his steps round the *Franklin J. Smith* and fade away She gathered the camouflaged shawl around her shoulders and bracing herself on her spread hands, rocked forward and stood with a grunt. Tottering forward she moved between the hatches until she reached the square bow. She looked down, her single eye winking in controlled drunkenness. The water stretched dark

448

head, creased by the December wind, and vanished in an even
ne under the fog. The broken heels held her back in an oblique
ne. She stepped forward, the shelter-half dropped to the deck
oor, she hummed in time with the lapping waves, she stepped
rward, humming, and stepped forward, humming . . .

. . . Someone was running up the street. Someone alone. In
vershoes. His feet were pounding on the cobblestones, his shoes
apping wildly. Ruby half turned and saw Sam Crawford fleeing
ist the *Franklin J. Smith*. Behind him a window banged shut.
She saw him and recognized him, and something in his sweat-
g face drew her from the line of mist and black water.

Sam saw she saw. He did not recognize her, but as she lifted
> her poles of arms and staggered back across the deck, he slowed
id drew up at the barge stern, waiting.

"I'm wore out," he gasped. He was. He was shaking all over.

"C'mupa hole," she called, pointing.

When he emerged from the hatch she saw the blood. It had
me through as he wrenched off his overcoat, smearing his
ouse in a slanting line from shoulder to hip like a ribbon on a
iled shirt.

"You got hurt."

"No." He made a fist of his left hand and held it across the
in and shaped his lips silently in another No.

She sat slowly by the jar and picked it up, sipping and choking
d watching him. His hands played lazily over a frozen smudge
his thigh. He was looking through her.

"Siddown, Sam."

He jerked, startled. "How you know my name?"

She forced a twisted smile. "Cupa Joe, Sam?"

Then he saw, sunk to his haunches, and looked her over
nderingly. "You sick?" She nodded, coughing. "How come
u here?"

She shrugged: "How come you?" They fell silent.

From another cove came three short honks: a police boat,
ecking. Sam looked around nervously. "Whatsa day?"

"Day 'fore Christmas." She drank deeply.

He tapped his temple, as though sounding it. "Missed a day," he said to himself.

"Ever'body misses a day now'n then. Good rid'nce." She drain the jar. "What'd you do witha day you lose?"

He tapped his temple again and shook his head slowly. "We to church, heard bells, saw buhds, swimmin' . . ."

Ruby hiccupped into laughter. "Same's me."

"You hear them bells?" he asked, perking up.

"Diff'rent bells, same church."

He frowned, perplexed, and rubbed his groin. She crossed h tubular legs awkwardly, and looked around. "Do me a fav Gemme a cigar."

"Seegar?"

"Dow'stairs." She told him where.

He brought back two and lit them and they sat on the c deck, smoking and soaking up the little sunlight. Sam kept f gering himself, and she, watching him, vaguely wondered wh

Then she stopped wondering and began thinking about h in other ways. He was so exhausted. His head seemed to h him. He was dizzy. He was in trouble: she sensed that. S groped for a way to help.

She had an illusion of falling and reaching for something to gr

The police-boat station was three blocks from Sloane Squa on the edge of the packing-house district. Cameron had est lished his headquarters across the street, in Louie's Bar & Gi and had left for only a few hours early that morning, to nap the room Morelock had ordered for him in the station hous

Morelock was playing it close — the longer he played it, closer it became. He was openly setting himself against Zip in the Department. Zipski knew that, and Morelock knew did. Since the afternoon of the day before, he had, on his o responsibility, countermanded a dozen of the commission orders. Ordinarily he could have done as he pleased in East P but two emergencies had undercut him — the night riots in Seventh and the knifing of a child that morning near Ken quare. At 11 A.M. Zipski sent out a teletype message to all aptains east of Stuart Street: they were to contine operation with keleton forces, sending all other men to headquarters for special ssignment. Morelock persisted in drawing details from his capins. The night before, the commissioner, in sheer desperation, ad toured the station houses commandeering men. Morelock, perating now from the police-boat station because he thought ipski would look for him there last, knew there would be another ich tour and probably a showdown. He dreaded it. But if he und the girl it was worth it. Finding her was of the first imortance to him — or to her father, which made it important to g Ed, which was the same thing.

Cameron had aged. His cheeks, normally bland, were shaggy ith beard, his hair stuck up on one side, and his eyes were dark uises. Christmas Eve was a packing holiday: Louie's was derted. He ate a greasy lunch, called Wallace, who hurriedly plained he was in conference with a State Representative named ormley and would be out when he could, and Madelaine, who id collapsed on the street not far from Sloane Square and was bed with fever. He had just decided to recross the street and rch on Morelock's desk when the grill door opened and his n came in.

"Hello, hello," Fred said, rubbing his hands together and blow-g on them.

Cameron examined him peevishly. "How did you get down re?"

"In a cab. How's business?"

"Lousy. Cops! Jesus." He sunk despondently to a stool.

Fred ordered coffee. It came steaming, and he was sipping it utiously when his father's mind found an old track. "Don't ur agency, or whatever it is, work today?"

"*It* does. I don't."

"Why not?"

"I just quit."

Cameron bounced against the counter edge. "Quit!"

"Sure," Fred said calmly, gulping coffee. "I been there three years. Time to move on. I figure the experience has been good though."

"Ye-es," his father agreed tentatively, deferring to the familiar saw. "I suppose so."

The man behind the counter had been watching them impatiently, waiting for one of them to plug the nickelodeon. Now he gave up and did it himself. The machine hummed and record slid into position. A vocalist cooed softly.

"I don't think she's even down here," Cameron blurted out.

Fred set his cup down thoughtfully. "They're looking in the right place, I think."

His father shook his head decisively. "What would she be doing down here? With these people!" He gestured inclusively, and the counterman looked up resentfully. "It doesn't make sense."

"I don't know. She's been living close to this for a long time."

"To *this?*" Cameron pounded the counter. "I don't believe it. No sir. She's been a little wild, but that's all. Nothing's wrong with her except a little pampering. You too. Both of you."

Fred bit his lip. He was here because his mother had asked him to come, and before he left she had pleaded with him not to argue with his father.

"She's a good child." Cameron's tired voice cracked. "And she's only a child. Everybody forgets that."

"She's twenty-eight," Fred reminded him, wondering as Wallace had at the difference her disappearance made. He does care, he thought, marveling; he really does.

"She was framed!" Cameron almost shouted. "It was a frame-up against me! That bastard did it! Kidnapped her!"

"Watch yourself, mister," the counterman said coldly. "This ain't no dive."

"Don't be impertinent. Get me a glass of buttermilk."

The door opened. A lieutenant put his head in. "Mr. Cameron?" Cameron braced himself against the counter. The lieutenant touched his cap respectfully. "Inspector Morelock would like to see you."

"Come on, boy," Cameron said unevenly.

Morelock was in the station office, questioning the Sloane quare cop, when they arrived. A thickset sergeant in ear muffs tood deferentially to one side.

"Officer Eaken, Sergeant Cannon," Morelock murmured. "Mr. Cameron and — ah ——"

"My son, Freddie." Fred winced at the diminutive.

"— Freddie Cameron," Morelock finished. "I think we've hit omething. Your daughter is definitely in this area." Fred glanced t his father, who stared stolidly at Morelock, who went on. "Fact , we'd've had her by now if Eaken, here, had been on the ball couple of hours ago."

Eaken sagged. The sergeant coughed. They looked at him.

"Want me to bring in the man, sir?"

"Yes." Morelock pointed at Cameron and then at a chair. Better sit down. This guy's a friend of your daughter's. At least e think he is."

Cameron sat. Fred withdrew to a corner. The door opened d the sergeant reappeared, leading The Angel Salesman.

The Salesman was furious. The mesh of vessels in his face owed angrily. "This is a outrage," he spluttered. He appealed Cameron, who cringed. He drew himself up. "I got connec-ns," he said darkly. "Downtown."

Morelock picked up a pencil. "Name?"

"William Ernest Wheeler," the Salesman replied mechani-lly, falling into a position of attention.

"Age?"

"Forty."

"Or fifty?"

"Forty or fifty."

"How long you been living with Ruby?"

"Since oney yesterday."

Morelock tossed his pencil aside and looked apologetically at ameron, and simultaneously the Salesman realized he had been pped.

"I ain't livin' with her!" he squealed. "I oney am takin' care er!"

453

"She needs taking care of?"

"Course. She's havin' a kid soon."

The room whistled with a suck of breath. Fred patted the back of his head and Morelock closed his eyes and rubbed the lids slowly with his forefingers.

"A — a what?" Cameron asked brokenly.

"A kid. She tole me." He added hastily: "Ain't mine. I oney found out yesterday."

Cameron stared at the floor.

Someone rapped on the door. Immediately it opened and a lieutenant came in urgently. "Commissioner's on his way," he told Morelock. "Just left headquarters."

"The knifing?" the inspector said, looking up quickly.

"I guess. It was a nigger, by the way. We got a description."

Morelock rose. "Well, Mr. Cameron, if we're going to get your daughter it'll have to be now, right now."

Sergeant Cameron jerked his head toward the Salesman. "Want him?"

"Bring him along."

"How 'bout my stature?"

"Leave it here. We'll watch it."

Patrolman Eaken grabbed the Salesman's arm and pushed him toward the door, and as he did, the Salesman broke wind.

In Morelock's limousine Cameron shook uncontrollably. Fred asked anxiously whether he felt well, whether he thought the ought to stop, whether he wanted to borrow his overcoat as laprobe. But Cameron shook his head tightly and said nothing.

They parked on the edge of the square and proceeded on foot in pairs — first Morelock and the Salesman, then Fred and the sergeant, with Cameron and Eaken last. Eaken had sought Cameron out.

"I'm really sorry I didn't pick him up earlier," he fawned. "I should of been more careful."

"It's all right." Cameron shivered.

"I guess I'll get put on report," he said gloomily.

"No, you won't." Cameron bent his head and hugged his shoulders. "I'll speak to the inspector."

"Gosh!" Eaken made grateful noises.

As they passed the row of condemned houses the window flew open, the ragged white head appeared. "Nigger stole Salesman's girl! Nigger stole Salesman's girl!" the mite chanted.

Cameron frowned deeply as the window shrieked down. "What's he mean?"

"Well," Eaken said carefully. "I'd say she might have a visitor."

Cameron's face went gray. "Get your gun out."

"Yessir." Eaken unhooked his holster. The barrel gleamed dully in his cocked hand.

Morelock and the Salesman were thirty feet beyond the others, Morelock stepping along quickly, the Salesman running beside with a stiff-legged little trot. At the Franklin J. Smith they stopped and the Salesman pointed, talking. Morelock listened, bobbing his head to show he understood.

Suddenly he froze. "Hey!" he yelled ahead. "Hey!" He spun round and beckoned.

The sergeant left Fred, hurrying forward. As he rounded the bulk he saw a coatless black man wearing overshoes scoot out of an opening in the bottom of a beached barge just ahead and run down the street. On the deck above, the grotesque figure of a tattered, misshapen woman swayed in the bitter wind, flailing her arms.

"Get that guy," Morelock snapped. The sergeant sprinted after the fleeing form.

Behind them a siren shrilled across the square. Morelock tilted his head toward it. It grew, approaching. "Oh, God," he muttered and walked back, brushing past Fred, past Eaken and Cameron, rushing up.

Fred cleared the bow of the Franklin J. Smith and beheld the black, in headlong flight, and Sergeant Cannon, pumping in pursuit. Then he saw Ruby weaving on the barge deck and ran toward her.

The Salesman had stepped upon an old hitching block and

was shifting his bright eyes excitedly from the flying black to the sergeant to Fred.

He cheered them all: "Go! *Go!*"

The siren, very close now, whined into a lower key and died. A black Lincoln appeared, careening down the street toward Morelock, puffing exhaust. It braked to a stop before the condemned houses and the old window above went up in greeting.

At that moment Eaken and Cameron reached the stern of the *Franklin J. Smith*, skidded around it, and looked out on the wild street.

Fred had overtaken his sister on the barge prow, locked his arms around her thick waist, and was dragging her backward toward the center of the hull.

Far ahead, where the dark sky was laced with broken spars and the narrow street disappeared in a thick mist, the black was zigzagging with an odd, shuffling run.

Fifty yards behind him Sergeant Cannon plunged furiously over the broken stones. His shoulders were bent forward and he had lost his cap. He was losing ground.

Cameron raised a clenched fist. His face went dark red. "That's the bugger! *Shoot!*"

Eaken took a little step to the left, whipped sideways with his free arm, caught the Salesman in the slack of his stomach and sent him sprawling, with a little cry, to the street floor. He stepped up on the block, aimed stiff-arm, and squeezed the trigger.

The bullet went *psseeeeeoooow* and the ricochet broke flatly. He had missed.

The sergeant, carried forward by his momentum, peered over his shoulder like an outfielder looking for a fly. He saw Eaken, saw the glint of his gun. His face opened in surprise, he stumbled, fell, scrambled on all fours, fell again, and lay hugging the cold street.

"*Get him!*" Cameron bellowed.

The shadow was disappearing into the fog, a dark patch dodging among swirling haze. Eaken aimed again carefully. From the barge came a throaty, incoherent shout. He squeezed slowly.

Psseeeooow went the bullet.

The shadow crumpled, went down, straightened, lurched forward into the scudding mist and vanished.

Eaken lowered his arm. "Winged him," he said under his breath. "I think."

But Cameron could not hear him. He was staggering toward the barge, where Fred had come out of the shelter of the hull with his sister's hand folded in his like a child's. Cameron moved slowly, wiping his eyes on his coat sleeve. They waited motionless, and when he reached the girl and threw his arms around her Fred stepped aside. But she collapsed, sacklike, against her father, and immediately Fred wrenched them apart and stepped between them, gesturing angrily. His father drew back, confused, and then the three of them came toward Eaken in a line abreast, Cameron wiping his eyes again and falling farther and farther behind.

The Angel Salesman pulled his knees to his stomach and folded his arms over them. Sitting on the street, in that disorder, he looked strangely comfortable. He glanced around, birdlike.

"Ossifer, you got company."

Eaken turned. All four doors of the Lincoln were open, and a half dozen policemen were piling out. One remained: a small man wrapped in a steamer blanket, sitting squarely in the middle of the back seat. Eaken recognized the commissioner with a pang. Beside the limousine Morelock was standing, hanging forward, listening to him.

Three of the policemen detached themselves from the purring radiator and approached Eaken. "C'mere," one of them called harshly. "The old man wants to see you."

The other two passed him, passed the broken line of Camerons, and moved toward Sergeant Cannon, who had risen, dusted his coat, and was again advancing on the wall of fog.

Zipski's face never changed. But sometimes it would go rigid, though the muscles were twisted by a single cramp. When Eaken came up to the car and looked into the back seat he had something of the feeling of looking at the Salesman's Angel. That feeling. Multiplied by horror.

457

The voice was quiet. "You fired two shots."

"I ——" Eaken cast around at the wall of blue uniforms, at the dirty snow beyond, at the open window and the waggling blur of white hair. "Yessir."

"Upon whose orders."

"Si — sir?"

"Who ordered you to fire those shots."

Eaken half turned to the bent figure of Morelock, now studying an ice-caked hub cap.

Zipski leaned forward. "Was it Mr. Morelock?"

Eaken started. "Mr. ——"

"Mr. Morelock, a recent member of the Department?"

"No." Eaken shook his head dumbly. "It was ——" he wheeled and pointed at Cameron, trailing his children around the stern of the *Franklin J. Smith* "— it was him."

The wall of blue quivered. Zipski paused. Then: "Do you mean Mr. Cameron?" Eaken nodded, and Zipski paused again. Then: "Very well. You are expelled from the Department and under arrest. Captain!"

An older man in a gold badge stepped forward and took Eaken by the arm. They brushed past Morelock and he nearly fell into the car.

Zipski issued new orders as he tucked the steamer blanket under his thin legs. Two patrolmen detached themselves, passed Fred and Ruby, and, turning about, took each an arm of Cameron and half carried him, spluttering, to the limousine.

The voice came evenly. "You are Jarvis Cameron?"

Cameron was stunned — his astonishment quieted his hysteria. "I'm who?" he said stupidly. A policeman tittered briefly.

"Your name is Jarvis Cameron."

"Why — of course it is. What ——"

"You directed Officer Eaken to fire his revolver."

"Well, I ——" Cameron swallowed "— I don't remember his name, but ——"

"But you did direct him."

"Certainly I did! Any citizen ——"

"Thank you. You are under arrest."

Cameron took a step back. "I'm *what?*"

"You are under arrest."

"You damned fool!" Cameron laughed harshly. "You think you can get away with this?" The blue wall stirred uneasily. "I'll have your badge tomorrow!"

"That may be," Zipski said softly. "But as of now you are under arrest."

"On what charge, may I ask?"

Sergeant Cannon and the officers who had followed him were now returned and waiting by the front bumper. The commissioner beckoned to them. "What did you find?"

"A little blood, sir," the sergeant replied. "Nothing else."

"Who is he?"

Cameron cleared his throat, but one of the policemen nudged him violently, and before he could regain his balance the sergeant had answered.

"No one knows, sir." He glanced hesitantly over his shoulder, where Fred again held his sister's hand. "That woman living on the barge might, but she's, well, sort of upset."

"Upset?"

The sergeant tapped his forehead with a mittened forefinger.

Zipski returned to Cameron. "The charge is conspiring to assault with intent to kill. When we find the man we may change it." Cameron wet his lips, but Zipski was talking to a lieutenant on the other side of the car. "You have men out? Good. Stay here. I'll notify radio."

Again Cameron gathered himself together. "Now goddam it ——" he began.

But Zipski was calling over his shoulder. "Who're you?" he asked Fred.

"I'm — her brother."

"Is that the bail jumper?" Fred did not answer. "I take it she is. Better take her to a doctor. I'll release her in your custody. Give your name to the lieutenant."

He slammed the door and spoke to the chauffeur. The motor

459

roared. The car backed away, turned deftly in a narrow alley, and was gone, sliding toward the square in a cloud of exhaust.

"Well, I'll be *god*damned!" Cameron exploded.

He was nudged again, nudged back, and was abruptly shoved across the street, spun around, and thrust against a vacant house front. Beside him were Morelock and Eaken, badgeless and hatless and silent. Cameron started to say something to Morelock, thought better of it, started again, again thought better of it, and then realized he had nothing to say. He stood listlessly, slumped forward a little, staring at the broken cobblestones. His center of gravity had shifted.

The headquarters party left with its three prisoners, trooping with broken step toward the square. The lieutenant took Fred's name. Then he and his search party fanned out.

Fred rubbed Ruby's hands between his own, one at a time. He spoke gently. "They're gone. Hadn't we better go, too?"

She took an uncertain step forward and set her shapeless, wasted face toward the river. Her neck had swollen until it wasn't a neck at all, and her open eye peered out through the slit of false fat, without expression, like the eye on an iced mackerel.

"Hadn't we better go?" he said again.

She folded her bluish hands over her stomach. "Sounds like onea them c'mmercials," she said. "Onea them Calvert ads." Her voice came muffled and indistinct, as though she were calling into the end of a broken megaphone, from far away.

"I beg pardon?"

But she did not answer.

The Angel Salesman watched the last policeman disappear into the mist. Then he cried "Merry Christmas!" cheerfully and swung across the rutted street.

Fred had never seen anyone so disfigured. He could not imagine what was wrong with her. It was getting colder. He had quite forgotten his father.

"I could use a drink," the Salesman said thirstily. "How 'bout you?" Fred shook his head. "How 'bout you Rube?"

Fred was about to reply for her, but just then the voice came again through the broken megaphone. " 'Member Ira? Ira was a pal."

"Yes, he was," Fred said kindly.

"But he wouldn't do nothin' nice."

"Beg pardon?" He dropped one hand and reached for the other, but she drew away.

"Go with Willie if I want. Don't b'lieve me? Let 'em try. Jus' let 'em."

Fred managed a strained smile. "Try what, Jan?"

She lifted her hands, clumsy as workmen's gloves, to her mottled throat. "Shoes clean. Didn't I hafta keep my shoes clean? Course I did. But we didn't have a clue. No clue!"

The Salesman shook his head sadly. "So many times I seen it." Then, irrelevantly, he added, "I really got to get a drink."

"So long," Fred said without looking at him.

"What're you gonna do?"

"That's my problem."

"What a problem." He executed a smart left face and stepped off with a full thirty-inch stride toward the *Franklin J. Smith*.

"We had some good times then. Didn't even break. Not even after I tried. Really tried. Had to. Don't b'lieve me?" Something jiggled in her throat, but there was no sign in the torpid face. "Had to if he wanted to. In th' john. Witha waitress." Fred slipped an arm around the enormous waist and turned her slowly toward the square. "Candy was good. 'Member Candy? Made him love t. Witha waitress. After dark. But I tried. Don't b'lieve me? I ried. I tried! After dark. No clue. No clue at all."

Down the shattered old street they hobbled, Ruby babbling, Fred urging her forward with his shoulder against hers and his arm across her back. They reached the square, crossed it, and on the far side he found his parked car. But when he reached to open the door her polelike legs buckled, she fell across the mudguard, and he had to push her awkwardly into the back seat, head first. He drove furiously to the hospital under a sullen afternoon sky torn by a fierce wind.

At the clinic the resident reassured him. Her dropsy was not serious; they were feeding her blood proteins intravenously, and the child was apparently sound. But there was this other thing, her incoherence. Would he mind stepping into this office, with this doctor? Just to answer these questions, these few questions . . .

The hospital was never entirely dark. After seven o'clock the lights in the patient buildings began to go out, one by one, until there were only a few on the sickest wards, but the tiers of operating rooms glittered all night, every night, and the emergency room never slept.

Tonight it was mobbed. The plain board benches were crowded with newspaper reporters, policemen, and special investigators smoking, working crossword puzzles, and demanding information.

Periodically they got it. Periodically an intern arranged his duck jacket, appeared briefly, and made a grave announcement.

"The situation is unchanged. Still critical. Dr. Frank is operating upstairs. That's all I can say." It was all he knew.

"Frank's middle initial H as in hat?" asked one of the reporters.

"That's it," the intern said briskly and left. Leaving, he glanced at an open copy of the morning paper's first edition and carried back to his colleagues the gist of the triple-deck headline:

BOND CHILD NEAR DEATH
HUNT BLACK TRASHMAN
CAMERON BAIL $5,000

"When's their next edition?" asked an apple-cheeked youngster from Harvard, looking up from a cut lip.

"That was it," said the returned envoy.

"Too bad they couldn't wait," the youngster said confidently, capping a hooked needle to his finger and beckoning to a nurse. "Bottom's dropped out of systolic — Spence just heard. She going any time."

462

Spence stared hostilely. There was money on this one. He dried his hands in the blowing machine and turned professionally to a smashed finger. "She's all right," he said over his shoulder. "Frank's massaging her heart. Just what she needs."

The envoy looked from the youngster to Spence and shook his head skeptically.

Five floors up, in a waiting room, another copy of the paper lay neatly folded on a table covered with many magazines. On either side the Bonds sat in straight chairs, listening to the buzz of the electric clock on the wall opposite. In the quarter hour since the doctor's last brusque visit, neither had spoken.

"Dr. Frank is a very famous man," Charlie said abruptly. His voice alarmed him. He looked around the room anxiously.

"Seems to me I've heard of him." She hadn't, but she was straining to keep the conversation going.

"Oh, I've heard of him many times, many times. Read about him, too."

"He must be real famous."

"Oh, he is. No question about it."

Silence closed in. The clock hummed. It was the loudest electric clock Charlie had ever heard. He wondered if it were broken.

"We were very lucky to get him," he said earnestly.

"I guess so."

"I mean, with the holiday."

"That's right, I hadn't thought of that."

"Oh, yes. No doubt about it, we were real lucky."

Footsteps came down the buff corridor. They turned eagerly toward them, then shrank back, afraid. But the steps went away, and they relaxed with a common sigh.

Charlie was determined. "That was the biggest man I ever saw, that cop with all the questions."

Loretta uncrossed her legs and recrossed them the other way. "Wasn't he big?"

"Big?" It was inadequate. "He was *huge*."

"Yes," she said vaguely, ready to give up. "He was big, all right."

"With all those questions!" As though that made him larger.

"He sure had a lot of them."

"He certainly did."

Charlie glanced at the window, where the night lay black against the old panes, then down at the paper with a twinge of false uneasiness. If he could just keep his mind crammed with the little fears he would be all right. So he forced the worries, trying to control them: he might have forgotten how to slice poultry, there might not be an opening, he might need references. Lucy might not give back the money, the bank might foreclose, they might not find another place. The description might have been wrong, many blacks wore overshoes, he could be sued for false arrest. The cops might check the Elbow, find he had not paid off, take him to court again. Dr. Frank might want too much money, the hospital bill might be too large, Dulcy might . . .

The clock buzzed hysterically. Time whined on.

Loretta recrossed her legs and recrossed them again, smoothing her skirt each time.

The newspaper lay neat and unread.

Somewhere a door opened and the hall outside was noisy with voices. This time the steps did not turn off. This time they came right up to the archway.

It was the surgeon, pajamaed in rumpled white, haggard and smelling of chemicals. The others passed on, talking of technicalities.

"Mrs. Bond? Mr. Bond?" Loretta bent forward in a sharp jackknife, her face scarlet. Charlie rose bravely.

"I'm sorry," the doctor said flatly. "We couldn't save her. There was too much trauma."

They did not move, and so he put it another way. "She's gone. I am sorry."

He was about to leave mercifully when Loretta sprang up and ran toward him, her face clenched like a fist and crying. He stepped awkwardly aside and she ran by him and out into the hall, making odd, mewing little sounds.

Charlie shuffled his hands together, apologizing for her. "I guess you did everything. That you could, I mean." It was a formality. Formalities were important.

The doctor puckered, considering what might have been left undone. "Everything," he concluded.

The corridor was torn with shrill sobs and the clatter of high heels running, stopping, and running again. Charlie looked troubled.

"She can't find it, where it is. Nobody told us."

The doctor put his head outside and simultaneously the clatter slowed and the sobbing stopped. "A nurse found her," he said. "She'll show her."

But Charlie was still concerned. "We never been in here before, I don't know how to get out." It was a terrible thing, not knowing how to get out.

"There's an elevator at that end of the hall." The surgeon pointed. "It runs all night."

"Oh, thank you." That was comforting.

Dr. Frank rocked in his wrinkled gown. "I — ah — have to go. Have another case."

"Don't let me keep you! I know you're busy. We're, that is, we're grateful for — for everything." The gowned figure bowed silently. Charlie studied for a moment. "We really do appreciate it," he added and looked up and was astonished to find the doctor had gone.

He was alone again with the clock.

Carefully he walked across the room, reached up, opened the case, saw the plug inside, pulled it out, and watched the sweep second hand stop. He breathed deeply. "Should've done that before," he scolded himself aloud.

He frowned at a sudden thought and hastily dug a hand into his trousers pocket. It came out with two dollar bills, squeezed together, and he pulled them apart, shaking his head unhappily.

The trolley fare would be twenty cents. Conductors hated bills. Sometimes they were nasty about it. He really should have brough change.

The windows rattled before a gust of wind, and he turned to them anxiously and peered out. Now that was foolish. He had forgotten his rubbers, and it was trying to snow.

He groaned. The groan grew and grew louder.

Suddenly, convulsively, he lurched against the wall and rolled along it, face first, back first, face first, toppling clumsily into chair with a thump. His face opened in horror, he clawed at it with trembling clawlike hands . . .

Now that was foolish.

He had forgotten his rubbers, and it was trying to snow.

His bowels were turning to water.

It was trying to snow, and across the city children called excitedl to parents who came running, looked out with dissolving alarm checked locked doors and windows, and withdrew to firesides an stovesides and treesides to roll their eyes and speak in hushed voice of Santa abroad, thinking of another abroad, another wanderin stranger prowling catlike after no one knew whose child.

And the holiday eve deepened and darkened, and mothen carried sleepless tots protesting up Valley stairways and behin Elbow partitions, and fathers slid sealed packages against snu evergreen boles, and the Christmas lights went out one by on and the city waited open-eyed in silent beds, children hopin happy hopes, men and women unhappy and afraid.

At police headquarters a thousand office windows winked fierce at the thin flakes fluttering through the night. There was n Christmas here, save in wistful thoughts brushed impatient aside as the business of strengthening search details, and checkin their reports against the great master map of the city, and siftin the hundreds of crank rumors — as the thousand-windowed busi ness of tracking down the crippled fugitive went on.

Zipski knew his man. He was sure of it, and had been sinc an hour after he had returned from the waterfront, shut himse in his office, and joined together the separate pieces of the puzzle. It was pathetically easy — so easy that Mike Holloway, the Department clown, had done it before him and, in his absence, set in motion the forces of justice.

Shortly after nine o'clock that morning a distraught black woman had come to the Thawe Street station house and asked help. Her husband had not come home the night before, and because of the excitement over policy, which he had always followed, and because he had been mysteriously beaten the week before, she suspected he had been attacked. Specifically she distrusted one Thomas Sanders, black, a poolroom operator known to be connected in a small way with Ben Erik's political organization. A routine check of station dockets showed the woman's husband had not been picked up in the riots, and so Sanders was brought in. He admitted knowing the missing man — had, in fact, sold him his house — but denied having seen him. He understood, from neighborhood gossip, that the truant was a steady customer of Charles F. Bond, who had been fined in criminal court two days before on a lottery charge.

It happened that Captain Hardy remembered the missing man as the key figure in an outrageous decision handed down the week before by Magistrate Paul Gormley and therefore took a special interest in the case. He checked Records by phone, found a previous conviction for assault upon a little girl, and was pouring over this when word reached him of the Linvale Place stabbing. Immediately he sent everything — the woman's description of her missing husband, Sanders's statement, and the conviction reference — over the teletype to Holloway, his immediate superior.

Holloway had just come in from a fruitless interview with shaken little Kenny Carter. He had returned to Linvale Place at once, questioned Charlie, and elicited from him an account of the previous afternoon's flight from Sam. Moments after the inspector had backed out of the Bond house with a clumsy expression of sympathy, a homicide sergeant was laying before Lottie the bloody coat found by the old railroad tracks. She identified

467

it with a wordless nod and collapsed. Ten minutes later her description, so innocently given, was dispatched to all station houses, and the first searching parties went out.

It was this description Zipski had ordered circulated among the barges after learning that Ruby worked in a diner a block from the truant's home. The agreement which followed was remarkable for hazy Sticktown. Four dogfish, peering out between the cracks of their listing homes, had seen the coatless figure rush up the street in flopping overshoes, rest on the barge with her, and flee into the fog before Eaken's gun. No one had seen him drop, for when Eaken started firing they all dodged for cover, but the stains on the cobblestones clearly indicated he had been hurt. The Physicians' Exchange and all emergency rooms were alerted for a wounded black man, ticket salesmen at the railroad stations and the airport were told to watch for a black who favored himself in any way, and from Sloane Square to the Elbow shivering police details cast hopeful flashlights on the banked snow looking for a bright wet track.

They found none. First to last, from his bastard birth to his flight across the frozen barrens of the waterfront, the wounds of Sam Crawford were internal, the bleeding inside. He had spilled all the blood the frightened city would see.

Sam had been hit in the spleen. Ruby's warning cry reached him a step from safety and wrenched him around, startled, in just the position to receive Eaken's second shot between the ninth and tenth ribs of his left side. The bullet passed through his clothing, struck into the abdomen, and lodged in the splenic pulp. He went down, wavered for a moment in pain and unbalance, and then plunged on, oozing a vivid splatter on the street below. Then the muscles closed over the surface wound, shutting off the blood, leaving Sam with a bullet in the cavity of his gut and a ruptured spleen.

And as he ran under the shield of fog, the slow leak of life into that cavity began — began with a faint burn under the heat that flashed and went away — and flashed again and again wer

468

away — and flashed and went — and flashed and went — like that, at intervals — labor pains of the last great birth, pounding in the womb of death.

Down the twisted street he ran, past the stolid shadows of the barges, until he reached a wasted slough of beach, licked by the brackish river. There he turned left, heading back into the city. A wave of false energy surged in him, he dug in with his tattered overshoes and flew north, over a plain of wry seaweed, through a city dump brown with rusted tin, into the warehouse district. Rushed blindly on, leaping over piles of lumber and oil drums, coming suddenly upon a clump of frame tenements. Stopped short, panting, glancing warily about, and walked carefully through a driveway, coming out upon a deserted street. Slipped across, sucking air, and on the other side entered a narrow alley, feeling the brush of the rough walls on his trembling shoulders.

Sam was two miles from Sticktown now and as safe as he would ever be. His strength was gone, his chest was stitched with pain, and his left shoulder hurt. He looked for a place to rest and halfway down the alley found a raised shelf between garages wide enough to admit him. He slid in head first, and just before he collapsed he had a thought: he should cover himself up. But before he could move he was asleep, dreaming his dreams, his strange dreams.

Sam slept, and life drained down around the dead lead in his gut and ran in a widening trickle across the smooth muscle of his stomach lining, into a jungle of intestine. Darkness fell and lay clean about him, and into the greater darkness of his pelvis life flowed redly and wetly and stickily, pooling against his shrinking bladder.

He awoke at eight o'clock with a tremendous need to urinate — rose, urinated, and almost immediately felt the need again. He was giddy: something was wrong. He was spent and starved, but it was something else — something which drew sweat in little balls on his frostbitten hands and weakened his wrists and quickened the pulse there and shrouded his mind with a soft smothering cloud. He shook his head groggily and fell to his knees.

469

He tried to think: tried to remember where he had been and how he had arrived here, what he had done and what he was afraid of and why — tried to trace the withered thread back into the cavern through which he had run here. He screwed up his streaked face and tried hard. But he could not concentrate, and as he staggered to his feet, still trying, life leaned on his bladder again and the urge welled in his groin.

He could not stay here. This was no place to be. He gathered himself together, attempted to button his fly, and toppled off the shelf, down the alley, to the sidewalk. On the corner a street lamp shone feebly. He stared dully and saw it framed in murky red, blinked and the frame turned blue, squeezed his eyes shut and nearly fell again.

He would go home, that is what he would do. He wondered why he was not there now. Again he tried to think, and again the suffocating cloud closed in, baffling thought. He turned west, ignoring the fresh swell in his bladder, and stumbled toward the haloed street light, toward home.

Down the sidewalk he reeled, feeling the tug at his heart, the hammer in his throat. And every other block he stepped haltingly into an alley, fumbled with his pants, soiled the cold brick and stepped out again and reeled on until he ran into Striker Street wide and bright with the lights of many stores and bars. The sidewalk was swarming with cheerful people, and the frame of Sam's sight was a double frame now, red and blue and closing in

It had begun to snow. Pale flakes flickered down the neon chasm, salting the gutters with a fine powder, and Sam was tired

He drew away from the crowd, into an eddy before a hock-shop window cluttered with the rubbish of the destitute — cameras, radios, cigarette lighters and watches out of pawn — and squinting, forced himself to read the signs: Your initials Lodge Or Service Emblem FREE On Any Leather Items Purchased Here, Simulated DIAMOND Rings 98¢ & Up, Hand Painted Souvenir Lockets, Statue of OUR LORD $2.95, Quick & E–Z Loans On Anything Of Value CUT RATE STORE CUT RATE STORE CUT RATE STORE CUT . .

A pink-fringed silk pillowcase in the window wore a message

suddenly important. He pressed his face against the glass and made out:

SWEETHEART
Love unending, warm and true
Sweetheart mine this brings to you
Love which hopes that happiness
All your daysssssssssss ——

It was gone in a swim of roses. His belly swelled again and he turned away, looking for a place. His eyes cleared, blurred, cleared and blurred again, like binoculars with a loose focus, and in the next block he lifted slit eyes and made out the dazzling sign:

<pre>
           M
HELPINGUP
           S
           S
           I
           O
           N
</pre>

He went inside. Upstairs a dozen voices chorused:

Away in a manger, no crib for his bed
The lit-tul Lord Jesus lay down his sweet head . . .

On the right a faded sign invited MEN. The toilet was empty. Sam dropped his trousers and sank to the single dusty stool. His shirt parted and he saw the little black hole between his ribs. It frightened him. He ought to get a doctor, get it fixed. But the only doctor he knew was Pellie's father, and he could not go there.

His pants fell from his knees to his ankles and one of the pockets bulged. He fumbled awkwardly, nearly tumbling from the stool, and drew out a wad of bills. Five one-dollar bills and a dime wedged between two of them. He blinked. Whose money? His. How come? He wobbled his head in confusion. The red and blue frame shifted and picked up a crumpled newspaper on the cement floor, the first page up. The headlines ran together, but under them he saw two pictures, one of a stocky man manacled to a policeman, surrounded by other policemen and holding his hat before his face with his free hand, and the other of himself.

It was him, all right. He remembered the pose, full face, with the number hanging from his neck on a brass chain. They were printing his picture in the papers. *Why?* The page was just out of reach. He lunged with his scabbed left fist, fell off the stool, and kneeling barelegged on the cold concrete held the type close to his face, squinting painfully. But the harder he looked the more it bleared, until all he was holding was a sheet of red, streaked with blue.

He folded the paper clumsily and thrust it under his shirt, over the wound, struggled to his feet, buckled his belt, and felt his way out into the hall. His sight cleared a little. He could see the door, he shuffled toward it.

Upstairs the chorus was gay:

> *All the other happy reindeer*
> *Used to laugh and call him names*
> *They would never let poor Rudolph*
> *Join in any reindeer games . . .*

. . . Life flowed in a thickening stream over the smooth muscle lining, through the cords of bowel, into the pelvic dike, ballooning the belly and sending burning flashes up the trunk cave while the sweat beaded on the icy flesh and the pulse beat savagely and the stifling cloud gathered, snuffing out the wicks of thought, one by one . . .

He was in the alleys, staggering down the cheerless backways of the downtown district, feeling his way up the trash-littered gullies he knew while the snow sifted down, crusting the shag of his hair with a hoary cap . . .

— Past Stuart Street . . .

— Past Howell Street . . .

— Toward the Seventh District . . .

— Toward home.

Once he saw a squad of policemen standing under an arc light diagonally across from an alley mouth, arguing which way they should go. He lurked behind a rainspout until they were gone and then shifted three blocks south, moving westward from there.

And once, before the last flickering wicks went out, he stopped before a blazing theater front, pulled the newspaper from his shirt with stiff fingers, and tried to read the smudge of print, and did read a paragraph before the twin frames swept over the page, but could not understand what he had read.

He should be nearly home. He had come far enough. Any moment he ought to come upon the face of Swinton's, Kelly's, Ollie's, the Unique. West Concord lay just ahead. There. Behind that jut of fence. But it wasn't there. But it should have been. Well. There. Beyond that green police call box. Behind that brick privy. Around that corner. The Elbow would be there. It must be, had to be . . .

But it wasn't. It just wasn't there at all.

He pitched forward, shifting frozen overshoes through the thickening snow, past the 50¢ 30¢ 25¢ parking lots walled with peeling billboards hawking dead brands and forgotten candidates, past the darkened Esso Servicenters and Bargain Harry's and Money Back Mac's, up the endless U of the lightless loveless hapless alleys, into the foul crypt of the old Seventh, into the tortured swamp of sanded sugar watered milk kerosene coal oil Merito Tawny Port Madeira Pure California Sherry Wine and Funk's World's Finest Hair Straightener, into the land of windows without glass cheap funerals and Hadacol, land of cold water walk-ups rusting basins and rotting roofs, land of swift justice for the poor . . .

— and there . . .

— In that place . . .

Justice delivered one last mighty wallop and sent him to his knees crawling up the lanes between high board fences through

473

a soft cold red and blue powder falling gently AS LIFE SURGED
wading through the bright confetti of death CRYING INSIDE
it's somewhere around here LIKE WATER FROM A BURST
MAIN beyond that line of stiff wash *There There There* SWIM-
MING DOWN INTO THE DARK TROUGH OF HIS
DROWNED LOINS.

Fink Kerby, stealing toward West Concord in the still shadowy
dawn to forage firewood from Charlie Bond's gutted grocery,
stumbled across the body and awoke the Elbow with his yells.

"He daid! Daid!" he shrieked. His voice crashed against a wall
of houses and he ran into the back yards screaming.

Lottie's spangled kitchen window opened and a gun was thrust
out, followed by a hand, followed by the white face of a policeman.

"Who?" he barked. Over the cop's shoulder Fink saw another
cop and, in the kitchen behind him, Lottie, bobbing up and
down by the shiny Christmas balls, trying to see.

"Sam!"

"*What!*"

"Him you want! Daid up a way!"

The first policeman sent the second to see, then the second
stood guard while the first went to the station house for help.
Lottie crept down the automobile doors, her sneakers slipping in
the new snow, and crouched by the body, brushing the flakes
from the frozen face and crooning.

The policeman looked at her sharply. "I'd be careful if I was
you. He ain't what I'd call popular."

But she did not hear him. She went on crooning and brushing
with her hand cupped against the cold.

Windows were opening, scared faces were peering out. A few
men edged into the alley, shoved from behind. The policeman
slipped the safety off his revolver. "Get back, now," he warned
and wished help would come.

Then a whistle blew at the alley mouth and a swarm of blue-
coats came rushing and four cops picked up the rigid, heavy-

bellied load and carried it to the station house. The policeman followed them, and Lottie followed him, and behind her ranged the people of the Elbow.

In the hall outside his office Captain Hardy took over. The captain had not stayed home this Christmas Day, and he searched the stuck pockets himself, digging out the effects. And Lottie stood back, watching, shaking her head gently and moaning.

Hardy heard her, looked up and saw her.

"Who're you?"

"Miz Crawford."

"Wife?"

"Sholey."

Hardy nodded, remembering. Then he shook his head vehemently. "You can't stay here."

So she went out the battered double doors and waited on the steps. Fink came and told her Emma had taken Peter Paul and the baby and she did not worry about that.

In the snow around her a crowd gathered, slowing traffic, and there were many curious faces there. In a little while an ambulance came, and two men went in with stretchers, but when they brought the body out it was shrouded in blankets, so she did not see his face again. After the ambulance had gone she left too, slipping home on sneakered feet, and the crowd began to break up, though there were many who lingered by the stationhouse steps, many who did not go down to West Concord.

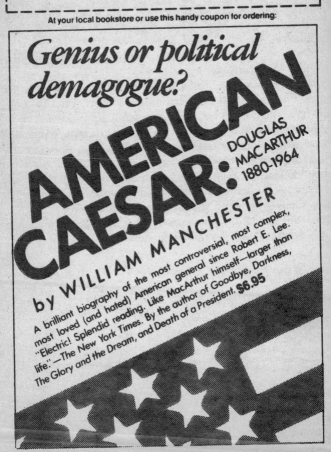

The National Bestseller!

GOODBYE, DARKNESS

by WILLIAM MANCHESTER
author of *American Caesar*

The riveting, factual memoir of WW II battle in the Pacific—
and of an idealistic ex-marine's personal struggle to understand
its significance 35 years later.

"A strong and honest account, and it ends with a clash of
cymbals."—*The New York Times Book Review*

"The most moving memoir of combat in World War II that I
have read. A testimony to the fortitude of man. A gripping,
haunting book."—William L. Shirer

A Dell Book   **$4.95**   **(13110-3)**